Part VI of the American Kitsune Series

By Brandon Varnell

ISBN: 1519111010
ISBN-13: 978-1519111012

DEDICATION

I feel like I'm doing dedications every single book—oh, wait. I am doing these every single book. Never mind.

The first person I would like to dedicate this to is my mom, whose helped me with everything outside of my book. Seriously. Aside from writing, I'm pretty much useless. Were it not for her letting me live with her after I graduated from college, who knows what would have happened. I would also like to thank my dad for supporting my desire to write and giving me advice when I need it, along with my step-mom and my step-dad. Both of them have been a really big help.

Following this, I would like thank my sister and her husband, who will be having a kid this year. I'm mostly thanking them because I'm gonna be an uncle—and you all know that uncles are the coolest gig ever. We don't have to be strict like the parents, and we don't have to spoil the child like grandparents. All I need to do is thoroughly corrupt their child by teaching them everything they need to know about geek fandoms: Star Wars, Naruto, DBZ, Sailor Moon, Cowboy Bebop, and every new anime that's come out since the old days. It's going to be a blast. My niece is going to be well on her way to nerdom in no time!

And finally, I am dedicating this story to my readers. When I first started writing, I was frightened and uncertain, but thanks to the people who read my stories and told me that they loved them, I've since gained the courage to try and reach for the stars.

Without all of you, I would never be where I am today.

Thank you.

CONTENTS

Others books to the American Kitsune Series

A Fox's Love

A Fox's Tail

A Fox's Maid

Chapter 1

The Passage of Time is Transient

As was per the norm since her daughter's disappearance, Camellia found herself sitting on the balcony to her clan's estate in Tampa Bay. Situated on the table next to her was a hot cup of tea, from which a beautiful fragrance wafted, relaxing her mind, even as the worry she'd been feeling for the past three months continued to plague her.

She looked down at the garden below, expansive and lovely, filled with a wide variety of well-maintained and beautiful flowers. Even though it was fall, the flowers continued to bloom, courtesy of her maid's prodigious gardening abilities. They were some of the loveliest blossoms she'd ever seen, and once upon a time, Camellia would have already been down there at this early hour, admiring them up close.

Despite staring straight at them, she did not see the wondrous array of colorful blossoms and hadn't for a while now. Unable to grasp the complexities of multiple thoughts at once due to the degradation of her mind, Camellia could only focus on a single subject. Her missing daughter, Lillian.

On August 4th, Lilian had disappeared from the grounds of this very mansion, vanishing without a trace. While some worried that she might have been kidnapped, the general consensus was that she had run away.

Neither Camellia nor anyone else knew how the young kitsune had managed to escape without being noticed. Evidence pointed towards excessive use of her Celestial abilities, which could, in the right circumstances, render Lilian all but invisible. Since then, Camellia had done little more than fret.

She might have had a mind reminiscent to that of a child, but she was still a mother.

"My Lady," a voice came from behind her. "You have not touched your tea. Is it not to your liking?"

"Hmm?" Camellia looked down at the tea, blinking. She then looked at the woman standing by her chair, a female with hair the color of midnight and three fox-tails waving about behind her. "Ah! Sorry, sorry. Camellia got lost in thought. Tee-hee!" After gently knocking her knuckles against her head, the five-tailed kitsune took a small sip of her tea. "It's very good."

Her complimentary words earned a gentle smile from the fox-woman dressed as a French maid. "I am glad to see that you still enjoy my tea. For a moment, I was worried that my skills might have slipped."

Camellia felt a small sense of dread well up inside of her at the maid's mention of "slipping skills." A shudder coursed through her body for reasons she couldn't understand.

The shudder went away, as did almost everything else, when a hand covered in a white glove began petting her on the head.

"Hawa…"

"Still so easy to please, My Lady." The kitsune maid was nothing if not amused by her mistress' reaction towards something as simple as head petting. It reminded her of, well, it sort of reminded her of a dog, though she would never say that out loud.

As the utterly blissed out Camellia enjoyed having her maid's fingers scratch behind her ears, a familiar presence appeared before them, floating just a few feet from the balcony.

"Oh. It's one of my sister's Kudagitsune."

The wraith-like fox-spirit with the pipe-like body couldn't have belonged to anyone but the maid's elder sister. The scroll, ghostly and translucent, much like the creature carrying it, told them as much. Kotohime was the only Pnéw̲ ma clan vassal who still used scrolls to deliver messages.

Most kitsune made do with simple envelopes these days.

After the fox-spirit dropped the scroll on the table and vanished back into its ethereal existence, the three-tailed maid unfurled the object and read its contents. Her eyes widening in a mixture of surprise and delight, she rolled the scroll back up, and then looked at the woman she served with a warm smile etched upon her fetching lips.

"My Lady, it appears Kotohime has found your daughter."

"My daughter?" It took Camellia a second or two to get out of the blissful state that her maid's head petting had put her in. It took another second for her to hear the words spoken, and then one more to process them. "H-hawa! You mean she found Lilian?!"

"Yes. According to my sister's report, Lady Lilian is currently living in Phoenix, Arizona."

"I can't believe it... my daughter's finally been found..." Tears leaked from Camellia's carnelian eyes, and a smile so joyous and bright it put the sun to shame appeared on her lovely face. "Camellia... Camellia needs to tell Iris that her sister has finally been found!"

Camellia scrambled out of her chair, stood up—

"H-hawa!!"

—And then promptly spilled to the floor when she tripped over her own five tails.

"M-My Lady!" A very worried maid knelt next to Camellia, who pushed herself into a seated position. "A-are you alright?"

Like every fall she'd taken this past century, Camellia took this latest one with good humor. "Ah. Don't worry. Don't worry." She looked down at her chest. "Camellia's breasts broke her fall."

The maid felt a small drop of sweat trail down the right side of her face.

"R-right...

***

"A strong body is a necessary component to becoming a balanced warrior. It doesn't matter how good your technique is, or how fast you can throw a punch, if you lack the strength needed to harm your opponent. A thousand punches at the speed of light will mean absolutely nothing if each punch has all the power of a fly. There are ways around this, of course, such as using weapons, but that's not always a viable option. You can't carry a sword or a knife everywhere you go, after all."

While Kiara spoke of warriors and swords and the necessity of being physically fit, Kevin Swift grunted and whimpered as he did push-ups. Doing a couple of push-ups normally wouldn't be too much of a problem for him, but several extenuating factors were currently making this exercise exceedingly difficult.

Kiara was making him do 200 hundred of them.

She was also standing on his back while he did them.

And there was a floorboard covered in nails directly underneath him.

Kevin stared at the spiky floorboard, his eyes wide and his pupils dilated. Sweat dripped off his nose, splashing against a nail, making it glisten brightly and bringing a stark reminder of what would happen should his arms give out.

His arms shook from having exerted them so much. It felt like his triceps and chest were being ripped to shreds from the inside out, contracting and expanding painfully each time he completed a push-up. The only reason he hadn't fallen flat on his face yet was because he feared being impaled by the hundreds of tiny nails.

He was really beginning to regret asking Kiara to help train him.

"Please make me into a man!"

His words were met with an awkward silence. Sitting behind her desk, staring at him with unusually wide eyes, Kiara F. Kuyo looked like someone had just blindsided her. The moment soon passed, however, and the woman gave him a feral grin that caused chills to run down his spine.

"I could make you into a man if you want me to, but I don't think your mate would appreciate me taking away her chance to steal your chastity."

Kevin gave the woman a vacant stare for several seconds, the time it took for him to realize what she'd said and why.

His eyes promptly widened.

"Ah!" He squeaked like a rat trapped by a cat—or a small fox kit trapped by a great dane. "T-that's not what I meant!"

"Ho?" Kiara's eyes glinted with an animalistic viscosity. "Then what did you mean, boya?"

4

"I-I m-m-m-meant that I wanted you to make me s-stronger!"

"Stronger, eh?" Kiara rubbed her chin and studied Kevin, who did his best not to look away, even though his face was about ready to explode. "Tell me, boya, why do you want to become stronger?"

The question sobered him. Embarrassment gave way to solemnity. Kevin looked down at his feet, unable to hold Kiara's gaze. "Because I'm tired of being weak," he confessed, his voice a soft murmur that made Kiara's ears twitch.

"What was that?" she asked, even though Kevin was sure she'd heard him. "Speak up, boy!"

"I said it's because I'm tired of being weak," Kevin practically shouted. "I'm tired of having to rely on Lilian for protection. I'm tired of not being able to help her when she needs me. I want to be able to stand by her side as an equal. I want to be able to help her. I want her to be able to rely on me."

"So you're doing this for Lilian?" Kiara raised an eyebrow at Kevin, who shook his head.

"Not just for Lilian. I'm also doing this for myself. I made a choice. I chose to become Lilian's mate, and that means I'm now a part of the world you and she belong to, but I'm... I'm still just a human," he choked out, as if admitting this fact physically hurt. "I don't have any supernatural abilities that would let me stand up to a yōkai..."

Kevin looked at his hands, clenching them both into fists, before looking back up to present Kiara with his determined glare.

"I don't want to be weak anymore. I'm sick of it. That's why I want you to make me stronger." He then bowed to the woman, a formal bow at the waist. "Please help me get stronger."

Kevin clenched his eyes shut and didn't look up, which was why he nearly squealed like a little girl when a hand landed on his shoulder.

He looked up to see a grinning Kiara staring down at him.

"All right. I'll help you get stronger," she said, causing hope to swell within Kevin's chest. "Come back here tomorrow morning and we'll begin your training. Be sure to dress for the occasion. You're gonna want something that you don't mind getting ruined."

Kevin would have wondered what she meant by that, but was honestly too happy to care. "Okay. I'll do that. Thanks!"

"You're welcome, boya."

As Kevin left, he never noticed the devious grin that nearly split Kiara's face in half, nor did he hear her diabolical chuckling.

"Ku ku ku... training a human to fight yōkai, huh? Sounds like fun."

A grunt escaped Kevin's lips when Kiara dug her heel into his back. "Come on! Keep going, boya. You're not even close to being done yet."

"I don't." Grunt. "See how." Whimper. "You can." Kiara dug her left heel into his shoulder blade. Kevin nearly squealed. "Expect me to." Kevin's face became a deep scarlet when something hard ground into his back. "Do push-ups." Sounds reminiscent of a dying cow escaped his mouth when his chest scraped against the bed of nails, drawing blood. "With you on my back!"

Even though he couldn't see her, Kevin could practically feel Kiara's grin. "It's all part of your training."

Kevin would have cursed, but since he didn't swear, he settled instead of spewing insults within the confines of his mind. Due to his mild nature, they weren't particularly mean insults.

Despite the fact that his body ached like nobody's business, as if he'd been chewed apart by an inu yōkai, Kevin continued doing as many push-ups as possible. Oddly enough, his current exercise was one of the easiest Kiara had given him thus far.

He didn't know whether that should please him or not.

Kevin still remembered some of the exercises she'd had him do these past two weeks. Hellacious did not even begin to describe them.

"Um, are you sure this is a good idea?" Kevin asked as he stood outside with Kiara. His new trainer in the ways of badassery had strapped a harness to his torso, which was attached to a tire that she sat upon soon after. In her hands was a whip.

"Of course it's a good idea," Kiara said, talking down to him like he was some kind of idiot. "You wanna get stronger, don't you, boya?"

"Well, yes, but—"

"The fastest way to get stronger is through intense physical

training," Kiara interrupted. *"It is only when a warrior pushes their body to the brink, when they take themselves to the edge of their physical limits, and then shatter those limitations, that they gain the strength they so desire."*

"Um, if you say so."

"I do say so. Now…" Kiara's eyes gleamed as she pulled the whip back. *"Start running!"*

The sound of a whip cracking, followed swiftly by a number of girlish squeals, echoed throughout the city. Rumors would eventually spread about a masochistic young man who let his mistress tie him to a harness and pull her around while she whipped him. Eric would not be happy when he learned that someone had beaten him in the masochism department, and no amount of denial would convince him that Kevin was only letting Kiara do this so he could become stronger.

In the end, Kevin couldn't get to 200 push-ups. He couldn't even break past the 100 mark.

"Eighty-eight," Kiara muttered, mostly to herself, though Kevin heard her all the same. "Not bad, boya. It's definitely an improvement from the twenty push-up limit you had when you first started." She looked down at the young man laying on his back, his tongue lolling out of his mouth as he gasped for breath, and his body covered in a thick layer of sweat. "Good job."

"Gu… ugh…"

Kevin could not answer. For obvious reasons.

***

After taking a shower, Kevin, having donned his outfit of faded leather jeans, a white T-shirt and sneakers, left Kiara's mercilessly untender hands.

He didn't ride his bike back home, mainly because he couldn't ride his bike. His body was in too much pain for that. His arms were sore, his legs were burning, and his chest felt like someone had injected acid straight into his muscles.

And yet, despite the pain, he felt good. Maybe not physically good, but mentally, emotionally, Kevin felt incredible. Accomplished. It wasn't noticeable yet, but he felt like he was getting stronger.

Arriving home and grunting his way up the stairs, Kevin

entered his apartment to find Kotohime cooking breakfast. He knew it was her before even looking in the kitchen, as he could smell the Japanese cuisine being prepared. Lilian rarely made Japanese food these days, preferring to try new dishes each time she cooked. She had a predilection for American breakfasts.

"Good morning, Kevin-sama." Despite her greeting, Kotohime did not look up from her task of setting the table.

"Um, good morning," Kevin muttered a tad shyly. Even after two weeks, he still couldn't get over the new suffix she had added to his name. He remembered asking her why she'd decided to switch from using "-san" to "-sama" once. Her answer had been rather enlightening.

"Because you have officially become Lilian-sama's mate. I must afford you the respect that comes with such a position, even if you are not quite deserving of such respect yourself."

Kotohime was a very traditional woman, believing that respect must at least be afforded to the position, if not the person who held it.

"I hope your workout with Kiara-san was productive," she continued as her tails reached into a cabinet and pulled out several plates.

"Uh, yeah, I like to think it was pretty productive." Kevin rubbed the back of his head, and then winced. It seemed even the simplest of movements hurt. "Kiara's tough, but thanks to her, I think I'm starting to get a little stronger."

"That is good. You're going to need that strength if you plan on standing by Lilian-sama's side."

"Believe me, I am already well-aware of that," Kevin said with more than just a hint of dryness.

"I'm sure you are." Kotohime's demure smile held an amused gleam, and her eyes glimmered in ways that still bothered Kevin. He felt like she was taking pleasure from his predicament.

After he had decided to become Lilian's mate, Kotohime had taken him aside and informed him of the dangers he would face— some of them anyway. She had not been pleasant about it either. There had been no reassurances, no "don't worry, I'll protect you" speeches or anything of the sort. Just straight up, brutally honest information given to him in a way that made the whole issue seem almost mundane.

Kevin was sure Kotohime had gotten a kick out of the whole thing.

"Breakfast will be ready soon," Kotohime's voice interrupted his thoughts. "Could you please wake up Lilian-sama for me? I believe she will enjoy being woken up by you more than she would me." Her smile as she said this was more than just a little devious. The way her eyes sparkled with a strange sort of mischief didn't help.

"Don't I always wake Lilian up?" Kevin retorted, "And of course she'd prefer me. I'm her mate."

"Ufufufu, indeed."

Kevin left Kotohime to her cooking and entered his bedroom. However, he paused in the doorway when he caught sight of his mate lying on the bed.

His heart skipped a beat.

Lilian lay on her back, her eyes closed. Even from a distance he could see her thick eyelashes, which presented a stark contrast to her fair skin. Her pink lips that looked far too kissable to resist were slightly parted as she rhythmically breathed in and out. Her breathing also had the added benefit of causing her bountiful chest to jiggle enticingly within the confines of the overly large shirt she wore, which looked far better on her than it ever had on him.

The covers had been thrown off at some point after he left. He knew this because he'd made sure they were covering her before heading off to Mad Dawg Fitness. Her left leg had fallen off the bed, and her right hand rested on her flat stomach. Crimson locks of hair fanned across the white sheets like an additional layer of silk, each strand shimmering in the morning light, haloing Lilian in a curtain of fire.

Even though Kevin had born witness to scenes like this for over two months now, it never got old. Everything Lilian did, even something as simple as sleeping, managed to combine astonishing sensuality with an innocence that was nothing short of criminal. He was sure that no one else in the entire world could pull off something like this.

***

Camellia let out several sneezes.

"Kuchu! Kuchu!"

It was an oddly cute sound coming from a woman with such a killer body, though those who knew her would not be surprised, given her childlike personality.

Unfortunately, she happened to be walking down the stairs when she sneezed and, as her sense of balance was like a child just learning how to walk, she ended up slipping. With a loud cry, Camellia tumbled down the stairs.

"HAWA!!!"

"M-My Lady!"

Fortunately for the poor maid who hurriedly rushed to her mistress' side, Camellia's breasts broke her fall. Again.

***

Sitting down on the bed, Kevin's right hand almost absently went to Lilian's cheek. His fingers tingled at the feel of her smooth, unblemished skin, so unlike his own rough and calloused hands. Lilian leaned into his touch, her full lips opening a bit more as she released a delicate sigh.

The urge to kiss her right then was almost overwhelming.

His thumb softly grazed over her lips. Her skin pursed slightly as she kissed the digit, sending a jolt through him, which traveled from his thumb down to his feet and then up to the crown of his head. This sensation! How could something as simple as a kiss on the thumb feel so electric?

As he admired the young woman he'd officially become, well, mated to, he guessed, he noticed something about her that he hadn't several seconds ago.

It wasn't the smile. She'd been wearing that since before he left this morning.

It was her eyes. Her left eye, to be exact. It was cracked open and staring at him.

He and Lilian gazed at each other for several silent seconds, after which, she seemed to realize that he'd noticed her staring and closed her eye again.

Kevin nearly snorted.

"Come on, Lilian." He removed his hand from her cheek and placed it on her shoulder, where he lightly shook her. "Time to get up."

"Zzzzz...."

"Fake snores aren't going to work on me, you know."

"Lilian can't get up. She's asleep."

"Talking in third person definitely isn't going to work. Come on. You have to get up. Kotohime has breakfast ready and we've got our first day of school to attend since its reopening."

"Lilian won't wake up until she receives a kiss from her mate."

Kevin sighed. He really didn't mind kissing her awake, the same way he didn't mind when she kissed him awake, but they had school today and, well, nothing they did ever ended in a single kiss. Lilian never allowed it to.

"Lilian…"

"Nope."

"Ha…"

Another sigh. Lilian could be really stubborn when she wanted to be. Knowing the vixen like he did, Kevin knew that she really would just lay there until he gave in.

He smiled. Just a bit. There were worse things he could think of doing than kissing his mate-slash-girlfriend.

Leaning down, Kevin let his lips caress Lilian's with the softest of touches. His plan was to give her a small peck and nothing more. He might not have minded kisses, but he didn't want to be late for school, or be forced to skip breakfast so they wouldn't be late. That would have sucked, especially because his workout with Kiara had left him starving.

His plan to just brush lips ended when delicate, feminine fingers wove into his hair, grasped the back of his head, and pulled him down. Kevin, in his surprise, opened his mouth to release a yelp. A tongue pushed its way into his mouth, leaving him with no time to fight back as it began exploring, like a excavator journeying deep into an unexplored cavern.

Kevin groaned as his mouth was filled with a most pleasurable sensation. He could feel Lilian's small tongue rubbing against the inside of his mouth in all sorts of mind-blowing ways, as if it was intent on sending him into a euphoric state of rapture.

If asked, he would never be able to adequately explain what it felt like to kiss Lilian. Words would never be able to accurately describe the feeling of her lips on his, of the wet heat generated from their kiss as his mouth became filled with her tongue and saliva. He could say it was passionate, or that it was hot, sexy, or any other number of words, but they would have been misleading simply because her kisses were all that and more.

However, he would easily tell anyone who asked that Lilian was the best kisser in the world, even if he'd never kissed anyone else and therefore had no frame of reference to back up such a claim.

This would be, of course, after he stopped blushing and stuttering from being asked such a personal question.

The world suddenly spun around. Kevin felt a disorienting sense of not-quite-vertigo, and then something soft pressed against his back, while something else just as soft pushed down on his front.

It didn't take long to realize he was lying on his bed, and that Lillian was now on top of him. He could feel her breasts smashing into his chest as she rested against him. Her legs became entwined with his, skin on skin action that created a delicious friction as her shapely calves and thighs caressed him. Her hands were still buried in his hair. They made a mess of his blond locks, nails scraping against his skin and leaving a pleasant tingle.

"Lilian..." Kevin mumbled breathlessly as Lilian went from kissing him to sucking, nibbling and licking his neck. He'd found out early on in their relationship that Lilian, for whatever reason, loved licking him. Consequently, she also loved being licked in return.

She pulled back to stare into his eyes. They were incredibly clear; bright green orbs more beautiful than any emerald could ever hope to be, shining with an effervescent luster akin to the light of twin celestial bodies. Her nose grazed his, and he could feel her hot breath caressing his lips. It was enough to make him shudder, and his need to feel those lips back on his became almost overpowering.

"I love you so much, Kevin," she told him, and the earnestness in her voice made his heart melt and his body quake with an emotion that vaguely resembled awe.

Kevin still didn't know how she could say something so easily, but then, maybe he wasn't supposed to understand. She was a kitsune and he was a human. Hers was a mind that couldn't be fathomed by someone with his mortality.

"I know," Kevin whispered, "I... I l-love you, too."

Lilian closed her eyes and arched her back like a cat, a sigh of bliss escaping her delicately parted lips. She wasn't wearing a bra, so the action did some wonderful things to her chest.

She opened her eyes again, capturing him with her viridian gaze. As she leaned down and claimed his lips once more, Kevin forgot about the reason he'd come to this room. His hands settled on the small of her back, still too shy and embarrassed to place them anywhere else. Lilian didn't seem to mind. She moaned into his mouth, a delightful sound that was muffled by their passionate, if inexperienced, kisses.

One last thought came to him before he succumbed to raging hormones.

Deciding to become Lilian's mate was the smartest choice I've ever made.

***

Nearly half an hour later, Kevin and Lilian sped down the bike lane like a pair of young fox kits being chased by a boarhound.

"We're so late! Dang it! You see, Lilian? This is what happens when I let you have your way!"

They were, quite obviously, running late. After their gods-only-know-how-long makeout session, Kevin had realized how late they were and made a frantic effort to get Lilian ready for school. He'd practically shoved her into the shower, chosen her clothes while she washed up, and then forced them both to eat breakfast posthaste before dragging her out the door.

Lillian didn't seem upset by his words, despite their harshness. Giggling, the redhead kept her arms wrapped tightly around his chest as she pushed her bosom into his back. She giggled even more when his spine stiffened like a metal rod.

"You weren't complaining before you found out we were running late."

Kevin nearly crashed into a light pole when he momentarily lost control of the bike. "Y-y-yes, w-w-well, w-who would complain about something like that?"

Lilian just smiled while nuzzling his back with her nose. She inhaled his scent. She loved his scent, and the warmth his body emitted, which had become her bastion of warmth in Phoenix's increasingly cool weather.

October had finally come, and with it, autumn had truly come to Arizona. Many of the leaves had lost their color and fallen to the ground. The air was not yet cold, but chilly enough that Lilian could feel the coolness seeping into her bones. As a kitsune, she was very susceptible to even mildly cold weather and had a predisposition towards warmer climates, such as the warm humidity of Tampa Bay and her clan's estate in Greece.

"Ha... ha..." Kevin breathed out deeply as he pedaled down the road. "Almost... there..."

Despite how sore he felt, Kevin still managed to haul major butt. One of the many benefits to Kiara's training was that his legs, which had already been exceptional for an athlete, had grown even stronger than before. He proved this by making it to school in record time.

Hopping off and locking down his bike, he and Lillian rushed hand-in-hand to their first class of the day, bursting into the room with all the subtlety of a rhino dancing in a ballet.

Kevin took deep, gasping breaths as he hunched over and rested his hands on his knees. Lilian only appeared mildly flushed. Then again, she also hadn't done a near suicidal workout routine with a merciless trainer that morning.

"You two are both late!"

If Kevin were not so breathless, he would have sighed. He really wished he had a different homeroom teacher.

Ms. Vis stalked up to them, her face scrunched up in a facsimile of outrage, her outlandish anger appearing almost comical, like some B-budget horror movie makeup artist on drugs had gone to town.

The pale woman hadn't changed much since the last time they saw her. Her clothes remained the same, her attitude remained the same, and she still looked like a Twilight reject. If there was one person he hadn't missed during his hiatus from school, it was her.

"Yeah." Kevin tried to play the diplomat. "Sorry about that. We, uh, got lost on the road of life."

Kevin would never make a very good diplomat.

Ms. Vis' face scrunched even more, becoming almost pinched, like a pug with clamps stuck to its face. It was also beginning to turn a rather repulsive shade of puce.

"Why I never! I cannot believe that you, of all people, would arrive late to my class, interrupt my lesson, and then have the audacity to give me such a horrid excuse," Ms. Vis hissed, her voice sounding similar to a bed of angry snakes. "I expected something like this from Ms. Pnéw ma, but not from you! It seems that…"

And that was about as far as Ms. Vis got before Kevin tuned her out. His eyes scanned the crowd of students sitting at their desks. He recognized the many faces present, even if he could not recall their names. Over by his and Lilian's assigned seats, he could see Lindsay at her desk, smiling and waving at him.

"And you!" Ms. Vis whirled on Lilian, an accusing finger pointed at the twin-tailed vixen. "Do not think that I am going to let you get away with corrupting my student! I do not know what you've done to pollute Mr. Swift's mind, but if you think I am going to let you cause the degradation of one of my student's intellect, then you are sorely mistaken, young woman!"

"I'm sorry, but I don't know what you're talking about." Lilian's eyes glowed a bright green as she cast an enchantment on the pale-skinned teacher. "I have not corrupted Mr. Swift at all."

Ms. Vis' eyes became dull and lifeless. "You have not corrupted Mr. Swift at all…"

"In fact, I have been doing all I can to educate him on all of the important issues he needs to know."

"You have been educating him on important issues…"

"Now, you will let us sit down and continue your lesson as if we were never late."

"Go sit down. I need to continue my lesson…"

"Oh! And by the way…" Ms. Vis, who had turned around, looked back at Lilian, who waved her hand in a vaguely mysterious fashion. "These are not the droids you're looking for."

A pause.

"These are not the droids I'm looking for…"

With that, Ms. Vis turned and walked up to the front of the classroom.

Kevin and Lilian shared a quick grin and a high five, before making their way over to their respective desks.

Or at least, they were going to, until they noticed how everyone else was staring at them. No, not just staring at them. The other students were giving them wide-eyed looks of incomprehensible shock, as if they had walked into class wearing matching green spandex, orange leg-warmers, were sporting a bowl-cut hair style, and shouting about their "flames of youth."

"That was a terrible anime reference."

… Sorry.

"It's fine, but please don't do it again."

… Okay.

"Lilian…"

"Come on, Kevin." She grabbed his hand and, ignoring his "who the hell are you talking to?" expression, dragged him further into the classroom. "Let's find a seat."

Kevin shook his head in a resigned manner as he and Lilian sat down. He greeted Lindsay, who appeared both amused and annoyed for some reason, and then turned to Ms. Vis as she lectured the class on Differential Equations.

* * *

Unlike most of the students who attended Desert Cactus High School, Lilian actually liked school.

It had nothing to do with learning, however, and everything to do with what school represented to her: Freedom. For Lilian, school was the embodiment of freedom. When she was at school, she could do what she wanted, be who she wanted, spend time with her friends, and meet interesting people.

There were also a lot of kinky scenarios that she and Kevin could get up to at school. Unfortunately, she had yet to convince her beloved that mating in the nurse's examination room (and also in the school lockers, the gym, and on Ms. Vis' desk) would be fun. Of course, considering she and Kevin had yet to actually do the deed, perhaps she was asking for too much.

A lot of people would have called her strange. She had learned from Kevin that most teenagers disliked school. Even Kevin considered it an obligation that he could do without.

However, Lilian was not like other people, be they human or kitsune. She was someone who, above everything else, enjoyed the freedom to make her own choices, a person who sought adventure in all its different forms and loved trying new things. That was also why she loved anime, manga, and video games so much.

The first few decades of her life as a supernatural being had been spent within the isolated grounds of her clan's estate in

Greece. Those years had been terrible. They'd been boring and lonely and hard. Her only companions had been Kotohime, Iris, her mom and Kirihime. They were nice, and she loved them, but they couldn't give her what she had now.

Kevin had saved her from all of that. Meeting him had been what saved her from that loneliness. He didn't know it. He couldn't possibly understand even if he still possessed his memories of that time, but he had been her salvation, her savior. She would always be grateful to him, even if he didn't remember the reason for her gratitude.

After class ended, she and Kevin parted ways with Lindsay and went to their next class. For the next several hours, Lilian spent time with Kevin in each class. While her mate mostly focused on taking notes and getting his work done, he did converse with her by sending covert messages through a notebook they had decided to share. After French, Physics and Social Sciences, she and Kevin walked across the courtyard toward the newly repaired gymnasium.

"Ne, Kevin?"

"Hm?"

"Is it just me, or is the roof a different color than it was before?"

Kevin looked at her out of the corner of his eye, then at the roof she was talking about.

"I think you might be right," he muttered, his eyes squinting. "It's still the same color, just... less worn, I guess. It looks like they ended up replacing the roof with a brand new one. I'm not surprised. It was probably easier to replace it than repair it after the damage you and Kiara caused."

As her face reddened, Lilian puffed up her cheeks like two balloons. "It wasn't my fault. Kiara's the one who tore a hole in the roof."

"And you're the one who fought her."

Lilian had nothing to say to that.

As they walked, Lilian noticed how they seemed to attract everyone's attention. She didn't know why, but a lot of people appeared to enjoy talking about them.

"Can you believe that someone as hot as Lilian is still dating a kid like Kevin?"

"Not really, no. I thought they would have broken up weeks ago. I wonder what she sees in a scrawny little kid like him."

"I'm just surprised he hasn't passed out yet. Wasn't he supposed to be afraid of girls or something?"

If she weren't in her human form, Lilian's ears would have twitched as she listened in on the many conversations happening around her. She didn't like how these boys were talking about Kevin like he wasn't worth her time or attention. Deciding who was and wasn't worth her affection was a privilege that belonged to her and her alone. These people should've kept their opinions to themselves!

"Something wrong, Lilian?"

"Oh, no." Lilian smiled at Kevin. "Nothing's wrong. I was just... thinking."

"About?"

"About how strange it feels to be back at school." Kevin raised an eyebrow, prompting Lilian to elaborate. "I know I haven't been going to school for very long, but it still feels weird coming back after not attending classes for a whole month."

Kevin nodded several times. "That's understandable. Most students feel that way after summer vacation ends."

"Summer vacation?"

"Mm. School lasts exactly nine months out of the year. However, the school closes down during the three months of summer, which we call summer vacation." Kevin paused and looked up, as if a thought had occurred to him. "Of course, I don't think we'll get much of a summer vacation this year, since we just had a month long break."

"Oh. That's kind of disappointing."

Kevin shrugged. "That's life. We're actually one of the luckier schools because we still have summer vacation. Most schools have become year-round schools, which people attend, well, year round. They don't get summer vacation at all."

"Owch." Lilian winced. She enjoyed school, but to have it all year? "That sucks."

Kevin's lips twitched in amusement. "Indeed."

***

Iris impatiently tapped her foot as she stood by the door, waiting for her mother to arrive. Really, how long did it take for that woman to get ready?

"M-My Lady! Please be careful!"

"Hawawawawawa!"

Iris sighed as her mother tumbled down the stairs for the second time that day. This time, she also had a large suitcase with her, which burst open, spilling the contents all over the floor. One of Camellia's panties flew through the air before fluttering to land on her head.

"Geez, Mom," she said, exasperated. "Is there ever a time when you aren't tripping over your own two feet?"

"Hawa…" Camellia looked up at her daughter from where she sat on the floor, tears gathering in her carmine eyes and a pair of white panties lying on her head. "Sowwy."

Kneeling behind the klutzy five-tails, Kirihime looked up at Iris as she comforted the older woman with some gentle head petting.

"P-please, Lady Iris, do not be rude to your mother," the demure maid pleaded. "You know it is not My Lady's fault."

"Yeah, yeah." Iris waved off the woman's words with an air of indifference. "Whatever. Look, can we just get a move on? The more time we spend standing here, the longer it'll be before I can see my sister."

Kirihime frowned at Iris, whose two tails writhed behind her in agitation. "I know that you are excited to finally see Lady Lilian after so long, but please be patient. Our flight doesn't leave for another two hours, and the airport is only thirty minutes away."

Crossing her arms under her bust, Iris huffed. Meanwhile, Kirihime helped Camellia to her feet. Her three tails also extended to impressive lengths and gathered up the luggage her mistress had dropped.

"That reminds me… just why are we taking an airplane again?"

"Because we're not allowed to set up Spirit Gates in the United States," Kirihime answered as she dusted off Camellia's clothes. "The United States has been claimed by the Four Saints and, as per the agreement set down after the war of 1868, no yōkai clan is allowed to claim any state within the United States as their territory. That's why we had to travel here by boat when we first arrived. Wasn't Lady Iris taught this already?"

"Maybe," Iris admitted with an uncaring shrug, "but it's not like I ever paid attention to what that shriveled prude, Daphne, ever said."

"L-Lady Iris, you shouldn't speak of your elder sister so disrespectfully."

Iris waved a hand through the air. "Whatever. Can we get going now?"

Kirihime sighed. There was just no pleasing this girl.

"Of course, Lady Iris. Shall we get going? I have hired a taxi that will meet us at the front gate in a few minutes, if it isn't already here."

"Finally." Iris lifted her small duffel bag, which contained all she'd be bringing with her. "Let's get going."

Camellia sniffled as Iris stalked off. "Iris doesn't like Camellia."

Kirihime winced at the sheer amount of hurt in Camellia's tone. It pained her to see what this once amazing woman had been reduced to. Unfortunately, there was little she could do to help her mistress, except comfort the woman using the only tried and true method she knew of.

Kirihime reached up and began gently petting Camellia's head.

"Hawa," the five-tails muttered in a blissful voice.

***

It happened while Kevin and Lilian were walking to the school locker rooms. One minute they were minding their own business. The next, Eric appeared before them as if by magic.

"It is a pleasure to see you, My Lord."

Kevin stared at his friend with his best "why the hell are you calling me that?" look. The lecherous young man knelt before him, reminiscent of a knight kneeling before their king.

It was all kinds of disturbing.

"Um, Eric, what the heck are you doing?"

"What do you mean, My Lord? Is something troubling you?"

"Yes. Yes, there is."

"What is it? Please tell me so that I might help fix whatever is ailing you, My Lord."

"You are." Kevin gave the still kneeling Eric a flat look. Lilian just looked vaguely amused. "Seriously, Eric, get up. You're freaking me out."

"Okay—I mean, very well, My Lord."

"Stop calling me that!"

With an unusual amount of pomp, the physical embodiment of lust and perversion stood to his feet. "If that is what you desire, then I shall do my best to comply with your wishes."

"Uh huh…" Kevin leaned in towards Lilian so he could whisper into her ear. "Do you have know what's up with Eric?"

"Mm mm." Lilian shook her head. "The last time I saw him was when he and everyone else came over last week, remember? And I didn't see anything happen to him that you didn't see yourself."

Kevin nodded. He remembered the last time they'd seen Eric quite well. He and Lilian had invited everyone to their home again for a movie night. All of their friends had shown up, including Christine, who'd told them she only showed up because it was common courtesy.

"D-d-don't think I'm here because I like you or anything! I-I-I-I'm only here because you invited me over and I have nothing better to do! Hmph!"

Something like that.

He still recalled the beating Christine had given Eric when the lecherous boy managed to successfully cop a feel. Kevin still shuddered every time he remembered what happened. Humans just weren't meant to bend that way.

Deciding to ignore his friend's strange behavior, he and Lilian renewed their walk to the locker rooms with Eric in tow.

"So," Kevin started, eying the pervert walking alongside them, "mind if I ask why you're calling me 'My Lord?'"

"I've decided to turn over a new leaf," Eric declared. Kevin and Lilian shared a brief look before focusing back on the pervert.

"A new leaf, huh?"

"That is correct. I have decided… from this day forth, you are my new lord!"

"Uh huh… wait." Kevin blinked. So did Lilian. "What?"

"Yes, I will become your lackey, and score any tail that you decide to spare me."

"Um..."

"I can't believe he just said that," Lilian commented, idly wondering if Eric had finally lost it after learning that she and Kevin were officially a mated couple, even if they hadn't actually mated yet.

Kevin used his free hand, the one whose fingers were not laced through Lilian's, to facepalm. "I can. I can so believe he just said that. I merely wish he hadn't."

"Yes!" Eric clenched his fist, a diabolically pervy grin etched upon his face. It was disturbing enough to make eldritch horrors look like cute, fluffy white bunnies. "This plan is foolproof! Women always seem to flock to you for some reason!"

"Uh, no. Only Lilian's really shown any interest in me..."

"And knowing your luck, it won't be long now before even more women flock to you!"

"Are you sure you're talking about me?"

"And since you're dating Lilian, that means every other bodaciously-bodied babe will be up for grabs!"

Kevin turned a desperate look towards his mate. "Lilian? He's not listening to me. What should I do?"

"Why are you asking me?" Lilian looked honestly confused. "I don't know how to make him stop. Maybe you should see if he has an off switch or something."

"I think any switch he might have only comes with two settings: perv and pervier."

"That means every sexy bitch coming your way will become mine! Yes! I will finally obtain my goal of becoming a Harem King! Mwahahahahahahaha-BWUAHAHAHAHAHAHA!"

By this point, tears of joy were streaming down Eric's face. He raised a hand to the ceiling, as if he was trying to reach out and grasp heaven.

Kevin and Lilian noticed all the people stopping to gawk at Eric as he stood in place, right hand on his hip, left hand raised toward the ceiling, his laughter reminiscent of a stereotypical anime villain.

Slowly, ever so slowly so to as not attract attention to themselves, the kitsune and her human mate began walking away from the scene.

As they walked further away from Eric, they could hear his

maniacally perverse laughter becoming softer and softer until, eventually, it vanished altogether.

"Kevin…"

"Let's just pretend this whole incident never happened," Kevin said.

Lilian tilted her head, a thoughtful frown marring her pretty face until, ever so slowly, she nodded. "Agreed.

***

Had he not been present to see the aftermath of Lilian and Kiara's battle, Kevin would have never believed the gym had once been the location of an epic showdown between yōkai. The once ruined floorboards were pristine, glistening with a lacquered finish. Brand new bleachers lined two sides of the interior, and the girders overhead gleamed with the luminosity of new steel.

Kevin and Lilian stood with two dozen other kids. Most of them were in groups of two or three, talking amongst themselves about one thing or another. Over to their left, a couple girls were staring at them. Whenever he or Lilian looked their way, they would giggle and go back to their conversation, which Kevin suspected he and his mate were the topic of. Standing several feet to his right was yet another group of kids, boys this time, all of whom were glaring at him. Kevin matched their glare with a stare of his own, which just caused their attempts to kill him with their eyes to grow more fervent.

"I never thought I'd see you look so confrontational," Lilian said, studying his expression.

Kevin turned away from his peers and looked at her, his head tilting. "What do you mean? I'm not being confrontational."

"Yes, you are," Lilian rebutted, smiling as if she was pleased about something. "Maybe you're not trying to bring about a physical confrontation, but you're definitely showing these other boys more hostility than before. Back when we first met, you always did your best to avoid the looks they sent you. Now you're returning them."

Kevin turned his head a bit, mostly to hide his blush. "I'm just sick and tired of people looking at me like I've committed some great crime. The only reason they're glaring at me like that is because I'm dating you and they're not. I'm tired of dealing with their petty jealousy."

"I never said there was anything wrong with it." Lilian placed one hand on his right shoulder while the other began to run up and down his left arm. "I like that you're not letting these people get to you like you used to. It's really hot."

Kevin rubbed the back of his neck, his cheeks growing even darker. "Y-you think so?"

"Oh, yes."

The world around him faded as Lilian's trapped him with her gaze. Slowly, she leaned up on her tiptoes and gave him a soft, almost delicate kiss. Kevin closed his eyes and kissed back. He didn't hear the girlish squeals that erupted from nearby, nor did he feel the increased killing intent pouring off the boys. Everything except him and Lilian vanished from his perception.

"Not you two again! Knock it off, lovebirds! Go play tonsil hockey on your own time!"

At least until a familiar shout interrupted them.

Kevin and Lilian pulled away from each other. While he blushed and tried to pretend that he hadn't been exploring the inside of Lilian's mouth with his tongue, his twin-tailed mate glared at Coach Raide, who hardly even seemed to notice the angered look she assailed him with. The large wookie of a coach blew his whistle and started shouting.

"Alright, brats! Line up!"

Standing so close their shoulders were touching, Kevin and Lilian stood in line. Eric, who must have appeared around the same time as Coach Raide, moved to stand on Kevin's left.

"I've got some news for you kids," Coach Raide began. Everyone looked surprised. Their PE coach wasn't one for giving speeches, so if he actually had something to tell them, it must have been important. "We've got a new assistant coach today. She's going to be in charge of all female PE activities, so you little valley girls had better listen to what she says! Got it?!"

Coach Raide got several glares from a couple of those "valley girls," who didn't appreciate the insult one bit.

"Now I want you all to welcome... Ms. Heather Grant."

Kevin only had a moment to wonder why that name sounded so familiar, because seconds later, a woman who looked vaguely familiar walked in through one of the gym's double doors.

Her short blond hair framed a pleasantly smiling face. She

wore a pair of blue sweatpants with white lines running along the outer legs, and a blue t-shirt that conformed to her generous frame. Despite himself, Kevin noticed that her bust, while not the same size as Lilian's, was still quite large. Light bluish-green eyes looked upon the group of students with a strange sort of dazzle, as if they were a pair of sparkling gems. Several boys held a hand to their nose as blood seeped between their fingers.

The only nosebleeder who didn't hold a hand to his nose was Eric, and that was because he was already on the move.

"Oh, baby! Where have you been all my life, you boobilicious blond sex machine! Come to papa—Gurk!"

Everyone watched in mute shock as Eric was clotheslined by a deceptively delicate arm.

It was almost amazing how the lower half of Eric's body continued moving even while his neck and head remained practically stationary. Due to the built up momentum, his feet left the ground, swinging about in a surprisingly graceful parabolic arc. The rest of his body soon followed, rotating along the central axis provided courtesy of the woman's arm.

Time, which seemed to have slowed down as Eric soared through the air in an out of control spin, reasserted itself as the licentious boy hit the ground. Hard.

"Urk!"

Several people winced at the strangled gurgles that escaped the boy's mouth.

"I give you an A for effort, but an F for execution," Heather said. Kevin's brows furrowed some more. He felt like he should know this woman. "Seriously kid, what were you thinking, going for a frontal assault like that? Everybody knows that when you want to properly grope a woman, you need to sneak in behind them and attack when they least expect it."

"Urk... ugh... ooh..."

Kevin wondered if anyone else was sweatdropping as much as him. Did this woman seriously just give Eric Corrompere, the epitome of concupiscence, groping advice?

Heather looked up, an amused smirk on her lips.

Then she made eye contact with Kevin and Lilian.

The smirk vanished.

"AAHHHHH!!!" Kevin and Lilian pointed at the woman, who

pointed right back, all three of them shouting at the same time. "IT'S YOU!"

***

The boys and girls split up after Heather was introduced, with Coach Raide taking the boys outside while the girls remained indoors.

"Alex."

"Rodriguez."

"So…" Eric placed his hands behind his head. "That Heather chick with the mean WWF skills is the woman in charge of those people who tried kidnapping you and Lilian, huh?"

"Seems that way," Kevin grunted. He and Eric were standing in yet another line, this one on the basketball court.

I hate basketball.

"Philip."

"Brian."

Eric whistled. "Damn. Never thought we'd bump into one of those people. Wonder how she got a job working at this school. Then again, that Japanese professor guy—"

"Inagami Takashi."

"Right, right, him. Anyway, he also worked at this school. Maybe she had her super secret spy agency or whatever create some false identification stating she was a teacher."

"Or maybe your dad let her have the job because she's hot, and we all know that your dad's as lecherous as you are."

"Christian."

"Zach."

"That's a harsh thing to say, My Lord," Eric muttered. "My old man might be a perv, but there's no way he's anywhere near as perverted as me!"

"That's not something to be proud of, idiot! And don't call me 'My Lord!' It's creepy."

"Francis."

"Jack."

"So, what do you think's going on with the girls?" asked Eric.

Kevin ran a hand through his hair. "I don't know, but I'm worried. That woman was the one who ordered my kidnapping, or at least I think she was. Either way, she was the one in charge of those people, which means she's the one who wanted to capture

Lilian. Who's to say that's not still her goal?"

"You could always call the police."

"And say what? 'Hey, Mr. Police Officer. I've got this woman teaching my gym class. I think she's actually a spy sent by a secret organization to capture my kitsune girlfriend. Could you please send someone over here to arrest her for me?'" Kevin snorted. "Yeah, I can see that going over really well."

"You know, you've become awfully sarcastic in the past two weeks, My Lord." Kevin twitched. "Are you feeling alright?"

"Just dandy."

"Haden."

"Eric."

"Heh, looks like they're calling me." Eric stepped out of line and tossed his friend a wave. "Catch you later, My Lord."

"Oh, for the all the gods' sakes, would you stop calling me that?!"

***

"Shouldn't you be playing dodgeball with the other girls?"

Lilian didn't answer Heather's question, instead choosing to glare daggers at the blond-haired woman. The new assistant coach appeared more amused by the redhead's attempt at making her spontaneously combust via her eyes than bothered. She was even grinning.

"Now there's a dangerous look. You weren't wearing that look the last time I saw you." Heather lifted her eyes to the ceiling. "Then again, I couldn't really see you all that well, since you were being supported by your boy toy."

"Don't you dare call Kevin that!" Lilian spat.

"Oh, so you can talk. I was beginning to wonder."

Lilian and Heather sat on the bleachers. Well, Heather was sitting. Lilian stood several feet from the woman, hands clenched into fists so tight that it was a wonder her nails hadn't broken the skin.

"What are you doing here?"

"My job." Heather raised an eyebrow. "You know, assistant PE coach?"

"That's not what I meant and you know it!" Lilian's already narrowed eyes became fierce slits. Her transformation slipped for a second, whiskers appearing for a brief instant before vanishing.

"What are you doing here? Are you here to try and kidnap me again? Or are you going to try and use Kevin as a hostage like you did last time? I swear, if you hurt even one hair on his head, I'll—"

"Whoa! Whoa! Whoa! Slow down, girl." Heather raised her hands in a "settle down" gesture. "I have no designs on kidnapping either you or your boyfriend. I'm not even a member of that group anymore."

Lilian remained tense, still feeling wary of letting her guard down around this woman. "What do you mean?"

"I mean they fired me," Heather stated flatly. "People who don't accomplish their mission objectives aren't people they can afford to keep. When I failed to capture you, they decided I was no longer fit to be a member of their group and they dropped me faster than yesterday's trash."

"So, if you're not after me and Kevin, then what are you doing here?"

"Didn't I just tell you? I'm the assistant PE coach." Heather shrugged. "I needed a job, so I applied."

"And they let you work here just like that?"

"Yep." Heather nodded. "The principal said 'you're cute, so I'll hire you!' and that was how I got my job."

Lilian took a second to think about that statement.

A drop of sweat soon appeared near her temple, trailing down her face and neck, rolling across her clavicle bone, before dipping into her PE shirt.

Lilian remembered; she had been allowed to enroll despite not having any of the necessary background information for that very same reason.

"Right. I forgot the principal here is a complete pervert."

***

Sitting in his office, behind his fancy desk made of the finest mahogany, Principal Corrompere giggled. Several feet away from him was a television, and on that television was porn.

What? This was the guy who birthed Eric. Are you honestly surprised?

"Kukukuku... oh, yeah.... you girls are looking mighty fine... oh, yes... just like that... you can do it, baby!"

As he giggled some more, mumbling out words no principal in their right mind should ever say out loud—especially at a school—

a strange sensation came over him, like a feather tickling his nose.

He sneezed. Then he looked around. After several seconds of nothing happening, Eric's father shrugged and went back to watching porn.

And people wondered why this school was so messed up.

***

Gym eventually ended.

Kevin and Lilian met up after changing into their regular clothes. Eric probably would have been with them, except he'd been sent to the nurse's office after trying to sneak up on Heather and grope her from behind. Too bad the woman was a former secret agent of some kind. Not even the Deus Sex Machina that allowed all perverts to recover after a massive beating seemed capable of healing the grievous injuries she had dealt to him.

Almost as soon as they left the gymnasium, Kevin noticed his mate's mood. "Are you worried about that Heather woman?"

"Yes. No. Well, maybe a little." Lilian furrowed her brows and frowned. "I don't like the fact that she's working here at our school. That woman's already kidnapped you once."

"Ugh, please don't remind me."

"Who's to say she won't try it again?"

"Yeah, I thought the same thing, more or less." Kevin paused. "Only our roles in the entirely hypothetical second kidnapping scenario were reversed. Anyway, there's not much we can do unless you want to pick a fight with her or something. We'll inform Kotohime about Heather becoming our new teacher. That way, if something happens to us and we don't show up at home, she'll know who the most likely culprit is. Really, that's about all we can do."

"I guess…"

They stopped in the middle of a busy sidewalk. All around them, their fellow students walked. A few glanced at them, and more than a few whispered as they walked past, but Kevin did his best to ignore them.

Kevin placed his hands on Lilian's shoulders, a reassuring gesture that did an admirable job of making the two-tailed vixen relax. His touch was like a panacea for her tumultuous mind. "Try not to worry too much, okay. If anything happens, we'll deal with it just like we've dealt with every other problem that's come our way."

Lilian's eyes glanced up at her mate. Long strands of silky red glittered as sunlight reflected off her hair, framing her face with sparkles that enhanced her beauty beyond what mere eyes could see.

"You really have grown a lot more confident these past two weeks, haven't you?" Lilian's lips gently curved up into a warm, inviting smile.

Kevin's cheeks darkened as he quickly turned his head, even if he already knew that hiding his blush was impossible. "Y-yes, well, I'm trying to be, at least."

Slender arms slid around his neck and a lovely, alluring face came ever closer as Lilian leaned up on her toes. Kevin was forced to look back at the young woman when she placed a hand underneath his chin and turned it.

"I like how confident you've become."

As if they possessed a mind of their own, Kevin's hands settled on the curve of Lilian's hips. Even separated as they were by the fabric of her jeans, he could feel the delightful and artistic curve of her waist.

Kevin's face became a bastion of red, and his body twitched as if fighting against the compulsion to run away. "R-really?"

"Oh, yes."

The arms around his neck drew him in closer. Lilian's breath hit his lips, and the delectable scent of mint and vanilla caused his mind to grow fuzzy.

"I like it a lot."

Kevin allowed Lilian's arms to pull him down, closer to her face. His eyes, just like hers, began to flutter closed.

"You two really don't know the meaning of the word discretion, do you?"

Jerking apart like someone had struck them in the face with an overpowered kitsune-bi, Kevin and Lilian looked to their left and right respectively.

"Lindsay." Lilian did not know whether to be happy at seeing her friend, or angry at the tomboy for ruining her and Kevin's moment.

"Hey."

Standing a few feet away, Lindsay waved at the pair. Like

most days, she had chosen to wear clothing that suited her tomboyish nature. Her black skinny jeans fit snugly on her hips, and the white T-shirt and jean jacket combo reminded Kevin of the clothing he wore back when he was 12. Walking beside her was a silent Christine, whose expression Kevin could not identify.

Smiling brightly at the girl in lolita clothing, Kevin greeted the Yuki-onna the same way he alway did.

"Christine, good morning. You look nice today."

"W-w-what are you saying, idiot?!" Christine sputtered, her face steaming. She crossed her arms over her chest and turned her head. "D-d-d-don't think th-that saying—that being nice to me and giving me c-compliments and stuff w-will make me forgive you!"

"Huh?"

And as always, Kevin had absolutely no idea what she was talking about.

Lindsay chuckled. Lilian was just thankful Christine was so tsundere. If the goth girl actually acted nice and tried earnestly earning Kevin's affection, well, it wouldn't haven't really changed anything, but it would have bothered her.

"It always amazes me to see how you can be so oblivious sometimes."

Kevin stared at Lindsay like she'd just told him that he had the power to control vectors. "Um, what?"

"Exactly my point." Lindsay shook her head. "Oblivious to the feelings of everyone except your girlfriend's."

Kevin somehow managed to look both embarrassed and confused.

"… Huh?"

***

Iris observed her surroundings with an amused glance. Everywhere she looked, men stared. Children, adults, teens, it didn't matter, all males stopped whatever they were doing when she walked past them. A man pushing a cart full of luggage ran into a pillar, while another standing with what appeared to be his significant other began drooling. Even the man's girlfriend stared at her like she was the rarest delicacy on earth.

She shook her head. These people, humans, were so pathetic. She wasn't even using her **Call of Ecstasy**, and they were still tripping over themselves just to catch a glimpse of her.

Not that she blamed them, of course, but it was still annoying. Couldn't they be a little more sporting and at least try to resist their hormonal response in the face of someone who embodied female perfection? It was no fun if they didn't struggle against their natural impulses at least a little bit.

"Come on, Iris," her mother called out to her. The older kitsune was walking in front of her, the ever faithful and kind Kirihime at the woman's side. "Hurry up or you'll fall behind—hawa!"

"M-My Lady!"

Iris wanted to facepalm, but that would have been redundant. Instead, she just sighed, watching Kirihime set down their luggage and helping Camellia back to her feet.

"Geeze, mom. You're a complete embarrassment."

"Th-that's not a very nice thing to say about your mother," Kirihime muttered, wearing a forlorn expression.

"That doesn't make it any less true," Iris retorted.

"H-hawa... I'm sowwy, Iris..." Camellia apologized, dewy tear drops in her eyes.

"Whatever. Let's just hurry up, okay?"

"Hawa..."

Several more trips and a lot more staring later, they eventually made it to their terminal.

Iris' stomach chose that moment to growl. "Ugh, I knew I shouldn't have skipped breakfast."

"Would you like some of my Teriyaki?" Kirihime asked, pulling out a steaming plate of food from between her bosom and offering the fragrantly appetizing dish to Iris.

The girl's face turned green. "There's no way in hell I'm ever eating anything you make. Never again."

Kirihime's shoulders slumped. "That's not a very nice thing to say..."

* * *

Kevin and Lilian were joined by their friends as they sat at a stone table underneath the gazebo for lunch.

"So... crap, do we even have a lunch?" Kevin asked, remembering what had happened this morning. His face warmed up and his heart threatened to explode as he recalled Lilian's warm tongue exploring his mouth. He shifted uncomfortably and hoped no one could see the way his pants tightened.

Curse you hormones!

"Don't worry," Lilian reassured him, "Kotohime foresaw that we wouldn't have time to make lunch and packed one for us. She made sure I grabbed it before we left."

"How come I didn't notice this?"

"You were too busy freaking out."

"O-oh. I see."

Kevin tried not to blush as Lilian reached into her cleavage and pulled out a large lunchbox. His eyes widened when he saw the box itself. Three-tiered and shaped like a square, the lunchbox had a lacquered finish and Sakura blossoms swirling along its surface like a mosaic.

Watching as Lilian arranged the food, Kevin saw that each story contained something different. The top story contained eggs and a variety of meats, the second held pickled vegetables, and the third was filled to bursting with rice.

Everyone gawked at the massive lunchbox, though Christine was the most vocal. "What the hell kind of lunchbox is that?!"

"It's called a bento box," Kevin answered, somehow resisting the urge to facepalm. "A Japanese lunchbox with several stories that can contain a variety of different foods."

Lindsay stared at swirling pink petals and beautiful designs like they were something out of a horror movie. "Why is it that everything you do these days has something to do with Japan? We don't live in Japan, you know."

"I am well aware of that," Kevin's reply made deserts seem lush. He looked back at the bento box and sighed. "Seriously though, I know Kotohime's into the whole 'adding random Japanese suffixes to people's name' thing, but I had no clue she was this into Japanese culture. If she wasn't from Japan herself, I would almost think she was a Japanophile."

"A what?"

"Nothing."

"Hey, I just noticed we're missing someone," Alex said, "where's Eric?"

"Who cares?" Christine said rudely. "I'm just glad that idiots not here to perv on me like he usually does. Damn, dirty lecher."

***

Eric Corrompere giggled with all the perversity of a dirty old man.

He'd woken up from his female-induced coma to find himself resting in the nurse's office. After waking up and realizing that the nurse's office was connected to both the male and female locker rooms, Eric had decided to use this opportunity to partake in his favorite hobby.

No, it wasn't playing H-games. That was his second favorite. His real favorite hobby was, of course, peeping.

After sneaking into the girl's locker room, Eric had swiftly hid himself in one of the many lockers. With his back pressed against the metal and his eyes peering through one of several small slits, the epitome of perversion, the entity of lecherous intent, watched as several girls entered the locker room.

Clamping a hand over his mouth to stifle his perverse giggling, Eric ignored the fluids running down his face, both the drool coming out of his mouth and the blood leaking from his nose. This wasn't the first time he'd drooled, gotten a nosebleed or had both happen at the same time, and it wouldn't be the last.

"Oh, yeah..." he whispered to himself, giggling some more. "Come to papa... that's right..."

His eyes zeroed in one girl who stepped in front of him. She turned away and opened the locker immediately across from the one he'd secreted himself in. A few of her friends stepped up with her and also opened their lockers.

"Like, can you believe the nerve of that new assistant coach? She, like, totally made me run, even though I told her I didn't want to," one of them complained. Eric couldn't figure out which one had spoken, and he honestly didn't care. The girl on the far left had just slid her shorts off, revealing cute white panties. Her butt had nothing on Lilian or Christine, but still, a butt was a butt was a butt, and if there was one thing Eric liked with the same zeal as boobs, it was butts.

"Like, I know. I tried to tell her that I just got my nails done, and like, she was all 'I don't care' and I was like, you're a total bitch."

The girls all laughed as one.

"I know, right? And then she forced us all to, like, play that

36

game of dodgeball. My hair is now totally ruined, and I'm all sweaty."

"Eeww!"

Eric squinted as he recognized the voice, or at least the type of person the voice belonged to. These girls sounded like the stereotypical valley girl cliche. How surprising. He didn't think girls like that existed anymore. They weren't living in the 90s. People should've learned how to speak proper English and not act so air-headed!

Weird thoughts coming from a boy who spent most of his life trying to peep on women.

He continued listening to the girls complain, or rather, he completely ignored the complaining in favor of watching them strip. He was a bit disappointed that none of these girls had much to flaunt. They didn't have the astoundingly large and unusually perky boobs of Lilian, nor did they have the marvelously flat chest of Christine. They were all in between, never going for one extreme over the other, thereby making them normal.

For some reason, normal had become awfully boring these days.

He blamed Lilian and Christine.

"Come on, girls!" a familiar voice shouted out. Eric also heard clapping coming from somewhere out of his field of vision. "Hurry up! Another class is coming in soon, so you girls need to clean up, get dressed and get out in five minutes!"

"Tch! Can you believe that woman? She doesn't honestly think we can do all that in five minutes, does she? Like, it takes me at least thirty just to do my makeup!"

"Totally, and it takes me fifteen to get my hair just right. That bitch totally doesn't know how easy she has it with her short hair."

"I don't think she even takes care of her hair. I mean, just look at it. It's all stiff and greasy, like she washes her hair in a tub of oil or something."

"Like, totally."

"Hey! Move your butts, girls! I don't pay you to sit around talking!"

"Like, you don't pay us at all!"

"Totally!"

"Ugh, I've got to take a shower. My skin is, like, absolutely sweaty and gross. I can't wear my clothes like this!"

"Me neither."

"Good thing I, like, brought a towel."

Eric's grin widened as he realized what was going to happen. These girls were going to strip naked! What a treat!

Contrary to the popular beliefs most men had of what transpired in a female locker room, girls didn't just randomly strip naked for no apparent reason. Eric had been most depressed when he had first learned this fact. All women should get naked in a locker room just like they did in anime! Why didn't these girls know that? Still, he'd grown used to seeing, at most, a pair of well-filled panties, and learned to make up for this deficiency in his Perv-O-Meter with hentai and H-games.

But now, none of that mattered! Because he was going to finally see a pair of real-live breasts!

"Hell, yeah! Bring on the boobies!" he shouted.

"Did you hear that?!"

Eric clamped a hand over his mouth.

"Like, it sounded like a shout!"

"You don't think…?"

"I do."

Eric "eeped!" when the door to his locker was suddenly and violently wrenched open. A hand grabbed a fistful of his hair and yanked him out. The young pervert went tumbling to the ground, where he soon found himself surrounded by a bunch of angry females in various states of undress.

"Any last words?" one of the girls asked, cracking her knuckles.

"I regret nothing!"

"Wrong. Answer."

Five minutes later a bruised, battered and thoroughly beaten Eric lay on the ground, twitching and groaning in pain. He looked like, well, like a bunch of women had unleashed their Righteous Female Fury upon him. His cheeks were swollen like a chipmunk whose mouth was full of acorns, and both of his eyes were black. His left eye looked worse, as it was swollen completely shut and beginning to turn purple. He was also missing several teeth and had a split lip that bled profusely.

Standing above him, hands on her hips and the most amused

smirk quirking her lips, was none other than Heather Grant.

"So… was it worth it?"

Eric groaned in pain, but was still able to slowly raise his shaky left hand into the air, where he gave a thumbs up… and then let it drop back to the floor with a dull thud.

Heather nodded approvingly. "Good man."

***

From the moment the plane took off, Iris had decided that she absolutely hated flying. There was just something unsettling about the whole thing. Maybe it was the knowledge that she was hundreds if not thousands feet above ground, or maybe it had something to do with how the plane would jostle and shake whenever they hit turbulence. Either way, she decided right then and there that flying sucked.

Iris sat in the seat closest to the aisle. No way in hell was she getting anywhere near the window. Kirihime sat beside her, humming a gentle tune to herself as she flipped through the pages of a magazine, which, judging from the front cover, was about knives. After reading over Kirihime's shoulder in an effort to distract herself, Iris shuddered and looked away, disturbed by the maid's fascination with pointy objects. Over by the window, Camellia had her face pressed against the glass, gazing at the vast sea of clouds with a child's curiosity.

Trying to ignore the way her stomach flip-flopped the longer she stayed in this death machine, Iris swallowed the bile attempting to rise in her throat and closed her eyes.

Within the darkness of her mind, an image appeared, of a beautiful girl with hair the color of crimson flames and eyes that sparkled brighter than a pair of emeralds.

Wait for me, Lilian. We'll be reunited again soon.

Chapter 2

Not All Surprises Are Good

"So, how is it?"

Kevin looked at Alex, blinking several times as he processed his friend's words. "How is what?"

Alex rolled his eyes, as if amazed by Kevin's ignorance. "Don't give me that 'how is what?' crap. How is dating Lilian, like, really dating Lilian and not that weird runaround thing you two were doing before?"

Kevin's cheeks flushed a dark shade of crimson as he opened his locker. "W-why do you want to know about something like that?"

Alex gave his friend a flat stare. "Are you seriously asking that? After over two months of listening to you claim that you didn't like her, you're finally dating Lilian. You can't expect me to not be curious."

As his other friends nodded, Kevin conceded that Alex had a point. If their positions were reversed, he'd probably be curious, too.

He paused halfway through getting changed. His track pants were on, but his shirt remained in his hands.

"It's… pretty amazing, actually." His blush didn't recede, but a soft smile did appear on his face as he thought about Lilian. "She's a really amazing girl, you know? She's vibrant, fun, cheerful, and is always optimistic about everything. She's like… like a bright ray of sunshine. Everything just seems so much more vibrant whenever she's around."

"Don't forget she's also hot," Andrew added.

"There's that, too," Kevin conceded. While more interested in Lilian as a person, he would be stupid to deny her general…well… hotness. The two-tails was, quite frankly, one of the hottest examples of the female species he'd ever seen. Oh sure, Kotohime was really attractive--gorgeous even--and she had a mature air about her that Lilian lacked, but she also carried a katana and wore a kimono everywhere she went. Plus, she scared the crap out of him.

Kevin put his shirt on and began lacing up his shoes. "Sometimes, I feel almost like I'm living in a dream, you know? I'm always expecting to wake up one day and discover that none of this ever happened."

It wouldn't have been a hard thing to do, considering all the crazy stuff that had happened to him in the past two and a half months. His life had been one zany disaster after another ever since Lilian's arrival. He felt almost like one of those harem protagonists in a shōnen romantic comedy.

Which was, of course, patently ridiculous. He wasn't some kind of shōnen manga protagonist, no matter what crazy things Lilian or Kotohime said to the contrary…

… Right?

"Listen to you, bragging about your love life," Chase scoffed. "From the way you keep talking about Lilian these days, you'd think she was the greatest chick in the entire universe."

Kevin's blush receded as he finished tying his shoes. "Well, if there was a contest for greatest woman in the universe, she'd definitely have my vote."

"Whatever," Chase grumbled. "For someone who used to be so hung up on Lindsay, you've become awfully lovey-dovey with a girl you claimed to not like two weeks ago. What changed your mind?"

Kevin shrugged as he, Alex, Andrew and Chase made their way out of the locker room with the other track members. "I couldn't say. I guess it's just, well, maybe I just realized that Lindsay wasn't the only amazing girl out there. Like, there are more fish in the sea, or something, you know?"

"Expanding your horizons."

"Studying abroad."

"Searching the market."

"… Women…."

Everyone stopped talking and stared at Justin very oddly for a second…

… And then went back to their conversation.

"You know, I just realized something." Kevin turned his head left and right, searching for something that wasn't there. Or rather, someone who wasn't there. "Eric still hasn't joined us."

Alex, along with his fraternal twin brother and Chase, also scanned the area. "Huh? You're right. That's really weird. I mean, Eric is a pretty unreliable guy at times, especially if he's given the choice between perving on women or hanging out with friends, but he'd never miss a track meet, and he definitely wouldn't miss out on the last one of the season. Where do you think he is?"

As if summoned by their words, a loud, familiar voice shouted from behind them.

"LOOK OUT, EVERYONE!!! COMING THROUGH!!"

And then another voice shouted, this one female.

"IF YOU PEOPLE DON'T WANNA GET FLATTENED, YOU'D BETTER MOVE OUT OF THE WAY!"

The entire male track team looked behind them to see Eric and…was that Heather Grant? Yes, it was. Their new PE assistant coach was also running down the hallway, and there was a large cloud of what looked like dust chasing after them.

Everyone present jumped away, their backs pressing against the wall, just as the two ran past them.

"There they are!"

"Get them!"

"Hurry up! Don't let them get away!"

"Come back here, you stupid perverts!"

"I can't believe we trusted you!"

"KILL THEM!!!"

Before anyone could even think about relaxing, the track team was forced back against the wall as a horde of outraged teenage girls rushed by. Several drops of sweat rolled down Kevin's face as he noticed that every girl was carrying some kind of household appliance: a broom, a mop, a rake, a strange pole thing, and...

"Holy shit! Is that chick carrying a claymore?!"

Kevin nearly did a double take when he saw that one of the girls rushing past them was, indeed, carrying a claymore: a two-handed longsword with a cross hilt of forward-sloping quillons with quatrefoil terminations. The weapon was gigantic, literally a foot or so longer than the girl was tall. That she carried it so easily spoke much of her strength, or her anger, or both.

Angry women tended to gain a substantial increase in strength proportionate to how upset they were. It was one of the basic laws of shōnen manga.

"Is that a prop? Please tell me that's a prop!"

"I don't know... it looks pretty real to me."

"B-but just look that that thing! It's huge! And look at the way she's carrying it! There's no way a waif of a girl like that could possibly carry a real sword that large!"

Kevin had to agree. Claymores were heavy. While he didn't know exactly how much they weighed, he knew that a full-tang steel claymore was, at the very least, somewhere around 60 to 80 pounds, if not heavier. It was probably a prop of some kind—although he couldn't recall ever seeing a prop like that being used in any of their school's plays.

Maybe that girl's a fan of Claire and that's just her cosplay sword... yeah, that's gotta be it. No way someone would be carrying around a real claymore like that.

The horde of murderous teenage girls dwindled down to a trickle before ceasing altogether. Alex, Andrew, Chase and Kevin all looked at each other with matching "WTF?" expressions.

"So, what do you think that was about?" Alex asked.

"No idea," Chase muttered, staring at the last place they'd seen the girl wielding the giant claymore.

Kevin shook his head. "I don't think I want to know."

"... Peeping..."

Once again, Justin received nothing but odd looks, even though, for once, the group completely agreed with him.

***

"Ha... ha.... I think... we lost them..."

Eric was hunched over on his hands and knees, breathing heavily as if he'd just run a marathon—or been chased by a horde of angry teenage girls. Sweat dripped down his brow and his shoulders heaved as he tried to regulate his breathing.

He looked at his partner in crime, the gorgeous blond teacher whose lecherous streak was even wider than his own, and he couldn't help but wonder: where had this woman been all his life? Why had she just revealed herself to him now? If only they had met sooner!

Unlike Eric, who looked ready to keel over, Heather hadn't broken a sweat. She appeared right as rain and ready to bolt at a moment's notice. "Hmm… I don't know. We women are a tenacious bunch, especially when angered. Trust me. I've been doing this for years."

"Wait, wait, wait, wait, wait!" Catching his second wind, Eric stared at the woman in shock. "You mean to tell me that you've been peeping on girls in the locker room for years? Seriously?!"

Heather's chest swelled with pride. "Of course! I've been peeping for years for my research and inspiration!"

"Research? Inspiration?"

"That's right. You see, I am not just a pervert who enjoys peeping on women in the locker rooms. Everything I do is for the sake of my art." Heather held a clenched fist up to her face. "I am the trailblazer, paving the way for men and women everywhere who enjoy reading about sexy shenanigans and bouncing boobies! I am an author! A writer of erotica! Peeping is my passion and writing is my craft, and I will hone both until I become a master!"

By the end of her speech, Heather had raised her clenched right fist into the air. The fire in her eyes, the physical manifestation of her determination and lustful desires, had turned into a raging inferno. Bright orange flames surrounded her body, a conflagration wreathing her in a strange, Saiyan-esque blaze of energy derived from her own perverse intentions.

Eric was in awe. This woman was truly a pervert among perverts. And she was a woman to boot! A hot woman! That alone caused her Pervy Power Levels to rise past 9,000!

Eric bowed before this messiah, getting down on his hands and knees, bowing so low that his nose scraped the tiled floor. "Oh, great and powerful one, please take me under your wing! I wish to learn your ways! Please share your knowledge with me!"

Heather smiled benevolently. "Very well. Rise, my young

apprentice. Rise and follow me into the world of perversity and peeping! It is only through me that you shall become a master!"

"Yes!"

The newly appointed master and apprentice smiled at each other, glad to have finally found someone they could share their salacious antics with.

This moment of bonding, which would have been touching had the pair's antics not been borderline criminal, was interrupted when a horde of furious females turned a corner.

"There they are! Get 'em, girls!"

"Oh, god! They found us! Run for it!"

As Eric and Heather began to run, the blond-haired assistant PE coach turned to her apprentice.

"Now then, apprentice, I believe it is time for me to teach you my first lesson."

Eric somehow managed to look incredulous. "What? Now?"

"No time like the present."

Eric looked behind him at the horde of outraged high school girls, and then back at his new master.

"Um, okay. So, uh, what's this lesson you want to teach me?"

Heather nodded, pleased to see someone so receptive to her teachings. "Whenever you are being hunted by a mob of angry women, you never have to outrun the mob. You just have to outrun the person next to you."

"Huh?"

Before he could decipher that statement, Heather stuck her foot out and Eric suddenly found himself eating pavement. Ignoring the pain, he looked up at the blonde woman, who grinned and winked at him, before hauling butt out of there.

And then the horde was upon him.

"Now we've got you!"

"Don't think we're going to let you get away with this!"

"You damn pervert! DIE!"

Eric's shrill screams echoed across the campus.

***

Lilian sat on the bleachers, waiting for her mate's track meet to begin.

All around her people spoke with increasingly rising volume. Having so many people talking at once, all of them trying to be heard over the other, caused her eardrums to hurt something fierce. While her ears weren't as sensitive as a dog's, they were still better than human ears.

Her "Go Beloved!" sign was conspicuously absent. She would have brought it with her, but didn't know where it was anymore. She had asked Kevin, but he'd just looked away and said that she must have misplaced it or something.

"But I know I didn't misplace it," Lilian muttered to herself, frowning. "I could have sworn I had it in my Extra Dimensional Storage Space. That's where I put all of my paraphernalia."

"Lilian?"

Turning to the speaker, Lilian saw Lindsay sit next to her.

"Hey, Lindsay! I didn't realize you would be here, too!" Lilian greeted her friend cheerfully. She then saw who else was with the tomboy and her face went flat. "Christine. What are you doing here? Don't you prefer hanging out in your cave to being surrounded by people?"

"I'm not a vampire!" Christine growled. "And I'm here because, because I... I—w-well it's because..."

"She's here to support Kevin," Lindsay answered for her friend.

"Right." Christine nodded. "I'm here to support Ke-Ke-Ke—no I'm NOT! W-w-w-why the hell would I support that jerk?! H-he's nothing but a loathsome, foolish little prick who's too taken in with big tits to notice when there's someone else much better for—I-I-I mean he's an idiot!"

As Christine's tsundere protocols activated, causing her to sputter out her usual diatribe, Lindsay continued talking. "That's also why I'm here. You didn't think I'd be willing to miss my friend's last track meet, did you? My support might not mean as much to him as yours does, but I still want to support my friend."

Lilian smiled at the tomboyish blond. It was hard to believe that she'd hated this girl as little as one month ago. "I'm sure Kevin will appreciate your support. He still cherishes your friendship a lot, and I know he appreciates you." She paused, her eyes flickering from Lindsay to Christine, and then back again. "By the way, I've noticed that you and Christine have been spending a lot more time together. What's up with that?"

"Ah. Well..." Lilian blinked. Was it just her, or was Lindsay blushing? "I just sort of thought she could use a friend, you know? Christine is so rude and abrasive."

"Who's abrasive?!"

"And she's always scaring people away because she scowls so much."

"I do not scowl!"

"And she's really, uh, what's the word I'm looking for? It's the one you used a while ago..."

"Tsundere?" Lilian supplied.

Lindsay snapped her fingers. "That's the one. She's really tsundere."

"I AM NOT TSUNDERE!"

Lilian and Lindsay stared at Christine, who squirmed under their deadpan looks.

"W-what are you two staring at? I'm not tsundere."

"You are totally tsundere."

"Completely tsundere."

"So tsundere you make Taiga look like a kuudere."

Lindsay stared at the redhead. "Who the heck is Taiga?"

"No one you would know." Waving her right hand in the air, Lilian got back on track. "Anyway, you were saying something about Christine? I think you were telling me why you're spending so much time with her or something?"

"Don't talk about me like I'm not even here!"

"Right. It's sort of like, even though she acts all rude and stuff, Christine is still a really good person, you know? I-I mean..." Lilian noticed that, indeed, Lindsay was actually blushing. "I think she's really kind of cool and nice once you get to know her, and her clothing is really pretty. Totally wouldn't wear them myself. Never in a million years. But, still pretty."

Lilian stared at her friend and her... not-friend with the observant gaze of someone trying to solve a puzzle.

"You... are you two into each other?"

"WHAT?!" Christine shot to her feet. "I am not into Lindsay! She's just a friend! A FRIEND! I am completely straight and in love with—" Her eyes widened. She looked at the kitsune and the tomboy, who were giving her strange looks.

"Are you telling me that even though Kevin and I are now dating, you still have a crush on him?" Lilian shook her head.

"That's... shouldn't you try and, I don't know, find someone else?" she asked, not condescendingly, but out of honest curiosity. "I don't mean to be rude, but Kevin is my mate, and he's finally returning my feelings. There's nothing on this entire planet that could ever take him away from me." There was a very brief pause as Lilian tilted her head. "And I don't think Kevin wants to take the harem route, so you're kinda out of luck there, too."

Christine's face morphed into an icy shade of blue. This time, it wasn't because she felt embarrassed, but because she was angry.

"Just because he's yours now doesn't mean he'll stay with you forever. He's a fifteen year old boy. They're prone to falling in and out of love every other week."

Lilian shook her head. "You don't understand anything."

Christine's eyes narrowed. "And what am I supposed to understand?"

"It would take way too long to explain, and I don't feel like repeating information that was already in the last book."

Christine and Lindsay blinked.

"What?" Lindsay looked nonplussed.

"The hell are you talking about?" a flabbergasted Christine asked.

"Let's just enjoy watching my mate beat everyone here, okay?" Lilian ignored her friends' questions, smiling at them before turning back to the track field.

The meet was about to begin.

***

Coach Deretaine marched in front of Kevin and the others, back straight, chest out and hands clasped behind his back. He reminded Kevin of a military sergeant about to drill his troops.

"Okay brats, listen up! This is the big one. The last track meet of the year. We've done well so far. This year we've had more success than any other year. However! I don't want any of you to become complacent just yet. Just because we've done well doesn't mean we can afford to become lax. I expect all of you to give twice the effort today that you've given for every other day..."

Kevin zoned out as Coach Deretaine continued his spiel. He'd heard this speech, or others similar enough, so many times that he could have probably quoted it by heart.

His gaze traveled to the bleachers. Even without her banner, spotting Lilian amongst the crowd was simple. All he had to do was look for her vibrant red hair. She was sitting with Lindsay and Christine, which brought a smile to his face. It was nice to know that his friends had come to support him.

"Swift!"

Kevin focused back on his coach.

"Yes, Coach?"

Coach Deretaine stared at Kevin, his eyes harder than diamonds. "You can make googly eyes with your girlfriend later. Right now I need you to stay focused. I'll be counting on you out there."

Several giggles broke out amongst the female track members. Kevin blushed. "R-right."

"All right!" Coach Deretaine barked. "Let's shows these pansies who's top dog around here!"

"OORAH!"

The track meet soon started. As per the usual, women's hurdles was the first competition. Kevin and his friends sat down on the bench and observed the girls while they raced. He ignored the comments from his friends about which girl's boobs bounced the most and instead focused on his own thoughts.

Perhaps not so surprisingly, most of his thoughts were centered around a certain fox-girl and what they would do after this track meet. He didn't know what the plan was, but Lilian had apparently prepared something special for him.

"Ufufufu, I would wish you luck, but I know you don't need it. You should also know that I have something fun planned for us after your track meet. Please look forward to it, ufufufu." As Lilian giggled in the middle of the hallway, several people who were standing next to them began slowly backing away.

Those had been her words right before the track meet. He assumed she had made plans for some kind of celebration and had asked Kotohime to gather ingredients for a feast, which explained why the maid-slash-bodyguard wasn't present.

On a side note, even though Kevin loved Lilian, he still thought her laugh was creepy.

"All right, Swift! Chase! You two are up! Show those lousy, good for nothing bastards who's boss!"

Kevin sighed at his coach's potty mouth and stood up. He and

Chase made it to the track field, where several other runners also stood, waiting for the race to begin.

"I've got nothing to say to you," Chase told Kevin as he stretched. "You might have gotten a lot faster somehow, but I'm still going to beat you."

"I thought you had nothing to say."

"Tch!"

Everyone got into position. Kevin knelt down, eyes and mind focused on his goal with laser-point precision. His breathing slowed and his mind became calm. This was the last track meet of the season, so he wanted to make it count.

A gunshot rang out. Kevin blasted off the ground and tore across the track. He pushed the muscles in his legs. Harder. Faster. His arms swung, his legs strained, his chest tightened. The world around him blurred.

80 meters…

Several people tried catching up to him. Kevin saw them out of his peripheral vision.

60 meters…

Kevin ran faster. Pushed himself harder. He wouldn't be beaten here!

35 meters…

The world came to a crawl. Time seemed to slow down. Several people on either side of him tried to race ahead, but he refused to let them pass him.

5 meters…

His chest became unbearably tight. His breathing turned ragged. His lungs burned like never before as he rushed across those last five meters.

And then it was over.

***

Lost in her own euphoria, Lilian had completely forgotten herself.

"WHOO! Way to go, Beloved!"

She stood on the bleacher to better see her mate run the one- and two-hundred meter dash, watching as he blitzed past his fellow runners. A few people kept pace, but it wasn't long before Kevin pushed himself harder, slowly widening the gap between him and everyone else.

Sitting on the bleachers beside her, Lindsay watched her with a face that seeped amusement. Christine just looked repulsed.

"Ugh, could you shut up and sit down?" The Yuki-Onna groused. "Seriously, fox-skank, everyone's staring at us."

Lilian cast a mild glare at the goth tsun-loli. "Then don't sit near me. I don't care about these people or what they think. My mate is out there doing something he loves doing, and I am going to show my support whether you like it or not."

"W-whatever," Christine scowled, but didn't say anything else. Lindsay shook her head.

The tomboy had noticed the distinct differences in personality between Lilian and Christine—aside from the whole "tsundere" issue, which she still didn't really get. Lilian was bright, cheerful, and always looking forward to each new day with excitement. Christine, in contrast, was kind of dark, easily irritated, and generally anti-social. Perhaps that explained why Lindsay had been so surprised to discover that Christine, for all her irritable behavior, was actually really nice.

"Ah, there you are!" a voice with a horribly fake Spanish accent said. Lilian's body shuddered from head to tails. "My *Preciosa de Flor*! How I've missed you these past few moons!"

Lilian turned around, Lindsay and Christine following her gaze. Several seats up stood the weirdest-looking boy Lindsay had ever seen. He had large, pompadour style hair and wore what appeared to be a matador costume. The neon pink and obnoxious blue of his outfit contrasted horribly with his bright blond hair and olive colored skin. He looked like a Spanish bullfighter who had picked a fight with a tie dye filled spray hose and lost.

"Not you again," Lilian groaned.

Juan ignored her. "My dear, my love, my sweet *más bella flor de loto*!"

"Would you stop it with the internet-translated Spanish already!" Lilian paused to draw breath. "And I am not your love!" Another pause. "And for the love of Lord Inari, stop calling me flour!"

Lindsay wondered who this guy was. Sitting by her side, Christine's eyes had widened in horror. The yuki-onna stared at Juan like he was an eldritch horror born from the transient nightmares of HP Lovecraft.

"You have no idea how much I've missed you," Juan continued. "Every day since last we met, you have been all that I can think about."

Lilian's face turned green. "Um. Ew. That's just creepy."

"My heart, it has ached without your presence to fill it with your sweet *apetecer*." Juan held both hands to his chest.

"Yeah, well, my heart hasn't been aching at all. Not until you showed up at least."

Lindsay watched, partially amused but mostly creeped out, as this strange guy continued spewing corny lines that sounded like something from a Harlequin romance novel. Actually, thinking about it, those lines might have been even worse than the corniest, trashiest romance novel around.

Juan sighed, looking ready to swoon as he stared at Lilian. "Ah, you are like a ray of bright sunshine caressing my skin, *ma hermosa de flor*."

That seemed to be the final straw for Lilian. Her already green face turned even greener and, before anyone could say another word, the beautiful vixen rushed off.

"Scuse me."

Lindsay watched as Lilian shoved her way through the crowd and jumped off the bleachers, heedless of the nearly fifteen foot drop. She, Christine and Juan all rushed over to the railing, and were just time to see the redhead run into the women's restroom.

"I wonder why she was in such a hurry?" Juan pondered out loud, causing both Lindsay and Christine to stare at the boy like he'd just offered them a packet of used condoms. The young man turned to them, his hair bouncing with the motion. "Do you think it was something I said?"

***

"Hey man, good job today."

"Nice work, Kevin."

"Man, you were fast, dude."

Ever since the track meet had come to an end, Kevin had been congratulated by just about everyone on his team. He would admit that it felt nice to have so many people appreciate and respect the effort he put into running, but it also made him feel more than a little awkward. His head seemed almost ready to burst, and there was this inexplicable feeling in his chest, a most bizarre warmth that caused him to feel elated and uncomfortable.

"Ha ha! You should see how red your face is!"

As Chase pointed and laughed at him, Kevin felt his face, which had already been fit to fry eggs on, burn hot enough to put the sun to shame.

"Be quiet," Kevin snapped. "You're just jealous because I beat you in both the one-hundred and two-hundred meter dash."

"Hmph! Whatever." Kasey Chase crossed his arms over his chest and looked away. "All that means is I have to work harder to beat you next time. Nothing more."

"Keep thinking that. Maybe one day it will come true."

Chase scowled at Kevin, who pulled down his eyelid and blew the older boy a raspberry.

After taking a shower, Kevin donned his normal clothes; faded blue jeans and a dark orange T-shirt. He laced up his sneakers and was about to make his way outside, when several members of the track team intercepted him.

"Hey man, we're all about to head over to Katherine's house to celebrate," one of them, a tall guy Kevin thought was named Ian, said. "You wanna come?"

Kevin was startled for a moment. Although he got along well enough with the other track members, they were all older than him. He and his friends were the only sophomores on the entire team, so while everyone was nice, the older members tended to exclude them from their after track activities.

"Uh, thanks, but Lilian and I actually made plans tonight. Sorry."

Ian chuckled. "Spending some time with your girl? I completely understand. Your girlfriend's a fox."

Kevin felt wry amusement at that comment, even as his cheeks heated up. "You've got no idea."

Heading outside after saying goodbye to his friends and the other track members, Kevin went to meet up with Lilian.

Unfortunately, Lilian wasn't alone.

"I told you to stop following me."

"Now don't be like that my *más eróticamente maravillosa harina*. There is no need for such harsh words. Not when it is just the two of us."

Kevin stared at Juan as he annoyed and harassed Lilian. The

two were standing in a hallway off to the side, and he correctly concluded that Juan had intercepted the redhead on her way to the lockers. The boy stood before Lilian, keeping her from passing by moving to block her way every time she tried walking around him.

His right eye began to twitch.

"Lilian."

Juan turned in his direction, and Lilian used that moment to slip past the big-haired boy.

"Kevin!"

Despite having been prepared for it, Kevin was still in no way ready for Lilian's pounce, which was so powerful that he had actually christened it with a name. He called it **Lilian's Secret Technique: Pnévma Pounce**.

Lilian jumped on him with all the strength of an oni on steroids. Only Kevin's increased strength, gained through hours of grueling training with Kiara, kept him from crumbling like a house of cards.

A pair of legs locked around his waist, forcing Kevin to place his hands on Lilian's shapely bottom so she wouldn't fall. He barely had time to grunt before his mate began a coordinated assault on his mouth.

Kevin tried to keep up with the girl's raw, undiluted passion, but he still lacked the ability to put up much of a fight. All Kevin could do was ride out Lilian's latest lip-lock and hope his legs, which already felt like they were turning into jelly, didn't fail him.

"Whew! Look at those two kiss!"

"I see some tongue action there!"

"Holy shit, that's hot!"

"Since when did Kevin learn to kiss like that?"

"I think his girl is the one doing most of the kissing."

Upon hearing the voices, whistles and catcalls, Kevin let out a loud squeak, only slightly muffled by Lilian's mouth. He tried to unsuccessfully jerk his mouth away from the two-tails, but she kept him in place by grasping his head in her hands, which consequently caused him to lose his balance as he tripped over his own two feet.

As Kevin crashed to the floor, shame filling him as the other track team members laughed and jeered and catcalled, one thought rose to his mind.

I'm never going to live this down, am I?

Somehow, Kevin felt like he could live with that.

***

Arriving home later that day, Lilian and an embarrassed Kevin found themselves being greeted by a kimono-clad vision of loveliness.

"Welcome home, Lilian-sama, Kevin-sama."

Kotohime offered them a bow. Well, she offered Lilian a bow. Kevin was pretty sure the woman would only bow to him after he proved himself to her, and the gods only knew when that would happen.

After rising from her deferential bow, Kotohime offered him a conciliating smile. "I believe congratulations are in order. Am I correct in assuming you won first place in your races?"

"Of course he did!" Lilian exploded with enthusiasm--a lot of enthusiasm. "He was incredible! The moment the gun went off, he was speeding down the track! I almost thought he was using Shunpo, he moved so fast."

Kotohime stared at her charge with a single, delicately raised eyebrow. "Indeed? That is most intriguing, but might I suggest you keep real life anime references to a minimum? Author-san has recently been getting complaints that he breaks the fourth wall too much, and so he's been trying to keep any cracks from appearing within the fabrics of this fragile reality."

"I don't see why he would bother with something like that." Lilian waved her hand dismissively. "Everyone knows he doesn't have the talent to write anything good."

D-Do you have to put it so bluntly?

"And you have no room to say anything. You're just as bad as I am."

I think you're both terrible.

"Shut up."

"Indeed, if you wish to continue living, I suggest you not talk any more than necessary."

My own characters hate me!

"We don't hate you," Lilian said reassuringly. "We just find you very annoying."

U-ugh...

"Would you two stop that already!" a red-faced Kevin

shouted. "Stop talking to someone who isn't real!"

Kotohime and Lilian looked at Kevin like he was an idiot.

"What are you talking about?" Lilian asked. "Of course he's real."

"Indeed." Kotohime nodded her agreement. "We wouldn't exist if he wasn't real."

The next morning, the complex manager would arrive at their doorstep after receiving numerous complaints about strange banging noises, as if someone had been slamming their face into a wall, coming from the Swift's apartment.

***

Kotohime led the pair onto the balcony, where she had prepared what appeared to be a romantic dinner for two.

A small round table with a white cloth placed over it sat in the center of the balcony, with two comfortable-looking padded chairs situated on opposite ends of the table. Kevin didn't question where Kotohime found the table and chairs, which he knew they hadn't possessed this morning. In the table's center, a single candle burned, its flame wavering and dancing to a transient tune beyond human perception.

"Oh, um, wow." Kevin didn't know what to say. "This is, uh…"

"I didn't really know what we should do to celebrate your last track meet," Lilian admitted as Kevin gawked at the scene before them. "My first idea was to invite all of your friends over and have a really big party, but we did that last time."

Kevin remembered that. They had done really well on their second to last track meet, getting first place in almost all of the competitions except for pole vaulting and the shot put. Having been so elated by their success, Eric had invited all of them to his house for a party.

He also recalled how that particular celebration had ended with Eric and his pervy old man being laid flat by an irate Christine, who'd shown up halfway through the party.

A small droplet of sweat trailed down the left side of his face. "Yeah. I think not having a party was a good decision on your part."

"Thanks. Anyway, that's why I decided on doing this. I thought it would be nice if we celebrated your success, just the two of us."

When Lilian's cheeks tinged a soft pink, visible even in the moonlight, Kevin thought he would die of moe. Some things existed in this world that were just criminal, and a drop-dead gorgeous girl like Lilian possessing such an enthralling look of sweet demureness was one of those things.

"Uh… ah…"

When Kevin opened his mouth and only got a few monosyllables for his trouble, he realized how close he was to losing it. He quickly closed his eyes and concentrated on his breathing. He would not allow himself to act like a jabbering idiot. Not anymore. He refused.

Opening his eyes, Kevin showed Lilian his best smile. "I like this idea. It's sort of like we're on a date at a nice restaurant."

Lilian's smile made Kevin feel both lighter than air and like there was a lead bowling ball in his stomach.

"I'm glad. Now then, shall we sit down?"

"Oh, um, right!"

Remembering his manners, Kevin held Lilian's chair out for her before sitting down in his own. Kotohime walked onto the balcony, carrying a tray of food. Kevin followed the tray with his eyes, trying not to let his mouth water as a delectable aroma wafted into his nose.

With her usually placid smile, Kotohime set the tray down, and then placed two glasses on the table, which she filled with what Kevin really hoped was sparkling cider.

"For a side dish, I have prepared *tiropsomo*, warm bread stuffed with feta. For Lilian-sama, I made *bourtheto*, and for Kevin-sama, *spetsofai*—sausages with bell peppers."

"You've really outdone yourself, Kotohime." Lilian sniffed the food, her own mouth watering. "This looks delicious!"

The perennial smile on Kotohime's face grew at her charge's words. "Yes, well, it is a special occasion, after all. Now, please enjoy the meal."

With one final bow, Kotohime retreated into the living room, leaving Kevin and Lilian alone once more.

***

Dinner that evening was a surreal experience.

He and Lilian had gone on dates before, but those had mostly been the kind of dates that all high school students went on: the movies, a picnic, ice skating and so on. None of them had been super-serious romantic dinners complete with candlelight and a table for two.

Kevin didn't know if this counted as one of those dates. But, even if it didn't, it had enough necessary components to be considered as such. That alone made him nervous.

He still did what he could to make it enjoyable, remembering to use his best manners and doing everything possible to keep Lilian engaged in conversation throughout dinner. It was more difficult than he thought it would be. While talking to Lilian was surprisingly easy, coming up with topics to discuss was tough. The butterflies fluttering about in his chest and the scorpions poking his intestinal tract certainly didn't help.

"How is your training with Kiara going?"

Kevin was so surprised by the question that he almost choked on his food. He banged on his chest several times to dislodge a bit of sausage before looking at the red-haired vixen, his mouth hanging open as he stared at her in stupefaction.

"I'm… sorry, but, did you just ask about my training?"

Lilian puffed up her cheeks, her pout filled with enough cuteness to suffocate a man from too much fluff. "What's with that response? I'll have you know that I am very interested in your training."

After a moment's hesitation, Kevin reached out and placed a hand over one of Lilian's. "I'm sorry. It's just that you've never asked about my training before. You always said that you weren't interested in the 'stupid training I did with that dumb mutt,' remember?"

Lilian's cheeks flushed upon hearing his words, just a bit. "Y-yes, well, t-that's just because I don't like you spending time with her. She's an inu, and even though she doesn't have any romantic intentions towards you, I still don't like how you're spending time with some filthy dog. You're mine, not hers."

"O-oh…"

Kevin and Lilian stared at each other, their faces growing more and more red as the seconds ticked by.

"S-so!" Lilian tried to get her groove back. "A-anyway, I've calmed down since then, and am now curious to know how your

training is going."

"Well," Kevin stretched out the word, thinking about how to best describe his training with Kiara, "it's... productive, I guess." When Lilian stared at him with an astoundingly blank expression, Kevin felt his cheeks burn. "W-what I mean is that Kiara hasn't been teaching me how to fight or anything. She just has me doing strength training exercises. She runs me through drills and routines that are designed to strengthen my muscles and increase my speed while not gaining any extraneous muscle mass."

"Uh huh..."

"Yeah. According to Kiara, having big, bulky muscles actually puts fighters at a disadvantage against their opponents, and that large muscles not only cause your movements and reactions to become sluggish, but that having them can also restrict your range of motion, limiting the number of ways your body can move and bend."

"That was a terribly long run-on sentence."

Kevin nearly faceplanted into his food. "You're not even listening to me, are you?"

Lilian dipped a piece of bread into her soup. "Of course I am. You said that Kiara is increasing your strength through exercise." She took a bite out of the bread and moaned at the pleasant taste filling her mouth. Upon swallowing, she continued. "And that having large muscles is a bad thing for fighters. See, I was listening."

Now it was Kevin's turn to pout. "It didn't seem like you were."

"That's because I'm an excellent multitasker. I can eat bread and listen to you at the same time."

"If you say so."

"I do say so."

Kevin and Lilian stared at each other for a second before, ever so slowly, matching smiles crossed their faces.

After they finished dinner, Kotohime served them baklava.

Wanting this moment to be romantic, Lilian tried convincing Kevin that they should feed each other. Because he didn't have any experience at being in a romantic relationship, Kevin agreed, even though the idea of him and Lilian feeding each other was kind of embarrassing.

When dinner concluded, Kotohime took their plates away. Lilian and Kevin moved to the couch where they watched an anime that Lilian had been wanting to see. Kevin didn't know why, but as they watched the anime, which featured a kid who'd been turned into a zombie by a necromancer with godlike powers, he felt a strange sense of deja vu, like he'd seen or knew someone who had been in a situation similar to the main character's. Weird.

Several hours later, as the twilight hour dawned, Kevin and Lilian prepared for bed. After their nightly ritual, Lilian donned plain white panties and a large white T-shirt, while Kevin put on black boxers and a T-shirt of the same color.

Kevin laid down on the bed with Lilian cuddled up to him, snuggling into his side and using his left shoulder as her pillow. Despite his body burning like a furnace, Kevin still responded to her affection, wrapping around her and letting his hand rest on the curvature of her hip.

Lilian sighed in contentment, kissing his chest and falling asleep seconds after saying goodnight, Kevin's warmth lulling her mind and body into a sense of peace and tranquility that she only felt in his presence.

On the other hand, Kevin was wide awake and suffering from a small (not so small in his opinion) problem. He stared down at Lilian's lovely leg, visible as a lump underneath the blanket covering them. While he couldn't anything more than an outline, he could feel her leg just fine, along with what it was grazing.

Lilian's leg rubbed against him, causing his body to respond. He rose to the occasion. Lilian shifted some more, her bare leg caressing him and causing a delicious sort of friction that he felt even through his boxer shorts. Kevin thought his face might undergo spontaneous combustion at any second.

Despite it only being 9:45, Kevin could already tell.

It was going to be a long night.

***

A sea of velvet blanketed the night sky, complemented by the twinkling of several million stars.

Justin leaned against a pillar located in a small park near his house. The pillar was connected to a pavilion filled with metal tables and benches.

He could have sat down, but he honestly preferred standing.

With a cell phone held to his ear, the young man waited patiently for the person he was calling to pick up.

"..."

"Good to hear from you, Commander. I was beginning to wonder if you'd answer my call."

"..."

Justin listened, waiting until the person had finished before chuckling. "I assure you, this isn't a social call. I just thought you would like to know that one of your former associates who went against the grain and tried kidnapping the kitsune, Lilian Pnévma, has managed to slip through the cracks and is still hanging around. She's currently teaching at my school as an assistant PE coach."

"..."

"Her name? I believe it's Heather Grant."

"..."

"Yes, it's the same Heather Grant who spent almost half the Arizona Branch's—excuse me, I meant, the now defunct Arizona Branch's budget on eroge."

"..."

"Never knew you were capable of such expletives, Commander."

"..."

"The point of my call? I just wanted to know if you would like me to take care of her for you. She could cause some serious problems if not disposed of soon, you know--especially if she decides to speak with Davin Monstrang."

"..."

"Very well. I'll let your people take care of her. Who do you plan on sending?"

"..."

"None of my business? Right. Okay. You know, that untrusting nature of yours will eventually be your downfall if you're not too careful."

"..."

"There's no need to get upset. I was simply stating a fact. People don't like it when they feel like you don't trust them. It makes us wonder if the reason for your lack of trust is because you plan on double-crossing us at some point in the near future. Besides, wasn't it your inability to trust others that caused your wife to leave you? Oh, wait. It wasn't lack of trust that made her leave, but because you experimented on her unborn child, wasn't it? My bad."

"…"

"You'd be surprised by the things a person can learn if they ask around enough. It's not like what happened between you two is a closely guarded secret. I'm pretty sure everybody knows about that incident and just refuses to speak about it."

"…"

Justin examined his nails. They'd need to be clipped soon. He'd have his mom do it tomorrow after school or something.

"Yes. Yes. I know. You've given me that same speech several times already. There's no need to give it again."

"…"

"Fine. Out."

Justin sighed as he hung up the phone.

"'Stay out of the way,' he says. 'You'll only cause problems in the future,' he says. Does he really think I'm so incompetent that I would allow myself to get caught by some hentai-watching floozy?"

Looking up, Justin admired the astral beauty of the phantasmagoric night sky, his mind tracing intricate shapes using the stars as waypoints.

"I guess there's nothing to it."

Pushing off the pillar, Justin shoved his hands into his pockets and began walking home, his mouth twisting into an unpleasant facsimile of a smile.

"I wonder who the Commander plans on sending after Heather? Whoever they are, I hope they're strong. I could really use some entertainment right about now."

***

Kevin didn't know when he had gone to sleep, nor did he know how long he had slept for. It couldn't have been that long though, because when he woke up to use the restroom, the clock told him it was 1:45 am.

Lilian stirred as Kevin tried to extricate himself from her grip, an exceedingly troublesome task. Lovely eyelashes fluttered open, revealing irises that glittered like precious gemstones. The twin-tailed kitsune blinked the sleep out of her eyes as he sat up.

"Kevin?"

"Go back to sleep, Lilian, I'll be right back. I just need to use the restroom."

"M'kay..."

Lilian complied and went back to sleep. Smiling as he looked at her, Kevin, in a rare moment of courage and initiative, leaned down and kissed Lilian on her right cheek. The emerald-eyed vixen smiled in her sleep, settling deeper into their large pillow.

Kevin left the bedroom and was soon draining the dragon. Upon revealing the tension in his bladder, he entered the hallway and was about to head back to bed, when a noise caught his attention.

Halting in his tracks, he strained his ears, listening for... there it was again! What was that? It sounded like something was... shaking? No, it sounded like crashing.

Looking around for a second, Kevin noticed that Kotohime was not in the hall. She also wasn't in the living room when he arrived. He frowned, but figured she must be out doing something. He didn't know what she might have been at this time of night, and truthfully, he didn't want to know.

The sounds grew louder, and Kevin determined that they were definitely from something crashing into something else, though he couldn't determine what. They came from outside his apartment and were getting closer.

Kevin approached the door slowly, cautiously, like a real life ninja and not those shōnen ninja who wouldn't know stealth if it hit them in the face. Having already dealt with several life and death situations, he had no desire to find himself on the receiving end of a kidnapping, a violent yōkai who wanted to kill him, or both.

The door loomed ever closer. His footsteps were as silent as he could make them. Not that it mattered. Whatever was causing that racket was making enough noise for the both of them. He soon discovered other noises mixed in with the crashes, which he realized must have been something banging against the stairs. It sounded like... voices?

"M-My Lady! Please be careful! I don't think these stairs are safe! Just listen to how much noise they're making."

"Tee-hee, don't worry. Camellia's fine. See? She's graceful."

"The reason they're making so much noise is because you keep banging our luggage against them."

"I-I can't help it. This luggage is really heavy…"

"Inari-blessed, you're almost as useless as Mom!"

"Th-that's not a very nice thing to say…"

Kevin blinked at the odd conversation taking place. He reached the door and, remaining vigilant, peered through the small eyehole.

"Hawa!"

His eyes promptly widened.

"My Lady! Please be careful or you're going to—"

"Hawan!"

Unlocking the door and swinging it open, Kevin was just in time to receive a face-full of two large, round things.

"Mmph!"

His back hit the floor as he lost his balance, the person who'd slammed into him falling on top of him, further depriving his lungs of oxygen. Because the two somethings smothering his face seemed to possess a circumference that was twice the size of Sanosuke Sagara's zanbato, he couldn't regain his breath either.

"Hawawawawawa!!!"

"Useless woman!"

"M-My Lady!"

As voices shouted and darkness encroached upon his vision, Kevin Swift had but one thought.

Sometimes, it just didn't pay to get out of bed, no matter how badly you had to take a leak.

***

Lilian was woken up by the sound of screaming.

"MMRPH! MHRGGLEEMPHHH!"

It was extremely muffled screaming, but screaming nonetheless. It was also very familiar screaming.

"Beloved!"

Jumping out of bed, Lilian rushed into the living room, where she presumed the screams had come from.

"Don't worry, Beloved! I'm coming to rescue you! I'll—eh?"

Lilian didn't know what to expect when she arrived in the living room. An intruder trying to kidnap her Beloved? An assassin trying to kill her Beloved? A crazy psychopath wielding a spear that always struck a fatal blow by reversing the nature of causality? She didn't know. It could have been anything, so Lilian prepared for the unexpected.

Unfortunately, no amount of preparation could have helped her come to terms with what she saw in that living room.

The first thing she noticed was that, indeed, Kevin was in danger--well, potential danger. He was being smothered by a large pair of boobs. This marshmallow hell was the result of having a woman with long black hair and wearing a white toga laying on top of him. Lilian watched as Kevin kicked and floundered and struggled underneath the woman, who seemed to be freaking out just as much, if not more, than her beloved mate.

"Hawawawawawa! Hwawawawawawawa!"

Like that.

Lilian looked at the next person in this unprecedented scenario —the woman in the French maid outfit who was running around her mate and the woman, making a complete fool of herself.

"Oh, dear! M-My Lady! P-please get off him! You're going to suffocate him!"

"Hawawawawa! HAWA!"

However, it was the last person who truly caught her attention, a stunning and vivacious young woman who looked to be the same age as her. Long strands of hair like silk the color of twilight framed a face that looked nearly identical to her own--all except for one important aspect.

The eyes. While Lilian's eyes had often been described as innocent and pure, this girl's eyes were like the incarnation of lust, sex made manifest. Unlike Lilian's vibrant irises that reminded anyone looking at them of a fairytale princess, the eyes of the vixen standing several feet away were an alluring crimson. Those eyes exuded a sexuality that was unlike anything that Lilian would ever see in another person. With just a single glance, those eyes could capture a person, enthralling them with the promise of unfathomable pleasure.

Of course, that was not what captured Lilian's attention.

She knew these people.

"Mom, Kirihime, Iris! What are you all doing here?"

All movement ceased. Even Kevin stopped struggling, though that was more due to him losing consciousness than because of

Lilian. Camellia stopped floundering and looked up, her enormous tatas still smothering Kevin. Kirihime was also brought to an abrupt halt upon hearing Lilian's voice.

Iris had the most overzealous reaction of all.

"LILIAN!"

"W-wait! Iris! Don't—GOOF!"

For a second, Lilian wondered if this was how Kevin felt very time she glomped him. If so, she totally needed to apologize for that. Being on the receiving end of a glomp was not fun.

Lilian found herself lying on her back. Iris lay on top of her, smothering her with affection.

"Oh, Lilian! I've missed you so much!" Iris rubbed her face in her sister's cleavage. "I can't believe we've finally found you!"

"I-Iris! S-sis! St-ahn! Stop it! C-cut it out!"

Iris did stop. She looked up, her chin resting between Lilian's breasts. Her eyes leaked tears, which descended down her cheeks like glistening moon drops. "I've missed you so much. Do you know how long I've gone without seeing you? Three months! Three whole months without being able to spend time with my darling Lily-pad."

"U-ugh." Lilian's cheeks became flames of red. "Please don't call me that ever again. That nickname was fine when we were children, but… no. Just no. And you can't do this anymore. I have a—" her eyes widened. "—KEVIN!"

Before Iris knew what was happening, Lilian threw her off, sending her crashing to the floor. Lilian jumped to her feet, red hair whipping about her like intense flames caught in a strong wind. Green eyes zeroed in on her mate's prone form before she rushed over to her mother.

"Mom! Get! Off! My! Mate!"

"Mate?"

"Eh?

"Hawa?"

***

Kevin awoke to the sound of voices.

"I can't believe you three came all the way here. How did you even find me?"

"What do you mean how did we find you? Isn't it obvious? Kotohime sent us a message."

"Damn that woman."

"H-hawa… p-please don't be angry, Lilian. Camellia… Camellia was just worried. Camellia wanted to see her daughter again…"

"What she said. Only without the daughter part. And not in third person."

"Please do not be too upset with us, Lady Lilian. We have missed you very much. All of us were incredibly worried when you disappeared."

"Ha… all right, all right. I understand. Look, I'm sorry for vanishing like that. It was never my intention to make any of you worry. I was just… I'm sick and tired of having every aspect of my life, from how I'm supposed to act to who I mate with decided for me."

"Hey, we understand perfectly. Well, I understand. I don't want you mating with some asswad who thinks he's hot shit just because his old man's the Bodhisattva."

"Lady Iris… p-please don't swear so much."

"Hmph. Whatever."

Kevin slowly opened his eyes, which felt like they'd been glued shut with rubber cement, and was greeted to the sight of two boobs covered by a white T-shirt.

"Lilian."

"Ah! Kevin! How are you feeling?"

Kevin made a face. "I can't see your face."

Lilian's smile was one of definite amusement. "I can't see yours either."

Sitting up, Kevin soon noticed several things about his new situation. First, he and Lilian were on the couch. Second, they weren't alone.

The first woman to catch his attention was the one wearing a French maid outfit, if only because the entire concept of a French maid being in his house made him do a double-take. She looked sort of similar to Kotohime. She had the same eyes, the same skin tone, the same facial features. Really, there were only two differences between this woman and Kotohime… aside from the fact that one wore a maid costume and the other a kimono. The first difference was that this woman had shorter hair with a single antenna-like strand poking out of her crown.

The second difference was that her boobs were smaller.

Not that smaller boobs meant much here. That was sort of like comparing watermelons to cantaloupes.

She also had three tails waving about behind her, and her fox ears seemed a little perkier than Kotohime's.

Shifting his gaze from the maid, Kevin's eyes immediately caught sight of the next woman in line. It was beginning to feel a bit redundant, but this woman was also very beautiful. Her features sort of reminded him of Lilian, only a bit more mature—at least as far as facial structure went. Her smile and the unusually naive light in her eyes as she looked at him presented a startling contrast with her womanly body.

The body of a woman with the eyes of a child.

Her boobs were also big. Really big. Like, as large as his head.

She had five tails.

The last person his gaze locked onto was a girl who looked so much like Lilian that it startled him. Everything about this girl, from the way her face was shaped to the sensual curves of her incredible body and even her two tails, reminded Kevin of his mate. There were just two differences: Her black hair and her feline-like crimson eyes that seemed to seductively whisper "come and get me, if you can."

He shook his head, blinked, and then looked at the girl again. For a second he thought that she had... but it must have been his imagination.

"So... Sleeping Beauty finally awakens, I see." The raven-haired succubus' curved lips seemed to seep amusement.

Kevin blushed at the "sleeping beauty" comment, but just because this girl embarrassed him with her words didn't mean he was willing to put up with them. Two could play at this game.

"W-who the heck are you?" his voice cracked.

Way to go, Kevin. You sounded so manly just now.

The vixen smirked at him. Kevin gulped. She placed a hand on her chest, her index finger absently brushing against her right nipple, which he could see through the fabric of her clothes. "Why, I am just Lily-pad's most humble and sexy sister. Nothing more, nothing less."

"I thought I told you not to call me that!" a thoroughly mortified Lilian spat.

"And I don't think humble and sexy can be used in the same sentence," Kevin muttered, doing what he could to regain his wits, what little he had. "So, you guys are Lilian's family, then?"

"No. We're Lilian's fairy godparents." Iris' sarcastic reply was met with a glare from Lilian and Kevin.

"Y-yes, we're Lilian's family," Camellia tried to play the diplomat. "The girl with black hair is Camellia's daughter, Iris, and the person next to Camellia is Camellia's maid, Kirihime."

"Uh huh..." Kevin eyed the kitsune strangely. "And I'm guessing that makes you Camellia?"

"H-hawa?" Camellia seemed startled. "That's right. How did you know?"

"Lucky guess," Kevin said, his voice dryer than a desert. Lilian and Iris facepalmed at the same time.

***

A problem arose with the arrival of Lilian's family. Actually, their arrival came with many problems. However, on that night, one particular issue stood out the most.

Sleeping arrangements.

The Swift residence wasn't that large. It had two bedrooms, a living room connected to a kitchen, two bathrooms, and an office attached to the master bedroom. It was an apartment meant for two people.

Fortunately, Kevin had a solution to this problem.

"I'm sorry I don't have a bed or anything for you to sleep on," Kevin said as he put several sheets, blankets, and pillows on the couch. Once finished, he stood up and looked at Lilian's raven-haired sister. "This is the best I can offer right now. If you want, though, this weekend, we can go shopping for some furniture. I'm sure we can find something more comfortable. Maybe a nice futon or something..."

Iris shrugged. "Meh, while I'm used to sleeping on a comfortable bed, so long as I'm with my Lily-pad, it doesn't where I sleep."

"Would you stop calling me that!" a discomposed Lilian hissed. "Inari-blessed, it's like you're purposefully trying to embarrass me!"

"Aw!" Lilian suddenly found herself caught within the fierce and overly affectionate embrace of her sister. "You know it's never my intention to embarrass you. You're just so adorable that I can't help but want to give you a cute nickname."

The redhead's face flushed deeply as Iris rubbed her cheek against Lilian's. "W-would you stop holding me like this! And besides, I can't sleep with you."

"Eh?" That stopped Iris in her tracks. She held Lilian at arms' length, staring into the other vixen's eyes, her own wide with shock. "What do you mean you can't sleep with me? Why can't you?"

"B-because I have a mate." Lilian peered over Iris' shoulder to look at Kevin, who watched the pair with a raised eyebrow. "I-I always sleep with Kevin these days, so…"

"Oh…" Iris shuddered. "I… I see… hehehe, right, I-I guess that makes sense… he is your mate, after all…"

Her grip on Lilian's shoulders tightened, prompting the other girl to squirm.

"I-Iris, y-you're kinda hurting me…"

"Am I? Hehehe… my bad… kukuku…"

As Kevin stood there, shuddering at the sound of Iris' laugh, which was way creepier than Lilian's, he couldn't help but think his life was about to get hectic again.

***

In the end, Iris had gone to sleep on the couch.

Kevin had finally relented on his "don't enter my mom's room" policy and allowed Camellia to sleep in it. He had also apologized profusely to Kirihime for not having anywhere for her to sleep. The three-tailed kitsune had assured him that she would be fine, and thanked him for his concern and hospitality. After that, he and Lilian went back to bed.

"I'm really sorry about this," Lilian apologized. She was straddling his body. Her arms on either side of his head kept her from falling on him, and her hair created a curtain that trailed across the bed like fiery threads of silk.

"What are you apologizing for?"

"For all this, for what happened tonight." Lilian didn't make any grand gestures towards the living room, but Kevin didn't need them to know what she was talking about. "I should have realized my family would find me eventually. While Kotohime is my maid and bodyguard, she's still a vassal of the Pnéyma clan. She would have told them my location sooner or later."

Kevin gave Lilian a reassuring smile. "It's fine. I don't really mind meeting your family. Actually, I was kind of hoping that I would at least get to meet your mom and sister at some point."

"Really?"

"Of course," Kevin paused, his face scrunching in an amalgamation of amusement and abashment, "though I would have liked to know they were coming beforehand. A little warning would have been nice."

"Muu. Don't look at me like that. I didn't know they would be coming."

"Right. Right. Kotohime's the one who called them over. I know that." He raised his right hand and waved it about in odd, circular gestures. "I'm not saying it's your fault or anything, just that I wish I'd known they were coming." Another pause. Kevin switched topics. "So… that girl in the living room is your sister?"

"Yes. Iris is my fraternal twin."

"Is this the same Iris that you shared your first kiss with?"

"Gurk!"

"Oh, we shared a lot more than that, uhuhu."

"Quiet, Iris!"

"Lilian…"

"D-don't look at me like that, Beloved. A-anyway, I was really hoping you'd forgotten about that," she mumbled.

"I don't think there's any way I would ever be able to forget about something like that," he replied, lips curling in amusement.

"Ugh, mou, you're becoming mean." Lilian pouted at him, her lower lip jutting out and trembling. "Meanie."

Kevin chuckled. "Yes, yes, I'm a big meanie. But seriously, your sister, she's kind of odd, don't you think?"

Lilian's bright green irises took on a curious quality. "You think so? She's never seemed odd to me."

"Well, yeah, but you grew up with her. You're probably used to her personality. I only just met her and I already think she's kind of weird." Actually, Lilian's entire family was weird, including Lilian herself.

"Now that's not very nice." Despite her words, Lilian didn't seem upset by what could have been perceived as him insulting her sister.

"We should probably try to get some sleep," Kevin changed the subject again. "It's getting late, erm, early, and we have school tomorrow—I mean today." Thinking about school reminded him of another issue that needed to be solved, but they would have to fix that problem later.

"Right."

After one last lingering kiss, Lilian slid off him and found refuge snuggling into Kevin's side. Her eyes closed and the twin-tailed kitsune nodded off seconds later.

Kevin wondered how Lilian could fall asleep so easily. He looked at the clock, which told him it was two in the morning, and sighed. This night had been really long. He didn't really know what to think about everything that had happened, so he tried not to and just closed his eyes to get some sleep.

Yet, even as the sandman came to claim him, one last thought pervaded his mind.

With the inclusion of Lilian's family into his life, things were definitely going to get hectic again.

And to think, all this had started because he'd gone to use the restroom.

***

Iris sat up in her makeshift bed about an hour after Kevin and her sister left.

She glanced around the dark room, taking note of the silhouettes of various objects. Kirihime sat in one corner of the room, soundly sleeping.

Slowly slipping off the couch, Iris made her way down the hall and stopped in front of Kevin and Lilian's bedroom. She paused with her hand on the doorknob, ears twitching as she channeled youki into them, enhancing her already prodigious hearing. When she received no indication that her sister or her sister's mate were awake, she slowly entered the room.

Iris' heart clenched when she saw them lying on the bed. Kevin was on his back and Lilian was snuggled securely into his side, with one of his arms wrapped around her, pulling the girl close.

Whispers filled her head as she stopped in front of the bed. They were soft, however, barely audible and thus easily ignored.

She stared at Kevin, watching as he breathed in and out, her frown growing more prominent by the second. One second turned into a minute, which soon became two minutes. Finally, after nearly five minutes had passed, Iris left, closing the door behind her and climbing back onto the couch.

She laid down, her eyelids fluttering closed, her mind slowly sinking into the murky depths of her soul where the whispers were at their strongest.

Kevin Swift, she thought to herself, *you are an obstacle in the path to my sister's love.*

Chapter 3

A Family of Foxes

The sun had just risen above the event horizon when Kotohime returned home.

She had been out gathering information on the current happenings in the yōkai world—an important task, considering she was charged with protecting Lilian.

It hadn't been easy, especially because she didn't like dealing with Valsiener. While he might have been the greatest source of information this side of Phoenix, she didn't trust him. That boy bartered information with impunity. He would give his intel to anyone who was willing to pay his price. It was better to gather intelligence from other sources.

As she entered the Swifts' apartment, her eyes caught sight of someone she hadn't been expecting to see for at least another few days.

"Kirihime?"

Sitting in the corner of the living room, her legs crossed and her back leaning against the wall, Kirihime appeared both similar and diametrically opposed to Kotohime herself. Even the way she sat showed that, while they bore a family resemblance, their demeanors were quite different.

"Oh, sister." Kirihime's smile was truly wondrous, full of energy and compassion. Kotohime didn't let that fool her, though she did return the smile with her own. "It's so good to see you."

"And you," Kotohime said. Her sister stood up, stretching out some of the kinks in her back and neck. Sitting like that wasn't very comfortable, something Kotohime knew from experience. "I have missed you. I gather from your presence and the mess on the couch that Camellia-sama and Iris-sama are here as well?"

"Of course. My Lady Camellia is still sleeping, but Lady Iris woke up a while ago and is taking a bath." Kirihime looked up, her mien thoughtful yet cute. "I'm somewhat surprised that she's up so early. We went to bed very late last night—ah, but then, I am told that traveling via human transportation can mess up a person's sleeping patterns, and Lady Iris already has issues sleeping."

"Indeed."

"So where were you last night? I expected to see you here with Lady Lilian and her, uh, mate."

Kotohime waved her hand, dismissing her sister's question. "I was simply taking care of a few errands. In either event, I believe I shall begin preparing breakfast."

"Very well. In that case, I think I'm going to go hunting."

With that, Kirihime pulled an eight inch long serrated knife out of her Extra Dimensional Storage Space and left, closing the front door behind her and leaving the room in stillness once more.

Kotohime shook her head and went into the kitchen. She really hoped Kirihime would be cautious during her hunt, but Lilian's attendant knew better than to expect a miracle.

***

Kevin wondered if he was destined to be caught in every awkward situation imaginable. Really, how else could he explain the embarrassing predicament he currently found himself in?

It all started that morning. His morning had gone the same way it always did when his body was recovering from being brutalized by Kiara. He woke up, extricated himself from the sleeping Lilian, and then made his way into the bathroom to take a shower.

That was when he ran into his current problem.

Someone was already in the bath.

Why don't any of these fox-girls lock the stupid door? It's not that hard.

Kevin swore he could feel his brain frying as he gazed at

Lilian's sister. He knew it was wrong. He was dating Lilian, so he shouldn't be looking at another woman, but if anyone else saw what he was seeing, they would have understood why he found it impossible to look away.

Unlike her sister, who seemed to prefer showers, Iris lounged in the tub. Warm water lapped at her breasts, the steaming surface and bubbles preserving her modesty while somehow enhancing her aesthetic appeal by adding an aura of erotic mysticism. One of her shapely legs rose up from the water and rested against the lip, bent at the knee, her calf rocking gently back and forth with a hypnotic sway. Water clung to her body, a combination of coalescing steam and sweat. He watched one particularly adventurous droplet slowly leave a glistening trail down her neck and clavicle bone before disappearing into the valley of her breasts.

Kevin tried to ignore the sight. He told himself that he needed to leave, that this was wrong, but something kept him pinned to the spot. It could have been shock, it could have been fear, it could have been something so incomprehensibly simple that it was staring him in the face. Whatever that something was, it kept him rooted where he stood, unable to tear his gaze off the alluring beauty lounging in the tub.

While he stood there and gaped like an idiot, a pair of eyelids slowly opened, revealing dark crimson irises. Those deep red eyes met his, and Kevin felt as if all the air had been sucked from his lungs. His legs threatened to topple as something primal and powerful threatened to consume him. Desire. Need. Want. Hunger. His body betrayed him, even as his rebelling mind shouted at him. He wanted to scream. He wanted to run. He couldn't, however, because those eyes, beautiful in the same way a King Cobra is beautiful, froze him solid in a block of ice.

The moment passed.

Kevin sucked in a deep breath.

And then realization set in. He was in a bathroom. With a girl. He was in a bathroom with a naked girl and oh-my-god-what-the-heck-was-he-doing?!

"S-sorry!"

Squeaking like a frightened rat ensnared by the claws of a cat, Kevin rushed out of the room and slammed the door shut. He pressed a hand to his sweaty face, gasping for breath, his mind making every attempt to figure out what had just happened and failing. For reasons he couldn't quite grasp, his mind appeared incapable of coming to terms with what he'd just done. He had been gawking at Lilian's sister!

I think I'm going to be sick.

The door opened. Kevin "eeped!" as Iris stepped out. Her narrowed, feline gaze oozed with a sexuality no girl her apparent age should have been able to exude. Kevin's spine snapped as his back tried to straighten, and his heart leapt into his throat when those succubus eyes locked onto him.

"Uh... hi?"

Iris' smirk made him want to shudder. He would have done so, too, but her gaze still had him immobilized.

"Hmmm..." Kevin felt a tremor run through his body when Iris hummed. Dear God! How could such a simple noise from this girl sound like a siren's call? "So, you're Lilian's mate," she murmured, her lips curving into a delightfully devilish smile. Kevin's mouth went dry. "I suppose she could have done worse for her first mate. Still..." her eyes surveyed him from top to bottom, studying him, dissecting him. Devouring him. "...I don't know what she sees in you exactly. You're handsome enough, sure, but you're not anything special."

And just like that, with those words and that condescending look in her eyes, the allure of her gaze and erotic beauty vanished like heat in the Arctic Circle.

Kevin's face went flat. "So I've been told, but really, I don't think my and Lilian's relationship is any of your business, sister or not."

Iris' eyes flashed. Something dangerous flickered in those irises. A smirk twisted her lips into a veneer that looked off somehow. He couldn't explain why, precisely, but her smile unnerved him.

Kevin did his best to hold her gaze, to show this vixen that he wouldn't be intimidated by her. He didn't know if he succeeded but, after a moment, Lilian's fraternal twin sister nodded.

"It seems you've got some bite to you, kiddo." With a supercilious chuckle, Iris patted him on the cheek as if he was a child. Kevin scowled and batted the hand away, causing her smile to grow. "Not bad. Not bad at all. I still don't know what she sees in you, but I guess that's because I'm not Lilian."

Holding his gaze a moment longer, she airily waved a hand at the door.

"Anyway, you can use the restroom now. I'm done with my bath, in case you couldn't tell." As she said this, her hands slid down her towel-clad figure, delicately roaming over the swell of her breasts, the dip of her slim waist and the curve of her shapely hips.

Kevin clenched his hands so hard his knuckles turned white. Iris noticed this, for she gave him one last wink before walking off, her hips swaying with exaggerated motions.

He waited for a moment, his mind and body slowly coming down from the adrenaline that his confrontation with Iris had caused to storm through his bloodstream. Shaking his head to dispel the last bit of… whatever had clouded his mind, he proceeded into the bathroom, entered the shower, and turned the water onto its coldest setting.

I can already tell, Kevin thought as he stood there, shivering, *this day is not going to be the least bit pleasant.*

***

Fifteen minutes after Kevin got out of bed, Lilian woke up. During that time, Kevin finished taking a shower and donned jeans and a T-shirt. Lilian got dressed after she had finished taking a shower herself.

Kevin looked at his girlfriend-slash-mate's clothing. Her jean shorts fit her shapely hips better than any glove, almost like they were painted on. They were also very short, which allowed an expansive view of her stunningly long legs. She wore a green off the shoulder crop top that exposed much of her flat stomach, which Kevin found distracting in ways he could scarcely comprehend. He then looked at her gladiator sandals and groaned. He was not becoming a foot person! He wasn't!

Kevin preferred tails.

"Do you like my outfit?" Lilian asked.

"Uh…" Kevin shook his head, shedding the fuzziness clouding his mind. "It's nice," he eyed the redhead some more. "Really nice," he amended, his face scrunching up. "But, um, aren't you going to be cold?"

Lilian shook her head. "It's not that cold yet. Besides…" she looked down at herself. "I kind of have to wear these clothes now. They're my signature look."

"Your what?"

"My signature look." She stared at him, as if doing so would somehow make Kevin understand what she was talking about. He didn't. "These are the clothes I wear on the back cover."

Kevin pressed a hand to his forehead and gave her a deadpan stare. "The back cover?"

Smiling, Lilian walked up and gave him a quick peck on the lips. "Don't worry about it too much, Beloved. Now then," she grabbed his hand, "let's get some breakfast. I'm starving."

Kotohime had breakfast ready by the time they arrived. Iris was also present, sitting at the table and slowly eating her salmon. When she saw Lilian, her face lit up like a million watt bulb. "Morning, Lily-pad. I hope you slept well."

"Don't call me that."

"Come on, sit and eat with me." Iris patted the seat next to her, and then slowly panned her face towards Kevin, the smile leaving. "I guess you can eat with us, too."

"Gee, thanks," Kevin's voice actually contained a surprising amount of sarcasm. "I'm so pleased that you're comfortable enough to tell me when I can and can't eat in my own apartment. Truly, your generosity and humbleness knows no bounds."

Iris snorted. Kotohime, who had moved to set their plates of food on the table, gave him an odd look. Kevin couldn't place it, but it almost felt like she approved of his attitude.

Lilian was much more vocal in her thoughts.

"I think that was the hottest thing you've ever said in this series. Ever."

"Uh…" Kevin blushed. "Thank you?"

Sarcasm, the hottest thing since Scarlett Johansson played Black Widow.

***

The problem Kevin realized they would have earlier that morning came to a head after breakfast. It was a multi-layered problem, one that he really didn't know how to solve.

"Ugh, what am I supposed to do now?"

"Kevin?"

"There's no way I can let those three live here without some adult supervision."

"Kevin?"

"I mean, sure, Camellia's an adult... sort of. But, she acts so childish. I mean, just listen to her. She talks in third person and has the dumbest catchphrase I've ever heard. How is that adult?"

"Hawa?"

"Beloved?"

"And then there's Kirihime. She seems nice enough, I guess, but she doesn't appear to be very reliable. I don't know, maybe I'm being too hard on her, but she wasn't very much help last night, and that French maid outfit is just weird."

"You're not listening to me, are you?"

"And don't even get me started on Iris."

"I'm right here, you know."

"She might be hotter than sin, but God, does she have a disgusting attitude."

"Still right here. Thanks for the compliment, though."

"There's no way I can leave them alone in my apartment. Who knows what kind of chaos they'll cause?"

"KEVIN!"

"Huh?"

Kevin blinked, his mind snapping back to reality. He looked around and noticed that he was standing in the living room. Lilian, Iris, Camellia, and Kotohime were with him. They stood off to the side, watching with various expressions that contained either amusement, exasperation, or a combination of both.

Except for Camellia. She just did what she did best: smile and look innocent.

And then Kevin realized what he'd been doing.

"Did I say all that out loud?"

"Yes." An amused Kotohime held the sleeves of her kimono up to her lips, demurely hiding her smile. "Yes, you did."

"Oh..." Kevin scratched the back of his head. "Whoops."

"Are you alright, Kevin?" Lilian's eyes shone with concern. "You seem a little... stressed."

"That's certainly one way of putting it." Lilian's words were completely disproportionate to the amount of stress he felt at that moment. "We've got a problem."

"I've noticed," Lilian said with just a touch of amusement.

"I'm not sure how we should handle this. I can't in good conscience let these three stay here without someone around. I don't want to come home and find that my place has been struck by a supernatural disaster."

"Seems like someone has trust issues."

Kevin glared at Iris. "If I have trust issues, then it's because I don't know you that well. You'll have to forgive me if extending trust to a couple people I've never met before last night is difficult."

"Whoa there, kiddo." Iris held her hands up defensively. Kevin glared at the "kiddo" comment. She might have been over a hundred years old, but by kitsune standards, she wasn't much older than him. "No need to flip. I get it. I really do."

"Whatever."

"I have an idea." Everyone turned to Lilian. "Why doesn't Iris come with us to school? That would solve at least some of your dilemma, right?"

"That's… actually not a bad idea," Kevin admitted slowly. Iris looked like she wanted to say otherwise, and only didn't because Lilian was the one who suggested it. "If Iris came to school with us, that would mean Kotohime only has to look after Camellia and Kirihime, and I think Kirihime can take care of herself."

"Hawa." Camellia's pout reminded everyone of a child who'd been told they couldn't have ice cream. "You make it sound like Camellia can't take care of herself. Camellia's a responsible adult, too, you know."

Everyone stared at Camellia with matching deadpan expressions. When it became clear that she was being serious, they decided to ignore her.

"Ufufufu, I had not realized Kevin-sama trusted me this much."

Kevin shrugged. "Lilian trusts you, and you haven't done anything that would warrant me distrusting you."

"Ufufufu, I'm honored."

"Please stop with the 'Ufufufu' already. It's not funny anymore. I'm pretty sure the fans are getting tired of your laugh."

… A pause.

"Wait. What did I just say?"

"BELOVED!"

"Wha—mmrrgggllle!"

Camella, Iris and Kotohime watched as Lilian pounced on her mate, sending him to the ground and smothering him into blissful oblivion.

"Oh, Beloved, you're so amazing!"

"Mrph! Mggrrrlllee! Mph! Mmph!"

"I'm so proud of you!"

"Hmph! Mm mmm mmph!"

"Truly, you're the best mate a kitsune could ask for!"

"MPH!"

"Um, Lilian-sama," Kotohime actually looked kind of worried, "not to be rude, but I think you're suffocating him. He might die if you keep that up."

Lilian didn't appear to have heard her. She continued holding Kevin's head to her bosom, heedless of the fact that her mate was slowly losing his tenuous grip on consciousness.

"Death by symmetrical docking... he can't complain." Iris cracked her knuckles. "And if he does, I'll kill him."

"Oh, my."

"Hawa?"

***

After solving the first part of their multi-layered dilemma, Kevin had to solve the second part: getting to school.

Kevin rode his bike to school--a bike only meant for one person. Somehow, he managed to fit Lilian on without too much trouble. Large breasts aside, his mate was actually quite thin. However, now there were three people going to school, and his bike could not carry three people—at least not safely.

They had to take the bus.

Kevin hated riding the bus. Back when he was in middle school, he remembered riding the bus. It was hot and loud and frenetic, with children running around and the bus driver yelling at them for doing so. People threw stuff all over the place, from pencils and erasers to gum and food. Unpleasant really did nothing to describe how horrible riding the bus truly was.

Kevin, Lilian and Iris sat on one of several benches. Because the bench was so small, his girlfriend sat in his lap. He didn't mind this, or he wouldn't have normally, except that the number of stares he received that day was disconcerting. It felt like there were nearly twice as many eyes on him than normal.

Kevin did his best to ignore the looks that ranged from downright murderous to "I'm gonna fucking kill you!" as the bus drove down the street.

He could not ignore the whispers, however, and there were many of them.

"Hey! Pst! Isn't that Kevin?"

"Yeah, I think it is. Certainly looks like him. Wonder what he's doing on the bus? Doesn't he ride a bike or something?"

Kevin wondered how these people knew so much about them, when he was positive that he'd never spoken with any of them before.

"Who the hell cares about that? Look at who he's with! Lilian and some other hot chick! Look at her! Shit, I wish I could get a piece of that!"

"Damn, that girl is fine."

"I'd tap that in a second."

"Do you think she's a virgin?"

"Are you freaking kidding me? You think a girl that hot is a virgin? Keep dreaming."

"I wonder, what's her relationship to Kevin and Lilian?"

"I wonder where she came from."

"I wonder where Kevin's getting all these girls from. What, does he make them fall from the sky or something?"

"I just wanna kill him. It's not fair that he's hogging all the babes for himself. Damn, greedy son-of-a-bitch!"

"Something wrong, Kevin?" Lilian asked as Kevin buried his face in her hair.

"Nothing. It's nothing."

"Hmm…"

While the bus shook and jostled as it drove along the bumpy road, Kevin felt something come over him. He felt cold, chilled, like someone had shoved him into a freezer. A shiver ran down his spine.

He looked around and his gaze landed on Iris. She was staring out the window, her left leg crossed over her right, with her left elbow resting against her thigh, and her chin sat on the butt of her hand. She seemed bored.

Silently, he went back to staring at the red hair of Lilian, who was enjoying her time on his lap.

Had he looked back at Iris again, he would have noticed her attempting to bore a hole through his head with her gaze.

***

When they exited the bus, Kevin led Lilian and Iris to the principal's office.

"Lilian already knows this, but I feel I should warn you; be careful around the principal."

"Oh?" Iris raised an eyebrow. "And why is that?"

Kevin just shook his head. "You'll see."

They arrived at the main office building and, upon speaking with the PA, were allowed to enter the principal's office and talk to the man up top.

Principal Corrompere was Eric's old man, which explained a lot, like why Eric was such a perverted lech, as well as why he hadn't been expelled for doing things that should have put him in prison.

Principal Corrompere looked like an older, fatter, more lecherous version of his son. While it seemed impossible for someone to look pervier than someone else, it wasn't. Anyone could tell from looking at the principal's drooling face and lustful eyes that this was a man whose perversity knew no bounds. His image wasn't helped by the porn magazine in his hands.

The lecherous old man giggles he periodically released didn't help anyone's perception of him either.

"Principal," the PA ignored the porn mag in her boss's hands, "you have a couple of students who would like to speak with you."

"Oh?"

Principal Corrompere looked up...

... And froze when his eyes locked onto two girls who created a sweet and sexy dichotomy that he'd never imagined possible in real life.

His face flushed. His breathing became heavy. Steam shot from his nostrils like erupting geysers. His irises, once a dark brown bordering on black, suddenly transformed into large pink hearts.

Without warning, he shot to his feet and ripped off his shirt, revealing a chest that made Chewbacca look like he shaved daily. The fat perv jumped onto the table and then leapt off to pounce on the two girls.

"Where have you two been all my life?!"

Lilian and Iris, upon seeing the danger presented to them, swiftly stepped out of the way.

Kevin wasn't so lucky.

"Come to papa!"

"NNNOOOO!!"

***

"I can't believe you!" Kevin did not look pleased as he, Lilian and Iris walked to class. It looked like someone had set a nuke off on his face. "That idiot jumped on top of me, and you did nothing!"

"I said I was sorry," Lilian mumbled sullenly, poking her index fingers together.

"Sorry doesn't cut it," Kevin snapped. "That man tried to kiss me! And he drooled all over my face. Do you know how disgusting that is? It took me fifteen minutes to wash the drool off in the bathroom."

Iris' chuckle was cut off by Kevin's venomous glare. She held up her hands, and though her expression was bland, her eyes twinkled merrily. "Hey, don't look at me. I'm not your mate."

"I fail to see how that matters. You were every bit as complacent as she was. I wouldn't be surprised if you had a hand in what happened."

"Now that's just rude." Iris decided not to tell Kevin that the reason for the fat principal's behavior was, partly at least, due to her **Call of Ecstasy**. She didn't use it often, mostly because she could easily seduce whoever she wanted without it. However, the opportunity for a prank had been too strong to ignore.

Lilian looked at him, her lips trembling. "I would have done something, Beloved, but that man scared me. I was so frightened. I thought he might do something pervy to me if I so much as moved."

Kevin crossed his arms. "That look's not gonna work on me."

Lilian's eyes grew wide and dewy.

Kevin's stern expression wavered for a second before he put his mask back in place. "Still not gonna work."

"Muu, Kevin." Lilian clasped her hands in front of her, the act causing her breasts to push themselves together. "Please forgive me? Pretty please?" She tilted her head for maximum adorableness.

Kevin's defenses crumbled.

"Ugh, uh, auu…" His shoulders slumped. "All right, fine. I forgive you."

"Yay!" Lilian threw a fist in the air.

Iris shook her head. "You're a pushover, you know that, kiddo?"

"… Shut up."

***

Arriving at the door to Ms. Vis' class, Kevin knocked exactly three times.

The door opened and Ms. Vis glared at him, as if he had just interrupted the most important moment of her life.

"Mr. Swift." She pushed her glasses up the bridge of her nose with her middle and index finger.

"You shouldn't do that."

Ms. Vis looked startled. "Pardon?"

"That," Kevin indicated how she'd been pushing her glasses up her nose. "You shouldn't do that."

Ms. Vis huffed irritably. "And why not?"

"Because you're not a Badass Bookworm like Gendo Ikari."

"Heh-heh. Nice one, Beloved."

Lilian and Kevin shared a grin and a high five. Ms. Vis stared at him for a few seconds longer, then promptly ignored him and switched her glare to Lilian.

"Ms. Pnéyma…"

"Good morning!"

Ms. Vis twitched, her neck muscles spasming as if she was trying to resist the demonic urge to strangle the Celestial Kitsune. Apparently deciding to pretend that Lilian didn't exist, her eyes landed on Iris. "And who might you be?"

Iris smirked. "I'm your new student, teach." She presented the teacher with her transcript and acceptance letter. Ms. Vis snatched the paper from Iris' hands and read it, her ghostly white face becoming increasingly red.

"I see." Ms. Vis glared at the vixen. "Everything appears to be in order, so all I can do is give you a warning. Do not follow your sister's example and do something that would interrupt the learning process of my class, or I will kick you out faster than you can say mathematics."

"Right. I got it. No worries, teach. I'll be on my best behavior."

Ms. Vis huffed and whirled around, walking back into the room. As he, Lilian, and Iris followed her, Kevin saw the raven-haired succubus' grin and had a startling premonition.

I get the feeling that something extremely erotic is about to happen.

Very genre savvy, this Kevin Swift.

***

"Settle down, class!" Ms. Vis shouted as Kevin and Lilian took their seats. "I know this might come as something of a surprise, but it appears we have a new student. I would like everyone to welcome Ms. Iris Pnéyma, who is here to further her education."

Iris strolled forward with a predator's grace until she stood in front of Ms. Vis, ignoring the indignant squawk from said teacher. She bent over and put her right hand on her knee. Her shirt, an arched black crop top that revealed most of her stomach and a more than healthy portion of her cleavage, caused her breasts to practically spill out. She then placed the index and middle finger of her left hand against her lush crimson lips, blew everyone a kiss and winked.

"Hi there! I came here from Florida to spend time with my sister, so I don't know this state very well. I hope I can count on all of you to take good care of me."

The reaction was instantaneous. Every male student minus Kevin was jettisoned out of their seats, launched across the room, where they smacked against the back wall as geysers of blood blew out of their noses like a broken fire hydrants.

Kevin clamped a hand over his nose, covering up the suspicious red liquid that leaked between his fingers.

After discreetly wiping her nose, Lindsay leaned over to whisper in Lilian's ear. "That's your sister?"

"Yep."

"Damn… she could make straight women gay."

Lilian looked at her friend, raising an inquiring eyebrow. "That was some very suspicious wording there. Is there something you'd like to tell me?"

"N-no." Lindsay's cheeks flushed. "Nothing."

"Hehehe…" Iris chuckled as she sauntered over to an empty seat next to Lilian. "Damn, I'm good."

While all this was going on, Ms. Vis looked at her class, her eyes twitching and her face quickly turning a bright shade of steaming red.

"Detention! Detention immediately after school! You're all getting DETENTION!"

***

Eric and Heather stood just outside of a vent leading to the girl's locker room.

No one else was present, which was good, because they could get into some serious trouble if other people learned of the operation that was about to commence.

Eric stood at attention, his back straight, hands at his sides. He looked like a soldier standing before his commanding officer.

"All right, my young apprentice, are you ready for your next lesson?"

"I'm ready, Master!"

"Very well." Arms crossed under her chest, Heather stared at her apprentice with all the seriousness of Jabidaya getting ready to face against Lord Pain in the ultimate peep off. "Stealth is the most important aspect for any peeper. After all, you can't peep if the girls you're trying to peep on can hear you. Do you understand?"

Eric finished writing her words on the notepad he had brought with him for just this occasion. He straightened his back and snapped off a salute. "Yes, Master."

"Good." Heather pulled off the grate blocking the vent. "Now, while a lot of people think hiding in a locker is the best place for a peeper to hide because of the up-close and personal view, it's actually the worst. You see, a locker is very conspicuous. It's the first place a girl will look when trying to sniff out a peeping Tom. The vents are much better. Not only do they offer you an aerial view to survey the entire locker room, but you'll also be able to see down their shirts."

Eric cried manly tears as he listened to his master. Truly, this woman was a peeper of unparalleled talent!

Heather looked at Eric and gestured to him. "Now then, climb through here, my young apprentice. Climb and discover paradise!"

With tears in his eyes, Eric saluted again. "Yes, Master! Thank you, Master!"

Heather's smile was benevolent. "You are very welcome, my young apprentice."

Eric disappeared into the vent. Heather stood outside, arms crossed under her chest, listening. One second turned into five and five turned into ten. After thirty seconds, she heard it.

"Come to papa, you magnificent mammaries!"

"AAHH! IT'S A PEEPING TOM!"

"KILL THE PEEPER!"

"Eh?! No, wait! I didn't mean to come here! I was supposed to peep on you through the vents!"

"Like that's any better! Die peeping Tom!"

"OH, MY GOD! OH, GOD PLEASE! NO! IT HURTS! MOMMY! HELP! OH, THE PAIN! THE PAIN, IT'S—OH, PLEASE GOD I'M SORRY! SOMEONE! ANYONE! HELP!"

From that moment on, all words faded away into a threnody of hoarser and hoarser screams. When Eric's screaming started to fade, Heather started picking up other noises accompanying the screams. The sounds of flesh beating flesh, metal beating flesh, wood beating flesh. She even heard crunching sounds that reminded her someone crushing peanut brittle under their feet, as well as loud banging reminiscent of someone's face being smashed against a metal surface.

Several seconds later, the freshman girls in PE walked out of the room, their faces etched and twisted into a facsimile of disgust.

"Can you believe that guy? Did he really think he could peep on us?"

"I know, right? Doesn't he know we were all warned about him by the older girls?"

"Of course he does. He's probably a masochist. I bet he was getting his rocks off while we beat the crap out of him."

"Ewwww! Jess… no, just no. Don't even go there. God, that's so gross…"

The girls' voices vanished as they entered the gym. Heather chose that moment to walk into the locker room, where she found Eric exactly how she expected to find him: beaten, battered, bruised, missing several teeth, and with his face so swollen it could have passed for a hot air balloon.

She marched up to the lump of barely conscious meat once known as Eric and gave him a disappointed look.

"You just had to jump out of the vents, didn't you? Remember what I told you? Stealth is a peeping Tom's best friend."

Eric just groaned.

***

The entire first half of school went the same way as their first class. Everywhere they went, their group—which now included Lindsay—was subject to the gawking of idiots who would either drool, nosebleed, or both.

Kevin couldn't blame them. He wanted to, but really, given the circumstances, it would have been hypocritical to accuse them of being a bunch of morons who thought with their dicks instead of their brains.

There was a lot of pretty in his group. No doubt about it. There was the cute tomboy, the porcelain-skinned doll in classic lolita dress, the vivacious redhead with an enchanting smile, and the seductive vixen who defined sex appeal. Really, it was only natural that the teenage males walking past their table gawked, suffered nosebleeds, or did both.

Matters only became worse when they were joined by the rest of their friends for lunch.

"We are not worthy! We are not worthy!"

Kevin's right eye twitched. "Would you two get up already. God, you two are so embarrassing right now! You're almost as bad as Eric!"

"We cannot do as you command, Master." Alex, along with his brother, were sitting *dogeza*, a Japanese bow where one prostrated themselves on the ground before those above their station. "We're unworthy of even looking at your divine presence."

"What he said," Andrew added.

Kevin pressed both of his hands against his face and groaned. What had he done to deserve this?

"They've got a point, you know," Iris chuckled when Kevin gave her a flat stare. "Don't give me that look. You know I'm right. You just need to think about this from their perspective."

"Is that so? And what, pray tell, is their perspective?"

"The perspective is that they think you," she pointed to him, "are currently in the process of creating standard harem dynamics."

"Haa....?"

"You're going the H-route."

"He's getting a harem!"

"I can't believe it!"

"Would you two shut up already?!"

"... Foxy..."

Kevin gave Justin an odd look. His friend was seriously starting to scare him.

"You're disgusting." Christine wrinkled her nose.

Kevin could have sworn that something sharp and pointy had just stabbed him through the chest. "Don't tell me you're taking their side, Christine? I need your support here."

"W-w-wha—" Steam burst from Christine's ears as her face transformed into a popsicle. "H-h-how shameless can you be?!"

"Eh?"

"Y-you don't—I mean, you can't just—KEVIN, YOU IDIOT!"

"Woah!" Kevin ducked as several shards of ice tried to impale him through the head. "W-what did I do now?"

"DIE!"

"Eek!"

While Kevin dodged icy death and Christine chased after him, Lilian, Iris and Lindsay watched. Iris also cast a minor illusion over the trio of boys at their table, making it look like Kevin and Christine were frolicking together.

"Aren't you going to rescue your boyfriend?" Lindsay asked. Lilian looked up in time to see Kevin roll across the ground, several ice shards impaling the place he'd been standing.

"Naw." She went back to her food. "He'll be fine."

"He's awfully good at running away," Iris commented. Lindsay stared at the two, a trail of sweat meandering down her face, before she turned to look back at Kevin and Christine.

"W-why are you so angry?" Kevin leapt away from more ice shards, one of which came suspiciously close to impaling his crotch.

"Why am I angry? WHY AM I ANGRY?!" Christine's face had turned purple by this point. "I'm angry because you're a disgusting lecher who's trying to make a harem! And you deserve to die!"

More ice shards tried stabbing him. They missed when Kevin leapt backwards. He was about to try and defend himself from Christine's untrue accusations, but another voice spoke up before he could.

"H-harem?"

As if time had come to a standstill, everything stopped. The twins stopped fighting, the trio of girls stopped chatting, even Christine had ceased with her ice shard blasting.

Kevin's eyes widened. Oh, god. No. Please no. There was no way, just no way this person could be here. Not now.

He turned around.

Yes, way.

Eric Corrompere had definitely seen better days. His face had multiple contusions and what almost appeared to be claw marks. Blood leaked from numerous wounds on his body, gashes so deep they should have killed him. How he wasn't dead was beyond Kevin. How come no one was freaking out over this?

"You... you have a harem...?" Like a zombie, Eric began to walk, his steps slow and halting, arms hanging uselessly by his sides as if they no longer worked properly. "You have a harem... hehehe... harem..."

"Eric, I don't know what you just heard, but I'm going to tell you right now that whatever it is, it's not... eh?" Kevin's eyes widened. "E-Eric... a-are you... crying?"

Indeed, Eric was crying. Like two large waterfalls, tears streamed from his eyes in a never ending flow. Miraculously enough, his shirt remained dry.

Eric stopped in front of Kevin and raised placed his hands on Kevin's shoulder.

"I think I just found my new god."

Everyone stared at Eric very, very oddly.

* * *

Ever since she had begun living at the Swift residence, Kotohime had created a routine that allowed her to maximize her time in the most efficient manner possible.

After waking up and making breakfast, she headed to the grocery store or went out to gather intel as needed. She then returned home and cleaned the apartment before making dinner.

After dinner, when Kevin and Lilian went to bed, she would go out onto the balcony and enjoy the Arizona night sky. It was mundane, but she enjoyed the simplicity of her new life.

As Kotohime put away the groceries from her latest shopping trip, her sister walked into the apartment. Camellia, who'd been watching TV, stood up to greet her.

"Kirikiri," Camellia smiled a dazzling smile at her maid… until she saw the blood covering the entire front of Kirihime's outfit. "H-hawa! W-what happened?! Are you okay?!"

Kirihime gave her mistress a gentle look. "Do not worry, My Lady. I am perfectly fine."

"B-but you're bleeding!"

"Bleeding? Oh, no." Smiling her lovely, brilliant smile, Kirihime gestured to the splatters of dark crimson covering her clothing. "This isn't mine. I was out hunting."

Camellia tilted her head. "Hunting?"

"Right. Hunting."

It was at this point that Kotohime finished putting the groceries away and walked into the living room. "Please be careful, Kirihime. This isn't like the old days, and I would hate for you to get arrested for manslaughter."

Kirihime was quick to reassure her older sibling. "There's no need to worry. I don't intend to do anymore hunting. Not for awhile. I just needed some rough leather for a project I'm working on."

Kotohime stared at her sister for a long time before nodding ever so slowly. "Very well. I won't say anymore on that matter. Oh! Before I forget, I must tell you not to let Kevin-sama know about your… hobby. I do not think he would appreciate the knowledge."

"H-he wouldn't?" Kirihime seemed shocked. "B-but he was so nice last night." She paused. "Well, actually, he seemed kind of frustrated, but he was nice for the most part. He even let us stay with him, despite not knowing we were coming."

"Indeed, Kevin-sama is a kind and courteous young man." It was one of the few points Kevin had in his favor, at least as far as Kotohime was concerned. "And that is why I am kindly asking you not to let him know of your hobby."

"I—okay. If that is what you want me to do, sister, then that's what I'll do."

"Thank you." Kotohime placed a hand on her sister's shoulder. "And do not worry. I am sure that Kevin-sama will appreciate you, even if he doesn't know about your love of hunting."

The smile Kirihime gave her sister was a wondrous and enchanting thing to behold. "Thank you. You always know just what to say to make me feel better."

"Ufufu, of course." Kotohime's demurely curved lips greatly enhanced her natural beauty. "You are my sister, after all."

***

Kevin rested his head on the table. His eyes were open but stared at nothing. They were the eyes of a defeated man, someone who, after years of hardship and struggle... or five minutes of the most humiliating experience of his life, had finally decided to give up and quietly die.

"There, there, Beloved," Lilian murmured gentle reassurances to her mate, running her fingers through his hair. "It's okay. If you don't want a harem, I'll make sure you don't get one."

Kevin looked up at her, his hopeful eyes boring into hers with an almost frightening intensity. "Really? You promise?"

"Of course. You're my mate," Lilian declared passionately. "If you don't want a harem, then I won't let anyone else have you."

"Oh, thank god," Kevin muttered in relief. "I was really worried for a second there. The last thing I need is to become one of those bumbling, idiotic, harem protagonists. I know people think they're awesome and everything, but seriously, have you seen the crap those guys have to go through? It might be entertaining to watch, but I can't imagine it's very fun to experience firsthand."

"Don't worry about a thing. If that's what you want, I'll never let you become a harem protagonist for as long as I live."

Kevin's eyes became warm pools of gratitude. "Thank you, Lilian. I love you."

Lilian's heart fluttered at his words. "You're welcome, Beloved. I love you, too."

"Lilian..."

"Kevin..."

The two leaned in, their lips moving ever closer...

Sniffle.

Kevin froze.

"It's." Sniffle. Sniffle. "It's so beautiful." More sniffling. And a sob. "To think his divine power expands." More sobbing. "He can make girls fall for him just by talking to them. Truly, My Lord's greatness has no limits."

"We are not worthy! We are not worthy!"

"Would you three knock it off already?!" Kevin shouted as Lilian crossed her arms and huffed, annoyed at how their moment had been ruined by a trio of fools.

Christine facepalmed as she watched the idiocy happening in front of her. "I'm not sure whether I should laugh or cry."

"I think I'm gonna go with laugh myself."

Christine glared at Iris. "I wasn't talking to you, fox!"

"Ha! Damn right I am!" Dipping her finger into the dressing on her salad, Iris turned to the three idiots bowing reverently to Kevin. "Oh, boys!" They looked up and Iris slowly stuck her finger between her lips, erotically sucking on it. She moaned around her finger before removing it, the digit coated in her saliva, which she then used to blaze a trail down her neck and collarbone, stopping only after it had reached her cleavage.

Alex, Andrew and Eric were felled immediately by a nosebleed. Even Justin was taken down in the same manner despite not actually watching it happen. The four boys laid on the ground, twitching as blood spurted from their noses like leaking faucets.

Iris nodded in satisfaction before turning to a pissed off Christine and smirking. "And that's how it's done."

Christine gritted her teeth, eyes alight with fury. "This is why I hate you foxes! You're always acting like a bunch of skanks because you think the way to a man's heart is through his dick!"

"The way to a man's heart is through his dick." Iris' alluring crimson eyes glinted mischievously. "Didn't you know that?"

"Kevin's not like that." Lilian smiled at her mate as she gripped his hand. He blushed, but smiled back. "He didn't become interested in me because I'm pretty. It wasn't until two months after we met that we started, um, dating, despite my countless attempts to seduce him."

"Tch! We'll see how long he lasts against me…"

"Did you say something?"

"Nope," Iris responded, going back to her salad, not letting anyone know what she was thinking.

Within the confines of her mind, a plan began to form.

***

Watching the group of humans and yōkai eat lunch from a distance, Valsiener sat in the library and looked out the window. With his youki-enhanced eyes, he could easily pick out the details of their faces, and with his talent for reading lips, he knew exactly what they were saying.

"Seems the group has expanded. Things are definitely getting interesting for Kevin and his entourage." He paused, his eyes lighting up. "If I'm not mistaken, I believe I remember hearing about how some big-shot clan heir was looking for Lilian. That should keep things interesting. Kekeke…"

***

"Achoo!"

"Bless you, Beloved."

"Thanks." Kevin sniffled as he rubbed his nose. "Wonder what that was about?"

"Maybe someone's talking about you," Lindsay suggested.

"I hope not."

"Here, a napkin for you, My Lord." Eric appeared before Kevin with a napkin in hand.

"Oh, thank you—no. Wait. Stop calling me that!"

"Very well, Harem Lord."

"Don't call me that either!" Kevin's wail went ignored. It was going to be a long day.

A really, really, really long day.

***

Kiara sat behind her desk, reading over reports and statements about her fitness centers.

A lot of people thought it was easy to own a business like hers, that all you had to do was sit through a few meetings and have others do the the grunt work. All those people were a bunch of idiots who had watched way too many movies.

Owning a business meant putting a lot of time and effort into your career. It meant spending hours listening to people bicker over inane and senseless issues, reading over reports to see how the business was doing, and then making decisions that you felt would best help expand your business.

There was also the whole decision-making process itself. Every decision she made affected her fitness centers, from the centers themselves, to her employees and the customers. Even a single careless mistake could cost Kiara her dream, and hurt the people relying on her to provide them with a stable source of income, not to mention their jobs. It required more than just hard work to excel at owning a business like hers. It required grit, determination, and a business acumen that few people ever acquired.

Her intercom beeped, interrupting Kiara's musings. She set her paperwork down and accepted the incoming call.

"Yes, Lisa? What is it?"

"You have a visitor here to see you, ma'am."

"I see… send her in?"

"Yes, ma'am—wait. How did you know it was a she?"

"Lucky guess. Now send her in."

"… Okay. She'll be up in just a minute."

Kiara smiled as the door opened and a familiar, kimono-clad, katana-wielding vixen walked into the room. She was honestly glad to see the woman. She and the four-tailed kitsune shared an odd relationship. They weren't really friends, though they got along in a strange way. They also weren't enemies, as none of the fights they got into were ever done with the intention of maiming the other.

"Kotohime. I'm surprised to see you here. Have you come for a quick sparring session?"

"Unfortunately not." Kotohime walked up to Kiara's desk, set her katana against the chair situated in front of it, and then sat down herself. "I am actually here for other reasons."

"Ah." Her eyes glimmering with the barest hint of amusement, Kiara placed her left forearm on the desk and leaned forward, meeting Kotohime's steady gaze with one of her own. "I see what this is about. You want to know about the boya's training, right?"

"Indeed."

"I didn't know you cared." When Kotohime said nothing, merely staring at her with that placid expression, Kiara pouted. "You're no fun."

"Ufufu, I believe you and I have very different definitions of fun, Kiara-san."

Kiara snorted. Leaning back in her seat, she tapped her fingers against the desk in a staccato rhythm.

"The boya's training has been progressing well. His strength, speed and endurance have increased a great deal these past two weeks. I'm not surprised, though. The kid's got guts, is determined, and has some serious motivation to get stronger." Kiara paused to look at Kotohime. "Is that a smile I see?"

Kotohime's lips flattened. "I don't know what you're talking about."

"You sure about that? I'm pretty sure I saw a smile."

"You must have imagined it."

"Of course." Kiara chuckled.

"Do you think he's ready to begin combat training?"

"Mmm... hard to say. I suppose I could begin teaching him, but I would like to raise his physical stats a little more before I start training him to fight. Why?" Kiara studied Kotohime, her eyes keen and sharp. "Is something going on?"

Kotohime waved away the woman's words. "Not at all. I simply want him to be prepared. The yōkai world is a dangerous place for humans to tread. You know this as well as I do. In order to ensure that Lilian-sama's mate remains alive long enough for them to, well, *mate*, I need him to become as strong as possible."

"Ha... if you don't want to tell me anything, that's fine, but don't make up such a terrible excuse. We're living on the fringe of that world, so unless something is coming for one of us specifically, then the boya shouldn't be in any danger." Kotohime clenched the fabric of her kimono. Kiara saw this and placed her hands on the desk. "Still, since you want him to start learning how to fight, I'll begin training him in unarmed combat this weekend. How does that sound?"

"Perfect. Thank you," Kotohime said quickly, perhaps even a little too quickly.

"Yeah. Sure."

Kotohime stood up, grabbed her katana, and prepared to leave. When she made it to the door, however, Kiara's voice stopped her.

"You know, Kevin reminds me of someone I knew a while back. Another young human who fell in love with a kitsune around two-hundred or so years ago."

Kotohime did not respond. She just left.

In the silence of the room, Kiara chuckled. "Really, you're just too easy to see through, my old friend."

With a heavy sigh, she cast one last look at the door before picking up her next report. This paperwork wasn't going to get itself done.

***

Kevin was exhausted by the time he arrived home—no, he was beyond exhausted. Tiredness seeped into his very bones, making them feel more fragile than glass. All he wanted to do was lay down and go to bed.

Too bad Kotohime had other plans.

"Lilian-sama, Iris-sama, I am pleased to see you two have arrived home safely. I trust your time at school was eventful."

"Eventful, now there's one way of putting it," Iris snorted in amusement. Kevin cast her a minor glare that went ignored.

"I am pleased to hear that." Kotohime ignored the byplay between the two. "Kevin-sama, are you ready for your lesson?"

"Ugh," Kevin groaned, "I guess…"

"You don't sound very excited," Kotohime said with a dangerous edge in her voice.

"Ah! No, no!" Kevin frantically waved his hands in front of his face. "I am excited! I'm super excited! I just, uh, it sort of slipped my mind because of all the stuff that happened last night, ah-hahahahaha… ha… ha…"

Kotohime gave Kevin a look hard enough to make him break out into a cold sweat. He tried to keep his eyes from straying off hers, knowing that to do so would mean pain—and humiliation, but mostly pain.

"At least you're honest." Kotohime eventually sighed, prompting Kevin to follow suit. He was safe, for now at least. "Now then, come here. It's time for your lesson."

Understanding that he wouldn't be getting out of this, Kevin turned to his girlfriend and her sister. "Why don't you two do some sisterly bonding or something? I doubt you want to be here for this."

Iris grinned, her eyes lighting up like a billion stars. "That's the best thing I've heard you say yet, kiddo. Come on, Lily-pad, we're taking a bath!"

"We're what? H-hey! Quit pulling on me! Kevin, make her let

go!"

Kevin watched as Iris began dragging her sister off.

"Sorry, Lilian," he said, "but you can consider this payback for not helping me when the principal tried to rape me."

"I'm sorry, alright! Please, help me!"

"No can do. I've got lessons, remember?"

"Don't be mean, Kevin! Kevin? Beloved!"

Kevin watched with solemn eyes as Iris and Lilian disappeared down the hall. Only after they were gone did he notice the observant gaze of a certain maid-slash-bodyguard.

"What are you looking at me like that for?"

Kotohime gave him a mysterious smile that he couldn't place. "Ufufu, I was just wondering if you might have some kitsune blood in you."

"Ha ha." Kevin's laugh was flat. "Funny. Can we get started on my lesson now, please? I still have homework to do after this."

"Of course." Kotohime guided him over to the couch. "We'll begin our lessons right now. Ufufufu…"

"That laugh of yours really doesn't inspire much confidence in me."

***

How long has it been since I've taken a bath with my sister?

The question stirred within Lilian's mind. It had to have been several years at least. She had stopped bathing with her sister immediately after meeting, at the time, a much younger Kevin. Her sister had never quite forgiven her for that.

Sitting at one end of the tub, her knees drawn up to her chest, Lilian tried to get comfortable with no success. Steam rose all around her. Iris lounged at the other end of the tub, one arm and one leg resting lazily off the lip.

"This is nice, don't you think?"

"I guess."

Iris cracked an eye open to look at her sister. "What's wrong, Lily-pad? I thought you would be happy. It's been so long since we've taken a bath together."

Her sister's left leg rose from the water's surface, the movement one of sensual elegance. Lilian adamantly told herself that she didn't find her sister's bare leg attractive. Iris bent her leg and set her foot on the lip of the tub, and then began rubbing her inner thigh while releasing a seductive moan that made Lilian look away.

"It's not that I'm not happy, but I have a mate now. Being with you like this, doing things like this with you, it doesn't feel right."

Wearing the flattest expression Lilian had ever seen on her, Iris set her leg back into the tub.

"Doesn't feel right? What is that supposed to mean? How could it not feel right?"

"Look," Lilian squirmed uncomfortably, "Kevin is a human. He... he doesn't really understand how kitsune relationships work, and he would never accept how close you and I are."

Iris raised an eyebrow. "So?"

"So, I love him. He's my mate, and I want him to be happy. More than that, I want him to accept me, but I don't think he can accept me if I'm, well, if my sister and I are... more intimate than sisters should be."

"Let me get this straight," Iris ground out. "You're going to throw me away like yesterday's trash because you have a mate now? Is that what you're telling me?"

"I-it's not like that," Lilian tried to say, but Iris was having none of it.

"It's exactly like that. This is why you've been ignoring me for the last six years, isn't it?"

"I haven't been ignoring—"

"Yes, you have." Iris' glare caused any words Lilian might give to die in her throat. "Ever since you started asking Kotohime about humans and their culture, you've begun ignoring me. You no longer take baths with me. You no longer sleep with me. It's like you've completely forgotten that I exist!"

"That isn't it..."

"And for what? Because you met some stupid human a couple of years ago and decided that he was more important than me?"

"Kevin isn't stupid," Lilian said through gritted teeth.

"Oh, come off it," Iris scoffed. "He's an ape, a lowly monkey. The only thing boytoys like him are good for is screwing."

Lilian snarled at her sister. "You don't know anything about Kevin, so I'd suggest you shut up!"

Perhaps she hadn't been expecting such a strong reaction, but

Iris grew wide-eyed at Lilian's snarling visage. "W-wha—"

"Kevin is an amazing person! He saved me! When I was at my worst, when our matriarch was trying to sell me off like a prized trinket, it was his words that saved me. Not yours. His. And where were you? Sneaking off to join Aster and Azalea for a little lesbian triple play!"

Now it was Iris's turn to be on the defensive. "That isn't what I was—"

"Kevin is the only reason I haven't been sold off to that idiot Jiāoào yet! Kevin is a kind and determined young man. He's accepted me even though I caused him nothing but trouble since I started living with him. I love him, and I'm not going to listen to you insulting him like this!"

Iris' eyes widened as Lilian stepped out of the tub. "H-hey! Where are you going?"

"I'm clean, so there's no point in staying in here," Lilian responded, wrapping a towel around her torso. "I'm going to see how my mate is doing with his lessons."

"W-wait a minute! You can't just leave like that! Damn it, Lilian, you're my sister! Why are you taking the side of some human?"

"If you can't figure out why, then telling you would be pointless."

I knew I shouldn't have let Iris talk me into bathing with her. She just doesn't understand.

Lilian stormed out of the bathroom and slammed the door before making her way to hers and Kevin's bedroom. After getting dressed, Lilian strolled toward the living room, where she could hear Kotohime lecturing her mate.

***

Kevin sat on the couch. In front of him stood Kotohime, her hands clasped behind her back, and her katana resting against the coffee table. She looked down at him, her gaze sharp and penetrating as any blade.

It was disconcerting, but Kevin didn't let her know that. He looked straight at her.

Kotohime nodded in approval.

"Why don't we start with a quick recap of what you already know about kitsune?"

"A recap? Why?"

"Because it's been a long time since any information on the different types of kitsune has been given. Three whole months, in fact. This is as much for your benefit as it is for the readers."

"I see," Kevin murmured, then frowned. "But wait, won't the readers get mad at us for repeating information?"

"T-they might," Kotohime stumbled over her words, but quickly recovered. She then gave Kevin an appraising look, as if seeing him in a whole new light. "However, the author also feels it would be good to start this lesson off with a recap, you know, just in case they forgot and need to have their memory jogged."

Crossing his arms over his chest, Kevin nodded. "That makes sense, I guess."

... A pause. Kevin blinked, his face scrunching up in confusion.

"What were we talking about again?"

"Nothing." Kotohime waved Kevin's confusion off as one might swat at a fly. "Now then, why don't you tell me about the different types of kitsune?"

"All right. Well, let's see... there's fire, earth, river, wind, and thunder. Those are the, uh, lower tier, I think..." He looked up at Kotohime, a question in his eyes, to which she answered with a nod. "And then, erm, there's the middle tier. That's spirit, forest, mountain, and sound."

"Good. Very good. And the last tier?"

"Celestial and Void. Those ones are easy."

"Excellent. It seems you remember your lessons well." Kotohime clapped her hands together. "I suppose it would be appropriate to tell you about the last tier of kitsune types."

"You mean there's a tier above the upper tier?"

"In a way. The last tier isn't really a tier because it only has one type of kitsune. Time Kitsune." Kotohime's nose scrunched up in a way that looked strangely adorable. "Time Kitsune are a complete mystery: a combination of myths and legends. Several times in the distant past, there have been people who claim to have seen or even met a Time Kitsune, but no one truly knows whether they exist or not. That being said, if they do exist, they would exist on a tier higher even than Celestials and Voids, simply due to the nature of their power. The ability to manipulate time is a frightening thing."

Kevin nodded. He thought it would be kind of awesome to control time, but he also knew how dangerous that kind of power could be.

"Now then, among the many hundreds of kitsune clans, there are thirteen that stand above the rest. These clans make up what is known as The Thirteen Great Kitsune Clans. They are the most powerful clans of their particular type. You will not need to worry about most of them. The lower tiers, for example, tend to stay as far from kitsune politics as possible, only getting involved when those they have made a pact with call on them for assistance, such as during a war between kitsune clans."

"Does that happen often?"

"You mean war between clans? Not anymore, no. It wasn't uncommon hundreds of years ago, but ever since the technological advancement of humanity during the early nineteenth century, kitsune—nay, all yōkai, have learned not to squabble as much. For our own safety, you understand."

Kotohime gave Kevin a moment to ponder her words.

"Of course, it does still happen on rare occasions. Just like human society, politics in our world are very cutthroat. However, unlike your human politics, ours are decidedly more deadly. If one kitsune clan wishes to usurp the position of another clan, then they may wage war, provided they do so in a way that does not reveal our existence to humans. Naturally, a clan from a different kitsune type, for example, a fire kitsune clan, cannot usurp the position of, let's say, the great water clan."

"Has that happened recently?" Kevin was captivated by Kotohime's words.

"Not recently, no. The last time this happened was around two-hundred years ago, when the Great Water Clan of Ślina was destroyed, and their position was usurped by an upstart clan called the Mul Clan." Kotohime paused for a moment, her eyes glazing over, before they regained focus and she continued. "While clan usurpation doesn't happen much anymore, there are still a lot of cutthroat politics going on behind the scenes; assassinations, backdoor deals, and political backstabbing to name a few."

"Sounds dangerous."

"It is indeed, and it will be more dangerous for you, seeing how you're human." Kotohime's intense stare made Kevin gulp. "Fortunately, you only need to worry about one clan right now. The Shénshèng Clan, the greatest clan of Celestial Kitsune in the entire world, has stood at the top of our race for many generations. They, along with the Great Void Clan of Gitsune, are the only clan to have never had their position as a great clan usurped. The ruler of the Shénshèng Clan is the Bodhisattva, Shénshèng Shinkuro-dono, who has been hailed as the most powerful Celestial Kyuubi to have ever graced the earth."

"And it's the son of this Bodhisattva guy who wants to marry Lilian, right?"

Kotohime nodded. "The kitsune you're referring to is a young two-tails around the same age as Lilian-sama. He's an impetuous child, and has a very strong sense of entitlement. That is, I believe, the entire reason he wants Lilian-sama so badly in the first place. She is one of the few people in the world who has denied him, and the only one who has done so with such vehemence. He will come for her, eventually, and you will need to be ready when he does."

Kevin breathed in, held it, and then breathed out. There was no need to be nervous or frightened. This was why he trained with Kiara, wasn't it? So he could stand up to this guy when the time came. Lilian was his. She had chosen him, had pushed her way into his heart with the subtlety of Eric in a girl's locker room, and he wouldn't let her go.

"Kevin-sama?"

"I'm fine." Kevin released a breath he didn't know he'd been holding. "Please continue."

Kotohime smiled, and this time, Kevin was certain of it. The smile was genuine.

"Kevin?"

Before the lesson could continue, Lilian entered the room, dressed in flannel pajama shorts and a spaghetti strap shirt. Kevin didn't know where to look; her legs, her ears, her tails, her butt, her swaying breasts, or her feet…

… Wait. What?

"Something wrong, Kevin-sama?"

"No." Kevin grimaced. "I'm fine. I just had a really disturbing thought is all."

"I see. Ufufufu…"

"I really wish you'd stop doing that." Kotohime merely smiled at him, which Kevin ignored and turned to face Lilian as she down on his left. "Not going to spend more time with your sister?" He was startled to see Lilian's face twist in a rictus of anger. It only lasted for a second, and when he blinked, the expression was gone, making him wonder if he hadn't imagined it.

"I would much rather spend time with you."

"If that's what you want…"

"It is."

Not satisfied with where she was sitting, Lilian crawled onto his lap. Kevin stiffened when she wiggled her bum against him to get comfortable. Grinning, the red-haired vixen wrapped her arms around his neck and rested her head on his shoulder. Kevin tried not to squirm and returned the gesture, his own arms going around her waist.

"Comfortable?" A vein throbbed on Kotohime's foreign as she stared at them, visible due to its bright red hue.

"Um!" Lilian smiled. "I'm very comfortable."

"I'm glad. May I continue with my lessons now?"

"Right. Go ahead and continue." Lilian waved her hand up and down from its position on Kevin's shoulder. "Just pretend I'm not here."

"Ha… right."

Kotohime was about to continue her lesson again—

"M-My Lady! Please be careful with those bags!"

"Don't worry. Don't worry. I've got—HAWA!"

"MY LADY!"

"Hawawawawawawa!!"

—When another interruption occurred.

Kevin, Kotohime and Lilian listened as a series of crashes and screams echoed from outside of their apartment. They winced as one when a particularly loud *bang!* signified someone hitting something hard and unyielding. Then the screaming and the crashing stopped, and absolute silence returned.

Several crickets broke the silence, chirping ever so quietly in the background.

"Please excuse me," Kotohime mumbled. "It seems we will have to continue this lesson some other time."

Kevin sweat dropped.

"… Right."

* * *

Iris stood on the balcony, her forearms resting against the wall, allowing her to lean forward. She stared up at the night sky, ignoring the almost loving whispers that wanted nothing more than the absolute and utter annihilation of everything she held dear. The stars were rather pretty that night, and she didn't want to ruin the moment by listening to them.

The door slid open. Iris did not turn around. What she did do was sigh. "Is there something you want, Mom?"

"Hawa… I just… Camellia heard that you and Lilian got into a fight. Camellia… Camellia doesn't think Iris and Lilian should be fighting. It's not good for sisters to fight, so please don't do it anymore, okay?"

Gotta give the woman credit for trying, I guess.

"Ha…" A longer sigh this time. "If this is your attempt at being a better mother to us, then I've got tell you that you're about sixty years too late."

"Hawa… Iris is so mean."

"Whatever. Look, just leave me alone, alright? I don't want to talk to anyone right now."

Camellia's eyes became dewy with unshed tears. Iris didn't care. This woman had never been a good mother, and even though a part of her knew it wasn't Camellia's fault, it didn't change the facts.

The door slid open again and Kirihime walked onto the balcony. She placed a comforting hand on Camellia's shoulder and offered the beautiful, if childish, mother a tender smile.

"Why don't you get ready for bed, My Lady? I will speak to Lady Iris on your behalf."

"Hawa…" Camellia wiped the tears from her eyes and gave her maid a bright smile that should not have been possible for a woman her age to produce. "Thank you, Kiri-kiri."

"You're welcome."

With Camellia gone, Kirihime marched up to her mistress' dark-haired daughter. She didn't say anything at first, just stood there with the younger kitsune, staring up at the moon and stars as they painted the velvety sky with their brilliance.

"Having a sister of my own, I can sort of understand how you

109

feel," Kirihime finally spoke. "Back when I was a two-tails like yourself, Kotohime had fallen in love with a young man, a human much like Lord Kevin. I remember how jealous I was of her new mate. He took up so much of my precious sister's time that I couldn't stand it."

Iris finally showed interest in what the maid was saying. "What did you do?"

"I tried to kill him. Multiple times."

In the presence of Kirihime's bright, wondrous smile, Iris felt a small thrill of fear traverse her spine all the way down to her tails.

"I failed, of course." Kirihime's smile turned both wistful and disappointed. "Kotohime foiled my attempts at every turn. It was frustrating at first, but I was eventually able to accept him after several dozen more failed assassination attempts, and life eventually got better."

She gave Iris a conciliating smile.

"It's okay to be jealous, you know?"

"Pfft!" Iris snorted and turned away. "Why would I be jealous of that kid? He's just a human brat."

"Just so," Kirihime agreed, "but he is also your sister's mate." Iris' face darkened at that reminder. "I am not saying you need to like him, but you should at least be nice to him. Right now, he is the most important person in Lady Lilian's life. However, that will not always be the case. Lord Kevin is a human, and he will die before Lady Lilian even gets her fourth tail. Do you really want to cause a rift between you and your sister over something as transient as this?"

Iris didn't respond, and Kirihime eventually left, allowing her to be alone with her thoughts.

Maybe I should apologize.

It would be hard, but she loved her sister dearly and didn't want Lilian to hate her because of something like this.

She blew out a breath and walked back inside, heading toward the room where her sister would most likely be resting.

***

Lilian and Kevin were lying in bed. Despite the late hour, neither of them could sleep. It wasn't that they weren't tired, because they were; they just had a lot on their minds.

"Kevin?"

"Hmm?"

"Have you ever gotten into an argument with someone you love?"

Kevin shifted to get more comfortable. Lilian, who lay on top of him, also moved to accommodate for the new position.

"Sometimes. Back when Mom was going to college, we would occasionally get into arguments. They were never anything big, just the standard arguments that a mother and son get into… I think. They were mostly about stupid things, and I don't remember them all that much because I was so young. Why do you ask? Did you and Iris get into a fight or something?" Lilian said nothing, but the way she tightened her hold around his torso told Kevin all he needed to know. "I see."

"I… I don't really know what to do," she confessed. "Iris has always been with me, and I can sort of understand where she's coming from, but things have changed. I have you now, and I don't think it's considered acceptable for sisters to bathe together."

Kevin was silent for a moment.

"I'm kind of surprised you even have something you consider unacceptable. Weren't you the one who told me that you and Iris used to kiss each other?"

With her face lying on his chest, Kevin could not see the adorable blush creeping across her cheeks, but he could imagine it easily enough.

"Muu, that's not something you should be saying at a time like this. I'm being serious here." She lightly slapped his chest. "Stupid Kevin."

"I'm sorry." Kevin chuckled. Lilian bit his nipple hard enough to earn a yelp. "Alright, alright, I'm really sorry. I didn't mean to laugh at you."

"You had better be." Silence ensued, but only for a moment. Lilian rubbed her cheek against his chest, enjoying the feel of her mate's warmth. "So, what do you think I should do?"

"I'm not sure I'm the best person to answer that question. I don't have any siblings, so I don't know what you should do. But, whenever Mom and I had an argument, we would always make up eventually. I mean, she's my mom. I love her, and I don't want us to hate each other because we were arguing."

He looked down at Lilian, who raised her head, bright green irises peering at him from beneath a curtain of crimson hair.

"It's the same for you, isn't it? Iris is your sister, and I'm sure you don't want to remain angry at her for the rest of your lives, right?"

"You're right. I know you're right." Pushing herself up, Lilian straddled Kevin's waist and graced him with a smile. "Thank you."

Trying—and mostly failing—to act nonchalant and cool, Kevin shrugged. "That's what I'm here for... sorta. I-I mean, as your mate, it's kinda like, you know, I should support you... and stuff."

"Hm, I suppose. Still," she whispered, leaning down until her lips just barely brushed against Kevin's, "I feel like I should show you my gratitude. That's also something mates do for each other, right?"

"Right," Kevin muttered before closing the distance, claiming Lilian's lips in a heated kiss.

Lilian moaned, the noise barely muffled by Kevin's lips, as a warm tongue filled her mouth. Times when Kevin initiated tongue action were rare, so it never failed to stoke the flames of her passion when he took the initiative.

She allowed him this moment, moaning at the feel of his tongue exploring the inside of her mouth. It was a shy, tentative reconnoiter, like a rookie spy who feared being caught and didn't want to penetrate enemy territory too deeply. Despite the shyness of his actions, Lilian loved what he was doing, and her own tongue soon joined in, caressing his as saliva was stirred up and shared between them.

Kevin's kiss heated up, taking Lilian by storm, especially when a pair of hands suddenly and quite unexpectedly landed on her rear. Lilian's surprised gasp became a lyrical symphony when those same hands decided to caress, knead, and squeeze to their heart's content. And when those same hands pulled her down until something hard and stiff came into contact with her sensitive lips, the music she sang into his mouth became louder still.

Her panties soon became damp, and the wet article of clothing clung to her skin and brushed against her folds. Perhaps it was simply due to the novelty of the act but, like ripples created by a stone as it hits the water's surface, a delicious and inescapable sensation spread through her insides.

Lilian decided to reciprocate the gesture.

"Hnnn!" Kevin's hips jerked against hers as he slid between her legs. The feeling of her, well, *her* rubbing against him in such deliriously pleasurable ways made whatever self-restraint he might have possessed evaporate. All that remained was his desire for the fox-girl on top of him.

Lilian's world spun. She could not see this, as she had closed her eyes, but the feeling of someone rolling her over was unmistakable. Her back hit the soft memory foam mattress, and Kevin's weight bore down on her, pushing against her. Tiny squeaks mixed with low notes escaped her mouth as Kevin ground against her overly sensitive nub.

And then it happened. Something unexpected. Something that had never happened before in all of their previous make-out sessions.

Her mate's left hand, which at some point had cupped her right breast, slipped underneath her shirt. The warm skin on skin contact caused her entire body to light up like a live wire. His thumb flicking over her stiffened peak made her body shudder and writhe in indescribable pleasure.

Lilian's breasts had been always sensitive, perhaps because of how large they were, and the act of Kevin fondling them, of his hand touching the bare skin of her breast, proved to be too much for her to handle.

"K-Kevin..."

Kevin stiffened when a pair of legs locked around his waist.

"Please..." It wasn't a word. It was a moan. Kevin thought he would die of sexy. "I need you... please..."

Before they could go any further, the door burst open with a loud *bang!* reminiscent to cannon fire. Kevin and Lilian froze. Their necks slowly craned over to see Iris standing in the doorway. With her hair overshadowing her face and her crimson eyes glowing with vicious malignance, the incredibly gorgeous kitsune looked like Sadako Yamamura—a very hot version of Sadako Yamamura, but still kind of *The Ring*-like.

"You... you two..."

"Uh." Kevin thought fast. "This isn't what it looks like."

Iris stared. Lilian stared. Kevin felt the combined weight of their stares and blushed a deep scarlet.

"… Okay, so maybe this is what it looks like."

Iris ground her teeth together."I can't believe you would do this to me! See if I ever decide to apologize to you again!"

The door slammed shut behind Iris, who they could hear stomping down the hall. When the sounds of her angry footsteps faded, they looked at each other.

"Sooo." An only slightly blushing Kevin raised an eyebrow. "Any idea what that was about?"

"Not a clue." Lilian shook her head. "Wanna start making out again?"

"After what just happened, I think we'd better not."

"Hawa."

"Don't steal your mother's catchword!"

***

Maddison used to be a member of a very small clan of Water Kitsune located at the edge of the Bodhisattva's territory—until her family sold her into slavery because the son of the Bodhisattva, Jiāoào Shénshèng, had decided that he wanted her for himself.

Her clan had been forced to sell her as a slave. Oh, they called her a vassal of the Shénshèng Clan, but she knew that was a very loose concept as far as Jiāoào was concerned. While everyone else in the Shénshèng Clan treated her with the respect deserving of a vassal, Jiāoào treated her like a toy.

She knew the reason Jiāoào wanted her. With her long red-haired, green eyes and lovely curves, she looked somewhat similar to Lilian Pnéyma. Of course, Jiāoào made sure to inform Maddison of her deficiencies at every opportunity; mentioning how her hair didn't have Lilian's otherworldly luster, how her eyes lacked the brilliant vibrancy of emeralds, and how her body didn't possess the luscious curves of the real Lilian Pnéyma. She didn't know what made it worse, that he told her these things to begin with, or that he was usually degrading her during intercourse.

She walked through the second home of the most powerful clan of Celestial Kitsune. Located next to the Tianmen Mountain, the Shénshèng Clan's second home held the appearance of a mansion from the Han Dynasty.

Only Jiāoào used this home. Here, away from the eyes of his father and sister and brothers, he could debase his servants—slaves

—to his heart's content.

Maddison eventually reached the room that served as Jiāoào's private chamber. She knocked upon the extravagant door, with its depiction of orchids and a nine-tailed kitsune sitting under a tree, and then she waited.

The person who greeted her was not Jiāoào, but another woman who, like her, had been enslaved to serve Jiāoào. Like all kitsune, she was quite beautiful, with purple hair, blue eyes, and a voluptuous body. Her three tails hung limply behind her.

She wasn't wearing any clothes.

"Yes? Can I help with you something?" Ling asked, and Maddison nearly shuddered. Ling Mei was a "vassal" who had served Jiāoào for far longer than her. The woman's eyes were dead, emotionless in a way that dolls would envy. How many decades had she been forced to endure under Jiāoào's yoke to have eyes like that? Maddison pitied her.

"Yes, could you inform Lord Jiāoào that a spy living in Arizona has uncovered the location of Lilian Pnéyma?" Maddison thought she saw a flicker in Ling's eyes, but that could have just been a trick of the light. "It appears that she and her immediate family have traveled to Phoenix, Arizona."

After taking a moment to absorb this information, Ling bowed to Maddison, who returned it. "I will hand this information to Lord Jiāoào at once…"

She trailed off when a cry of pain reverberated from within the room.

After a second of awkward silence, she amended her statement.

"Correction: I shall hand this information over to Lord Jiāoào once he has finished satisfying himself."

Maddison shuddered again. She thought Ling also shuddered, but she couldn't be sure. Either way, she had done her task and, seeing how she had no desire to become Jiāoào's plaything, she decided to leave before he became aware of her presence.

"In that case, I shall leave you to it."

With one final bow, she left, walking down the hallway as quickly as her legs could carry her.

Chapter 4

A Teacher's Closure... Sort of

The next day was an awkward one. Iris tried to pretend that what happened last night had never happened, and Lilian helped by claiming ignorance. There were still some problems, especially between the two sisters, but Kevin decided not to interfere for fear of exacerbating the issue. That, and Iris didn't seem to like him very much, so he thought it best to avoid her for the time being.

That morning Kevin rode his bike to Mad Dawg Fitness, which was only a few miles from his complex.

He really did love how everything was so close to where he lived: the mall, the gym, school, the park, the grocery store. Literally, every place he might need or want to visit was between ten to twenty minutes away.

The air that morning was crisp, cool and refreshing. It was still fairly early. The sun had risen but wasn't that high. It sat low on the peaks of a mountain range in the distance, barely a third of it peeking up from sharp spires painted in oranges and pinks.

As he pedaled, he thought about Kiara and his training. He trained with her four days a week: Monday, Tuesday, Thursday and Friday. He had actually wanted to do more, but Kiara told him that four days would be more than enough. She further explained that if he trained any harder it might actually damage his muscles, which would hinder his attempts at becoming strong enough to stand against yōkai. He complained in the beginning, but after their first week of training, he understood why she refused to train him more.

Kiara's training was tough. Really tough. Brutal even. Kevin never went home without feeling like someone had tried to tear his muscles apart from the inside out, like he'd been skinned and had his body dunked in rubbing alcohol. After experiencing her routine firsthand, Kevin was glad that he didn't have training with Kiara more than four days a week.

Mad Dawg Fitness was one of those gyms that could be considered truly gigantic. Not just huge, but monstrous. Spanning nearly 12 acres of land, the fitness center looked like a sprawling metropolitan mall instead of a gym.

The building itself had three stories. Having been there plenty of times in the past—especially recently—Kevin knew that each level consisted of different recreational activities. The entire second and third levels were dedicated to fitness classes like Zumba and stuff. It had all of the normal sports rooms that people expected from a gym: basketball court, tennis rooms and a swimming pool. Anything people could think of that dealt with exercise, it was probably there.

Already dressed in his workout clothes, Kevin arrived in the room that Kiara had dedicated to his training. Spacious and more than a little spartan, the large room's only real decorations were the large blue mat that covered nearly the entire floor and a mirror that spanned the entire northern wall.

Kiara was already there, standing in the center of the mat, waiting for him.

She also wasn't alone.

"Ack!"

The three jabronis who had tried to beat the crap out of him with little success just over a month ago grinned at him.

"Wh-what the heck are they doing here?!" Kevin's voice sounded quite shrill as he shouted, pointing to the trio of tall, taller and… midget. Seriously. Kevin had never seen someone so freaking short.

He's like a pint-sized meathead.

The fanged grin on Kiara's face did little to settle his nerves. In fact, it just made everything worse. "I called them here to help train you."

"T-train me?"

"That's right." Kiara crossed her arms, the smirk on her face widening. "I think your physical fitness is at a level where you can begin learning how to fight against opponents stronger than you. You're actually lucky to reach this point so quickly, but I think we can attribute that to you being on the track team."

"B-b-but why are these three here?! They're just a bunch of side characters with no real purpose!"

While Midget and Pimples scratched their heads with a witless look on their faces, Tall got angry. "Hey! Did you just insult us?"

"YES!"

Kiara looked amused. "You've been hanging out with those foxes way too much." Kevin glared at her, but she just chuckled. "Don't give me that look. You knew this was going to happen eventually. The only way you can learn how to fight properly is by fighting other people."

"I know that." Kevin's scowl did not leave his face. "I just don't know why I have to spar against those three. Why can't I spar against you?"

"Because even if I were to hold back, just a single punch from me would probably kill you. At the very least it would put you in a hospital and cripple you for life."

… An unsettling silence descended upon the room. Several crows cawed somewhere in the distance, which Kevin found strange because they were inside… and Arizona didn't have crows.

"Okay, you make a very good point," Kevin admitted reluctantly, "but I still don't understand why it has to be them."

"Aw, don't be like that, bud."

"Yeah, we won't hurt you… much."

"And I certainly won't break your teeth in for what you did to my tooth."

While the three jabronis cracked their knuckles, Kevin gulped.

Kiara did her best to reassure her disciple. "Don't worry, boya, I'll stop them before they do too much damage to you."

"Your words are like a bastion of safety in this sea of fear and uncertainty." Kevin deadpanned.

"Really?"

"NO!"

"Oh, well," Kiara shrugged, "can't say I didn't try. Now let's get to work. Boys?"

As the faces of Midget, Pimples and Tall split into wide grins, Kevin whimpered.

I knew I should have stayed home this morning.

***

That morning, Lilian went about doing everything she normally did. However, while she went through the motions of daily life, she was still very conflicted about what happened last night with her sister.

She remembered Kevin's words before they went to bed. She knew her mate was right. While there were several things about Iris that she neither liked nor approved of, Lilian really did love her sister. So, she planned on apologizing.

Unfortunately, apologizing proved to be more difficult than expected, especially since she didn't know how.

Sitting around the table with her family, Lilian's mind worked furiously on trying to think up the best way to apologize. Sure, she could just say "sorry" but, in all honesty, she really didn't know what she should be sorry for. The fact that she and Iris got into a fight? That she walked out on her sister while they were taking a bath? What about how she didn't think it was okay for her and her sister to bathe together in the first place? Two of those three were things she didn't really feel all that sorry about, and the last one wasn't even her fault.

As she sat there, gazing at the table in silent contemplation, Kotohime served them breakfast.

"You should have told me you were cooking breakfast, Kotohime," Kirihime said as a plate of broiled salmon and a bowl of rice was set in front of her. "I would have been more than happy to help you."

"The reason I didn't tell you I was making breakfast is because of your tendency to use questionable ingredients." Kirihime's shoulders slumped. "However, if you like, you can help me clean the dishes."

Kirihime perked up seconds later. "I'll help you clean up after breakfast, then."

Seated on Lilian's left, Camellia absently munched on her rice. Looking at her mom made Lilian feel guilty. Not just for running away and worrying her, but for a lot of other things as well. It was sad to see the woman who'd given birth to her and her sister reduced to such a pitiful state, especially since she had been so much more, once upon a time.

Kotohime used to tell her stories about her mom, tales of a once legendary kitsune who'd earned the title *The Dancing Lily*. Lilian didn't know how much of those stories were true, and she would likely never find out. Camellia's mind had degraded long before she and her fraternal twin gained their second tail and became supernatural creatures.

Lilian turned her attention away from her mom and looked at her sister, then looked away when Iris noticed her looking. Wanting to pretend she hadn't been staring, her eyes strayed to the empty seat beside her. Kevin's seat.

She stood up.

"Lilian-sama?"

"Do you think you can put some of this food in a lunch box for me?" asked Lilian. "I'm going to see how Kevin's training is coming along, and I want to bring him some food. I'm sure he's going to be starving."

"Always thinking about your mate, hm?" Kotohime's small smile actually made Lilian blush, just a little. "If that is what you want, then I can certainly put together a breakfast bento for the two of you. Just wait one moment while I grab one of my bento boxes."

While Kotohime went off to grab a bento box, Iris stood up.

"I'll go, too."

"Huh?"

Iris looked away when Lilian's eyes fell upon her. "I still don't know my way around here very well, so I'll come with you in order to get a feel for the city."

Lilian didn't need to think about her decision. If her sister went with her, then she could apologize during the time it took to travel from home to Mad Dawg Fitness.

"Okay."

"Great! Just let me put some clothes on."

It was only as Iris strolled out of the room that Lilian noticed her sister was wearing a very familiar negligee.

"What are you doing in my sexy lingerie?! Get out of that outfit right now!"

Iris' tinkling laughter echoed down the hall, causing Lilian to scowl.

Maybe she shouldn't apologize, after all.

***

"Hiiii!"

A wide-eyed Kevin stumbled backwards as Tall came at him in a swift charge. The man moved so fast! He was far faster than someone his size had any right to move. He was in front of Kevin within seconds, launching a quick and powerful straight with his right hand.

Adrenaline pumping through his veins, Kevin leapt to the right. His haste caused him to stumble and fall to the ground—which was fortunate, as it meant he avoided getting an elbow to the face when Tall realized his initial attack had missed and tried to do a follow-up.

Somehow managing to turn his fall into a shoulder roll, Kevin scrambled back to his feet... and was just in time to see another fist sailing at him like a loaded spring.

"Oh, God!"

He tried to move backwards, but ended up tripping over his own two feet. Instead of backpedaling, he fell onto his back. At the same time, his feet kicked up into the air.

Woosh!

All the air left Tall's lungs as a pair of feet were planted into his gut. Kevin, still rolling backwards, forced Tall to move with him. The much larger male soon found out that Kevin had an impressive amount of strength in his legs, as he was tossed over Kevin and hit the ground with a loud thud.

"Oof!"

Kevin scrambled to his feet and saw that his sparring partner was already standing again. Tall wiped away the bit of spittle that escaped his mouth and glared fiercely at him.

"That was your one freebie, kid. Everybody always gets one."

"Eh?"

"But now I'm getting serious."

"EH?!"

"Prepare yourself!"

Kevin screamed like a little girl when Tall charged him again. The muscular giant of a man came in with a two-three combination: jab, jab, hook. His fists moved so swiftly that all Kevin's eyes could make out were a pair of blurs.

Kevin moved faster than he ever had before. His mind could scarcely begin to comprehend the speed with which his opponent attacked him. However, while his mind seemed incapable of reacting in time, his body, it appeared, had no desire to get hit. It moved of its own accord, doing everything humanly possible to avoid having his face smashed in.

When his foe launched another combination, Kevin tripped again, this time while moving to the left. Rather than falling to the mat, he swung his arms wide in an effort to maintain his balance. His body spun about like a ballerina, only with far less grace. Despite his lack of elegance, he managed to do an admirable job of spinning around his opponent's body, avoiding all the strikes sent his way. He also managed to crack his foe in the back of the head with one of his wildly flailing arms. The older, more muscular and more experienced man was sent to the ground a second time.

"This is just like the time we were fighting him back at that school!"

"Did ya see that, Kiara? Ya saw that, didn't ya?!"

"I saw it." Kiara had her arms crossed as she stood by her other two former disciples. She observed Kevin with keen eyes, studying his movements, analyzing and cataloguing them for future reference. What she saw intrigued her.

"So, what do you make of it?"

"Hmm…" A thoughtful look. "Hard to say. He's definitely got some kind of natural talent for not getting hurt and hurting his enemies while he's at it, but I'm not so sure it's a natural talent for fighting."

"Wha… but you saw what he just did! That kid's got natural badass written all over him."

"Hmph. If you want to think that, then go right ahead. I've got a more realistic hypothesis in mind."

"What's that?"

Kiara didn't answer, so the one Kevin called Taller went back to watching the spar.

It was almost amazing to see how Kevin managed to dodge all of Tall's attacks. He didn't do so in a way that looked graceful or nonchalant, but awkward and graceless instead. He stumbled and tripped and generally looked like a fool, and yet, somehow, someway, it helped him avoid getting his teeth busted in.

That didn't mean he had an easy time of it. His strange manner of evasion may have helped him avoid Tall's attacks, but due to the difference in their levels of physical fitness, Kevin still had a difficult time of it. His lack of experience and ability to put his natural athleticism to good use also hampered his combat abilities.

Kevin might have been fast when it came to running track, but that meant nothing when he couldn't make use of that speed. He was used to moving linearly, not weaving around punches and kicks like a monkey on crack.

"Hya!"

Another attack came. A straight jab. They seemed to be Tall's favorite punch, and he used them quite often. Kevin tried to dodge, to get out of his sparring partner's range, but couldn't quite manage it.

He did manage to do something else, however.

Stumbling again from another awkward attempt at dodging, Kevin reached out with his left hand and tried to grab something, anything, in order to steady himself. And grab something he did. A thick, muscular forearm. Kevin, not even paying attention to what he had grabbed, tried to pull himself to his feet.

And then another miracle happened.

Because Tall had been rushing forward, he had a lot of built up momentum. When Kevin pulled on him, Tall stumbled. Kevin then shifted his feet in an unwieldy attempt at steadying himself, which resulted in Tall's momentum and weight being used against him.

The end result was Kevin shoulder-tossing Tall like he was a ragdoll. The muscled man hit the ground, his lungs emptying in a loud *whoosh!* as he lay on his back, staring at the ceiling, blinking his dazed eyes and trying to understand what had just happened.

Breathing heavily, sweat accumulating on his brow and dripping down his chest, Kevin watched his opponent gasp for a breath that would not come. He blinked the sweat from his eyes, and then wiped it away when that didn't work, all the while staring at his downed opponent in confusion.

What… what just happened?

Clap. Clap. Clap.

Kevin turned to the sound of clapping as Kiara walked onto the mat, wearing the feral smirk that made her seem like she was perpetually amused.

"I think I've seen enough." She turned her head as Tall climbed to his feet. "Take ten. I don't think there's much you can do here."

"Ugh… right…"

As Tall limped off the mat, Kiara turned to Kevin. "I think I'm finally beginning to understand why my boys thought you were some kind of master combatant."

Kevin scratched the back of his head. "Really? That's good, because I have no idea why—wait." His face scrunched up. "Master combatant?"

"Correct. I've finally uncovered your secret, which means that your real training can now begin." At Kiara's whistle, Midget strode onto the mat. "He'll be your new opponent." When she saw Kevin's incredulous expression, her smirk widened. "Don't let his appearance fool you. Of my three disciples, he is the best."

When Midget cracked his knuckles and gave him a look that promised payback, Kevin could only gulp in response.

I somehow get the feeling that this is going to hurt. A lot.

***

After Lilian and Iris left for Mad Dawg Fitness, Kotohime and Kirihime washed the dishes. Camellia had offered to help, but they had rather forcefully refused the offer, and not just because they were her vassals. Having a woman who tripped on air clean the dishes was asking like for disaster to strike twice.

When they finished the dishes, Kotohime suggested they go shopping, stating that they were running low on food. She also invited Camellia. Inari only knew what would happen if they let that woman stay at home alone.

Because they had no mode of transportation, the trio of kitsune had to take the bus, which took a little over fifteen minutes to arrive at their destination: Secure Shopping.

They became the subject of many stares upon entering the grocery store. People from all walks of life watched the trio, their eyes following the group like unbearably horny yōkai looking at their next conquest.

Kotohime wondered if it was their clothing. She had to admit that their outfits were quite eccentric. That morning she'd chosen to wear a kimono depicting a savanna landscape, and her sister wore her usual French maid outfit. Meanwhile, Camellia had donned something vaguely resembling a toga.

Yes, Kotohime determined, it was quite easy to see why people were staring at them. None of these outfits could be considered normal in this modern age, especially in the United States. They couldn't have been more conspicuous if they tried—except maybe if they brought their tails and ears out.

Don't do it, Camellia.

"Hawa?"

The group pretty much ignored the gawking. The only person aware of the many stares was Kotohime. Kirihime might have also noticed, but if she did, then she did an admirable job of pretending she didn't.

"What's on our list?" Kirihime looked at her elder sister. Behind them, Camellia tried to wander off, but Kotohime placed a hand on the woman's shoulder before she could get herself lost.

"Please do not leave my side, Camellia-sama. It would not do for you to get lost in this store."

Camellia pouted a bit, but relented. "Muu, okay."

With the threat of their childish charge wandering off gone, Kotohime addressed her sister. She pulled a list out of her Extra Dimensional Storage Space, unfolded it and looked over the contents. "We have a pretty large list. There's a lot of vegetables and meats on here, and we'll need to buy some seasonings. Come. I would like to get the shopping done by noon, so I can prepare dinner for Lilian-sama, Kevin-sama, and Iris-sama."

The trio were just about to begin shopping when someone spoke up behind them. "You know Kevin and Lilian?"

As one, the trio turned to see a woman with short blond hair and a cheerful grin. She wore the clothing of a clerk; black pants, khaki shirt and an apron thrown over it.

"Dawn-san, how are you this morning?" Kotohime gave the woman a polite bow. Kirihime followed her sister's footsteps and curtsied. Camellia just stood there. She wasn't even paying attention.

Dawn gave them a smile. "I'm doing good. You know how it is here, nothing ever changes."

"Indeed."

The smile vanished to be replaced by blatant curiosity. "I didn't realize you knew Kevin and Lilian. How do you know them? And who is this?"

"Ah, yes, please allow me to introduce my sister, Kirihime." Kotohime gestured toward her sister. "She and I work for Camellia-sama here, who is the mother of Lilian-sama."

Dawn didn't think she would ever get used to the strange suffixes Kotohime added to people's names.

"Um, where is this Camallia-sama you're talking about?"

"Camellia-sama is…" Kotohime looked behind her and froze. Camellia wasn't there. "Oh dear. It looks like she wandered off again."

At her sister's words, Kirihime spun around, her eyes growing quite large when she saw the empty space that her mistress should have been occupying. "M-My Lady? My Lady Camellia? O-oh no! Where did my lady go?!"

While Kirihime placed her hands on her cheeks and began to fret, Kotohime gave Dawn an apologetic bow. "I apologize, but while I would enjoy speaking with you some more, my sister and I really must be going. It seems our mistress has wandered off, again, and it is imperative that we find her."

"Mistress?"

"Yes. Now, if you'll excuse us."

Kotohime grabbed the cart and her sister before walking off, leaving a confused and somewhat embarrassed Dawn behind.

"What did she mean by mistress?" Her eyes suddenly became wider than dishpans and rounder than hockey pucks. "Surely it couldn't be… but no, I must be imagining things. That must be it. Those two look like maids, so they must work for that Camellia person as her servants. Yes, there's no way those two could be transvestite pleasure slaves who cater to the whims of their unusual and horny mistress. Definitely not."

Shaking her head one last time, the woman went back to work, and decided to forget this encounter ever happened.

***

Tension. Thick, cloying tension that threatened to suffocate her was what Lilian felt as she walked alongside her sister. Mad Dawg Fitness wasn't that far from where they lived, but at that moment, Lilian could have sworn it was hours away.

She wanted to say something, anything, if only to rid herself of this strange pressure that surrounded them, choking her like a tail around her neck.

Unfortunately, Lilian was having one of those rare occasions where she just couldn't think of anything to say. Thus, she remained silent.

She did, however, peer at her sister out of her peripheral vision. Iris walked by her side, black hair fluttering like elegant streamers in the wind, shining and lustrous as the rising sun's rays struck each strand and captured them within its luminescence. Her hips swayed from side to side with every step taken, moving with a natural sexuality that Lilian had never been able to accomplish, no matter how hard she tried.

Her sister's ability to do anything and make it look extraordinarily sexy had always amazed her. Unlike Lilian who, for one reason or another, had never managed to gain that kind of sexiness, her sister made everything she did look like something out of a teenage boy's wet dream. She was eroticism in motion.

It was actually kind of scary.

Iris noticed Lilian glancing at her out of the corner of her eyes, and the redhead quickly turned her head to look at something else.

I am not turned on by my sister's swaying hips, Lilian told herself. *I'm not. And I'm definitely not aroused by the way her breasts are bouncing. No way.*

"I want you to know that I still don't approve of you and Kevin."

The words made Lilian snap her head back toward her sister. "What? But why? Is it because he's human?"

"Don't be stupid. I don't care about that. It wouldn't matter to me if he was human, kitsune or any other kind of yōkai. He could be an alien and I still wouldn't care."

"Then why?"

"Because you're too good for him." Lilian wanted to look surprised, but somehow, she knew her sister would say that. It still embarrassed her, though. "You're too good for everyone. None of these people are worthy of being your mate. Not Kevin. Not that idiot, Jiāoào. No one."

"Iris…"

"The only person deserving of your attention is me."

And just like that, any warmth she might have felt at her sister's compliment died a horrible, horrible death.

"You're wrong," Lilian tilted her head down, long locks of shimmering red hair overshadowing her eyes and hiding a portion of her face from view.

"What was that?"

"I said you're wrong." Like a curtain, Lilian's hair parted when she looked at her sister, her eyes narrowed and her lips set into a thin line. "You're wrong about Kevin. He is worthy of being with me. You just don't understand because you don't know him like I do. And besides, who is and isn't worthy of being my mate isn't your call to make. It's mine."

Iris frowned, but didn't refute her sister's words—at least not out loud.

We'll see about that.

***

Kiara was right. Midget, despite looking weaker due to his shorter stature and large front teeth, was a much better fighter than Tall. His strikes were faster, more sure and packed a hell of a lot more punch. Kevin had tried blocking one of Midget's punches at the beginning of their spar. Now his right arm was numb and dangling uselessly at his side.

"Come on! Is that all you've got?!"

Midget came in hot. Two steps and he was in Kevin's guard. The air seemed to whistle as he extended his left hand in a punch, the fist corkscrewing as it rushed toward Kevin's stomach. It was dodged when Kevin stumbled to the left, but he soon discovered that the punch had only been a distraction.

"Gah!"

Kevin took two staggering steps backward after finding himself on the receiving end of a vicious headbutt. His vision blurred for a moment, the edges darkening as pain exploded in his nose. Something warm and wet trailed down his skin and onto his lips. Blood, he realized. His blood.

Blinking several times, he tried to rid the spots from his eyes

—

—And promptly wished he hadn't when he saw another fist filling his vision. He managed to duck the attack, but ended up taking a knee to the face when Midget took one step forward and raised his left leg. The attack slammed into him like a fat man body-slamming an ant.

Kevin rolled backwards, moving with the blow, and somehow landed back on his feet. He barely had time to regain his bearings, though, as Midget came in quickly, offering no reprieve and closing the distance between them in the blink of an eye.

A low kick aimed at taking out Kevin's left knee was avoided, but he could not avoid the follow-up, the brutal backhand jab that popped him across the face. Saliva mixed with blood flew from Kevin's mouth as his head snapped to the left like he'd just suffered whiplash. He did not fall, but that probably wasn't a good thing, because it meant Midget could still attack him.

A loud ringing entered Kevin's ears as another fist clocked him on the temple. Everything started to teeter. The world spun and strange spots appeared in his vision. He didn't have time to contemplate the oddity of what he was seeing because less than a second later, a pair of hands grabbed his head in a clinch and his face soon met another knee.

Kevin could have sworn he heard, as much as felt, his nose breaking. A loud *crack!* issued from his nose, echoing ominously within his mind. The pain escalated, becoming unbearable. Kevin imagined this is what it would feel like if Thor, Norse God of lightning and thunder, used his mighty hammer Mjölnir to bludgeon someone in the face.

Everything grew wobbly. Kevin's world began to spin. He barely even felt his back hitting the mat as his vision started fading…

"Beloved!"

Kevin's vision snapped back into painfully sharp focus as a familiar voice penetrated his ear canal.

A lovely face filled his vision seconds later. Perhaps it was because he felt slightly delirious, but Lilian looked even more gorgeous than usual. Her soft, unblemished skin shone with a healthy vitality, surrounded by glimmering strands of fire. Viridescent eyes gleamed with concern, calming his mind and somehow soothing the aches and pains in his body, as if just having her eyes on him made him feel a thousand times better. She was, without a doubt, an angel.

"Lilian…"

"Shh. Don't talk." Lilian shushed him as she set his head on her lap. The difference between the hard surface of the blue mat and the gentle softness of Lilian's thighs was like heaven and earth.

Kevin absently noticed through his darkening vision that Lilian's ears were out. A second later, two white-tipped fox tails appeared before him, their tips glowing with an iridescent golden light that soothed his wounds better than any healing balm.

"You can heal his bruises, but don't heal his muscles," Kiara's voice said from somewhere out of his line of sight. Lilian looked up at where he assumed his trainer was standing, her eyes burning like imploding twin stars.

"What did you do to him?"

"Just training."

"Training?! You call this training?! Look at him! Kevin looks like a horde of Oni trampled him!"

Kevin felt a rapid decline in his HP gauge.

Ugh, way to make me feel good about myself, Lilian.

A feminine snort sounded out. It was not Kiara. "He definitely isn't looking too pretty right now. Not that he ever did."

"Be quiet, Iris!"

Ah. So Lilian's sister was here, too. Did that mean they had made up?

"That's the price one pays to acquire strength." Kevin could almost imagine Kiara's uncaring shrug as she spoke. "You think gaining the strength and skill necessary to fight against a superior foe is easy? Don't be ridiculous. It takes hard work and effort. You've got to put your all into training, breaking your body down by putting it through hell, shedding blood, sweat and tears in the process. That's the only way to get stronger."

"I don't want to hear that from you, dog!"

"You're spouting some awfully harsh words to someone who's helping your mate get stronger." An amused chuckle. "You do know that Kevin was the one who came to me for help, don't you? He came in knowing full well what I had in store for him."

"But that's…"

"It's alright, Lilian."

Lilian peered down at him. Kevin tried to give her a smile, but from the grimace on her face as she looked at him, he realized that his smile probably didn't look too good.

"Beloved..."

"Kiara's right. I knew this would be hard the moment I asked her to train me. I accepted that, so try not to blame her for my condition."

"But..."

"If this is what it takes to get stronger so that I can stand by your side, then I will gladly accept whatever Kiara dishes out without complaint." He paused. "Well, without too much complaint. Anyway, I want to become someone you can rely on to have your back when things get rough. I don't want to be that human who constantly needs saving."

"Oh, Kevin..."

"Someone gag me, please."

Lilian glared at someone outside his field of vision, Iris, Kevin presumed, before she returned her focus to healing him.

"Okay." She sighed. "I understand that this is what you want, so I won't say anything more. Just... try not to injure yourself too much, okay? I hate seeing you like this."

Kevin revealed bloodstained teeth when his split lips peeled back into a grin, "I'll do my best."

**

Ms. Vis stood in line at Starschmucks. As per the usual, a fairly long line of people kept her from getting to the cash register and placing her order. Fortunately, it was early in the morning and school wouldn't start for another hour, so she had some time to herself and could afford to be patient.

Waiting in line didn't bother her. It might have three months ago, but having nothing better to do than stand around in a line gave Ms. Vis the opportunity to do some productive thinking. And she had a lot to think about.

Most of her thoughts centered around a certain trio of students. Her mind kept trying to figure out how Mr. Swift and that blasted redhead kept getting out of trouble. Just the other day she had given the class detention, yet somehow, those two managed to get out of trouble again. To top it off, that little educational disruptor's sister and Ms. Diane had avoided detention as well, and she didn't even know how it happened!

"Hawa…"

Ms. Vis blinked. What a strange sound.

"Hawawa…"

She blinked again. It sounded like a person, but what kind of person said… whatever this person was saying?

"Hawan…"

Turning to her left, Ms. Vis caught sight of a very pretty woman with long midnight hair. Adorning a figure that she most certainly did not feel envious of was what appeared to be a toga, or something similar. Ms. Vis found it to be a most unusual form of dress. It looked like something straight out of ancient Greece!

"Hawa…"

The woman, who was the source of the strange noise, stared up at the board, her expression reminding Ms. Vis of a little girl who'd been allowed to go shopping with her parents for the first time. Except this person wasn't a child. She was an adult, which made the expression on her face that much more disturbing.

Ms. Vis turned back to face the line. There were only two people in front of her now. She ignored the woman. Whatever this female's problem was had nothing to do with her.

"Hawa…"

Her right eyebrow twitched.

***

It took a long time to find Camellia, much longer than it should have. She and Kirihime checked everywhere they thought their mistress might have wandered off to—everywhere except the most obvious place, apparently. Only after exhausting every other option and concluding that she must have left, did they travel back to the front of the store, where they saw the woman in question standing next to the Starschmucks.

"My Lady!"

At the sound of Kirihime's voice, Camellia turned, the sweetest of smiles blossoming on her face. "Hawa! Kirikiri! Koto! Hello!"

Kirihime stopped in front of her mistress, worried eyes gazing at the childish woman with barely masked relief. "M-My Lady! Are you alright? Why did you run off like that?"

"Run off?" Camellia looked honestly confused. She put a finger to her lower lip, boosting her cuteness by a factor of 12.

Several men, and even a few women, were felled by massive blood hemorrhaging, as dark liquid blasted from their noses like the tail ends of several comets.

"You left us," Kirihime tried to look stern, but her demureness was such that she appeared more whiny than anything else. "We didn't know where you were. Did you know how worried I was?"

"Ah! Sorry, sorry." Camellia had the decency to look embarrassed. "I saw something shiny and decided to follow it, and then I ended up here."

While Kirihime merely seemed relieved to have found the five-tailed kitsune, Kotohime felt exasperated. Perhaps having Camellia travel with them while grocery shopping had not been the best of ideas. Then again, letting her stay at home by herself with all those amenities and other breakable objects would have been just as bad.

"From now on, please remain by our side, Camellia-sama. It would not do for you to get lost in a place like this."

"Hawa..." Camellia's shoulders slumped, her eyes becoming dewy as tears started to gather. "Sowwy..."

"It is fine. Do not worry about it."

"Kay." Camellia wiped a few errant tears from her eyes. She then presented them with a smile. "Thank you."

Kotohime felt eyes upon her and turned her head. She blinked. A woman whose skin was so pale that it appeared almost translucent was staring at her with a narrow-eyed gaze. Her outfit, an outdated skirt with an equally out of date collared shirt and black stockings, kept much of her body covered. She had no clue who this woman was, but that scrutinizing expression, those eyes that stared at her in distinct disapproval, bothered her.

"Can I help you, *Josei*-san?"

If Ms. Vis noticed Kotohime's use of the Japanese word for "woman," she did not let onto this fact. If she heard the tone of warning in Kotohime's voice, then she willfully ignored it.

"You..." her frown increased. It looked like she was thinking really hard. Kotohime could practically see the gears in her head turning. "Look awfully familiar. Do I know you from somewhere?"

Now it was Kotohime's turn to frown. "I am quite sure that you and I have never met before, though I must admit that you look familiar. Perhaps we have—ah, now I remember. You're Ms. Vis, if I am not mistaken."

Ms. Vis' eyes widened. "Y-yes, but how did you—"

"Lilian-sama has spoken of you quite often, and I recognize you from the description that she gave me." Kotohime eyed the woman before her with a studious gaze. So this was the woman that Lilian always complained about?

Hmm...

"Lilian-sama," Ms. Vis mumbled, her eyes blinking. "You don't mean Ms. Pnévma, do you?"

"Indeed."

"You... just how do you three know that girl?"

"Ah! That's easy! Camellia is..."

"Camellia-sama is Lilian-sama's mother."

"Hawa... Camellia wanted to say that..."

"My apologies, Camellia-sama."

"Hawawawa."

"M-mother?!" Ms. Vis seemed shocked. She even pointed at Camellia with a shaky finger. "You're that girl's mother?!"

"Um!" Camellia nodded with a happy smile.

The chalky math teacher pressed a hand to her forehead, as if she could already feel a migraine coming just by being in the presence of **Lilian's Mother**.

"And what about you two?" Ms. Vis tossed the sisters a stern look complete with thin, flat lips. "How do you know Ms. Pnévma?"

"Kirihime and I are this family's humble and hardworking servants." Kotohime, ever the proper *Yamato Nadeshiko*, bowed to the shocked educator. "I would like to thank you for taking care of Lilian-sama and helping further her education."

Having apparently not expected such a polite and proper response, Ms. Vis stumbled over her words. "I-it's... that's alright. You're welcome, I guess." A second passed before her glare returned. "If you know Ms. Pnévma, does that mean you also know Mr. Swift?"

"Yes."

"And what is the nature of your relationship with Mr. Swift?"

"Ah! Kevin is—"

"Lilian-sama's fiance."

"Hawa… Koto is being mean to Camellia."

"Ufufu. Please accept this humble maid's apologies again, Camellia-sama"

"Muu."

Ms. Vis stood before the strange trio of beautiful women, her mind blanking as the word "fiance" bounced in her skull like a linear equation.

"Is she going to be okay?" Kirihime looked worried as she waved a hand in front of an unresponsive Ms. Vis' face.

"Ufufu, I believe she will be fine."

"I don't know, sister, she looks broken."

Once the word "fiance" settled in her mind like an isosceles triangle, Ms. Vis snapped out of her fugue and began to sputter. "M-m-m-marriage?! Did you just say t-that girl is m-mar-mar-m-m-marrying Mr. Swift?!"

The three kitsune glanced at each other.

"Um, yes?"

"Not happening! No way. No way, no way, no way, it's not happening!" Ms. Vis showed just how much she disapproved of Kevin and Lilian's apparent union by crossing her arms in an "X" pattern. "They are too young to be thinking about marriage! Way too young! They haven't even been properly educated yet! And that girl is just no good for Mr. Swift! No good at all!"

Two of the three kitsune's eyes narrowed.

"Ne, Sister, can I cut her?"

"No." Kotohime sent her sister a glance. That odd glint in Kirihime's eyes. The strange smile on her face. She recognized those signs, and they meant nothing good. "There shall be no cutting."

Kirihime looked disappointed, but relented under her sister's unwavering gaze.

"I know! I'll give her detention!" Ms. Vis' eyes had taken on a maniacal glint as she continued raving like a lunatic. "That will teach her! I'll give her an entire month's worth of detention! No! I'll give her a whole year's worth of detention!"

"No, you will not."

Ms. Vis growled, an unusual sounding snarl that bubbled up from her throat. She turned to glare at Kotohime, and made the same mistake with the four-tailed kitsune that she often made with

Lilian.

She looked into the woman's eyes. Her glowing eyes.

Ms. Vis' own eyes glazed over.

"You will not do anything untoward to either Lilian-sama, Iris-sama or Kevin-sama."

"I will not doing anything untoward to them…"

"In fact, from this day forward, you will treat Lilian-sama with love and respect."

"Love and respect…"

"Kevin-sama, too. You will treat him as if he were your own son."

"My own son…"

Kotohime made a vaguely dismissive gesture with her right hand.

"Move along."

"Move along…"

When Ms. Vis turned around and walked away, disappearing down one of the store's many aisles, Kirihime turned to her sister.

"That was an impressive use of enchantments, sister. You really have that whole Jedi thing down to a T. Obi-Wan's got nothing on you."

"Please do not compare me to an old man in a bathrobe," Kotohime muttered. "Now then, let us continue shopping. We've already wasted enough time here."

"Sure." Kirihime was about to look back at the shopping list when she realized they were missing someone. Again. "Um, hey Sister, where is my Lady Camellia? I could have sworn she was right behind me."

Kotohime looked at where Camellia had been standing just a few seconds prior. When she saw that the space was unoccupied, she brought up a hand and used it to palm her face.

"Come on," she moved off, leaving their cart behind. "Let's go look for her before she breaks something or some human tries taking advantage of her."

Kirihime's eyes widened in alarm. "Y-you don't think that would really happen, do you? It wouldn't happen, right?" Kotohime said nothing. She was already walking off. "Sister? Sister? Wait up! Don't leave me!"

***

The first rays of light peeked in through Christine's window.

Unlike most mornings, when the rise of the sun would wake her up, Christine did not wake up from it this time—because she was already awake.

She sat on her bed, dark bags underneath her eyes. In her lap was a book, and her hungry gaze devoured the words written on each page with the vigor of a dog gnawing on a chew toy. However, despite how much Christine enjoyed reading, she was not doing so for pleasure. Not this time. She was a snow-woman on a mission. An important mission.

It had become increasingly obvious to her that if she wanted to get Kevin to notice her over that big-breasted bimbo, then she would need to step up her game.

She sat on her bed, holding a book titled "Five Easy Steps to Making Him Yours" and flipped through the pages, scanning the text like an alchemist searching for clues about the Philosopher's Stone. Situated around her person were numerous other books, all of them bearing similar titles: "So You Want to Get a Boyfriend?" and "The Best Way to a Man's Heart is His Through His Chode" were just a few of the titles stacked haphazardly on her bed.

Her eyes scanned one page and then she flipped to the next page. She didn't stop for anything. Not to use the restroom, not to get a drink. Nothing. When she finished reading the last page fifteen minutes later, she closed the book and released a sigh. Gods, she was tired. Her eyes felt heavy and thick. All she wanted to do was take a nap. In fact, that sounded like a really good idea.

Christine let herself backwards onto her bed. Her hair spread out around her, contrasting with the light blue sheets and her pale body. She prepared to close her eyes when she caught sight of the clock.

6:34 am.

She rubbed her eyes, then looked again.

Still 6:34 am.

"Shit!"

Jumping to her feet with an energy she did not know she possessed, Christine began throwing on her clothes. After spending nearly half an hour putting her ridiculously complicated gothic lolita outfit on, she rushed out of the apartment and sprinted to the bus stop as quickly as her dress would allow.

It was only after she had gotten on the bus that she realized something.

"Damn it! I forgot to take a shower!"

Six seconds later, Christine realized she'd just shouted and that everyone was now staring at her. Seven seconds after that, a blushing and thoroughly embarrassed Christine sat in a seat at the back of the bus, doing her best to pretend she didn't exist.

I hate my life.

***

Kevin bobbed in and out of consciousness as the car he was in drove down the road.

Lilian had managed to heal all of his injuries, but she hadn't healed the damage done from working out to his muscles. According to Kiara, having his muscles healed by a Celestial Kitsune would negate all of the effort he put in that day. This meant he would have to suck it up.

Lilian also couldn't heal exhaustion. Go figure.

He really didn't want to go to school today. A part of him felt tempted to ask Lilian if she would like to stay home with him and watch anime. He didn't, but only because the larger part of him knew that skipping school was wrong.

Curse his sense of responsibility.

Still, things could have been worse. He could have been riding his bike to school that day. Instead, Kiara had offered to give them a ride, which was good, because even if he had been in any condition to ride his bike, there were one too many people for him to travel with.

He sat slumped in the back seat, with Lilian sitting next to him and his head resting on her shoulder. Delicate, feminine fingers traveled through his hair, and long nails gently scratched his scalp. It felt good. Really good.

By the gods, he loved having a girlfriend.

Sitting on Lilian's other side, Iris seemed to be bothered by something. Her face had become pale and her eyes withdrawn. She kept glancing at Kiara every so often before shifting back to look out the window. Kevin didn't know what was bothering the girl, but he was too tired to care about whatever troubles ailed his girlfriend-slash-mate's sister.

Kevin jerked in his seat when the car ceased moving with

startling suddenness. The action forced his eyes wide open. He looked around, noticing the mass of people outside of the windows, and realized they had arrived at school.

"Come on, Kevin. Time to get out." Kevin groaned, causing the emerald-eyed fox-girl to smile as she gently helped him undo his seatbelt. "Don't act so glum. I'm sure once you've had a chance to relax in class, things will get better."

"Our first class is with Ms. Vis."

Lilian winced. "Okay, after our first class, I'm sure things will get better."

"I wish I had your optimism."

***

"What the hell is this?!"

Before he, Lilian and Iris could take so much as a single step from Kiara's vehicle, one of the few people Kevin could truly say he hated marched up to the group.

It was enough to make Kevin wonder if there really was such a thing as karma.

Chris Fleischer looked better than he had in months, which wasn't saying much because it was clear to Kevin that the inu no longer possessed the strength he once boasted. His body looked frail. Weak. His muscles had long since atrophied, and he no longer held the appearance of a hulking monstrosity. Now, he looked abnormally tall and skinny.

Was this the result of whatever technique Lilian had used on him those three months ago?

"Hello there, little brother," Kiara greeted the younger inu with a look that said, *I know what you're thinking, and I really couldn't give a damn.* It was an impressive look, to be sure. Kevin would have to remember it. "How are you doing this morning?"

"Don't fuck with me, Kiara!" Chris snarled. "What the fucking hell are you doing with Swift and that bitch of a fox—doof!"

Kevin and Lilian blinked when a black-furred tail shot out from underneath Iris' skirt, smacked Chris in the face, and then just as quickly retracted. No one seemed to see it aside from them, but there could be no doubt that everyone saw Chris stumble back.

"No one insults my sister when I'm around, dickweed."

"You fucking cunt!" Chris held a hand to his now split lip.

"Just you wait! I'll fucking murder you!"

"You won't be doing anything of the sort," Kiara interrupted the argument before it could become truly violent. "Go to class, you three. I'll deal with my foolish little brother."

Iris looked like she wanted to say something, but one glance from Kiara had the girl hiding behind Kevin and Lilian. Kevin glanced at his mate, who correctly interpreted the question within his gaze and shrugged, stating quite clearly that she didn't know what was wrong with her sister either.

"We'll leave this to you," Kevin decided.

Kiara grinned and waved them off. "See you kids later."

***

"Che, can you believe the nerve of that guy?" Iris ranted on their way to class. "I can't believe he had the audacity to insult my lovely sister like that. Who the hell does he think he is?"

"Definitely not Simone the Digger." While Lilian giggled into her hand, Iris gave Kevin a very flat look. In return, Kevin waved his left hand in a dismissive gesture. "Nothing. Just forget it."

While continuing to class, Lilian noticed a poster on the wall of a school building. It showed two people dressed as zombies, a vampire that didn't sparkle, and someone wearing a really cheesy werewolf mask, no shirt, and photoshopped abs.

"Hey, Kevin, what's this?"

Kevin stopped and looked at the poster. "That? It's for the Halloween party. Every year, the school has a party celebrating Halloween. We do things like dancing and bobbing for apples, and there's always a contest to see who has the best costume..." He trailed off when stars appeared in Lilian's eyes.

"Can we go? We're gonna go, right? We so have to go to this."

Kevin leaned back when Lilian invaded his personal space, her star-like irises boring into him like a legilimens invading his mind.

"We can go if you want to. I went to the one we had last year and it was pretty fun."

"Yes!" Lilian pumped a fist into the air. "But wait." The hand dropped. "You said it was a costume party?"

"Well, it's a Halloween party. Everyone there will be wearing costumes."

"I see." Lilian bit her thumb in thought, then her eyes lit up. "Kevin, we need costumes!"

"I'll see if we can go costume shopping some time this weekend," Kevin hedged.

"Okay! So, what kind of costumes should we wear? Oh! Oh! Can we get matching costumes?"

While Lilian talked Kevin's ears off about all of the different costumes she wanted to wear, which included everything from cosplaying as Lelouch and CC to dressing up as a schoolgirl and a perverted priest, Iris looked back at the poster.

"A Halloween party, huh?" A smirk that spoke of nothing good caused her lips to curve. "Sounds interesting."

***

Kevin plopped down in his seat with a boneless flop. His head and torso fell forward until his face planted itself against the desk, and then he started to snore.

Lindsay looked at Lilian as the redhead scooted her desk closer to Kevin's, while Iris sat directly behind Lilian.

"What's up with Kevin? He looks exhausted." A grin spread across Lindsay's face. "Don't tell me you kept him up late last night with some sexy shenanigans or something."

Lilian smiled at her friend. "I wish, but no. He was training with Kiara today."

"Kiara?" Lindsay looked nonplussed. "You don't mean Kiara F. Kuyo, do you? The owner of Mad Dawg Fitness?"

"That's the one."

Lindsay looked quite put out as she crossed her arms over her chest. "And neither of you thought to tell me this?"

"It didn't seem that important." Lilian reached out with her left hand and ran her fingers through her mate's hair. After the initial stiffening, Kevin relaxed under her ministrations and let out a low, pleased groan. "To be honest, the idea of telling someone else never really crossed my mind. Kevin might have been willing to tell you, but he's been so busy with training and learning kitsune culture that it probably slipped his mind."

Lindsay's cheeks swelled like someone had shoved grapefruits into her mouth. "It's still mean of you guys not to tell me about something like this."

Lilian didn't stop her actions, but she did look at Lindsay.

"Then how about I tell you something to make up for it?"

"Like what?"

Lilian made Lindsay lean in. Iris, curious to know what was being said, also leaned in.

"Like the fact that Kiara isn't human. She's an Inu."

Lindsay's eyes widened. Iris' eyes also widened, but for completely different reasons.

"That's why I felt so nervous around her," Iris muttered harshly, her face pale. "Damn it, Lily-pad! You're supposed to tell me these things!"

"Maybe I will when you stop calling me 'Lily-pad.'"

Iris grimaced, but didn't say anything.

"Are you serious?" Lindsay leaned back when Lilian nodded, her expression was akin to someone who'd been shocked by lightning. "I can't believe it. I mean, I can, but I certainly wasn't expecting it." She took a moment to gather her thoughts. "Wow. That's just... wow. To think that one of the women all the girls on my soccer team admire is an inu is... that's, I don't even know what to say."

"Uh, Lily-pad" With her pale face and jittery limbs, Iris appeared quite nervous. "Are you sure you should be telling her this? I mean, isn't she..."

"Lindsay already knows that yōkai are real," Lilian informed her sister before frowning. "And what have I told you about calling me Lily-pad?"

"Sorry, sorry, you're just too cute when you get all moody and pouty like that." Iris winked at the redhead. "Better be careful, sis. Keep looking so adorable and I might just gobble you up."

"W-whatever." Lilian turned her head to better hide the blush staining her cheeks.

At that moment, the doors to the classroom opened again and Ms. Vis walked in. She looked just as stern and no-nonsense as always—at least until she made it to the front of the classroom and saw Kevin sleeping on his desk.

"What is wrong with Mr. Swift? Is he alright?" Her eyes peered at Lilian, and the young vixen had to blink when she saw the honest concern in them.

What in the name of Inari's tails is going on?

"Uh..." Lilian found herself at a momentary loss for words.

"Y-yes, he's just tired from, um, working too much…"

"Working, she says," Lindsay mumbled under her breath.

"Oh, the poor boy!" Ms. Vis blubbered. "Ms. Pnéyma, why don't you be a dear and take Mr. Swift to the nurse's office, so he can get some rest? In fact, why don't you stay there with him? That way he will have a familiar face to greet him when he wakes up. I think he would like that."

Lilian stared. Lindsay stared. The entire classroom stared. The only people who didn't look like something had struck them between the eyes were Iris and Kevin. Iris because she didn't know how unusual this attitude was for Ms. Vis, and Kevin because he was asleep.

"Lilian?"

"Yes, Lindsay?"

"I think something strange is going on with our teacher."

"Me too."

"Also, the world seems to have suddenly gone dark."

"We seem to be experiencing an unprecedented solar eclipse. I think the celestial bodies might have also been knocked out of alignment."

"Uh huh."

"Ms. Pnéyma? Are you feeling unwell?" The concern Ms. Vis irradiated for her well-being made Lilian wonder if this person might have been a doppelgänger. "Do you also need some rest?"

"Um, no, I'm, ah, fine."

The relief Ms. Vis exuded was a palpable thing. It disturbed Lilian greatly. "I see. That is good. Do you think you can get Mr. Swift to the nurse's office, then?"

"Uh, I think can do that. Yeah, I'll definitely do that. Lindsay, can you, um, help me get Kevin to the nurse's office?"

"Help?" Lindsay blinked several times, her mind still clearly undergoing severe mental trauma from the sudden shift in their teacher's emotional paradigm. It took her mind a second to realign itself with reality. "Um, right! Help! Yeah, I can help you!"

She and Lilian both stood up and moved to Kevin's desk. Iris stood up as well.

"What?" the raven-haired girl asked upon seeing the two stares directed at her. "You didn't think I was gonna let you two go off without me, did you? I can help too." More stares. Iris actually began to feel uncomfortable. "Why are you two staring at me like that?"

"You're offering to help." Lilian scrutinized her sister. "You never offer to help with anything, and considering how much you dislike Kevin, I'm inclined to believe you're up to no good."

Iris clutched her chest, as if she was experiencing heartburn. "You don't really think I would do something like strip naked and climb into your mate's bed while he's unconscious, thereby instigating a sexy situation in which you would discover us in a most compromising position in order to create tension between you and him, do you?"

"That was an awfully specific scenario you presented, and yes, I do think you would do something like that."

"That's a harsh thing to say." Iris pouted. "I promise, the only reason I am doing this is because I want you to be happy. Fox's honor."

Lilian exhaled a soft breath before letting herself smile.

Her sister was abrasive, rude and way too arrogant for her own good, but she was also a good person—at least to her. To other people? Not so much.

***

Kevin woke up feeling refreshed. He didn't know how long he had slept, but he'd clearly needed it. Who knew fighting against someone who was short and had buck teeth could be so hard?

Wanting to know where he was, he opened his eyes… only to be met with another pair of eyes.

"Lilian…"

"Hey, sleepyhead." Lilian smiled at her mate. Kevin smiled back. "How are you feeling?"

"Better. How long was I asleep for?"

"You missed first period."

Kevin winced. "I bet Ms. Vis didn't like that."

"Actually, she was surprisingly concerned." The look on Lilian's face was half-amused, half-disturbed. "She was the one who suggested we take you to the nurse's office."

"Nurse's office?" It was only after she had spoken that Kevin realized he was lying on his back, on a bed, and that they were, indeed, in the nurse's office. How had he missed that? "And you're saying Ms. Vis suggested you bring me here? Wait." He stared at

Lilian, confused. "We?"

That was when he noticed the other two people with them. Lindsay and Iris stood off to the side. Iris had her arms crossed under her bust, while Lindsay's were clasped behind her back.

"Yo, Kevin!" Lindsay greeted him with a cheerful grin. "Glad to see you're back in the land of the living."

Kevin smiled uncertainly. "Um, good to be back."

"Great, you're awake and everybody's happy," Iris interrupted the moment between friends. "can we go now?"

Despite the rude words, the others decided to heed them and, together, they left the nurse's office and traveled to their next class.

Kevin, Lilian and Iris all shared classes together. Lindsay had PE. After saying their goodbyes, they parted ways with the tomboy and headed off to their French class.

"K-Kevin!"

A squeak like that of a frightened mouse caused the group to stop. Christine stepped out from behind a locker, her hands wringing together and her cheeks stained with the color of a frozen tundra. As she walked toward them, steam poured out of her ears, and whenever one of her feet touched the ground, an icy footprint was left in its wake.

"Hey, Christine." Kevin wondered if he should ask the girl if she was feeling alright, but then he remembered what happened the last time he asked that question and decided not to. "How are you doing this morning?"

Christine took a deep breath and tried to calm her boiling emotions. She could do this. She could.

"I-I'm... g-g-good. H-how is—I-I mean, how are you doing this, um, this m-morning?"

Damn it.

"I'm doing alright," Kevin replied warily. There was something horrifyingly familiar about this scenario, though he didn't know what. It made him nervous for some reason.

"R-really? T-that's good. So, um, uh... d-did anything interesting happen, you know, recently?"

Kevin thought about telling Christine that he had started sparring Kiara's jabronis, but then remembered how those same jabronis—or at least one of them—had beaten the crap out of him and didn't think his pride could handle her knowing.

He shook his head. "Not really? What about you?"

"Oh, uh, um, no-not really, no."

While watching the awkward duo stand around like a pair of idiots, Iris leaned over and whispered into Lilian's ear. "This girl... she's into your mate, isn't she?"

"Yep."

"Why?"

"Because he's the main character, obviously."

"Hm…" Iris pondered that for a moment, then nodded. "Yeah, I guess that makes sense."

Iris looked at Christine, whose face steadily grew a darker shade of blue with each passing second. She then looked at Kevin, who appeared wary, as if he was expecting the snow-maiden to erupt.

Raven hair fluttered as she looked back at Lilian.

"Aren't you worried that she might take him from you?" she teased, her mischievous crimson eyes glittering like diamonds.

"Why would I be worried about something like that?" Lilian asked. "I don't mind if she loves Kevin. However, I don't think Kevin is really interested in going the harem route, so I doubt anything will happen between them."

"… Right…"

"To be honest, I feel kind of bad for her," Lilian admitted. "She clearly likes him, but she's so tsundere that I doubt Kevin even realizes it."

"Hn."

Kevin noticed how Christine continued standing there, not speaking, the blue of her face spreading to her neck, and he became worried.

"Are you alright?"

Christine jumped in surprise. She looked at Kevin, and then looked away. Back at Kevin. Then away again. After doing this exactly six more times, she crossed her arms and tried unsuccessfully to look nonchalant.

"O-o-of course! W-w-why wouldn't I be?"

"Your face is blue."

"Wh-w-w-wha—IT IS NOT!" Christine exploded. Kevin winced as several strands of his hair froze like icicles. "And so what if it is?! It's not like that's any of your business, idiot! Jerk!

Stupid!"

"Woah!" Kevin held his hands up. "Look, I'm sorry. I didn't mean to upset you. Please don't be mad at me."

Christine's eyes widened. "I-I-I'm not—I mean, it's not like— IT ISN'T LIKE THAT!"

"Wow," Iris chuckled in condescending amusement. "She's got it bad."

Incapable of disputing that fact, Lilian could only nod.

Christine's face looked like an icicle ready to spontaneously combust. "T-that's—I'm s-s-s-s-s-s—"

"Christine?" Kevin leaned in closer. "Seriously, you're beginning to worry me. You don't have a fever do you?"

Christine froze when Kevin placed a hand on her forehead. Her eyes became the size of hockey pucks and her jaw started to tremble.

"Ten Midgets says she blows up on him?" Iris said to Lilian, who shook her head.

"I don't take sucker's bets."

"Tch. Spoilsport."

"W-w-wha…?"

"Hm," Kevin murmured as he placed his other hand against his own head, feeling the difference in their temperature. "You are awfully cold, but I don't think you have a fever."

"W-w-wha…"

"But if you're not sick, then why is your face all blue? Is this a yuki-onna thing?"

"W-w-w-wha…"

"Christine?"

"WHAT THE HELL DO YOU THINK YOU'RE DOING, JACKASS!"

"What the—gack!"

Kevin never managed to finish his sentence before Christine's swift uppercut slammed into the underside of his chin. He felt a brief chill, like the skin there was being flash frozen, and then came an unusual feeling of weightlessness.

Several seconds later, he hit the ground.

It really hurt.

"Gu… huu… uuhhh…"

Christine stared at Kevin as he lay on his back, his eyes

crossed. Her own eyes were wide, and they went wider still the longer she stared, as if she couldn't believe she had just hit Kevin. "This isn't what I—I mean, I didn't mean to—THIS IS ALL YOUR FAULT! JERK!"

"Kevin!"

While Lilian went to help her beloved mate, Iris watched the snow-maiden run off and disappear around the corner.

"So that's a tsundere, huh?" she pondered something for a moment before chuckling. "It looks like he really does have one of every type." She glanced at Kevin and Lilian to see her lovely sister place a kiss on the young man's chin, and ignored the irritation she felt. Now was not the time for that. "Hey, kiddo, do you plan on getting a kuudere as well? You know, to make your harem more complete?"

"Be quiet!" A thoroughly embarrassed Kevin hissed in pain, the act of moving his jaw hurting more than he expected it to. "Ow, ow, ow. Pain. My jaw. I think it's broken."

"Do you want me to kiss the pain away?" Lilian offered. Kevin blushed, but still managed to nod.

As Iris watched the two, the plan that had been forming in her mind began to solidify. She couldn't allow this to continue. She would prove to Lilian that Kevin didn't deserve to be her mate.

All she needed was an opportunity to put her plan into action.

***

After rounding another corner, Christine leaned her back against the wall and held a hand to her heart. It was beating so fast, like a hummingbird's wings with the strength of a battering ram. She could practically feel it trying to pound its way out of her ribcage!

Her legs, already weak from the nerve-wracking experience, gave out, and Christine slid onto her bottom. A shiver caused her to realize that she was also losing control of more than just her emotions. The concrete underneath her had frozen solid. Hoarfrost spread along the ground, slowly creeping across the pavement like an insipid creature of the deep abyss, and had even traveled up the wall behind her. Her breath came out as a thick white mist, and several people walking nearby shivered.

Why was this so hard? Confessing shouldn't be this difficult, should it?

N-not that I actually love Kevin! This is just a crush! A crush, damn it! I simply want my first dating experience to be with someone I know and trust! That's all!

Keep telling nyourself that, nya.

Shut up!

"Ha..."

Closing her eyes, Christine began several breathing exercises, the same ones she had been taught years ago when her benefactor adopted her. They helped her regain a semblance of control, both over her powers and her emotions. The hoarfrost receded, her breath ceased to produce mist, and her cheeks returned to their pale skin tone.

Standing up, Christine started walking to her next class. This attempt at talking to Kevin had been a bust, but she would try holding a regular conversation with him again at lunch.

"My Gothic Hottie!"

Eric Corrompere suddenly appeared out of nowhere and rushed Christine with the intent to... well, Christine didn't actually know what he planned on doing, and she didn't care either. His presence meant that she now had the perfect punching bag to rid herself of that last bit of pent-up embarrassment.

Tsundere Protocols: Activated.

"I'M NOT YOUR GOTHIC HOTTIE!"

And so the mighty fist of a tiny little girl flew straight and true.

***

"AAAIIIEEEEE!!"

Sitting at his desk, Kevin Swift looked up, his face etched in a stern expression more suited to a field commander than a 15 year old high school student.

"Is something wrong, Kevin?" Lilian asked.

"No," Kevin said after a moment, his body returning back to a more relaxed posture. "I just thought I heard Eric screaming in unimaginable pain for some reason."

"I'm sure you were just hearing things."

"Yeah, you're probably right."

Another moment passed before Kevin returned to taking notes, as Ms. Bonnet lectured them on proper enunciation and lexicon.

Lilian was right. He must have been hearing things.

Chapter 5

The Great Costume Disaster

When news that Lilian was no longer living in the Pnéyma estate reached Jiāoào, he had ordered his servants to begin departure preparations immediately. This was the chance that he'd been waiting for, and so, after making his servants gather the essentials that he would need for a trip to the United States, Jiāoào and his small entourage started their journey.

On October 8th, they left his family's second home without informing anyone that he would be leaving and made their way to Shanghai. His plan was to book passage on a seafaring vessel that would take him to the United States. He was eager to claim his prize.

Unfortunately, in spite of his impatience to arrive in Phoenix and acquire his soon-to-be mate, Jiāoào found himself facing several unexpected delays.

"What do you mean no ships can set sail?" A growl gurgled from within his throat as he glared at Maddison, who had prostrated herself before him. "Well?!"

"I—th-there's a storm, Lord Jiāoào." Maddison's voice quivered as she spoke. Fear permeated her being. That was good. She should have known better than to present him with information that he didn't want to hear. "A-a hurricane. Th-they said it's too dangerous to set sail."

"Tch!"

Jiāoào paced back and forth, his face twitching in anger. He couldn't believe it! He was this close to having Lilian in his grasp, and he couldn't even get to her!

He took a deep breath. There was no need to get upset. So, he would have to wait a little bit longer before collecting his prize. All was not lost. He was a patient fox. He had waited several years to claim Lilian already; waiting a bit longer wouldn't kill him.

He looked down at the Water Kitsune and licked his lips.

While he waited to meet with his Lilian again, he would entertain himself with this one.

It was the least she could do for presenting him with such distressing information.

***

Saturday morning was surprisingly gloomy. The sun hid behind the clouds, concealing the bright rays normally associated with the desert state.

Kevin was once again sparring against the one he called Midget. It had been getting a little easier with repetition, though only a little. Midget, like most people, seemed to have a pattern to his attacks, and if he could discern what that pattern was, they could better defend themselves against him.

His eyes narrowed in fierce concentration, Kevin focused all his efforts on not getting his face caved in by the stronger man's limbs and also tried to determine what this man's attack pattern was.

A right straight came flying at him. Kevin sidestepped to the left, his movements just a little awkward. He tried stepping into his opponent's guard, but had to halt his momentum when a knee suddenly threatened to render him a soprano.

While moving backwards, he tripped over his own two feet. As he fell down, however, his left leg shot out and he hooked his foot on the underside of Midget's knee. When his back hit the ground, his momentum, combined with the strange maneuver, gave him the strength needed to yank Midget's feet out from under him.

Rolling backwards, Kevin eventually landed on his feet. He staggered two steps when he couldn't quite regain his balance, but his sparring partner was having the same problem due to his unorthodox attack. They both reclaimed their equilibrium at the same time, but it was Midget who reinitiated the spar, stepping into Kevin's guard and launching a one-two combination of right straight, left hook.

Kevin avoided the straight by stepping to the left, and the hook was evaded when he ducked. This would have been the perfect maneuver to respond with a powerful uppercut, which had been his plan all along... except Midget fought using Muay Thai, a kickboxing style that relied on knees and elbows as much as it did hands and feet. When Kevin ducked low, a large hand grabbed a fistful of his hair and he ended up having a meeting of the nose-on-knee kind.

Pain exploded in his nose, but Kevin managed to keep it together. He moved with the attack, rolling backwards, and came up on his feet.

He wasn't given much reprieve, as Midget was already coming in swinging. His vision became filled with a large fist. Eyes wide, Kevin tried to sidestep, but his left foot caught his right leg and he tripped.

Fortunately for Kevin, he had something to grab onto.

Midget's forearm.

"What the—whoa!"

Using his own fall as leverage, Kevin swung the much wider male around by the arm. While Midget was not launched far, he did end up flying a few good feet before landing on his stomach. Not wanting to give his opponent the opportunity to recover, Kevin rushed forward, intent on ending the mock-battle.

He soon discovered that Midget had no intention of losing.

Before Kevin knew what had happened, something that reminded him of a steel vice grabbed onto his leg. There was a momentary feeling of being weightless as he was yanked off the ground. Several seconds later, his stomach rose into his throat, and then his back hit the mat hard enough that all of the air left his lungs in a loud *whoosh!* of breath.

"Gu... hu..."

It was a familiar feeling, not having any air in his lungs. Kevin would even go so far as to say he'd gotten used to it. That still didn't make it any better, though.

"Hu... hack... uh..."

"I think I broke him." Midget idly scratched his left elbow.

"Whoops."

"Ng…"

"Those are some awfully weird noises you're making, bud."

Kevin wanted to tell Midget to piss off, but all that came out was a strange, gurgling noise that sounded sort of like, "murgle."

"Alright, that's enough for today." Kiara clapped her hands together and gestured at her three stooges. "You three can head home now."

"You got it, Kiara."

As the trio left, Kiara walked over to Kevin, who pushed himself into a sitting position and leaned back on his arms. Her business suit ruffled as she stepped in front of him, arms crossing as she looked at the young man with a critical eye.

"You're surprisingly clumsy for someone who runs so well."

By now Kevin had become accustomed to how blunt Kiara could be.

"T-that—is that really something you should be saying to your disciple?"

"I feel that honesty is the best policy. You won't get stronger if I coddle you." Kiara ruffled Kevin's hair, making him scowl. "However, I wouldn't worry too much. In fact, I think this can work to your benefit."

"You're saying that my clumsiness can be an advantage?"

"Anything can be an advantage if you know how to use it," Kiara retorted, to which Kevin made a face. Seeing his obviously befuddled expression, she elaborated. "The key is figuring out how to turn your weakness into your strength. Even simple things like your personality, or your natural propensity for tripping over your own two feet can become your strength if you know how. Heck, even the way you dress can give you an advantage against your enemies."

Kiara paused, allowing Kevin a moment to absorb her words.

"Take Kotohime for example; if you didn't know how skilled she was with that katana of hers, and just saw her just wandering around town, you'd probably assume she was easy prey, right?"

"I… I guess so."

"No one would expect a woman wearing clothes that look more suitable in ancient Japan to be capable of fighting. Yet she is one of the strongest yōkai I have ever met, easily on par with myself, and maybe even a little better."

Kevin was surprised by how much praise Kiara gave Kotohime. He didn't know the exact nature of their relationship, though he'd sometimes see them talking rather amiably. However, he also remembered Lilian's words about how inu and kitsune didn't mix, so their strange friendship seemed kind of odd.

But then again, both Kiara and Kotohime were odd individuals. For a species who enjoyed combat so much, Kiara didn't display much bloodlust. She always spoke with a mostly polite, if somewhat gruff, tone. He had never heard her badmouth anyone either.

Kotohime was just weird.

"You can do the same thing," Kiara continued. "Your unassuming nature and general clumsiness when fighting would easily fool someone into thinking you can't fight at all. They would underestimate you and suddenly 'bam!'" Kevin nearly jumped when Kiara smashed her left fist into the palm of her right hand. "You hit them right where it hurts!"

"That makes sense… I think."

Kiara raised an eyebrow. "You think?"

His cheeks turning red, Kevin squirmed under Kiara's stare. "W-well, I've seen some similar stuff happen in the anime I watch, so…"

"You and your anime," Kiara sighed. "What is it with kids these days?" Shaking her head, as if dispelling her bemusement, she waved a dismissive hand at him. "Anyway, we're done for today, so why don't you take a shower and head home?"

"Right."

After taking a shower, Kevin hopped on his bike and rode home, his mind full of deep thoughts—as well as daydreams about kicking ass and taking names.

Although, just whose name he was taking and whose ass he was kicking had yet to be seen.

***

When Kevin returned home it was to see that everyone was already prepped and ready to leave. It made him very glad that he'd had the forethought to pack some clothes in a gym bag so he could change after his beating—uh, workout.

"I can't believe we're going shopping for Halloween

costumes!"

"Yes, yes, Halloween trip. Hurrah, hurrah. Look, can we get going now?"

Lilian looked at her sister with large round eyes that seemed to be begging for a hug.

"Mou, aren't you excited, Iris? We're going costume shopping for our first Halloween ever!"

"Aw!" Iris squealed as she wrapped her arms around her sister's shoulders and rubbed her cheek against Lilian's hair. "You look so adorable when you're excited like this, Lily-pad."

"I-Iris! Stop hugging me like this! And don't call me Lily-pad!"

"Ara, ara." An amused Kotohime stopped Iris from further embarrassing her sister. "Please calm down, you two. While this is indeed something to be exuberant about, please try and save your enthusiasm for when we actually start shopping, ne?"

"Have you ever gone costume shopping, Lord Kevin?"

Kevin didn't think he'd ever get used to the way Kirihime (or Kotohime, for that matter) addressed him. He just didn't feel very lordly. He still answered her, however. "Plenty of times. I'm a human, remember? I grew up celebrating Halloween."

A small frown crossed Kevin's face, something that Kirihime did not fail to notice.

"Are you alright, Lord Kevin?" she asked, concern radiating from her voice. Kevin looked at her and smiled a bit. He really liked this woman. She was so much nicer than her sister.

"Yeah, I'm fine. I was just remembering something."

Kevin looked back to Lilian and Iris. Lilian was chatting her sister's ear off about what kind of costumes she wanted to try on, while the raven-haired kitsune merely watched her with an amused smile. He didn't think Iris was listening.

She's probably too busy staring at Lilian's chest.

Kevin absently eyed his mate's chest, watching it bounce and heave as she made wild hand gesticulations.

There could be no doubt that it was what Iris was staring at.

"What were you remembering?" Kirihime asked. "If you don't mind my asking."

Kevin turned away from his mate and her sister. "You know how my mom is always out of the country for her job, right? I never really got to celebrate Halloween with her because of that. Sure, we celebrated Halloween together when I was really little, but I don't remember those times that well. I can't even remember my mom ever taking me costume shopping. All throughout elementary school, I went shopping with Lindsay and her family. And when I was in middle school, I went with Eric and his dad."

There was a moment of silence as the group of kitsune looked at Kevin. This silence broke when Lilian grabbed his hand and beamed at him.

"Don't worry! Now that I'm here, you don't need to worry about not spending Halloween with your family. I'm your family now!"

"Lilian," Kevin felt his cheeks grow warm. He wondered if he would ever get used to the feelings she evoked in him.

Probably not.

"Ah. Camellia... Camellia will treat you like a son!"

"Uh..." Kevin didn't know if Camellia even knew how sons were supposed to be treated. "Thanks?"

"Tee-hee!"

"It may not be my place to say this," Kirihime placed a hand against her chest, her lips curving in a gentle arc, "but everyone here, including Lady Iris and my sister, see you as a part of our family. I don't know if this will make up for not having your mother around, but I do hope that you will eventually see us as your family one day."

Kevin felt a strange warmth pass through his chest as she spoke. It was bliss, ecstasy in every sense of the word, this strange but pleasant feeling. He allowed himself a smile. Strange as it may have seemed, these people... kitsune, really were almost like a family to him now.

Hard to believe that I've only known three of them for about two weeks.

"Hey, Kirihime! I hope you're not making a pass on my mate!"

Lilian wrapped her arms around Kevin's left arm and glared at Kirihime, whose wide eyes reminded him of water balloons.

"N-no! Of course not, Lady Lilian! I-I would never—I mean—Kevin is handsome but, you know, he's just too young. Ah! Not that being young is a bad thing," she assured Kevin, as if he needed some kind of reassurance. "It's just that you're too young for me. Hm-hm." She nodded her head. "Don't worry, Lady Lilian, I would never make a pass at your mate."

"Good."

"You know that you really don't need to worry about that, right?" Kevin whispered in Lilian's ear. "Even if she did like me, it wouldn't matter. I'm your mate, remember?"

"I know," Lilian whispered back. "I just wanted to watch her squirm a bit. It's funny."

"Huh…" After a moment, Kevin chuckled. "I guess you really are a kitsune."

"But of course." Lilian's smile epitomized mischief. "In any case, I wouldn't mind if she did make a pass at you, just so long as she recognizes that I'm your mate."

"Hm-mm… wait. What?"

"Nothing."

"Would you two stop whispering over there!?" An irate Iris stared daggers at the duo.

"Sorry," the two said in unison.

Under Kotohime's guidance, the group exited the apartment and locked the door behind them.

Because the mall was too far to walk, they would be taking a cab, which Kotohime somehow managed to get for them. Kevin hadn't even been aware that Kotohime knew how to use the phone, much less hire a cab. But then again, she was over 200 years old.

As they made their way down the stairs, Kevin observed the family of kitsune. Lilian appeared to be the most excited of the group. She wore a smile that went from ear to ear and had a bounce in her step. Camella also seemed pretty excited, but…

"Hawa! Halloween!"

The eldest of the group—even if she didn't act like it—rushed down the stairs with an enthusiasm that could not be denied.

"M-My Lady! Please do not jump around so much! You might—"

"HAWA!"

"—trip." Kirihime flinched as the person she served took a spill, falling down the stairs and landing in a heap of limbs, tails, and ears.

Kevin and Lilian winced. That had to hurt.

"By Inari's saggy scrotum, can't you be a little more graceful?"

"Hawa..."

***

Spirit was a Halloween store, though it looked more like a warehouse than a place that sold costumes. Large and rectangular, it sat near a crowded parking lot, a lone building located several hundred meters from a mall. Made of metal, the structure would normally be gleaming in the sunlight but instead appeared dull due to the cloud cover.

Christine and Lindsay were already there, waiting in the parking lot as they exited the cab. Lindsay wore the bright grin that was so typical of her. Christine looked bored, though Kevin thought he saw hints of excitement dancing in her eyes, restrained by her need to appear aloof.

"Hey, you two!" Kevin greeted as he strode up to them, Lilian by his side and Iris by hers. Behind them, the two maids made sure Camellia didn't try to wander off as they trailed after him.

"Hey yourself." Lindsay took one look at them and shook her head. "That's quite the group you've got there." She paused to lean in, as if sharing a conspiratorial secret. "Are they all... you know?"

"Yeah."

With Lindsay's opening, introductions were in order. They had all met Iris already, but neither of them had met Lilian's mom or Kirihime. While Lindsay greeted the group of kitsune with her usual friendliness, Christine remained silent. Her eyes were a mixture of cold and uncertainty, and the temperature around the yuki-onna had begun to plummet.

"So, this is your family," Lindsay eyed the unusual gathering of kitsune.

Lilian nodded. "My immediate family, yes."

"Uh huh." Lindsay eyed Camellia, whose toga did little to hide her voluptuous body. "No offense, Lilian, but I think I'm beginning to hate your genetics."

Lilian pouted. "That's not a very nice thing to say..."

"Jealousy is such an ugly emotion," Iris shook her head pityingly.

"You have no right to talk down to people about jealousy," Kevin said dryly, ignoring the furious glance the raven-haired vixen cast him.

Alex and Andrew arrived next. They were dropped off by their mother, a nice woman who owned a bakery. She would often give Kevin cookies when he visited, which was why he didn't visit very often. Too many cookies weren't very good for the body.

The moment Alex and Andrew saw the large group of beautiful females standing around Kevin, the pair dropped to their knees in worship.

"Oh, wise master, please take us under your wing and teach us your womanizing ways!"

"Shut up, you two," a thoroughly shamefaced Kevin spat. "I don't want to deal with this crap so early in the morning. And get off the ground. Everyone's staring at us because of the scene you're making!"

Justin showed up after the twins, his father, a quiet and unassuming man dropping him off before leaving. The dull-faced boy took one look at all of the people gathered, and then cracked a small smile.

"… Doki-doki waku-waku…"

Needless to say, the boy got nothing but odd looks from everyone.

The last person to show was Eric. The perverted high schooler was not dropped off by his parents—neither of them owned a military style Humvee, especially not one with a large painting of Alice from *Monster Girl Quest* on it.

Eric stepped out of the vehicle, a pair of shades on his face. Kevin wondered if his friend was trying to look cool. It wouldn't have worked regardless, but it failed epically here. The moment Eric left the large military vehicle with the image of a super-sexy lamia emblazoned on its hood, he froze, the glasses falling from his face to reveal dishpan-sized eyes. He surveyed the crowd before him, taking in the curves of those present with a stupid look on his face.

Then he started drooling like an idiot.

"And this is your best friend," a grinning Iris said to Kevin, who merely facepalmed.

Eric wasn't alone that day. Clad in a black tube top, booty shorts and sandals, Heather Grant could have easily competed with the kitsune present in the beauty department.

"Hmmm… I like this woman's style," Iris muttered, mostly to herself.

"What's she doing here?" asked a mildly annoyed Lilian.

"You didn't think I could allow my young apprentice to go costume shopping without me, did you?" Heather's question was obviously rhetorical, as the woman spoke before anyone else could answer. "The number of sexy costumes in this store, the ability to peek on women while they're changing into those costumes…" She held a clenched hand up to her face, her eyes igniting with passion. "There's no way I could allow my impressionable apprentice enter such a place unprepared."

Like the ardent flames of a powerful wildfire, a flickering orange aura engulfed the young woman. It very much reminded Kevin of the main character from *Doragon Fighters X.*

While the others focused on Heather, their expressions ranging from bemused to "what the fuck is wrong with this woman?" Eric, who'd still been gawking at the women around him, exploded into action.

"Where have you sex-bots been all my life—GU!"

Everyone switched from staring at Heather to Eric after the woman gave her apprentice a chop to the back of the head, sending him face-first into the concrete in a twitching sprawl of limbs.

"Lesson number forty-two, my young apprentice. Control your lustful urges and wait for the right moment to strike."

"Ugh… got it…"

***

Spirit was a very large store. While it looked big on the outside, it somehow appeared even more massive on the inside. The floors were made of polished granite, while the walls gleamed with the color of steel.

The group stepped into the store as one, and Lilian, easily the most excited of the group, couldn't help but stare at their new surroundings with bedazzled eyes.

"Wow…." Lilian whispered. "It's so big."

"That's what she said—ouch!"

"Don't be such a pig," Christine retracted her hand from the back of Eric's head, which now had a massive welt covered in a layer of ice. "Idiot."

"Now, now, that is no way to treat my apprentice." Heather

admonished the scowling yuki-onna. "Unless, of course, you caught him peeping on you. Then he deserves to get beaten for getting caught."

"Hey!"

"So, what do you think we should get?" Alex asked his brother. "Matching costumes or go our separate ways?"

"We should definitely go our separate ways," Andrew determined. "I have no desire to match costumes with you."

"You're an asshole, you know that?"

"Ha! The only ass I'm seeing is you!"

"You wanna take this outside?!"

"Ara, ara." A smiling Kotohime stopped their fight in its tracks by shoving her katana between them. "There is no need to fight so early in the morning now, is there?"

The twins gulped.

"Kevin," Lilian looked at her mate, "what kind of costumes do you think we should get?"

Kevin cast her a sideways glance. "Weren't you the one who had all the costume ideas?"

Her cheeks turning a lovely shade of pink, Lilian drew circles on the polished granite floor with her left foot. "I do have a few ideas," she mumbled lowly, "but now that I'm here, I, well, I'm not really sure where to start."

Kevin felt his own cheeks become warm. Lilian's innocence was truly one of her most endearing qualities.

"Ah, well, I was hoping we could find costumes for couples, or something," Kevin admitted.

"Um," Lilian nodded and smiled at him, "I like that idea, so I'll follow your lead."

"Then I guess I'll have to do my best not to lead you astray."

The two shared a matching smiles as they gazed into each other's eyes.

"Someone please gag me."

Their moment was ruined by an obnoxious voice and several gagging noises.

Kevin and Lilian turned to glare at Iris, who looked unrepentant as she gave them a sickly sweet smile.

The group soon split up. Alex and Andrew went in one direction and Kotohime, on a suggestion from Kevin, followed after them to keep the two from fighting. Heather dragged Eric behind her after claiming that, as her apprentice, he had to wear something that matched her. Christine and Lindsay also wandered off together, though it looked more like the tomboy had decided to drag the snow-maiden off against her will. That left just him, Lilian, Iris, Kirihime and Camellia.

"M-My Lady? My Lady, where did you go? My Lady!"

Correction, it was just him, Lilian and Iris. Camellia had disappeared, though none of them knew when, and Kirihime quickly rushed off to try and find her wayward mistress.

"So…" Kevin glanced at the two sisters. "I think we should stop by the couples section first."

"I agree," Lilian nodded.

"Whatever," Iris waved one hand through the air while the other went to her hip. "I don't care where we start, so long as I get to see my Lily-pad dressed in something cute."

Lilian's red cheeks bulged like someone had shoved helium into them. "Why won't you stop calling me that?"

"Because it's fun," Iris admitted, tossing her sister a wicked grin.

***

"Alright, my young apprentice, it is time for your next lesson."

"You mean we're not going to get our costumes, Master?"

"That can wait. This is far more important. I may not get another chance to impart this lesson on you, so I need to teach it to you while we have the chance."

Eric and Heather stood facing each other in one of the many aisles. They were near the changing rooms, which could be easily discerned due to the shift from wall to curtains.

"If there is one thing I have learned about Halloween, it is that women wear some of the kinkiest outfits you can ever imagine during this time of year," Heather lectured her young apprentice. "And if you are skilled enough, then you can watch them change into those kinky costumes. No joke. I remember watching this one woman trying to dress herself in some kind of bondage cosplay or something; it had all these straps and stuff. It really was freaky, but kinda hot, too."

Heather placed her hands on the young pervert's shoulders.

"And that is why we must seize this opportunity! This is a

once in a lifetime chance to practice peeping on women while they get dressed in sexy cosplay! Carpe diem, my young apprentice, you understand?"

Eric looked up at his teacher, hearts in his eyes and tears creating streaks down his face. He could not help but be awed by this woman, who had more knowledge about peeping than even he, an entity of salacious desires. Truly, Heather was a magnificent, wonderful master.

"Yes, Master!"

"Excellent! Now let us be off!"

***

Lindsay traveled along the western wall, where most of the female costumes were located. She held onto a slightly dazed Christine who, after nearly five minutes of struggling, had finally settled down.

"What do you think I should get?" Lindsay asked, her eyes scanning the costumes as they slowly strolled down the aisle. "I want to go with something classic, like a zombie or a dead cheerleader, but I'm thinking those are too cliche…" She trailed off when she realized that Christine wasn't paying attention to her. "Christine? Hello?" She waved a hand in front of the girl's face. "Earth to Christine."

"Hmm?" Christine blinked, her mind coming back to the real world. "I'm sorry, were you saying something?"

Lindsay gave her friend a look. There was an odd glint in her eyes that Christine just did not like. "Thinking about Kevin again?"

"W-w-w-what the—WHAT THE HELL ARE YOU TALKING ABOUT?! I-I-I—that's not—I'm not thinking about that idiot!"

Lindsay watched Christine explode in an almost literal sense. Her face turned bright blue and steam poured out of her ears, becoming a strange foggy mist that crystallized as the temperature rapidly dropped to below freezing.

"Are you still trying to hide your feelings? Didn't you already admit to pretty much everyone except Kevin that you like him?" Her words made Christine blush that much harder. "Look, I know this isn't easy for you, but it's just us right now. You really don't need to hide your feelings around me. I'm not going to laugh at them. I once had a crush on Kevin, too, you know."

"I-I know that." Christine pressed her hands against her face, as if doing so would hide the icy hue of her cheeks. "It's just—it's hard for me. I've never—I mean I'm not that sociable."

"I can tell."

Christine glared at Lindsay, but there was no real heat in it. "Look, it's just not easy for me, okay? I'm not used to having friends and I'm certainly not used to expressing my feelings about the... the boy that, um, that I kinda like... and stuff."

"And how do you feel? When you're around Kevin, I mean."

"My body feels hot and cold at the same time," Christine admitted quietly. "Like my bakeneko side is warring with my yuki-onna side for control over my body. It's frustrating. It feels good, but at the same time, it's really irritating."

"Hm. Well, I don't know much about the whole yōkai thing." Lindsay shrugged. "That stuff is beyond me, and I'm not a Japanese nut like Kevin and the others. But, it seems to me like you're confused about your own feelings. I mean, you don't even know why you like him in the first place, right?"

"... No."

"Did you just look away from me?"

"N-no. Of course not."

"You did. You're looking away from me." Squinting as she leaned over, Lindsay got right in the startled Christine's face. "Is there something going on that I should know about?"

"O-o-o-of course not!" Christine's voice came out as a pitiful squeak. "I-i-it's not like I knew him years before coming to Arizona or anything! W-w-w-why the hell are you asking me something like that?!"

"I didn't ask you something like that," Lindsay's statement seeped amusement, "but it's pretty interesting to know that you two knew each other before you came to Arizona. Where did you two meet, if you don't mind my asking?"

Christine was silent for a moment. Her cheeks flushed a deeper shade of blue bordering on purple.

"... Alaska."

"Alaska, huh?" Lindsay hummed. "I do remember when Kevin took a trip to Alaska with his mom. I think it was four years ago?"

"Five," Christine said softly.

"Right, five years ago," Lindsay amended. "That would mean you were both ten when you two met." She paused, her head tilting for a second before nodding. "Yeah, that sounds about right. Kevin wasn't really shy back then. I actually remember him being really outgoing."

"He was."

"But you know, a lot can change in five years," Lindsay continued. "The Kevin you used to know isn't really the same Kevin who exists right now. He's different. Shyer. Less confident. Though I'll admit he's getting better. Still, maybe you should learn more about this Kevin, rather than relying on your memories of what he used to be like. You might find that the Kevin from your past and the present one are two completely different people."

"There's a lot more to it than that," Christine said. "If it was simply a matter of him being different, or of my feelings dissipating with time, then I wouldn't be having so much trouble."

Lindsay tilted her head curiously. "Then, what is the problem?"

"I-it's not important," Christine muttered. "Let's just drop the subject for now, okay?"

Lindsay looked like she might argue further, but then she shrugged and gave Christine an indulgent smile. "Sure, if that's what you want."

"It is."

The conversation ended as the two renewed their search for costumes.

***

"My Lady? My Lady, where are you?" Kirihime wandered the store, calling for her mistress. She was quite worried. Incredibly so. The store was large, and with her mistress' penchant for wandering off, she could have been anywhere. "Oh, dear. This is not good. My Lady, where did you go?"

Her mistress hadn't always been this air-headed and clumsy. Kirihime remembered a time when her mistress had been one of the most amazing kitsune she'd ever known; kind and compassionate, but also possessing a mischievous side and a fierce determination.

She did not know when exactly the change started. Her

mistress hadn't just woken up one day and suddenly become an air-head. It had been a slow, insidious process, one that must have started decades before anyone ever realized what was happening.

"My Lady Camellia, please answer me!"

Kirihime eventually found her mistress staring at some of the costumes.

Relief washing through her more swiftly than a river's current, Kirihime ran up to her mistress. "My Lady, there you are!" she exclaimed. "P-please don't wander off like that anymore."

"Oh! Kirikiri!" Camellia exclaimed, as if just now noticing the woman by her side. With a childish grin, she pointed to the costume she'd been staring at. "Don't you think you would look great in this costume?"

"U-uh." Taken off guard by the comment, Kirihime found herself at a slight loss for words. "W-well, I guess so… maybe?" She looked at the costume in question and had to admit; it did look good. It was a fairy costume; a shimmering blue dress with a sweetheart neckline, lace up bodice and a multi-layered skirt. It also had black garters attached to the skirt. It somewhat reminded her of her French maid outfit, only blue and black instead of black and white—and it had wings. And the headpiece had been replaced with one made of flowers.

"Camella thinks Kirikiri would look really good in a costume like that."

The enthusiasm being displayed by her mistress proved to be too much for her. With a gentle smile she asked, "Would you like me to try it on?"

"Um!" Camellia nodded joyfully.

Heaving a resigned sigh, Kirihime took the costume and entered one of the changing stalls. Once there, she stripped out of her clothes.

With prodigious use of the single tail she let slither out from underneath her outfit, she undid the zipper in the back. The dress fell away, revealing her voluptuous body. While not quite as curvy as her sister, Kirihime was still quite proud of her 97 centimeters of bust.

The changing room, while small, had a mirror that allowed Kirihime to see her reflection. Looking over her body, she absently hefted her chest, covered by a black lace bra.

"They feel heavier for some reason," she murmured to herself. "Odd, they shouldn't be growing. I'm not in mating season."

Kitsune ceased to grow after gaining their third tail. They stopped aging and their bodies stopped changing. That was because the third tail was when kitsune reached the peak of their physical and mental development, when they went from being adolescent kitsune to adults.

There was only one exception to this rule.

Mating season.

Because kitsune were, at their base, foxes, they had a mating season in which they would go into heat and seek out a mate. All animals had the instinctual desire to procreate, and kitsune were no different. During the time they went into heat, a kitsune's breasts grew as a result. This was done in an effort to attract a potential mate. After all, few men could resist the call of big breasts.

"Oh, dear. I hope I'm not gaining weight."

Kirihime looked herself over some more to see if she might be packing a few extra pounds somewhere. Kirihime trained and hunted often enough that she shouldn't have had this problem. However, she hadn't been able to do a lot of hunting since coming to Arizona.

"It doesn't look like I've gained any weight." Worrying her lower lip she turned around and looked at her backside. It didn't appear to have changed any. It remained just as tight and firm as always, so then, what was the... problem...?"

"Huuu..."

...?

"He he he..."

Kirihime cocked her head. What was that noise?

"Oh yeah... the stuff..."

There it was again! Where was that coming from?

"You... apprentice?... told.... kinky..."

Kirihime's ears twitched. She looked around the room, trying to ascertain where those voices were coming from. They were close, but sounded muffled, as if there was a layer of thick cloth, or perhaps a wall, separating them.

"Do... take..."

"... More... quiet... hear you..."

Narrowing her eyes, Kirihime looked up and saw a grate--a

grate with two pairs of eyes peering out from behind it.

"Crap! She saw us! Retreat! Retreat!"

"Oh, no you don't!"

All three of her tails suddenly appeared as Kirihime dropped her disguise. They extended at incredible speeds, spearing through the grate and grabbing onto the first thing they could--a leg.

"Oh, God! She's got me! Master! Help!"

"Sorry, my young apprentice, but you know how these things work. You should have been faster. I'm afraid you're on your own."

"No!"

It didn't take much effort to yank Eric out of the vents. The metal was smooth and there was nothing to find purchase on. In a few short seconds, the young man was wrapped up in some sort of furry bondage that would have probably been really hot, were it not for the look in Kirihime's eyes. Gone was the warmth, the compassion. Instead, her dark eyes were dead, blank, and emotionless in a way that made Eric tremble in abject fear.

"Um... mercy?"

In response to his words, Kirihime pulled a knife out of her Extra Dimensional Storage Space.

It was a really big knife.

A really, really big knife.

And it had serrated edges.

Eric whimpered.

***

Kevin walked with Lilian and Iris as they traversed the circumference of the store. They had found plenty of costumes: a sexy police officer and a convict, Harlequin Alice and the Mad Hatter, Harley Quinn and The Joker, a monkey and a banana... Kevin had found the Mr. and Ms. Pac Man to be interesting. However, none of them really stood out to either him or Lilian.

"I don't know why you two are getting so into this," Iris said as the couple stared at a Spartan warrior costume. "It's just some stupid human celebration, and these costumes look like crap."

"Muu," Lilian pouted at her sister, "do you have to be so negative all the time? So what if these costumes aren't the best? It's not the costumes that matter. This is the first time Kevin and I are going shopping for our Halloween costumes together. That's all that matters."

Iris sighed. Her sister was so naive. Still…

"I guess you have a point. And besides, I do think I would look rather good in this outfit." Iris pulled down a ruffled dress with a very low cut. She put the dress against her body and showed it off to Kevin, winking to try and get a rise out of him. "Don't you think so, Kevin?"

Kevin looked Iris up and down for a second, considering the question with the seriousness it deserved. "If you're thinking of dressing up as a barmaid, then you should probably wear darker colors."

Walking over to the rack where Iris had found the costume, he completely missed the shocked look that overcame her features. Lilian didn't, though, and she sent Iris a smug grin, as if to say, "did you really think that would work?"

Iris returned her sister's look with a frown.

"Something like… this one." Kevin pulled a black and red version of the costume off the rack. He then handed it to Iris, who stared at the costume with the same look she would give an amorphous alien entity. "I think that would look much better on you. The darker colors go with the mysterious allure you possess."

"Oh?" The subliminally divine curve of her lips reeked of amusement. Sinful red eyes narrowed in sensual seduction. Kevin's body stiffened as he found himself trapped within the vixen's gaze, enraptured by her smile. "You think I'm mysterious and alluring, do you?" she raised her right hand and placed it on his chest. Kevin shuddered as a thrill like sticking his fingers in a socket passed through him. "What a wonderful gentleman you are, to pay me such high compliments. It's that sort of treatment that could make a girl fall for you, you know."

"I… is that so…" Kevin felt himself falling deeper into her eyes. Why was it getting so hard to think? How come he couldn't… why was he…

A hand covered his eyes.

Everything became suddenly and startlingly clear, like a fog had been lifted from him mind.

"Why don't you get changed into that costume, Iris?" Lilian's voice. The hand must have been hers.

"Aw, come on, Lily-pad. Don't be upset. I was just playing

around."

"You were not playing around. Now go and get dressed," Lilian hissed. She sounded angry.

"Tch. Fine, fine, I can take a hint. I know when I'm not wanted."

Kevin heard the sound of footsteps getting further away. When he couldn't hear them anymore, the hand left his eyes and he could see again, which meant he could also see the green eyes mere inches from his own, staring at him in concern.

"Are you okay?" Lilian's voice was thick with worry.

"I... yes... I'm fine." Kevin shook his head. It still felt a little foggy. "What... what happened? When Iris stared at me, I felt..."

"Aroused? Turned on? Like Iris was the sexiest thing in existence? Like her eyes were gateways into a world of unfathomable pleasure?"

"Uh, yes." Kevin paused. "Except that last one. Her eyes kind of always look like that."

"Hmm, true enough."

Lilian looked like she wanted to say something, but didn't quite know how to say it, as if she was worried it might change something between them.

"Lilian?"

She sighed. "Iris used an enchantment when she was looking at you."

Kevin sucked in a breath. "You mean...?"

"Yes. It's called **Call of Ecstasy**. It's an enchantment unique to my sister. While there are many techniques that can be used to arouse or increase the lust of a target, they are mostly done through the use of pheromones. My sister's technique is different in that it doesn't use pheromones at all, but stimulates the part of the brain dealing with desires and specifically targets a person's lust. It's incredibly effective and almost impossible to break because it's not a chemically-induced reaction from an outside force, but a reaction from directly inside of the brain. It feels natural, like that's how it's meant to be, and so your brain doesn't interpret it as something harmful or wrong."

"I see." Kevin closed his eyes. "That's a pretty frightening technique."

"It's strange, though." Lilian's face had scrunched up in a

rather cute expression of confusion. "Iris has never used it seriously before. I once asked her why, and she told me it's because she doesn't need to use it to seduce someone. I think the only time I've seen her use it was on a three-tails the matriarch introduced. He tried to get grabby with me and she turned him into a slobbering mess."

Kevin scratched the back of his head. "Maybe it's because she wasn't trying to seduce me?"

"Eh?"

"I don't think Iris was using that technique to seduce me." Kevin tried to put his thoughts into words. "I think she just wanted to hurt me for being so close to you."

"T-that is a possibility," Lilian said. "I didn't think of that. Anyway, why don't we continue—"

"OH, GOD! GET AWAY! GET AWAY FROM ME!"

Kevin and Lilian's conversation was interrupted by Eric, who blitzed past them, his clothing ripped and several cuts visible on his flesh. They blinked when Kirihime also ran past them, chasing after Eric. They blinked again when they noticed that she was carrying a bloody knife in one hand.

"Please come back, young man. I still haven't finished punishing you."

"WHAT DO YOU MEAN YOU HAVEN'T FINISHED PUNISHING ME?! I'M BLEEDING!"

"You are not bleeding nearly enough for my tastes."

Eric soon disappeared around one of the aisles. Kirihime followed. While they could no longer see them anymore, the young couple could still hear them, and what they heard was disturbing.

"Oh, dear. It looks like you've run into a dead end."

"N-now, hold up, miss. Let's not do anything hasty now. Y-you can't just cut me up. It's illegal."

"So is peeping."

"Urk! T-t-that is true. Ah-ha… hahahaha! L-look, how about I just, uh, apologize and we let bygones be bygones, ne?"

"Oh no, I am afraid that just will not do." The sound of a blade sliding against metal echoed ominously in their ears. Eric squeaked. "You see, while I am quite proud of my body, I have a very strong dislike of being peeped on. It's insensitive, rude, and has caused many women to gain a strong distrust towards men. It is people like you who cause these problems. Your kind are the worst."

Despite the situation, Kevin pressed the palm of his right hand into his face. "Honestly, Eric. Do you really have to be so…"

"Perverted? Lecherous? Salacious? Hentai?" Lilian offered several very apt words to describe Eric.

"All of the above."

"Therefore," Kirihime continued talking, "in order to properly educate you on how to treat a lady, I believe that a little physical reinforcement is needed to… get my point across."

Looks of alarm spread across his and Lilian's faces.

"L-look, I-I-I'm sorry, alright? I—OH, GOD" Eric wailed. "WHAT ARE—NO! PLEASE NO! GET AWAY FROM—OH, DEAR SWEET—AHH!—P-PLEASE! HAVE MERCYYYYYYYYYYAAAAAHHHH!"

As Eric's voice trailed off into a series of agonized moans and groans, which soon disappeared altogether, leaving only an eerie silence, Kevin looked at Lilian.

"Would it be wrong of me if I decide to pretend I didn't hear any of that?"

Lilian thought about it for a moment, and then slowly shook her head. "I don't think so."

"Good."

***

It took a long time to travel from China to Arizona--two whole weeks, in fact--but at last, on October 15th, he had finally arrived.

Arizona, the state where his Lilian was currently residing with some inbred ape. Jiāoào wrinkled his nose in disgust. What his prize could possibly see in some filthy human was beyond him.

The chain in his hand clinked, the tension increasing. Frowning, he swiftly and brutally tugged on it, earning a pained rasp from the person whose neck it was attached to.

"I wouldn't move around too much, if I were you. You're already on thin ice for not being able to please me like the others. Don't push your luck," he said, not turning his head to look at the person he had addressed. He could see her just fine in the reflection of the window.

With her red hair in complete disarray, Maddison had never looked so defeated. Her eyes were blank, dead to the world, despite the tears leaking from them. Likewise, her arms were tied together with special fibers made from jorogumo silk, and a chain was attached to a metal collar around her neck. The chain went quite well with her maid outfit. He really did have to compliment himself on her wardrobe.

They'd gotten a number of looks from the humans they'd been forced to deal with while traveling. One of the humans who saw them even had the audacity to call the police and try to report him for abuse.

What right did those lousy humans have to reprimand him for what he did with his toys? They were just a bunch of lowly apes.

Jiāoào was a firm believer in yōkai superiority. They were the stronger race, the more intelligent species. Yōkai, and kitsune in particular, had it all; power, intelligence, abilities beyond mortal comprehension, and the longevity needed to truly master those abilities. What did humans have? Nothing. They only had their technology, which they thought was enough to protect them from beings like himself.

Truly, humans were a pathetic race.

With an air of disdain, Jiāoào observed his new, temporary home. It was disgustingly bare and much too small. The house, if it could even be called such, couldn't have more than fifteen rooms, and some of those rooms were even connected. Who'd ever heard of the sitting room being connected to the kitchen like that? Not only was it tiny and lacking any sort of decorations befitting a kitsune of his status, but the bed was miniscule. How could he be expected to enjoy his playthings properly in such a small bed?

"You see, Maddison?" Jiāoào finally turned his head to look down at the woman by his feet. She really did look quite miserable. "This is what you get for not finding me proper accommodations." With a *tsk* of disappointment, he smashed his heel into her back, eliciting a wail. "And you wonder why I am always comparing you to my Lilian. Not only do you lack her beauty, but you clearly lack her brilliance as well."

He looked back out the window, ignoring the muted sobs of pain. It was no less than she deserved. Everything wrong that had happened during this trip was her fault.

"I hope my other servants prove to be more useful than you. They are, after all, the ones that I have tasked with finding everything out they can about my Lilian and her living situation, as well as her... human toy."

Jiāoào grimaced. He refused to call that human her mate. His Lilian clearly did not know what she was doing. That, or she'd been brainwashed. Why else would a kitsune of her stature and ability be with a lowly waste of ape-flesh?

"I really do hope they return soon. Still..." His lips curled as he looked down at the girl. His two tails wrapped around Maddison, who tried to struggle but no longer possessed the strength to fight him. "... I suppose I shall just have to find some way to kill time while I wait."

As wails of pain turned into cries of agony, Jiāoào thought about his Lilian. Soon, she would be his, and then she would be properly broken.

***

Iris was not a morning person. She had never enjoyed waking up early, preferring instead to sleep in until around noon.

Too bad Kevin did not believe in doing the same. It was bad enough that he'd gone and stolen her sister from her. Couldn't he have the decency to at least stay in bed until she wanted to get up—or at least be a little quieter?

Her sleep-deprived eyes glared balefully at the ignorant Kevin as he put on his sneakers and exited the apartment, the *click* of the door being locked following his departure. It was only after Kevin left to do Inari-knows-what that Iris realized something. If Kevin was no longer sleeping, then it meant he wasn't in bed. And if he wasn't in bed, it meant Lilian was currently alone.

Several seconds later, an excited Iris wandered into Kevin's bedroom. She sat down on the bed, her added weight causing Lilian to shift and tighten her grip on the pillow she held. Lying on her side, the redhead's sensual curves were visible yet hidden beneath the covers.

As Iris watched her beautiful sister's sleeping face, a sense of longing swept through her. How long had it been since she and Lilian had slept together? Five years? Six? The matriarch had not approved of how close they were, claiming it would ruin their chances of finding a good mate. Iris snorted. That woman had just wanted to set her sister up with some douchewad from the Shénshèng Clan in order to gather more power to herself.

175

Reaching out with her left hand, Iris ran her fingers through Lilian's hair. Her fraternal twin mumbled something incoherent and shifted in her sleep again.

"I… I love you," Iris whispered. The words hurt for some reason. A tight pain entered her chest, constricting her like a snake coiled around its next meal. She held back tears she could not explain. "So much…"

"*Kill…*"

A cold chill swept through her arm, coalescing at her fingertips. Her eyes went wide in terror when she noticed that her fingernails had become tinged with a distinct ebony color.

NO! Iris pulled her hand back hastily. She gritted her teeth, struggling against a force that could not be seen, heard or distinguished; an intangible urge to destroy that which she cherished most. *I won't you let you take her!*

Unable to stand in her sister's presence without feeling the disgusting, implacable urge to stain the bed in Lilian's blood, Iris bid a hasty retreat from the bedroom.

The apartment was not silent, Iris realized. While she had not noticed, Kotohime was already up and preparing breakfast. Kirihime had also woken up and could be seen on the balcony hanging up clothes.

Iris went into the washroom, where all of the extra towels were kept. Maybe a shower to rinse off the accumulated sweat would help her regain her bearings.

As she neared the restroom, the sound of the shower running caught her attention.

***

Kevin rode his bike and tossed newspapers onto the driveways of the homes he passed. He shivered and took his hands off the handles of his bike long enough to zip his jacket closed, keeping October's chill from seeping into his bones.

Riding around and delivering newspapers was getting easier, Kevin had noticed. He wondered if this meant he was getting stronger. He hoped so. All that exercising and all those sparring sessions had to be doing something.

After he had finished delivering newspapers, Kevin arrived back at the distribution center where his boss, Davin Monstrang, presented him with the money he'd made.

"Here," the monstrously-sized man grunted, pressing a wad of bills into Kevin's hand. It wasn't much, about $50 all told, but that would give him enough money for what he had planned today. "Try not to spend it all in one place, brat."

Kevin rolled his eyes. His boss never changed. How many times had he heard Davin Monstrang say those exact same words? It had to be a couple hundred at least.

"Yes, sir."

Kevin was about to leave, his hand was even on the handle, when Monstrang's voice called out to him.

"I hear you've been keeping some unusual company." Kevin froze. "It's not my place to tell you not to get involved with people like them, but I do recommend remaining wary, especially around that mate of yours."

Kevin worked his mouth silently, his mind trying to grasp the immensity of that statement. Finally…

"Did you just…" He paused, then shook his head. "No, you know what? I don't want to know."

Kevin left the distribution center and rode home, his mind awhirl. He arrived at his apartment to find Kotohime cooking breakfast. Her kimono was different that day; a dark velvet made to look like the night sky. Starting from the hem and traveling up in an artistic display was what Kevin recognized as a depiction of the Milky Way Galaxy. He did not know if the presentation was astrologically correct, but he found it stunning nonetheless.

"Morning, Kotohime."

"Good morning, Kevin-sama."

"You're not making a traditional Japanese breakfast today." It wasn't a question.

"Indeed I am not. Iris has been complaining about the lack of variety in my cuisine. Again. I have decided to try my hand at making something new." Her lips twitched and, for just an instant, Kevin thought she was smiling at him. "I do hope that you, Lilian-sama and everyone else will enjoy it."

"Hm!" Kevin nodded. "I'm sure we will. You're an excellent chef." There it was again; that strange twitch. "Do you mind if I ask you a question?"

"Of course not."

"Thank you. I noticed Kirihime is hanging our laundry out to dry."

"Indeed she is. Is that a problem?"

"Not really, no. It's just… well, she does know that we have a dryer for that, doesn't she?"

Kotohime's conciliating smile put him at ease, oddly enough. Wasn't this the same woman who had threatened to clean his entrails with her katana if he didn't make a decision about his relationship with Lilian?

"I am afraid that you'll have to forgive my sister. She is not used to living in the human world. Most of the technology we have is very outdated. She doesn't even know how to use a washing machine, so you can't expect her to know how to use the dryer."

Kevin didn't really know what to say to that, so he changed the subject. "I see. Well, I think I'm just going to take a quick shower." He prepared to move off before a thought made him pause. "No one else is using the shower, are they?"

"Not to the best of my knowledge."

"Good."

It turned out the restroom was indeed empty—thank the gods for small miracles. After turning the water onto its hottest setting, Kevin stripped out of his clothes and entered the shower. Pressing his palms flat against the tiled wall, he allowed the warm spray to ease the tension and soreness in his muscles.

Kevin never heard the door click open and close. He did feel the pair of naked breasts pressing into his back, however.

Emitting a squeak akin to that of a frightened mouse caught by a tiger, Kevin scrambled away from the breasts. Unfortunately, the tub was small and slippery, and thus the inevitable happened.

He tumbled out of the bathtub when his legs hit the lip, landing on his back and cracking his head against the floor. Stars swam in his vision as an intense pain caused his head to explode in agony. He lay there, blinking and trying to stop the incessant rattling of his brain, and eventually succeeded.

A part of him wished he hadn't.

Kevin had seen many a sexy thing in recent times; Lilian wearing his clothes as nightwear, Lilian in skimpy lingerie, Lilian naked, Lilian in the shower naked. Yes. He'd seen enough sexy things that he could honestly say that Justin Timberlake didn't know the true meaning of bringing sexy back. Kevin had seen so much sexy that he'd been practically desensitized.

None of his past experiences could have prepared him for what he saw now.

She stood above him, bereft of clothing, her long raven hair sticking erotically to her skin. Droplets of water trailed down her body; over her breasts, her stomach, her hips and legs before dipping into the crevice between her glorious thighs. While Kevin had seen Lilian naked plenty of times, there was something intrinsically different between Lilian and her fraternal twin, something that he couldn't comprehend but understood instinctively.

Lilian, for all her otherworldly, inhuman beauty, was surprisingly innocent. Even when trying to seduce him, the girl retained an unusual sense of purity. Because of that, while everything she did had undeniable charm and sexiness, it didn't really hold a candle to the vision of otherworldly seduction standing before him.

Everything Iris did, from the way she cocked her hips, to how she crossed her arms under her bust with the obvious intention of bringing attention to her breasts, and even her facial expressions were designed to draw people's eyes to her. There was a strange sort of animalistic attraction to her that Lilian simply couldn't compete with.

"Now there's a reaction I wasn't expecting." Iris' sinfully sensual lips curved with wicked cunning. "How cute."

"I-I—what are you doing in here?!"

"The door wasn't locked, so I thought I'd invite myself in." Kevin knew that he had locked the door upon entering, which meant she had purposefully picked the lock and was lying to him. "You don't have a problem with that, do you?"

Kevin wanted to tell her that he did have a problem with her actions, a very big one. But he couldn't. His mouth wasn't working. It wouldn't even move. In fact, the moment they made eye contact, all thoughts tried to vanish from his mind like a cosplayer dressed as Miku Hatsune running from a horde of fanboys at an anime convention. All that remained was this woman, this creature of carnal desire.

One thought managed to penetrate the haze clouding his mind; a call for action. Kevin closed his eyes, a vain attempt to keep himself from responding to her. He'd been enraptured the moment their eyes met.

"Open your eyes." Responding to the command without a second's thought, Kevin snapped his eyes back open. Iris smiled. "That's better; we can't hold a proper conversation if you're not even willing to look at me."

With an unusual amount of grace for such a simple action, Iris stepped out of the tub and knelt beside him. Kevin struggled to think, to do something, anything. But he couldn't. Thoughts slipped through his grasp like water in his hands, and taking action was impossible when his muscles refused to work.

"W-what is…"

"Uh, uh, uh." She placed a delicate finger on his lips. "There's no need to think. All you need to do is feel. And see."

Kevin's pupils dilated as the blood rushed to his eyes… and he saw. He saw himself and this vixen in the heat of passion. He saw her riding him, her sharp nails raking against his chest and drawing blood. He saw himself, shoving her against the wall and brutally pounding into her. He saw and saw and saw, and there were so many scenes that he was seeing; of sex and violence and things that not even Eric in his freakiest state could imagine. It was too much. It was way too much. He couldn't… couldn't…

"Just let go…" a voice whispered in his ear. Warm breath hit his skin. Kevin shuddered, which intensified when a set of teeth gently nibbled on his earlobe.

"Nggg… gu…"

"Struggling is pointless," the voice whispered seductively, "just give in."

Kevin thought about doing just that. Why was he even struggling in the first place? It felt so good, this lust; it was incredible.

The moment his mind began slipping away to embrace the dark feelings, animalistic attraction and carnal desires, an image speared through the haze clouding his mind; of red hair and green eyes, of a beautiful girl who looked like she'd come straight out of a fairytale.

"My name is Lilian Pnéyma, but you may call me Lilly, or anything else you would prefer."

Lilian. That name. He remembered that name, and those

words. It was back when he and Lilian had first met.

"However, I would be particularly pleased if you called me You Sexy Thing, You."

Ugh. He wished he could forget that. It was so embarrassing!

"My three sizes are ninety-nine, fifty-eight, ninety. Oh! Wait. You Americans don't use the metric system, do you? In which case, my three sizes would be thirty-nine, twenty-three, thirty-five."

And he really wished he could forget that. Seriously, who reveals their hip to bust ratio to people?

"And my seiyuu is Yukari Fukui."

Kevin frowned. He didn't remember Lilian saying that.

"I don't really have much experience with this kind of thing, but then, given your age, I don't really think you have too much either. I'm really looking forward to learning more about you as we deepen and explore our relationship together."

Yes. That was what she had said.

"I love you! I love you so much, Kevin! I know you don't love me back. I realize that, but I... I don't care! I don't want to leave you! I want to stay with you forever!"

"But you're not just anyone. You're my mate. I love you."

More and more images bombarded him. Images of Lilian, of the times they shared, of the hardships they'd gone through, of the sexy and zany situations that had become a staple of his everyday life.

Kevin found the strength to move.

"St... stop... it... stop this..." He ground his teeth hard enough to draw blood. Hands scraped against the ground until the skin on his fingertips was rubbed raw. "Stop it...!"

"W-what...?" He glared at Iris, whose eyes had grown inhumanly wide. "How are you...?"

"I said... stop it... right... NOW!"

With one final push, Kevin shoved everything he had against the compulsion. All of his strength, all of his will was brought to bear. He pushed it into these carnal feelings with every ounce of willpower he possessed.

Pain exploded in his head. It was agony like nothing he'd ever felt before. It felt worse than if someone had shoved his brain onto a bed of hot coals. He would rather have his head dunked in a vat of acid. Nothing he could have thought up could've prepared him for the unimaginable pain he felt in that moment.

He felt liquid pouring out of every orifice. Thick and potent, it held a coppery scent. He felt himself falling, like a puppet whose strings had been cut. He heard his head cracking against the ground, but he could not feel it.

Everything was spinning. Darkness crept along the edge of his vision. Why was everything so blurry?

"Beloved!"

Was that shouting? It sounded so familiar, yet he couldn't... couldn't...

Darkness.

***

Lilian had never felt so exhausted before.

After waking up that morning, she had left the bedroom and headed for the kitchen, only to stop when she saw the restroom door ajar. Curious, she had glanced inside, and found Kevin undergoing seizures on the floor while Iris stood over him. It hadn't take long to realize what had happened.

She looked down at her mate. Kevin was lying on the bed, his breathing even and steady. He looked peaceful now, but there had been several close calls where she thought he might have gone into shock.

Wiping the sweat from her brow, Lilian completely missed Kotohime entering the room until the woman spoke up behind her.

"How is he?"

"I've managed to heal him," Lilian responded, turning her head. "I've stopped his blood hemorrhaging, and I've repaired the damage done to his mind as well." She reached out with her left hand and placed her palm over his forehead. "We're lucky I managed to get to him when I did. Had I not started healing him right away..." Lilian trailed off. She didn't want consider what would have happened had she found him a second later.

"Indeed, we are quite fortunate." Kotohime looked at Kevin for a moment, then shifted her gaze back to Lilian. "Your healing abilities have improved. I can see that you've been practicing."

"When I can." Lilian rubbed her arms to ward off the chill that came over her. "Kevin's spars have been getting dangerous. I've had to heal him a lot this past week. Without me there to heal him, he'd be going to school with broken bones and bruises."

"Hmm…"

Lilian looked at Kotohime with a curious frown. What was she smiling about?

"Anyway, would you mind looking after him?" she asked.

"Of course." Kotohime sat down on the bed. "If you want, I can even heal the part of his brain that ruptured. You seem to have missed it."

Lilian felt both horrified and embarrassed. "I would like that," she said softly.

Kotohime gave her charge a gentle look. "Do not worry too much, Lilian-sama. You did an admirable job on everything else. You simply need to remember to look deeper next time." As she spoke, a soft blue glow emanated from her hands. The swordswoman placed them under Kevin's head, where the rupture was located.

"I'll remember that next time, though I hope there won't be a next time."

"Of course. Might I ask where you are going, Lilian-sama?"

Lilian's face darkened. "To speak with my sister."

***

Lilian found Iris sitting on the couch in the living room. She appeared nervous. Her posture remained relaxed, but her eyes were flickering about, as if she was expecting something to leap out at her. Fingers occasionally twitched, and her left foot tapped incessantly against the beige carpet.

Normally, such out of character behavior from her sister would have thrown Lilian for a loop. However, she was angry enough right then that she found herself not caring.

She stomped into the room.

Iris looked up. Her eyes widened. She stood up from the couch and tried to speak. "Lilian, I'm—"

"You hurt my mate," Lilian's harsh whisper sounded out menacingly. "Do you have any idea how much damage you've done? I had to spend almost an hour just to stop the bleeding! He could have died!"

"L-Lilian, I—"

"And for what? Why would you do this to him? Why would you hurt him like that?"

"Because he was taking you away from me!" Iris shouted,

stunning Lilian into silence. "Ever since you first met him, he's all you would talk about, all you would think about. You started ignoring me in favor of him. Even when he wasn't around, you wouldn't think of anyone else. It's like you completely forgot I even existed."

"I never ignored you, Iris. I simply can't be what you wanted me to be. Kevin would never accept our relationship. And don't give me that speech about me being brainwashed by our matriarch; we both know that's a lie. I have never once let anything that hag has said guide my decisions. Every decision I've made is one that I chose myself."

Iris looked like she wanted to say something but wasn't sure what to say.

"Not that any of this matters anymore." Lilian narrowed her eyes into angry slits. "You and I are done."

"You don't mean that," Iris whispered, her voice conveying a sense of shock. "You don't mean that... you can't! I'm your sister!"

"Correction: you were my sister until you decided to hurt my mate. Now you're just someone I share the same blood with." Lilian turned around. "I could never be related to someone who would willingly hurt the person I love the most in this world."

"W-wait! Lilian! I'm sorry! I didn't mean to! Please, come back!"

But Lilian did not come back. She left the living room, leaving a distraught Iris in her wake and ignoring the way it felt like her heart was breaking.

She went back to her bedroom. Kevin remained lying on the bed, but Kotohime was sitting in seiza against the wall.

"Do you know how long it'll be until he wakes up?" Lilian asked.

Kotohime cocked her head to the side. "It's hard to say, as I am unsure of how much damage was done to him. However, he is a rather strong-willed young man. I imagine it won't be long before he wakes up."

As if on cue, Kevin groaned. Lilian rushed over to the bed and sat down. One of her hands reached for Kevin's face, cupping it as blue eyes slowly opened.

"Kevin?"

"Lilian?" he whispered, blinking. "Wha... what happened?" Eyes fluttered about in confusion as they took in their surroundings. "Why am I in bed? What happened? The last thing I remember is..." Something wet fell on his face. Tears. Lilian's tears. "H-hey now, Lilian, what's wrong? Please don't cry."

"I'm sorry," Lilian sniffled, wiping a few stray tears from her eyes before they could fall. "I'm just so relieved to see that you're not hurt. I was so worried. I've never been so frightened in my life."

Kevin still looked confused. At any other time, Lilian would have found that expression adorable. Not right now, though. Not after what had just happened.

"Lilian," Kevin placed his hands over hers, "what's wrong?"

Lilian tried to calmly explain how Iris had used an enchantment on him to increase his arousal and sexual desire. Kevin listened with an oddly calm face, as if he was not being told that someone had just tried to manipulate him by increasing his lust to levels even Eric Corrompere couldn't fathom. By the end of it, Kevin was sitting against the headboard while Lilian leaned against him.

"So all of that was an enchantment, huh?" He sighed in obvious relief. "I'm glad to hear that."

"Glad?" Lilian's brows furrowed. "How can you be glad? Iris tried to manipulate you. She used an enchantment, a very powerful one. You're lucky that your brain isn't oozing out of your ears right now."

Kevin smiled at her, and Lilian's breath caught in her throat. "I'm glad because I, well, I was worried. When I saw all those images in my head and felt those overwhelming desires, I thought that... I thought they were..."

"You believed they were your own feelings, yes?" Graceful as always, Kotohime rose to her feet and walked over to the bed, stopping at the edge and gazing down at the young man. "You need not worry, Kevin-sama. Those images you saw, those feelings you had, all of them were implanted within your psyche by Iris' enchantment. None of what you saw or felt came from your own mind."

"I'm glad to hear that."

"Still, I must say, I am most impressed." Lilian and Kevin

looked at Kotohime curiously. She saw this and gave the young man a warm gaze filled with pride. "Few humans can resist an enchantment, especially one that powerful. The fact that you were able to speaks highly of your willpower and mental strength. That's quite admirable."

"Ah-hahaha…" Kevin's awkward laugh made Lilian smile. His embarrassment at her maid's words was very endearing. "T-thank you. So!" Kevin coughed into his hand. "I believe we had some plans today, didn't we?"

Kevin tried to sit up, but Lilian put her hands on his shoulders and pushed him back down.

"Easy, Kevin. Don't try to stand up just yet," she fretted over him. "Even though I healed you, the damage done to you isn't something you can walk off so easily."

Kevin did his best to wave off her concerns.

"Ma, ma, I feel fine. Really."

He insisted on sitting up again. Lilian tried to stop him, but eventually gave up. Her mate, it seemed, could be just as stubborn as her when he wanted to be.

"There's no way you can expect me to lay around in bed all day doing nothing." He scooted over to the edge of the bed, his feet dangling off. "We made plans today, and I would hate to see those plans ruined because of something like this." Heedless of Lilian's previous protests, Kevin pushed himself off the bed—

"Now, let's—"

—And promptly fell face-first to the floor.

Lilian sighed. "Now do you see why I told you to remain in bed? You suffered a lot of damage and that damage has affected your motor functions."

Kevin rolled over onto his back and gave his mate a mild stink-eye. "I wish you would have told me that before I tried standing up."

Lilian had the decency to look abashed. "Um, whoopsies?"

"Ara." Kotohime was amused.

***

Because of Kevin's desire to not let what had happened that morning affect their plans, he and Lilian ended up doing what they'd intended. Iris had gone off somewhere, so she hadn't joined them, though Kevin had the feeling that Lilian wouldn't have let her sister come near him anyway. Kirihime had also vanished. He assumed she was following Iris. Kotohime had some errands to run, which meant it was just him, Lilian and Camellia.

Their destination for that day was called R-Galaxy, the largest store in Arizona for anime, comics, manga, movies, video games, and other types of nerd paraphernalia.

Kevin had agreed to take Lilian there after the kidnapping incident, but hadn't been able to find the time due to training with Kiara, track practice and meets, and his part-time job delivering newspapers. It was also further away from his apartment than the mall. Getting there required them to take a bus which, while inexpensive, meant spending an hour on a bus.

Kevin really, really hated buses.

For a place that sold nerd paraphernalia, R-Galaxy was surprisingly large. Then again, comics and movies had always been popular in the US, and anime and manga had been gathering in popularity for years. Kevin could still remember when *Pokemon* had swept through the nation and children everywhere were getting caught up in it. He even used to collect the cards for it—until they started making more than 151 Pokemon.

"Inari-blessed!"

Kevin almost chuckled as he observed Lilian's nearly bulging eyes after they had walked into the store. Not that he could blame her. *R-Galaxy* was like a massive dungeon, only instead of having monsters and dark hallways, it contained aisles, racks, and displays.

"Big, right?"

Lilian nodded absentmindedly, her wide eyes still exploring the large store and all the people browsing it. There seemed to be quite the crowd that day. Many of the aisles were filled with customers wandering through them, checking out the racks and rummaging around for whatever took their fancy.

"Come on, Beloved!" Lilian grabbed his hand. "Let's go!"

"Eh? W-wait, Lilian! What about your—"

But Lilian wasn't listening anymore. She'd already begun dragging him along behind her. All Kevin could do was pray to any god that was listening that Camellia would follow them.

***

From the moment Kevin had resisted her enchantment, Iris

knew she'd screwed up in a big way. The downward spiral of what happened afterward; her sister's rage, her sister's rejection, and the knowledge that it was her own fault, led to Iris running out of the apartment. After wandering around the streets for what felt like hours, she had eventually arrived at the mall.

Iris dragged her feet across the tiled floor, observing the shops through the display windows. There was a lot of different stuff being sold. She saw everything from toys and clothing to jewelry and makeup. Having been isolated in Greece and the Pnévma estate in Tampa Bay all her life, she'd never seen so many different items on display before.

Just another reason to hate that old hag.

Dozens of people stopped what they were doing as she walked by, no matter what they were doing or who they were talking to. Boys. Girls. It didn't matter what their gender, age, or sexual orientation was. All of them stared at her.

In most cases, Iris would have played it up. She knew she was sexy, and she loved letting everyone else know it, too. However, the events of a few hours ago had left her in a rather sour state. Much like that time at the airport when she'd wanted nothing more than to see Lilian, in that moment, all she felt was annoyance. Didn't these people have anything better to do than ogle her?

She sighed. Maybe she was being too hard on them. After all, they were just humans. Then again, Kevin Swift was supposed to be just a human, yet he'd managed to throw off her enchantment. Sure, it might have been at great personal cost to his physical health, but that he'd been able to shunt aside her most powerful enchantment was nothing short of astounding.

So lost in thought was she that, upon turning the corner, she didn't see the other person also turning the corner at that exact same moment.

"Oof!"

Iris winced as she fell onto her backside. It felt almost as bad as someone stepping on her tail.

"By Inari's left nutsack, that really hurt." She glared up at the person who knocked her over, a curse on her lips, only to die when she saw who it was. "Hey, I know you!"

"Ah…"

A pause. Bland, half-lidded eyes stared back at her.

"… Foxy…"

Iris stared at the young man, her face deadpanning. "You're a weirdo, did you know that?" When the young man said nothing, she sighed. "Ha… whatever. Get up. It's time for you to show me around."

Justin merely blinked.

***

"What should I get… mou, this is harder than it looks. There's so many choices. Tricky, tricky."

Kevin watched, somewhat amused but mostly exasperated, as Lilian perused one of the many shelves dedicated entirely to manga. They'd already been there for nearly fifteen minutes, yet his mate-slash-girlfriend still hadn't come to a decision on what she wanted to buy.

"Remember, Lilian, I only have enough money for two manga volumes at the moment, so be sure to choose carefully."

"I know that," Lilian replied absently, her focus still centered on her options. From what Kevin could see, she had narrowed down her choices to six different manga. "Let's see… *Fullmetal Alchemist* is supposed to be amazing, but I really wanna read the next volume of *Vampire Knight*. And then there's *Monster Musume*, mustn't forget that one and… oh! *Rurouni Kenshin*! That one is a classic!" Lilian paused. "Though I already have all the volumes for that one. Hm, I wonder if they have any *Negima Magister Magi*…"

Scratching his head, Kevin walked up to the redhead. He placed a hand on her back and leaned in to whisper in her ear. "I'm gonna go find your mom real quick. It seems we lost her when you ran off. Will you be okay on your own?"

"Hm? Yeah, I'll be fine." Lilian waved Kevin's concern off. Her eyes had yet to leave the shelf. "You go do what you have to."

Kevin shook his head. This girl actually seemed more interested in manga than even he was. It almost made him wonder if she loved manga more than she loved him.

He went off in search of Camellia, who proved to be quite elusive. *R-Galaxy* was a large place; with such a spacious interior and with hundreds of aisles, finding Lilian's mom became more than just a chore. She wasn't on the second floor, and she didn't appear to be on the first floor either.

"Ha... where did that woman go?" He asked himself as he looked around the store. "You'd think a woman wearing a freaking toga with boobs the size of Alaska would be easy to find."

Looking everywhere but in front of him, Kevin didn't see the woman turning a corner until it was almost too late.

"Woah!"

A quick burst of adrenaline rushed through his system. Kevin's eyes widened as he spun around the female who'd appeared seemingly out of nowhere. He managed to avoid running the poor woman over—only to smash face-first into a nearby support column. With a groan, Kevin fell backwards with a dull thud.

"Ouch..."

"Are you injured, young man?"

Blinking several times to clear his vision, Kevin saw the woman he'd nearly run into leaning over him. She was rather attractive, with long purple hair and blue eyes. Her figure was also quite impressive, though not as amazing as Lilian's. Her black pants were skintight, short, and left little to the imagination. An equally skintight crop top of the same color flattered her figure quite well.

"Don't worry." Kevin sat up with a groan. "I'm fine. This is nothing compared to some of the things I've been hit by recently."

"Pardon?"

"Nothing. Don't worry about it." A hand appeared in front of his face. "Oh, thank you." He allowed the woman to help him stand up.

"You really should learn to be more aware of your surroundings, young man," the woman lectured him. "You never know what kind of dangerous situations you might get into that could have otherwise been avoided."

"Um, thank you for the advice." Kevin frowned as he stared at the woman. Observing her more closely, he saw that her eyes were blank and soulless, like a doll. Talk about creepy. "I'll be sure to take that to heart."

"See that you do."

The woman walked away, disappearing down another aisle, and Kevin began his search anew. It took a while, but he eventually found Lilian's mom sitting at a table in the cafe, munching on a sandwich.

She wasn't alone.

"I don't think we were ever properly introduced, were we?"

"Hawa..."

Munch.

"I'm Heather Grant, full-time PE assistant at Desert Cactus High School and part-time writer."

"Hawa..."

Munch.

"Of course, I'm hoping to one day become a full-time writer, but it's been slow going even with all the inspiration I've managed to get so far."

"Hawa..."

Munch. Munch.

"I've noticed that you're a very beautiful woman, Camellia. I was wondering if you'd, hehehehe, allow me to use you as inspiration for my books?"

"Hawa..."

Munch.

A drop of sweat trailed down the left side of Heather's face. "You... I can't help but notice, but you really eat a lot."

Kevin stopped in front of the odd pair. "Ms. Grant, what are you doing here?"

"Ah! It's the kitsune boy."

"I'm not a kitsune!"

"No, but your girlfriend is."

"Whatever," Kevin grumbled, "and you didn't answer my question."

Heather opened her mouth to answer him, but was beaten to the punch.

"Hawa, it's Kevin-kyun!"

"Eh?! Camellia! Don't—mrphgglle!"

Everyone in the cafe watched in open shock as Kevin found himself being asphyxiated by two of the largest breasts any of them had ever seen. Heather managed to sum up everyone's thoughts on the matter quite succinctly.

"Damn, my young apprentice was right. It's like he makes women fall for him by simply existing."

***

After running into Justin at the mall, Iris and her new chaperone found themselves seated at one of the long tables in the food court.

"I'm awfully surprised to see one of the kiddo's friends here," Iris made idle conversation while they ate. She'd managed to coerce Justin into buying her lunch; a type of food called a hamburger, which she'd never had before. "I'm even more surprised it's you. You don't strike me as the type who'd wander around on his own for no reason."

Justin looked up from his food—a burrito—and turned his head to face her. His eyes met hers before they were invariably drawn down to her boobs.

"Ho?" Iris smirked when she saw where he was looking. "See something you like?" She placed her hands on the edge of the seat and leaned back just enough so that her chest strained her shirt.

While Justin's face remained bland, his cheeks did turn a bit red. He turned his head. "… No…"

"Huhuhu," Iris' chuckles sent shivers down Justin's spine. "If you say so."

She and Justin grew silent. Conversation continued around them, with people talking about this and that. Iris would have normally listened in, but she honestly didn't care. She had her own problems to deal with.

"Say, you're friends with Kevin, right?"

Justin looked up from his food. "… Yes…"

Smiling a devious little smile that caused Justin to actually show surprise, Iris leaned forward and allowed him to catch a tantalizing glimpse of her cleavage.

"What can you tell me about him?"

***

"Beloved! There you are!"

"Lilian—waagghh!"

For the second time that day, Kevin found himself lying on his back with a beautiful girl on top of him. Fortunately for his eroding physical health, Lilian did not smother him with her breasts. She merely sat there, straddling his hips and grinning in a vulpine manner that made her look very, well, foxy.

"I can see why Eric has so much respect for this kid," Heather said, mostly to herself. "He's quite the player to have all these

193

women jumping him like that." A perverted grin. "Hehehe, I can already tell this kid is going to give me loads of inspiration."

"Hawa?"

"Nothing," Heather waved at a hand at the confused Camellia, "just thinking out loud."

"Hawa."

"I've finally decided on the two manga I want!" Pulling two manga from her Extra Dimensional Storage Space, Lilian showed them off to Kevin. "These ones!"

After shaking away the stars floating around his head, Kevin looked at the manga in her hands. "So, you've decided to go with *Vampire Knight* and..." He looked at the other manga, his face slowly deadpanning. "*Gurren Lagann.*" His right eyebrow twitched. "Are you making fun of me?"

Lilian's smile was absolutely brilliant as she spoke, "Of course not, ufufufuf, why would you think that?"

Oh, yeah. She was definitely mocking him.

***

Kevin stood in line with Camellia, Lilian and Heather, who had decided to join them.

"I've got nothing better to do. Might as well join you. Besides, I need some more inspiration."

Kevin didn't really understand what she'd been talking about when she mentioned "inspiration," but decided not to bother with it. He was pretty sure he didn't want to know anyway.

While they stood in line, waiting for their turn at the register, Lilian wandered over to a small rotating display case that sold small trinkets. Kevin followed her with his eyes for a second, but didn't pay much attention to her until...

"Beloved! Beloved, look at this!"

Kevin didn't call Lilian out on using her old pet name for him. He knew she was just excited.

"Check it out!" She showed him the item she found. "It's an official *Shinobi Natsumo* kunai!"

"So it is." It wasn't a real kunai, of course, but it was still a pretty good replica. It was even made out of metal and not plastic. "Would you like me to get it for you?"

"Would you?" Her eyes widened with hope, and then dimmed when she remembered something. "No. No. I want it, but you're already spending your hard-earned money on my manga. I can't ask you to get something like this for me."

Kevin rolled his eyes. "You're not the only person who likes manga, you know. Besides, I've got enough money to buy that as well." Lilian opened her mouth to protest, but he cut her off. "It'll be fine. Really, I want to get this for you."

"A-are you sure?"

Kevin knew Lilian was on the verge of giving in. She was, in many regards, an open book.

And to think this girl is actually a kitsune.

"Really."

"Okay," Lilian said demurely, her large, innocent eyes looking at him from beneath a curtain of crimson hair. "Thank you, Kevin."

Lilian leaned in and pressed her lips against his. Kevin accepted the kiss, welcomed it even—despite the fact that they were in public and it was kind of embarrassing. He was beginning to get used to her public displays of affection.

"Huhuhu." Heather giggled in a most perverse manner. "Eric was right. This kid is solid gold! Gold, I tell you! Huhuhu!"

Camellia expressed her confusion at the lecherous woman's words in the only way she knew how.

"Hawa?"

Exactly.

***

Mei Ling watched as Kevin left R-Galaxy with Lilian and Camellia.

She'd been observing them for several days now, following from a distance, studying them to learn everything she could. Her master wanted to know about the human that the Pnéyma Clan heiress was so enamored with, and she did not want to suffer the consequences that would come if she failed him.

While Mei Ling acted like an emotionless doll to avoid having her sanity eroded by her master, that did not mean that she didn't have emotions. She merely hid them behind an inexpressive visage. It had helped to keep her alive and sane ever since she had become her master's slave.

Mei Ling followed the trio from a distance as they stepped onto a bus. She waited for a moment and then entered the bus as well, choosing to sit near the back where she could continue to her observations.

She would spy on them for a bit longer, just to be on the safe side. Then she would report back to Lord Jiāoào with her findings.

***

Kevin woke up to the fulfilling warmth of his mate's embrace. The hour was late, signified by the darkness outside his window. He stared at the ceiling, wondering why he'd woken up. Then his stomach growled.

"Ah. That's why."

He looked down at his mate. Lilian lay snuggled against him, her head on his shoulder, her arms around his waist, and her legs entwined with his. Soft snoring escaped her delicately parted lips.

She was also sleep talking.

"Zzzzz... munya-munya... you think you can beat me... silly Britannian homo... I'll show you... coz I'm the pyro-ninja... zzzz..."

Kevin felt some sweat accumulate on his forehead at Lilian's muttered words. This girl said the most bizarre stuff in her sleep sometimes.

After extricating himself from Lilian's grip, Kevin wandered into the kitchen for a midnight snack. The apartment was engulfed in darkness. None of the lights were on, and with the new moon out, it meant he only had what sparse starlight filtered in through the window to guide him.

He saw Kotohime sleeping over in a corner of the living room on a futon. It was almost unusual to see her asleep. While he knew that, logically speaking, Kotohime had to sleep sometime, the idea that she ever actually went to sleep was somehow shocking. Kirihime slept next to her sister, her arms and legs spread as she lay on her back, drool leaking from the corners of her mouth.

He shook his head.

After raiding the fridge in search of food, Kevin eventually decided on something healthy; carrots and celery with a little bit of peanut butter. He got himself a plate and was about to sit down when he saw that someone else was also awake.

Iris stood outside on the balcony. He couldn't see much because her back was turned to him, but knowing of the argument that had happened between her and Lilian, he easily determined

Iris's reasons for not being able to sleep.

Taking his plate of veggies, Kevin walked onto the balcony. "I didn't think anyone else would be awake at this hour."

Iris turned her head, startled. Red eyes narrowed and a frown appeared when she saw who stood behind her. "Oh, it's you."

"Do you have to talk about me like I'm some kind of pest? It's pretty rude, you know."

Iris snorted. "This is how I am. You don't like it, don't talk to me." She eyed him as he wandered up to her. "Is there something you want from me, kiddo?"

"I'd like a couple things, actually. I'd like you to stop calling me 'kiddo,' for one," Kevin quipped.

"Not happening," Iris declared. "As far as I'm concerned, that's all you are; a kid. While you and I may technically look the same age, I'm still over a hundred years older than you."

"It's that kind of attitude that keeps pushing Lilian away."

"Tch! I don't need a lecture from you!" Iris sent Kevin a vicious look mired by frustration. "I'm perfectly aware that things between my sister and I have not been... ideal."

Kevin snorted. "Ideal? What are you, the master of understatements? Your relationship with Lilian is so far from ideal it makes the relationship between Makotou Itou and Kotonoha Katsura look perfect."

"Ouch." Iris winced. "That's harsh."

"And no less true."

"Look, did you want something, or are you just here to gloat?"

"To be honest, I'm not really sure why I came out here," Kevin admitted, holding his plate of vegetables out to Iris. The fox-girl looked at him skeptically before taking a few carrots. "By all rights, I shouldn't want to have anything to do with you, not after what you did this morning. Yet, I'm not really angry at you. I mean, I am kinda mad," he added upon seeing her flabbergasted expression, "but I'm not that mad."

Iris looked at the cement underneath their feet. "I don't understand. Why aren't you angry at me?"

"I guess it's because I can kind of understand how you feel." Kevin admired the velvet sky. Without the moon, the stars shone all the more brightly. "Granted, I've never had any siblings, but I understand that you and Lilian were close before I came along. I imagine it can't be easy watching someone you love grow distant because she fell in love with someone else."

Iris didn't say anything. She didn't have to say anything. The look in her eyes, too wide and too round to be human eyes, said more than words ever could. She was stunned; completely and utterly astounded.

Kevin turned away from the sky to look at Iris. "I'm not going to ask you to like me. If you don't like me, that's fine. I'll understand. But I would like to ask that you at least hold off on judging me until you've gotten to know me."

"You…"

"Think you can do that?" Kevin held out his hand. "I don't think that's too much to ask for."

Iris stared at the offered hand. Kevin waited. Seconds ticked by, and all Iris did was stare. He began to feel like an idiot. Iris hated him for taking Lilian away. She wasn't going to accept his offering.

He nearly squeaked when something suddenly grabbed his hand. He looked down to see a smaller, more feminine and more delicate hand holding his in a soft grip. He looked from the hand to see Iris smiling at him.

And for the first time since they met, Kevin thought he might have just gotten a glimpse of the real Iris.

"Deal," she announced.

Kevin smiled. It wasn't much, but he felt like he was finally helping his mate with something. And really, what else could a guy like him ask for?

***

"Hehehehe… oh yeah… look at all those beauties… hee hee hee…"

Heather Grant was enjoying her favorite pastime—well, her second favorite pastime. Playing eroge was her all time favorite activity, but peeping still held a place close to her heart.

The world around her looked like something out of a jungle paradise; trees and shrubs of all kinds surrounded her, encroaching upon her from all sides. The steam rising up from the water's surface combined with the jungle theme of the hot spring masked her presence perfectly.

"Thirty-five, twenty-four, thirty-two. Not bad… hehehehe, not

bad at all."

She stood behind several large shrubs, which hid everything but her head from view. A pair of binoculars were pressed to her face. A dozen or so feet away, several women enjoyed the hot springs.

Heather could have joined them if she wanted, but that would have ruined what she was trying to accomplish.

One could not peep if they sat in the midst of those they wished to peep on.

"Hmm… fifty-seven up top, fifty-four around the middle, and sixty-six on the bottom. Oh my. You're a big girl, aren't you? Hehehehe…"

Heather had always loved visiting the hot springs. There were so many different body types to enjoy. So many women to sample. Few things could beat a good trip to a hot spring, especially for a peeper like her.

"You girls are going to make excellent resource material for my book."

Heather was a woman with big dreams. While she had, through a series of odd and unusual circumstances, ended up becoming a member of an agency bent on protecting the world from yōkai, her real goal in life had nothing to do with yōkai at all. She wanted to be a writer.

Of porn.

It was her dream to write the smuttiest, raunchiest books ever, which was why she needed inspiration.

And so, with a notepad in one hand and a pencil in the other, Heather Grant continued peeping, her perverted old man giggles heard by no one but herself.

***

Heather left the hot springs after deciding to spend a bit of time enjoying the water instead of peeping. All of the females had welcomed her, of course, being a woman herself. She doubted they had even suspected her of shamelessly ogling their naked flesh from a distance.

Eric would have been jealous.

While wandering the empty streets, a feeling came over her. The hair on the back of her neck stood on end. Her arms prickled curiously. She knew this feeling. It was a feeling that had saved her life a number of times when she had worked for the agency, and she knew what it meant.

She was being followed.

Pretending that nothing was wrong, Heather carefully observed her surroundings without turning her head, using windows and other reflective surfaces to see all around her. She couldn't see anyone; not behind her, nor to her left or to her right. There didn't appear to be any people hiding behind dumpsters or walls either. Heather looked at the roofs and frowned when she still couldn't see anyone. So then, where was…?

Her eyes widened.

Above!

Launching herself into a series of acrobatic back-handsprings, Heather barely avoided being flattened. The street wasn't so lucky. The pavement cracked and exploded outward in a shower of rubble. Heather clicked her tongue as she used her agility to dodge the rubble coming her way; ducking and dodging and weaving in a ceaseless, fluid motion.

The area soon cleared of dust and debris, and Heather caught sight of the large crater that had been created by whatever tried to flatten her. She could also see it, the thing that had nearly turned her into a pancake.

It was tall. Whatever the thing was towered above her by at least three feet. While it appeared vaguely humanoid in shape, with two arms, two legs and a head, the resemblances ended there. What she at first thought to be armor plating rippled when the creature moved, its metallic surface gleaming brightly in the moonlight, giving it an organic appearance. A sleek, bullet-shaped head swiveled in her direction, its red v-shaped visor flashing, presumably scanning the area. Clawed hands and feet clacked as it moved, scraping against the ground and gouging small strips out of the cement.

"What the hell are you supposed to be? Some kind of *Kamen Rider* villain reject? Wait, I know!" Heather pointed at it. "You're one of those human-sized *Gundam* things that ended up being scrapped because no one cares about human-sized *Gundams*. Am I right?"

The thing did not answer. Its head tilted this way and that, as if studying her from a different angle would help it figure out what she was talking about.

And then it charged. Without warning, without prompting, it rushed at her like a missile locked onto its target.

Heather rolled across the ground, avoiding what would have been a most painful shoulder ram. Coming back up on her feet, she twisted around to face this creature and reached behind her back, pulling out two weapons from hidden holsters; a 9mm handgun and a flashbang. She fired the already loaded gun several times, frowning when the bullets just sunk into the thing's armor.

Okay, so bullets won't work on this thing. That's fine, I have other weapons in my arsenal.

Clicking the button on her flash grenade, she fast-balled the object right into the strange creature's face. The explosion, while not harmful, was incredibly bright. Hopefully, that would scramble whatever this thing used to perceive its opponents.

With the thing distracted—hopefully—Heather turned tail and ran. She didn't know what that thing was, but it was already clear to her that, whatever it was, she would not be able to defeat it with her current arsenal. All she had were guns and stun grenades.

A sound from behind made her eyes widen. She threw herself to the ground just in time to avoid something with a fusillade shooting past her. A rocket. The wall several feet away exploded in a shower of flames and cement.

Heather scrambled to her feet just in time to avoid being impaled through the back. She warily eyed the weapon; made from the same organic material as the creature, it shifted and morphed. What had once been a clawed hand was now a large gun with multiple barrels. It pointed the gun at her, the barrels spinning with a loud *whirr!*

"Oh, shit!"

There was no time to think after that. Heather bolted. She jinked and juked left and right, zigzagging across the blacktop, avoiding the many hundreds of tiny bullets that pierced the ground and air around her. Thankfully, whatever this thing was, it didn't have very good aim.

She turned a corner leading into an alley. A ladder stood on her left. She took it, ascending as swiftly as possible. The thing also turned the corner and saw her. It aimed its gun and opened fire, but she was already on the roof, sprinting across the rooftop.

It followed her.

Heather hissed as bullets whizzed past her. She reached the end of the roof and leapt off, landing on the other roof. She stumbled, knees bending, then rolled along the ground and shot back up. She continued running and jumped to the next roof.

It continued following her.

Releasing a fierce groan, Heather put more effort into her running. It was gaining on her. She could hear its feet pounding along the ground in a series of loud *thack-thack!* sounds that struck her ears like a violent heartbeat. The series of roofs ended and Heather jumped down, rolling across the ground to absorb the shock of impact. She ran to the right, quickly turning a corner and ducking into an alley. There, she hid behind a large dumpster, ignoring the smell. She'd rather deal with the scent of rotten eggs and sulfur than whatever that thing was.

With her back pressed against the dumpster, she could not see the thing as it approached the alley. She could certainly hear it, though. Heather held her breath, careful not to make a sound. She waited and waited and waited, and after what felt like several hours of waiting, she heard it move away from the alley and walk away. She breathed a deep sigh of relief.

Striding out from behind the dumpster, Heather was just about to begin walking back home when a loud *click* echoed behind her. Eyes wide, she spun around just in time to see a gun pointed at her chest.

The sound of a gunshot rang clearly in the alley.

Chapter 6

Perverts and Precarious Predicaments

Kevin stepped out from one of many shower stalls at Mad Dawg Fitness. He grabbed the towel hanging from the nearest rack, wrapped it around his waist, and walked into the changing room. While changing into his normal clothes, Kevin noticed his reflection in the mirror and, being a teenage boy, he ended up doing what all teenage boys did when they saw their shirtless reflections in the mirror.

He started flexing and checking out his muscles.

Unfortunately, he was disappointed.

"Tsk. Doesn't look like I've grown much, does it?"

While his chest and shoulders seemed a bit broader, he couldn't see any major differences between now and before he'd started training with Kiara. His pectorals weren't any more defined and his stomach didn't have those washboard abs he had always wanted; he looked more or less the same as he always had. How disappointing.

With a sigh, he finished getting dressed, exited the locker room, and strode to the gym's entrance. Lilian stood near the door, waiting for him. Kiara was there, too, and Kevin noticed that his girlfriend kept as far from the other woman as possible.

His lips twitched.

Even though she dislikes Kiara, she still comes here to

support me.

Every day since the morning that she had first delivered breakfast, Lilian had started coming to watch him train. She woke up earlier than she used to, even though she didn't have to, and rode over on his bike, despite how cold it had become. It touched him more than he could say. His heart warmed up every time he thought about it.

"Are you ready to go, Kevin?" Lilian's eyes brightened like million-watt bulbs as he walked up to her.

With his gym bag slung over his shoulder, Kevin grinned. "Yep."

"Great! Then let's get going."

"Thank you again for training me," Kevin addressed Kiara, who merely smirked at him.

"Don't sweat it, boya. You're a good student. I don't think I've ever met someone as determined to get stronger as you. Keep at it and I'm sure you'll be strong enough to take on some of the less powerful yōkai someday."

Kevin blushed at the praise, just a bit. "Ah-hahaha, t-thank you."

"Come on, Kevin. Let's go."

"All right, all right, no need to rush."

He and Lilian left the gym and rode back to their apartment. Kevin didn't even need to enter to know what he would find; Kotohime cooking breakfast, Kirihime doing laundry or cleaning, Camellia still sleeping, and Iris taking a bath. He'd gotten used to their habits. It was hard to believe that they had only been living with him for three weeks now.

After locking up his bike, Kevin opened the door.

"HAWA!"

And suddenly found himself getting a face full of breasts.

The world around him spun as he and Camellia tumbled down the stairs. After smacking various limbs against the hard cement of the staircase, Kevin found himself sprawled on his stomach, on top of Camellia, with his face still embedded in her massive cleavage. Blinking several times, he looked up to see Camellia's not-quite-conscious face.

"Hawa," the woman mumbled in her semi-concussed state.

"M-My Lady! Lord Kevin!" Kirihime rushed down the stairs

in a panic, Lilian following close behind. "Are you two alright!? You're not hurt, are you?"

"Ugh, I'm fine," Kevin mumbled, sitting up. He looked down at Camellia, whose eyes held the glazed-over appearance of someone who'd been knocked for a loop. "Don't know if I can say the same about Camellia, though."

"Hawa," Camellia mumbled again, seemingly in agreement.

***

Kevin and Lilian sat at the table, the amazing food cooked by Kotohime arrayed before them. Camellia wasn't sitting at the table with them, and instead sat on the couch, watching some kind of early morning kids' cartoon, Adventure something or other. He didn't know what it was called, since he didn't watch American cartoons.

"Something wrong, Kevin-sama?"

"Hm?" It took Kevin a moment to realize that he'd been staring at the same space for over five minutes. Returning to reality, he tossed Kotohime a grin. "Sorry, I was just thinking."

"You seem to be doing that an awful lot in this story."

"What?"

"Nothing." Kotohime waved off his question while Lilian giggled into her miso soup. "What were you thinking about this time, if I may ask?"

"Just all the changes that have happened."

Kevin looked around. Lilian sat next to him, Kotohime stood by the redhead's side, Camellia sat on the couch while laughing at something he couldn't see, and Kirihime stood beside her while wearing a gentle smile.

"So much has changed. Even now, it's hard to believe that not even four months have passed since I met Lilian." Kevin sent the redhead a warm look which actually made the girl blush, allowing him to chalk up another point for himself. Kevin: Five. Lilian: Over 9,000. "I never imagined my life would take such a drastic turn, but you know what?" His warm look turned into a joyful grin. "I wouldn't trade it for the world."

"Kevin…"

"That's some pretty deep stuff you're talking about there, kiddo—I mean, Kevin."

Everyone looked up. Iris stood in the kitchen entrance dressed in a dark red skirt, tan winter boots with fur lining the top, and a red shirt with a black jacket thrown over it. Her hair was still wet from her bath.

"What do you want?" Lilian asked menacingly. Iris flinched, but tried to hide it. Kevin placed a hand on Lilian's left thigh and rubbed it in slow, concentric circles.

"Easy," he said. Lilian shuddered, her cheeks flushing just a bit as she released a breathy sigh, relaxing completely under his ministration. And with her no longer hissing like an angry viper, Kevin greeted Iris. "Morning, did you sleep well?"

Iris looked stunned for a moment, but recovered admirably. "Yeah, I slept fine… thanks for asking." She sat down opposite the two, dark eyes the color of blood peering at them; conflicting thoughts visible beneath her calm facade. "So… I imagine you slept pretty well, right? After our little talk, I mean."

"Talk?" Lilian snapped out of her pleasant fugue.

"Nothing important." Kevin tried to wave her question off.

Iris saw the opportunity for a prank.

"Oh? You didn't know?" A sinful smile. "Your mate woke up late last night and comforted me in my time of turmoil." A dreamy sigh. "He was so gentle and tender. I can see why you like him so much." Iris winked at the gobsmacked Lilian. "He's quite the charmer."

"That's not how it happened at all! Don't say things that could be so easily misunderstood!"

"Kevin…"

Wincing, Kevin turned to see Lilian. She was angry. Well, sort of angry. He imagined that if he ever saw an angry chipmunk, it would look a lot like Lilian did right then.

"Now, Lilian," Kevin wanted to run away, but resisted that particular urge. "Iris is just pushing your buttons. I woke up last night to get a midnight snack and saw her standing on the balcony. We talked for a bit and came to an understanding. That's all."

"He also offered me his carrot stick."

"Right." Kevin nodded. "I also offered her my—wait." He blinked. Then he blushed. "I did not! And it was just a carrot! A CARROT!"

"Beloved, I can't believe you would do this to me!" Tears sprang to Lilian's eyes. "How could you offer her your carrot stick when you haven't even offered it to me!'"

"Would you stop it with the carrot innuendo already?!"

"Huhuhu," Iris snickered behind her hand.

"And you stop laughing!"

While the three youngsters bantered amongst themselves, Kotohime placed her hands on her cheeks and smiled. "Ara. It's so nice to see these three getting along."

***

Despite the zaniness during breakfast that morning, Kevin, Lilian, and Iris made it to the bus stop with plenty of time to spare.

Upon their arrival, Kevin immediately started sulking several feet away. He crouched next to the stop sign and drew circles on the ground with his right index finger. His HP gauge had taken several hits that morning, and he needed some time to grieve. That meant Iris and Lilian were alone, which gave them a chance to talk.

"Why don't you tell me what really happened last night," Lilian demanded, not asked. It wasn't a request.

Iris sighed. "It's more or less exactly how Kevin put it; he woke up, got a midnight snack, saw me on the balcony, and we talked."

"About?"

"About how I shouldn't dislike him until I've gotten to know him better."

"And?"

"And I agreed to try and do that." When Iris saw Lilian smile in her direction, she looked away. "Don't look too into it. I doubt I'll ever like him. I just don't want you to hate me. I couldn't care less about your... mate."

"Hmm," Lilian looked pensive, "I guess... so long as you're willing to not interfere with our relationship, then I'm willing to let bygones be bygones."

"I won't make any promises."

"Ha... I suppose that's the best I can ask for."

An awkward silence fell upon them--until Iris broke it.

"By the way," she glanced down, "what's that in your hands?"

"Hmm? Oh, you mean these?" Lilian held up the objects in her hands.

"Yes."

"This one right here is a kunai." Lilian shook the leaf-shaped blade used by every shounen manga ninja in the multiverse, the same kunai Kevin had bought for her. "And this is a whetting stone to sharpen the kunai." She then shook the strange gray block in her other hand. "I'm going to use the whetting stone to sharpen my kunai."

An awkward silence ensued. During this time, Iris stared at Lilian like she was an idiot.

"There are so many things I could say to that, but I won't. It would be too easy," Iris declared. "And has anyone ever told you that you're beginning to take after Kotohime way too much?"

Lilian just tilted her head. "Hawa?"

***

School had yet to start, but there were still plenty of people milling about, both students and teachers alike. Sometimes they walked in groups, other times alone. A few sat at the stone tables littering the courtyard, enjoying the crisp morning air, while some went straight to their homerooms.

Christine stood near the entrance, trying to calm herself down with a pep talk.

You can do this, Christine. There's nothing to worry about. All you need to do is tell Kevin that you want to speak with him a-a-alone and—ah—a-a-and tell him that you… that you… that you hate his guts! No, wait! Tell him that you l-l-l—want to kill him! N-no, that's not it! That isn't—agh! This is so stupid!

Christine was trying for another confession. Despite the fact that Kevin was dating Lilian, she still felt confident in her chances of making him see that she would be a much better girlfriend than the redhead. Yes, she would not allow the person she l-l-l-lo-lov—sorta liked to be with someone other than her.

It took a while for Kevin to show up. Because of Iris, he no longer rode his bike, which was actually faster because there were no stops along the way. When the bus he rode in rolled to a stop, he disembarked, his left hand clasped in Lilian's right, with Iris trailing behind them. As they started walking to their homeroom, Christine walked up to them.

"K-K-Kevin!" she shouted, even though she was only four feet away.

"Um, morning, Christine," Kevin greeted warily. "How are

you?"

"I-I-I-I, uh… ah—I needed—I mean, I wanted…"

"Is she alright?" Iris asked Lilian. "She looks like she's about to explode."

"She's fine," Lilian assured her sister. "This is natural for tsunderes."

"Right, right. I forgot that this girl was a tsundere."

"Uh, Christine?" Kevin was looking more concerned by the second. "Are you alright?"

"I'm fine!" Christine snapped before calming herself. "I wanted to—I needed—I, ah, um… what I mean is… I-want-your-babies!"

A stiff breeze blew through the now silent clearing. A tumbleweed rolled between Kevin and Christine. Kevin tracked the tumbleweed until it rolled out of sight, and then turned back to Christine.

Um, what?" Kevin looked dumbfounded.

"Ne," Iris leaned into Lilian's ear again, "what's up with tsun-tsun over there? She looks like an ice cube."

"Just wait for it," Lilian whispered back.

"Um, Christine, can you repeat that?" Kevin rubbed the back of his head. "I didn't quite catch that?"

It took Christine exactly 2.6 seconds to register her own words. It took another 2.6 seconds to comprehend them. Exactly six seconds after that, Christine's face exploded with color as steam poured out of her ears.

Tsundere protocols: activated.

"Y-y-y-you… how dare you, ya damn beast!"

Kevin's eyes widened fractionally.

"What—Gu!"

He then received a brutal headbutt to the face, which sent him sprawling to the ground.

"Y-y-you stupid, IDIOT!"

"Holy crap!"

Kevin rolled to the left, avoiding the heel stomp that crashed into the pavement. He stared in horror as a spiderweb of cracks spread out from the point of impact, followed by a sheet of ice that crawled across the ground.

"HOW DARE YOU MAKE ME EMBARRASS MYSELF

LIKE THIS!"

Kevin scrambled to his feet, then got the hell out of Dodge when a fist sought to bash his face in. He avoided it. The poor light pole behind him wasn't so lucky. It emitted a loud metallic shriek as it bent where Christine punched it.

"I'LL KILL YOU!"

"Why are you being so violent?! What did I—Holy Berserker on a stick!"

"STAY STILL AND DIE!"

"How about no—sweet Mary MacBeth!"

Iris and Lilian, along with the other students present, watched as Christine chased Kevin around the courtyard.

"Aren't you going to help him?" asked Iris. "He is your mate, after all."

Lilian gave Iris a solemn look. "I love Kevin very much, however, even I am not stupid enough to get in the way of a tsundere and her target."

"Makes sense," Iris agreed, and then returned to watching Christine try to pound Kevin's face in.

I wish I had some popcorn.

***

Eric strolled around a corner and stepped into the courtyard.

He didn't normally come back this way since his class was located on the opposite side of school, but he felt obligated to greet his new lord these days. After all, it would be wrong of him to not pay proper homage to his lord, like those mongrels who didn't pay respect to Gilgamesh, a character from one of his favorite visual novels.

"My Lord!" Eric greeted in a booming voice as he stepped in front of Kevin—only to barely avoid being struck stupid when the boy in question nearly ran him over. "What the hell is—"

CRACK!

He never finished that sentence, because in less time than it took to say *"za warudo,"* Christine slammed her fist into his nose.

"My nose!" Eric held a hand to his now bleeding nose. "You just broke my nose! What did you do that for?!"

BAM!

"GA! You just headbutted me!"

"FILTHY, DISGUSTING PERVERT!"

"O-Oi! I take offense to—GAOI!"

"DIE, NEURONS! DIE!"

On that day, Kevin learned a very important lesson. *Whenever dealing with Christine, make sure to bring Eric along, so she can have a target to beat up when her tsundere protocols activate.* His perverted friend made a great scapegoat.

***

Classes passed quickly that morning, and soon enough, it was time for PE.

"Line up, brats!"

Kevin, Lilian, Iris, and Eric lined up with the rest of the students as Coach Raide blew into his whistle. The man looked at all of them, scowling more fiercely than usual. Perhaps it was just their perception of him, but the large wookiee-like coach seemed awfully angry about something.

"You'll all be doing drills today!" He received a chorus of groans. "Shut up! Anyone who whines or complains is getting worked twice as hard as everyone else! Now, you're all going to follow me outside to the track field, where we'll be doing a one-mile run! Well? What are you waiting for? An invitation? Move it!"

Spurred on by their coach, the group traveled outside.

"Is it just me, or is Coach Raide even more belligerent than usual today?" one of the male students asked.

"It's definitely not just you," another said. "He's pissed. Just look at that scowl. That's not his normal scowl."

"Really?" asked a girl. "I can't tell the difference between this scowl and his normal one."

"That's cuz you're an idiot."

"Hey!"

Kevin let the conversation flow over him as he walked to the track field, Lilian's left hand clasped in his. Iris strolled along on the redhead's right side. Eric frowned as he walked on Kevin's other side.

"Pardon me, My Lord," Eric was speaking formerly again, "but I was hoping you would permit me to ask a question."

"You can knock it off with the 'Lord' thing. It wasn't funny the first time, and it's not funny now."

"I think it's hilarious."

"You be quiet!" Kevin spat at Iris, seconds before noticing the stare Eric was giving him. He ran a hand through his hair and sighed. "Go ahead and ask, though I can't promise an answer."

Eric nodded as if he'd been expecting Kevin to say that. "I just wanted to know if you've seen my master anywhere."

"Your master?" Kevin blinked. "Do you mean Ms. Grant?"

"Hm. Master."

"Now that you mention it, I haven't seen her since we went shopping for Halloween costumes." Kevin's face scrunched up for several seconds before relaxing again. "To be honest, I thought she'd be with you."

"I'm not sure why you'd think any of us would know where she is." Lilian wrinkled her nose to show her dislike for the blond woman. "You're the one who's always spending time with her. Shouldn't you know where she is?"

"That's just it, I haven't seen her since Saturday. I don't know what's going on." Hanging his head, Eric appeared completely unaware of the large raincloud that randomly appeared above him. Kevin, Lilian and Iris moved several feet away as rain began pouring from it. "And Master promised to take me peeping today…"

Kevin facepalmed. "Of course that's what you'd be worried about."

Despite Eric's idiocy, their curiosity had been piqued. They decided to ask Coach Raide if he knew where Ms. Grant was. Unfortunately, the ornery man didn't seem to appreciate the question. Immediately after mentioning the assistant PE coach's name, his face turned a deep shade of puce.

"What the hell makes you think I know where that good for nothing slacker is, huh?! I'm not her goddamn keeper!"

Needless to say, they avoided Coach Raide for the rest of class.

***

School had ended, but Eric had been forced to stay after because he had gotten caught peeping. Again. His dad had spoken with him at great length, lecturing him on how he needed to stop spying on the girls because it was disrespectful. His old man had done this while looking through a porn magazine, thereby rendering everything he said null and void. What right did that old codger have to stop him from peeping? The old fool just wanted to stifle his peeping habits because he didn't have the guts to do it himself!

Getting off the late bus, Eric grumbled about the unfairness of the world as he walked up to his house. The lights weren't on, meaning that his mother must have still been at work.

He was surprised that his mom hadn't divorced his old man yet, what with his father's unrepentant perviness and all that. Perhaps she saw something special in the old man that no one did.

God only knows what she sees in the old fart.

He opened the gate and entered the courtyard. As he locked the gate behind him, the hairs on his neck prickled. He rubbed the back of his neck, wondering if the cold chill blowing through the courtyard was due to the weather or something else. It wasn't until he had reached the front door that Eric finally realized why he felt this way.

He wasn't alone.

"Ah... heh... apprentice..."

"M-Master!"

Eric rushed to Heather's side. She was resting against the cobblestone steps, her back leaning against the door. She held a hand over her torso, which was covered in filthy bandages. Crimson splotches seeped between her fingers, spreading across her skin and soaking into the fabric of her shirt.

Eric felt ready to hyperventilate.

"W-w-w-what happened to you?! Why are you bleeding?!"

"Later..." Heather grunted. "I'll tell you later..." She looked up, her half-lidded, partially glazed over eyes blinking at his. "H-help me... get inside..."

Eric quickly followed her command. Slinging one of her arms over his shoulder and foisting her up, he entered the house and staggered to the living room, Heather's feet dragging along behind him.

Because of his parents' jobs, they were quite well off, and the living room reflected their wealth. The furniture was comfortable and the appliances state-of-the-art. They even had a 76' flatscreen TV with surround sound built into hidden speakers all over the house.

He laid Heather down on the large leather sofa, ignoring the blood seeping into the material. He could worry about that later. There were more important matters at hand.

"Ha... ha..." Heather's breathing had grown heavy. A pained expression was etched on her fair features. "Apprentice... I need you..." She coughed, blood dribbling from the corners of her mouth. "I need you to get... contact with Lilian... tell her... need... help..."

"What do you mean, Master? Why would you—Master? Master!" When Heather's eyes closed and her body went limp, Eric freaked out. "Oh, god! What do I do? What do I do?" he fretted, running around like a chicken with its head cut off—at least until he ran into a wall. Then he remembered what his master had told him just before she passed out. "Call Lilian. Call Lilian."

He grabbed his phone and was about to dial Lilian's number when he remembered something else.

"Does Lilian even have a cellphone?"

***

After receiving a phone call from Eric, Kevin and the family of kitsune went over to the pervert's house.

He was beginning to think coming over had been a mistake.

"Oyoyoyoyoyo! Hello, beautiful girls!"

Eric's dad had come home just a few minutes after they had arrived. The moment he saw the five gorgeous females standing in his abode, the perverted principle stripped off his suit and bum-rushed them like a fat man at an all you can eat buffet.

Time seemed to slow as the man ran toward them, his flabby belly bouncing and jiggling in ways that made Kevin want to vomit. With a salacious grin, the disgusting principal leapt into the air with the obvious intention of pouncing on the family of female kitsune.

"Here I come—DOOF!"

Kevin watched in mute silence as Mr. Corromperre was smacked in the face by a large, fluffy black tail. The rotund man soared in a graceful parabolic arc until his grotesque body crashed into a wall on the opposite side of the room, causing the entire vertical surface to crack. He also had the unfortunate luck of slamming into it headfirst, which caused his fat little head to get stuck in the wall.

As the pervy principal struggled to pull his head out of the hole, Kotohime retracted her tail. "I believe having that happen once per novel is more than enough."

"I would be happy if it never happened again," Kevin added, shuddering as he remembered the fat pervert trying to jump on Iris and Lilian and landing on him instead.

"Hmm. Agreed."

"Enough fooling around." Eric was, surprisingly, not up for their antics. "I need you guys to heal my master."

He directed them to the unconscious Heather. Her skin, once a light tan, had become chalky-white and pasty. The vermillion liquid pouring from a gaping wound in her side had stained the leather sofa, and the repugnant coppery scent of blood filled the air, causing the yōkai amongst them to gag.

Being a Water Kitsune, and the only one present with four tails, Kotohime took to healing Heather. While she did that, her sister pulled Eric's dad out the wall and knocked him unconscious with an enchantment. Nothing good would come from a human walking further into the house and discovering the scene in the living room.

Healing Heather was an easy task for Kotohime. While not a healer by nature, Water Kitsune had the most powerful healing techniques of all kitsune types.

Kevin watched in fascination as the wound on Heather's stomach slowly closed, the skin sealing shut as if she had never been wounded in the first place.

"Is she going to be alright?" he asked.

Kotohime removed her hands from Heather's torso and stepped away. "Oh, yes. She will be fine. It appears she gave herself some basic first aid, which kept her from bleeding out. She's lost a lot of blood, but blood is made up of ninety-eight percent water. I replenished most of it and healed all of the damage done. She won't wake up for a while, but provided she gets a full eight hours of uninterrupted sleep, she'll recover."

"That's good." Kevin still didn't know how to feel about Heather, but he didn't want her to die if she could be saved. "You're really good at healing people."

"Ufufufu, why thank you." Kotohime hid a demure smile behind her kimono's left sleeve. "But I am truthfully just a novice. As a four-tailed Water Kitsune, I should be an expert healer, but my abilities are middling at best. Now then, would you mind helping me move her into a bedroom?"

"Oh, um, sure."

After Kevin helped Kotohime transfer Heather to an unused bedroom, the group adjourned to the living room.

"So, does anyone know what happened to Blondie?" Iris asked, trying not to frown as Lilian sat on a blushing Kevin's lap. Beside her, Camellia looked around the room, her eyes taking in their new surroundings with the kind of curiousness one might expect from a child.

"If we knew what happened, then we wouldn't be sitting here discussing it." Eric crossed his arms over his chest, looking surprisingly serious. Then again, the woman he looked up to had almost died. That was apparently enough of a reason for him to cast his salacious habits aside—at least temporarily.

"There's no need to get upset. I was just asking a question."

"Judging by the wound Heather-san sustained, I can only conclude that the weapon used to injure her was some kind of projectile." Kotohime cocked her head to the side, musing over something. "From the size of the wound and the damage inflicted on her internal organs, I assume it was a rifle, though I couldn't tell you which kind. There was an exit wound in her back, suggesting the bullet went straight through her body."

Kevin frowned. "As interesting as that information is, it doesn't really help us."

Eric nodded his head. "This is Arizona. Anyone can buy a rifle these days."

"Of course, we can probably dismiss this as a random shooting," Kevin added. "People who start shooting sprees prefer doing so in populated areas with a lot of people. We would have undoubtedly heard about something like that happening. That means whoever did this must have known Heather personally."

"What about those people who kidnapped you?" suggested Lilian, her brow furrowing thoughtfully as she bit her thumbnail. "That Heather woman worked for them at some point. She said that she got laid off when I talked to her, but what if she didn't? Maybe they tried to silence her, but she managed to escape before they could kill her off, and now they've come back to finish the job."

"That's…" Kevin paused, considering her words. "Completely possible," he admitted. Smiling, he leaned up and pressed his lips to her cheek. "Good thinking."

Lilian beamed at him.

"All this speculation is fine, but it still does not solve our immediate problem," Kotohime announced. "What do we plan on doing with this knowledge? Should we protect this woman from these people, or should we leave her to fend for herself?"

"Oi, oi, oi!" Eric stood up and gave Kotohime a glare. "How can you even think about leaving my master to fend for herself?"

"Easily," was the blithe reply. "That woman kidnapped Kevin-sama and tried to capture Lilian-sama. I do not care whether she lives or dies."

"Yeah? Well, I do!"

"That is not my problem."

"Why you…!"

"P-please stopping fighting, you two." Kirihime looked nervously between her sister and Eric. "U-um, Mr. Corrompere, Kotohime does not truly mean what she's saying. She just doesn't like people who try to hurt her charge." The demure woman addressed her sister next. "And Kotohime, please do not say such things in front of others who might care. I-It isn't very nice."

Everyone except Camellia stared at Kirihime, who looked like she was about to faint.

Kotohime smiled. "You are right, of course, Kirihime." She bowed her head to Eric. "I acknowledge that my words were in poor taste. Please forgive them. I was simply speaking on impulse due to my negative experiences with Heather-san."

"Negative experiences, she says," Kevin muttered in a soft whisper that only Lilian could hear. "She kicked Ms. Grant's butt back to the Stone Age and calls it a negative experience." Lilian hid her snickers behind a cough.

"Tch. I guess I can forgive you this once," Eric mumbled. "But only because you've got the largest rack I've ever seen!" A perverted expression overcame his features. "Now, if you really want me to forgive you, perhaps you should put out a little." Eric's fingers twitched as he brought his hands up, as if he was already imagining what it would feel like to grab Kotohime's superlative bosoms. "Maybe if you let me have a quick squeeze of your—oof!"

The group watched as Eric Corrompere received a very brutal smack to the chest by the same tail that put his old man through a wall. The dark-haired teen soared into the air and over the couch, smacked into the kitchen table, rolled across the table, and then fell to the floor, his head hitting the marble tiles with an audible *crack!*

As one, the group looked from Eric to Kotohime, who gave them all a dazzling smile.

They turned away again, swiftly coming to the conclusion that it would be in their best interest to forget the past sixty seconds of their lives.

It was safer that way.

***

Christine had never felt more awkward in her life. Lindsay had invited her over for dinner and she, like a moron, had accepted the invitation without really thinking about it. To be fair, she'd been a little busy berating herself when Lindsay asked if she wanted to hang out after school, but even she knew that excuse wouldn't hold up if used, which was why she didn't use it—at least not verbally.

Stupid. Stupid. Stupid. Stupid. Damn it, Christine, if only you hadn't been so preoccupied with your newest failure, than maybe you wouldn't be in this situation!

She sat at the table, trying to ignore everything around her. Lindsay's parents stared at her as if she'd sprouted half a dozen heads from her backside and all six had started shouting, "NOTICE ME, SENPAI!" as loud as they could. She felt like a circus freak show being put on display.

She was really beginning to regret accepting Lindsay's invitation.

"So, you're one of Kevin's friends?" Mrs. Diane asked in a poor attempt at making conversation.

Lindsay's mom looked nothing like her daughter. Where Lindsay possessed an athletic build, her mom was what many would call "pleasantly plump." She wasn't necessarily a large woman; she simply had more meat on her bones than most. Her hair was also several shades darker than her daughter's.

"N-no—w-well, sort of." Christine tried to control her natural urge to deny being friends with Kevin. "I-I mean, he and I, well, we've spent a good deal of time together, so I guess you could say we're friends…"

"That's nice. And how is that young man doing, if you don't mind my asking?"

Christine's mind went on high alert. Something about the way Mrs. Diane asked that question, or maybe the disturbing gleam in the woman's eyes, set her on edge.

"He's doing fine," Lindsay interrupted the conversation before anyone else could say something. "In fact, he's been doing great."

Mrs. Diane raised an eyebrow at her daughter. "Really?"

"Yep. The past few months have been really good to him. He's grown up a lot."

"Mm." Christine shuddered. That smile. Oh god, that smile! It made her feel like retching—and running away screaming, but mostly retching. "That sounds wonderful. You should invite him over for dinner sometime. I would so love to see him again."

Over at Eric's house, Kevin felt an icy chill run down his spine as he sneezed several times.

"Ugh, um, maybe… perhaps… eventually…"

Christine had the distinct feeling that what Lindsay really wanted to say was, "not a chance in hell."

Dinner continued in relative silence. Mr. Diane didn't speak, he merely finished his meal and set his plate in the sink before leaving. Mrs. Diane also said nothing—at least not until she, too, had finished dinner. She offered them both a good night, and told them not to come into the living room. Christine didn't know why she would give such a warning, and part of her feared knowing.

After they'd both taken a shower and donned their sleepwear, she and Lindsay sat together on the tomboy's bed. While her pajamas were black like everything else she owned, Lindsay's looked like someone had taken a Midgetet of neon orange paint and dunked them in it. Oddly enough, Christine thought those bright clothes suited the girl.

"What do you think about our new Social Studies teacher?" Lindsay asked from where she lay on her stomach, elbows on the bed, chin on the butt of her hands, and her feet kicking in the air.

"You mean Professor Collins?" Christine absentmindedly flipped through the pages of her book. "He's alright, I guess. I'm just glad he's not some crazy secret service agent who's in the habit of kidnapping teenage boys." A pause. The flipping stopped.

"At least I hope he's not."

"Hehe, yeah Me, too. He's not Asian, though, so I think we'll be okay."

"Hn."

Lindsay rolled onto her back and looked at the ceiling. Christine remained seated with her legs crossed, a book titled "Ten Things You Need to Know About Men" in her lap.

"Reading another one?"

"Of course." Christine flipped another page. "If I want to get Kevin to l-l-l-l-lo—like me, t-then I need to know how he thinks."

"Can't you just say love?"

Christine felt her face burn a fierce blue. "Wh—l-love—I could never—who's in love?! Just because I have a small, teensy, tiny crush on someone doesn't mean I love him!"

"Okay, okay, no need to get so defensive." Lilian raised her hands in a calming gesture, then lowered them back to the bed when it looked like Christine wouldn't verbally rip her head off. "Anyway, I'm not sure if those books are gonna help you."

"What do you mean?"

"I mean that I've known Kevin for a long time, and in that time, I've come to learn a few things about him."

"Like what?" asked a curious Christine.

"Like if you can't even admit you love him, then you're never going to get anywhere," Lindsay said bluntly. "Do you know why Lilian managed to earn Kevin's affection even though he had a crush on me?" A blushing Christine shook her head, too intrigued for her tsundere protocols to activate. "It's because I never did anything. I sat on my laurels, expecting that one day he would finally pluck up his courage and confess to me. And he did, but by then it was already too late, and Lilian had gained a foothold in his heart."

Her soft smile held a trace of bitterness.

"It wouldn't have been fair to either of us if I had accepted such a half-hearted confession. I didn't want to accept Kevin's feelings when I knew they were split between me and someone else. I expect any boy I'm dating to have feelings for me and only me."

Christine swallowed. "I think you told me something like that a while ago." She thought about Lindsay's words. "So, you're saying that if I really want to be with Kevin, then I need to con-con... tell him how I feel?"

"Honestly, I don't think you can be with Kevin anymore. He's not like other boys who'll have random flings with whoever he wants. He's a hopeless romantic who reads way too much manga and wants that kind of fairytale relationship." Lindsay paused for a moment, as if not quite sure about the veracity of her statement, but then just decided to roll with it. "He wants that fairytale ending; where he becomes the hero, sweeps the heroine off her feet, and they both ride off into the sunset." Another pause. "Or, you know, the anime version of that, where he and the heroine team up and defeat some giant robot or whatever, and then ride off into the sunset."

The book seemed to groan as Christine gripped it between her hands. "What exactly are you trying to say?"

Lindsay finally sat up and faced her friend. "That Kevin's not going to stop dating Lilian because you like him. Those two, I don't know, they just work. Kevin gets Lilian. He understands her in ways I can't even comprehend. And Lilian is dedicated to him; I mean really, REALLY dedicated to him. I don't think I need to tell you just how strongly she feels for Kevin."

"No," Christine begrudgingly admitted, "you don't."

She knew that Lilian loved Kevin. She had seen how the kitsune acted with him. It wasn't just how they held hands or how they stole kisses at school. There were times when those two would look at each other, and everyone around them knew they were holding a silent conversation that none of them would ever be privy to. They also shared a love for video games and anime, and she had caught them reading manga together several times during lunch. She didn't want to admit it, but seeing how they acted toward each other never ceased to leave her feeling envious.

"Exactly. Now can you say that your feelings for Kevin have the same depth and strength as Lilian's?" When Christine said nothing, Lindsay rolled onto her back again. "Before you think about trying to get between Lilian and Kevin, perhaps you should examine your own feelings first."

The rest of that evening was quiet. They talked for a bit, but conversation remained stilted. Eventually, the two girls crawled under the covers and went to bed.

***

After Eric recovered from being sent into blissful catatonia via Kotohime's tail, the group decided on their next course of action. Kevin, Eric and, surprisingly, Lilian, were all for helping Heather Grant. Kotohime disagreed and Iris didn't care. Kirihime had been neutral on the matter and only stuttered incoherently when they asked for her opinion, and Camellia... they didn't even bother asking for her opinion. She probably didn't have one anyway.

With a three versus two vote in favor of helping Heather, the group began their preparations for whatever danger they would face. None of them knew what had wounded the blond woman so grievously, but they figured the best idea was to prepare for the worst case scenario.

The group then split up. The boys went to set up the extra beds in the guest rooms, while the girls went to take a shower.

"I can't believe I'm stuck here with you while all those gorgeous babes are frolicking around in the shower, doing who knows what to each other." Eric bemoaned his fate—and then remembered who he was talking to. "No offense, My Lord."

"Oh, shut up," Kevin grunted. "Just so you know, girls don't actually grope each other when they take baths together. That only happens in anime."

"My Lord, you are wise and amazing when it comes to building your harem."

"I don't have a harem!"

"But, you clearly know nothing of women."

Kevin's right eyebrow twitched. "Who's the one with a girlfriend here?"

"Allow me to educate you on the elusive and mysteriously sexy creature known as the female, My Lord. Women are creatures with an undeniable need to touch each other; groping, squeezing and caressing each other's boobs is their panacea."

"You're completely ignoring me, aren't you?"

"They love playing together and comparing sizes by squeezing each other's jugs."

"Yep, you're ignoring me."

"I bet you those girls are having a great time groping each other's titties right now." Eric's cheeks stained red. He also started drooling. "Hehehe... I bet you they're moaning in delight as they caress each other's bodies..." His breathing became a deep, heavy rasp reminiscent of an old man whacking off to porn. Kevin actually saw steam blowing out of Eric's flaring nostrils.

Kevin sighed and resisted the urge to facepalm. He knew what was coming next.

"Boobies, here I come!"

Kevin was running almost before Eric could even bolt for the door. He stretched out his left hand—

"You can see some boobs... in hell!"

—and used it to clothesline Eric. The licentious teenager crashed into the ground with a harsh thud. Dark eyes bulged in asphyxiated agony, as his hands went to his throat, from which the sounds of hacking and wheezing emerged like the ribbets of a bull frog.

Kevin clapped his hands together. "I've always wanted to do that," he admitted, smiling. The smile left, replaced by a stern expression. "Eric, this is a law from your lord." Eric stopped choking. "You will not peep on those girls. To do so is a sin against your lord, and I will not stand for it. Do you understand?" Eric nodded. "Good."

Several minutes after—hopefully—beating some sense into Eric, Kevin stepped into one of the guest restrooms, a towel slung over his shoulder.

Setting the towel on a rack, Kevin stripped out of his clothes, and then turned the shower on to a mildly hot setting. Steam soon rose into the air, clinging to the walls and fogging up the mirror by the sink.

Kevin was just about to step into the shower when someone knocked on the door. Thinking it was Eric coming to pester him, he opened the door while giving a mild glare—only for it to vanish when he saw familiar bright green eyes and a vibrant smile.

"Lilian?" Kevin needed a moment to register that, indeed, Lilian was standing before him. "What are you doing here? I thought you were taking a bath with the others."

"I was going to," Lilian admitted, "but then I realized that my mate and I haven't been able to spend much time alone together because my family kept getting in the way, and I thought this would be the perfect opportunity for us to bond."

"Bond?" He studied the girl, and eventually realized that she wasn't looking at his face. Feeling a sense of unease growing in the pit of his stomach, Kevin looked down.

His face grew red.

He let out a loud "eep!" and tried to cover himself with his hands.

"Ufufufu," Lilian chuckled. "You're still too cute when you get embarrassed like that."

Kevin tried to glare at her, but the blush on his face lessened the effect. "It's got nothing to do with being embarrassed and everything to do with common decency," he insisted, lying through his teeth. "Most people don't stand around in the nude while someone else is present, not even if they're dating that person."

"Most people aren't mated to a kitsune."

"Ugh…"

She had him there.

"Kevin" Lilian's eyes were warm and so incredibly earnest that Kevin was unable to look away, "you are my mate; the person I love more than anyone else in this world." Delicate hands reached up and cupped his face. "This isn't some random person wanting to see you naked. This is me, your mate, who wants to become more intimate with you. If it helps, I promise not to touch anything below the belt."

Staring at the girl with an uncomprehending gaze, Kevin's mind became a warzone, a battle the likes of which no one had ever seen before—mostly because it was all happening in his mind.

***

The desolate wasteland spread out for miles, its borders traveling far beyond the distant horizon. Cracks traversed the ground like a myriad system of interconnecting spiderwebs. There was no flora or fauna in this wasteland. It was the perfect place… for war.

Two forces stood on opposite ends of each other, armies of nearly equal might. Multi-segmented plates clicked together as figures moved and jostled each other. Horned helms adorned the many heads, their faceplates masking their identities. Hands gripped massive halberds with leaf-shaped blades that gleamed like a thousand suns. The army on the northern border wore white armor, while those in the southern quadrant wore red.

A moment of silence swept through the clearing. A

tumbleweed rolled across the ground. It was the unspoken signal for the battle to start, and the two forces rushed in toward the center, yelling out their battle cries.

"For Lilian!!"

"For chastity!!"

Thunder struck the earth as these two titanic armies fought. Bodies were thrown into the air with impunity. Halberds clashed, the sound of metal on metal, steel ringing against steel, rang out in a symphony of chaos. Sparks flew and shouts accompanied the maelstrom of combat. It was, indeed, a battle worthy of being placed within the annals of history.

A third party soon entered the fray. From one of the many cliffs surrounding the battlefield, an army appeared. Unlike the two forces duking it out down below, this army was bereft of nearly all their clothes. Wearing nothing but simple loincloths and bandoleers similar to Tarzan's, the group of individuals looked identical. Messy blond hair framed bright blue eyes that glared down at the battlefield. With nary a thought, this force surged down the cliff, their own battle cry echoing across the land.

"DEATH TO THE CHERRY!!"

And so more chaos was unleashed upon the battlefield.

***

"Kevin? Earth to Kevin? Hello? Anybody home?"

"Wha—eh, what?" Kevin blinked several times, his focus returning to the real world. "I-I'm sorry, did you say something?"

Lilian frowned at him, but reiterated her question. "I asked if you would let me take a shower with you, remember?"

"Ah, r-right, so you did…" he blushed and looked at the ground, silently coming to a decision. "I… I suppose it would be alright… if we… you know… showered together…"

"Really?" The way Lilian's eyes lit up like fireworks on the Fourth of July was a sight to behold. The girl practically radiated happiness.

Unable to speak properly, Kevin merely nodded.

"Thank you! I promise you won't regret this!"

What followed their conversation was like something out of a dream. After allowing Lilian into the restroom, she stripped off her clothes and joined him in the shower.

The shower/bathtub was large enough to fit four people

comfortably. It also had a bench and a detachable shower head.

Lilian had Kevin sit in front of her as she lathered her hands with soap and began washing his back. Kevin's stomach twisted itself into knots as Lilian's tender hands roamed over his body. His heart thumped in his chest like the roaring engine of a 1965 Camaro as her delicate fingers ran through his hair. His entire body felt like a live wire. Every touch, every caress, the feel of her thighs touching his, of her breasts as they rubbed against him, sent his mind into a dizzying fit. Only an effort of sheer will on his part kept Kevin from passing out. After Lilian finished washing his back and hair, it was his time to return the favor.

"Make sure to wash every inch of me, okay?" The words were said so innocently that Kevin could do nothing but nod dumbly.

Okay, Kevin. You can do this. You and Lilian have done plenty of stuff together. This is just the next step up. Don't lose it now.

Lilian sat between his legs. Her long red hair hung over her shoulder, exposing her back and rear end to him. His gaze followed the curve of her spine; her perfectly straight posture drew his eyes invariably to the hint of her shapely butt. She sat so close that her scent addled his mind, and while not close enough that her backside was pressing into him, he was keenly aware of her thighs touching his. A pleasant shudder ran through his body.

Oh, God! I think I'm gonna die!

"Kevin?"

"Y-yes?"

"You're not washing my back."

"R-right... sorry..."

Hesitant at first, he placed a single hand on Lilian's back, right between her shoulder blades. A jolt shot through him. Her skin felt so soft, so incredibly soft.

He ran his hand up and down her back, slowly moving in greater and vaster sweeps. His hand would travel from the nape of her neck down to her tailbone. Her tail wasn't out right then, but a part of him wished it was.

"K-Kevin," Lilian moaned.

"Hmm?"

"Y-you forgot the soap."

Kevin needed a moment to process those words. "Oh, so I did.

S-sorry."

"Mm," another delicate moan, "that feels really good, so it's okay."

After lathering his hands in soap, Kevin began the process of washing his mate's sublimely stunning back. He burned the feeling of his soapy hands mapping the contours of her body, of her perfect, unblemished skin becoming covered in soap suds. He swept his hands over her skin in soft, gentle movements; transitory caresses that caused the young female kitsune to emit a dangerous moan.

Kevin had become entranced. His body was burning up from the intense visual stimulation, and his mind had blanked out some time ago. What little remained of his higher thought processes could do nothing but congratulate him on not passing out.

The process of "you wash my back and I'll wash yours" eventually ended. Rather than get out of the tub, Lilian proposed the great idea of lounging in a hot bath together.

"In Japan, the act of bathing together is very important for increasing intimacy between couples. I think it's called skinship."

"You do know this isn't Japan, right?" Kevin surprised himself by speaking. He hadn't believed himself capable of speech.

Lilian pouted, but didn't let his words deter her. "Regardless of which country we live in, I think it's important for us to do this so we can bond as mates. I want to grow closer to you. I want us to be more intimate."

Kevin didn't know if it was her words, her smile, or the way she looked at him with those radiant eyes of hers, but he found himself unable to deny her desire for physical intimacy..

"All... all right. We can, um, we can take a bath together, too."

"Yes!" Lilian pumped a fist into the air. "Beloved and I are taking a bath together!"

"Do you really have to say that so loudly?" Kevin grumbled.

After filling the tub with hot water, Kevin leaned against the wall while Lilian rested against his chest. If he thought washing Lilian's back had been torturous, that was nothing compared to having her naked body conform to his.

Kevin could feel everything; her back as it rested against his chest, her butt as it rubbed him in all the right—and wrong—ways. He could feel himself respond to her, could feel the surge of overwhelming arousal. And, judging by the way she wiggled against him, Lilian could feel it, too.

I need to calm down before I regret something. I know! Think unsexy thoughts. Think unsexy thoughts. Think unsexy thoughts. Eric's dad in a speedo. U-ugh, I think I just permanently scarred myself!

Despite his insecurity, Kevin slowly became more comfortable. He was still very much aroused. His body still felt like it had been lit on fire. But, it didn't affect him as much anymore. He found that he could even appreciate Lilian's beauty without his mind lagging like a crappy computer trying to stream anime at 1080p.

"Isn't this nice, Beloved?" Lilian's voice snapped Kevin out of his stupor. He realized with a start that he'd been nodding off.

"Yeah," Kevin agreed a little reluctantly, "it is kind of nice."

Lilian turned her head, green eyes gleaming in triumph. "See? I told you bathing together was a good idea."

"All right. Fine," Kevin grumbled half-heartedly. "You were right and I was wrong. Happy?"

"Very." Lilian twisted around until she was facing Kevin, who suddenly found his attention divided between her gorgeous face and her tantalizing breasts. "But you wanna know what would make me even happier?"

"Uh, um, no?"

Lilian's lips arced into the loveliest of smiles. Her arms encircled his neck, and her body molded to his. Kevin nearly went cross-eyed as he felt Lilian's bare breasts rubbing against him.

"If you would kiss me."

Kevin broke. His body responded without conscious thought; his arms tightened, pulling this divine creature closer to him. The feel of her body conforming to his sent what little was left of Kevin's restraint out the window.

Lilian didn't resist when Kevin kissed her. She moaned into his mouth as his tongue penetrated her lips and snaked past her teeth to gently caress her tongue, which responded with equal passion. Her mouth soon filled with saliva, which was stirred together by their dance. Loud noises permeated the air; the smacking of lips and the echoing moans. Water splashed against the tub, spilling over as his hands roamed along Lilian's back, while hers made a complete mess of his hair.

Oxygen soon became an issue. With the gasp of a man drowning at sea, Kevin and Lilian reluctantly parted. Yet even then their hunger was such that they continued giving each other intermittent pecks between gasps for oxygen, all to keep the fires in their loins blazing. The last of those annoyingly unsatisfying pecks was caught by Kevin's voracious tongue. The moans Lilian elicited provoked the flames burning in Kevin's gut, spurring him to continue.

While their mouths were occupied, their eager bodies were just as active. Lilian squirmed against him; her breasts rubbing against his chest, two stiff peaks causing a ceaseless sensation of never ending pleasure. Her fingers threaded through his locks of messy blond hair, turning them into a bed of wet spikes. In return, his hands occupied themselves with her shapely ass, grabbing and squeezing and caressing, much to the redhead's delight.

Kevin could feel himself losing control, could feel himself slipping further into the dream that was Lilian. His body craved her, had been craving her for a long time, and it seemed he could no longer resist the beautiful kitsune's shamefully innocent invitation.

"Kevin…" Lilian's moan was like a siren's call as he switched from kissing her mouth to suckling on her neck. One of his hands slipped between their bodies and fondled her breasts. Her nipples stiffened under his ministrations and her moaning became even louder.

One last thought managed to penetrate Kevin's mind, a pathetic plea to stop, to cease what he was doing and end this madness.

Stop this, Kevin! Cease what you are doing and end this madness!

Yeah, that.

Unfortunately, the logical side of his brain no longer functioned as it should have. Thoughts of decency, propriety, and waiting until he felt comfortable with Lilian vanished, and all that remained was his desire to experience all that Lilian had to offer. To please and be pleased in return. He wanted to—

"Damn, that's hot."

—Like a mountain of ice cold water being dumped on them, the young couple became painfully aware of the third presence in the room. Lilian and Kevin slowly craned their heads toward the new voice.

Eric stood in the doorway, hands on the handle. If his flushed cheeks and bleeding nose didn't tell Kevin what the boy was looking at, then the dark eyes planted firmly on Lilian did.

"Kya!"

"ERIC!"

In that moment, two things happened; Lilian ducked underneath the water's surface, covering her body as best she could, while Kevin roared and jumped out of the bathtub.

In a display of aerial acrobatics that should have been impossible without shonen manga mechanics involved, Kevin leapt into the air, his body twisting like a corkscrew until he was parallel with the ground, his feet pointing directly at Eric.

"Stop-ogling-my-mate-you-pervert Kick!"

The loud *bang!* of Kevin's feet impacting against Eric's chest rang out abnormally loudly due to the bathroom's acoustics. Seconds after being hit, Eric flew backwards with the speed of a cannonball. He blew right out the door and into the hall, crashing into the wall before crumpling onto his backside with a heavy thud.

"Ow."

He got back up, surprisingly.

"Oi! What the hell was that for, you—" was about as far as he got.

"Finishing move! Combustion of Manly Souls Uppercut!"

Eric's head jerked upwards, his teeth clacking together and his face scrunching up in stunned agony. His feet left the ground by at least a foot. Meanwhile, his spine curved painfully, traveling in the direction that the momentum of Kevin's fist took him.

Seconds later, Eric Corrompere lay on the ground, dead to the world around him. Standing above the prone pervert's form, Kevin took several heavy breaths, his right fist still raised above his head.

"Whoo! Now that's what I like to see! Take it off!"

With movements that were almost mechanical, Kevin turned to see four sexy vixens standing several yards down the hall, each one wearing a vastly different expression. Kotohime looked

amused, Iris' lecherous grin put anything Eric could give to shame, Kirihime's cheeks were flushed an adorable red, while Camellia stared at him with enough childish curiosity that he felt ashamed for some reason.

And suddenly, like a blaster bolt between the eyes, it hit him.

He was still naked.

"IYAHN!" Kevin cried out pathetically as he tried to unsuccessfully cover his body from view.

Chapter 7

The Katsura Sisters

Twilight had settled onto the valley of the sun several hours ago. The night sky, darkened by the vastness of space, appeared as a panoramic view of the unending and infinite phantasm; a reflection of darkness locked within a cruel and uncaring universe.

Within this dark night, two figures moved, their clawed feet clacking against the blacktop road. Their target was a house built within a cul-de-sac. The structure, like those around it, appeared to be that of a normal house; large with two-stories, a red-tiled roof, and stucco walls. There didn't seem to be anything out of place about this house.

Unless one knew about its occupants.

They had tracked their target's location to this house. After discovering her whereabouts, they began reconnaissance. According to infrared scanning, their target wasn't alone. Seven other heat sources could be detected inside at various locations.

Mission parameters stated that the target needed to be terminated. However, the standing orders programmed into their processors also stated that they were not to be seen by anyone. They would have to remain idle until their target was alone.

"Excuse me, but you two do know that it is rude to spy on people, do you not?"

Two heads swiveled on whirring servomotors. Red visors

focused on a kimono-clad woman carrying a katana standing several feet away.

Neither figure saw the knife that suddenly lashed out from the darkness, a mere flicker of light, which became embedded in the left side of the right figure's head. As the figure crumpled to the ground, the other figure was struck in the chest by two black furry tails. The swinging appendages had enough power behind them to send the figure skidding across the street. Its head swiveled to look at the one who had attacked it and its companion—another woman, this one wearing what its database tentatively identified as a French maid outfit.

Its head turned away from the French maid when its ultrasonic sensory system picked up vibrations traveling along the ground.

It looked at where the first woman had been and glimpsed a brief yet bright flash of light.

And then it saw nothing.

***

It happened within a split second. Kotohime had used the distraction provided by her sister to launch her own assault. Faster than the human eye could blink, her blade hissed out of its sheath, a mere reflection of glimmering moonlight. It was sheathed just as quickly, and upon hearing a soft *click*, the armored figure's head slid off its shoulders and rolled along the ground. Its body remained stationary for a moment before it, too, followed the head, crumpling into a heap of rippling silver.

"Nice job, sister," Kirihime congratulated her on a well-executed maneuver.

"Thank you," Kotohime nodded graciously. She then turned around and looked down at the armored figure. "That is odd…"

"What is?" Kirihime asked as she knelt down, presumably to pull her knife from the first thing's head.

"There is nothing inside," she gestured toward the metallic figure, "it's empty."

"Empty?" Kirihime took a closer look at the one she had killed, even going so far as to try banging on it, which caused its silvery surface to ripple like liquid. "This thing has an unusual composition. I wonder what it's made of."

"I do not know."

Kotohime looked curiously at the now headless "corpse."

What she had originally believed to be an armored human was completely empty. There was nothing inside of it—nothing except for the material it was composed of, which undulated in strange and aberrant ways.

After a moment's observation in which nothing happened, Kotohime shrugged and began to walk away. She had only taken several steps before her danger senses kicked in, screaming at her to move.

Spinning around, Kotohime slid her katana out of its confines. She raised the blade just in time to block a gleaming silver spear. Sparks flew as she rotated her wrist, redirecting the sharp object, forcing it along a circular path over her head. The spear retracted when its attempt at impaling her through the neck failed, and Kotohime frowned when she saw what had attacked her.

The thing that she had just cut the head off of was standing again. Its head was also back on, gleaming and seamlessly attached to its shoulders as if it had never lost it in the first place. A glance to her left revealed that the figure Kirihime had stabbed with her knife was also back on its feet, and it had already engaged her sister in combat.

With her left hand holding her sheath and her right hand gripping the hilt of her katana, Kotohime regained her placid smile as she stared the thing down. "Ara, ara. It looks like this will be a little more interesting than I first suspected."

The thing said nothing. It merely charged, and the sound of steel clashing against steel rang out across the empty street.

***

Though she was normally hesitant, Kirihime felt none of that as she attacked her new enemy. Just like when she was on the hunt, her blood was pumping, her heart was racing, and she was enjoying the thrill of mortal combat.

Her three tails slammed into the creature, whose undulating, anthropomorphic body continued to unnerve her. It flew for several feet before slamming against the blacktop. Sparks arced off its gleaming silver surface as it tumbled along for several dozen feet before coming to a stop.

While she hadn't expected that to be enough to kill this thing, Kirihime still felt surprised when it slowly picked itself off the ground and stood up.

Clawed feet slid across the road, emitting a horrendous squeal like her prey normally did right before she killed them. It turned to face her. Its rippling surface gleamed brightly within the night, the moonlight reflecting off its unblemished metallic body, which didn't have so much as a scratch on it, as if she hadn't sent it tumbling along the ground like a ragdoll.

What is this thing made of?

Frowning, Kirihime used the extension technique again. Her three black tails shot out from underneath her blouse, their tips attempting to spear the thing through the chest. It sidestepped her first tail, which pierced the ground it had been standing on, then backpedaled to avoid her second tail, which she tried to use as a bludgeoning tool. Her third tail came in, and this time, the thing's hand shot out and grabbed onto it, its fingers curling around her tail in a vice-like grip.

That's not good.

Kirihime yelped as the thing yanked on her tail, and she was sent rocketing toward it at dizzying speeds. Despite being surprised by the sudden maneuver, she did not allow herself to remain inert. Swinging her feet around, she pointed her heels at the creature, which either couldn't react in time or didn't realize the danger it was in.

She planted her heels into the thing's visored face, the heeled points digging into the metallic, bullet-shaped head with a loud *crack!* like rumbling thunder. Its head snapped back as it stumbled backwards. Kirihime used its head like a springboard, kicking off and flipping into the air before landing several feet away.

This… this is exciting.

Just like when she was hunting, Kirihime felt her blood pumping through her body at an abnormal rate. Her pupils had become dilated and her breathing heavy. A wide grin spread across her face, stretching from ear to ear.

People who saw this grin usually ran away screaming. The thing facing her did not run. Its servomotors whirred. Its red visor flashed. It almost looked like it was thinking about something. Kirihime did not know what it might have been thinking about, but she didn't really care. She charged at it, rushing toward it in a full-on sprint enhanced by her youki. Within seconds she was there, standing before it, her knives ready to tear it limb from limb.

She thrust the knife in her left hand, but the thing appeared to have finished thinking. It moved more quickly than she expected it to, deftly swerving around her attack, dodging it, and then trying to impale her.

Not one to be outdone, Kirihime bent her torso like a contortionist, the spear passing above her and cutting the air. She wrapped her three tails around the extended spear as it passed and tried to lift the thing off the ground, but the strange mercuric substance proved to be quite slippery. Like an eel it slid from her tails' grasp.

The thing attacked her again, thrusting out its left hand, which also morphed into a spear-like shape. Kirihime tilted her head, but the thing had anticipated her movements. Its right spear-hand suddenly filled her vision.

Kirihime's eyes widened. Pain flared across her cheek as she tilted her head to the left, the sharpened spear moving past her, grazing her skin, cutting into her flesh.

This pain... it feels good!

To keep the thing from attacking her again, Kirihime closed the distance between them.

"Water Art: Crystal Blade!"

Water coalesced around the knife in her left hand, hardening into a crystalline structure that glittered with the consistency of diamonds. That same knife was then thrust forward, her enhanced speed making it move more quickly than anything a normal human could match. The thing tried to block the attack, but one of Kirihime's tails wrapped around its arm, pulling the appendage away from its torso.

The knife pierced the armored body, slicing through it with ease. The blade carved a trail across the chestplate before making a violent exit when Kirihime yanked it out. No blood poured from the gaping wound, and Kirihime watched in silent astonishment as the metal undulated, becoming liquid, before closing around the vicious-looking slash mark.

"What the...?"

Shocked by how her foe had healed from what would have killed even a yōkai, Kirihime nearly missed the spear that the thing tried stabbing her through the head with.

Bringing the blade in her right hand up, Kirihime blocked the attack. However, the strength behind the blow pushed her backwards. She skidded along the ground for several feet, kicking up a light cloud of dust. She eventually stopped, but was forced to immediately move again when the spear quickly elongated, seeking to penetrate her flesh.

That… that looks just like the extension technique!

Kirihime swerved left. The spear followed, becoming liquid again and changing direction to keep her in its sights. It moved so fast it appeared as nothing more than a blur. Kirihime moved faster than she ever had before as she pumped more youki into her muscles.

"Water Art: Three-Tailed Crystal Whips!"

Three whips made of water formed on the tips of her tails and quickly solidified. They shot forth, lashing out at the metal spear, which fell to pieces as the incredibly sharp whips of hardened liquid sliced them into multiple segments. Unfortunately, this didn't seem to end the problem, as the spear simply grew back to its original length and continued extending.

Her mind working overtime, Kirihime began to move about more erratically. She juked and jinked, moving in increasingly complex patterns to avoid the spear that followed her like a male fox in heat. Sweat formed along her brow and threatened to sting her eyes. The patterns she made with her movements became increasingly more complicated as time went on.

It was only after nearly five minutes of evasion that her intentions became clear. The seemingly random patterns she traced while dodging had caused the spear to become tangled into a complicated knot. Kirihime increased her physical abilities with the enhancement technique after twirling around the spear again, her body vanishing into thin air before reappearing several feet away. She hoped that with the spear twisted into a knot, she would have a shot at taking her enemy down before it attacked her.

Her plan to have the strange mercury-like substance twist itself into a knot proved unsuccessful, however. The substance simply melded into itself without resistance, and then the spear continued following her.

"Water Art: Water Armor."

Appearing around her form, thousands of tiny droplets like liquid crystals glittered, their twinkling akin to stars of the Milky

Way galaxy. They moved and pulsed, rippling and shifting into a variety of shapes before amalgamating on her body. The many droplets of water combined to form segments of an armor both ancient and powerful. Each segment covered her body, connecting to each other like links in a chain and forming a set of traditional samurai armor. The armor rippled for a moment, its form seemingly not fully cohesive, before hardening into sparkling crystallized water.

Kirihime charged the spear. Not even bothering to dodge, she let the hardened point of sharp liquid metal hit her. Squealing erupted as the spear, unable to penetrate the diamond-hard armor, scraped along its surface. Sparks coruscated off the armor as the spear's course deviated, sliding across the armor until it no longer presented a threat.

As Kirihime closed the distance, a deranged grin appeared on her face.

"I would really like it if you died for me, please!"

The two knives, hardened water encasing them and lengthening the blades, struck the armored figure at the hips. The two weapons tore straight through the amor, bisecting the thing and causing the top half to fly away from the lower half. The legs, no longer supporting a torso, tumbled to the ground. Meanwhile, its torso soared for several feet before hitting the road with a loud clatter, its surface rippling like a placid pond disturbed by a rock.

Kirihime waited for several seconds. When it became obvious to her that the thing was dead, she dispersed her water armor and stuck the now waterless knives into the sheaths underneath her skirt. At the same time, her sadistic and cruel demeanor vanished.

"I-I am terribly sorry that you had to die." She bowed to the armored figure—or at least the upper half of it. The figure didn't respond, though she had not expected it to. With her apology said, she turned around and started walking away.

She never saw the spear soaring toward her unprotected back until it was too late.

***

Kotohime observed her opponent. Her keen eyes studied its gleaming surface, its sleek design, its clawed feet and strange abilities.

The battle had come to a standstill. This thing, whatever it was, did not have a very durable body. Her blade tore it apart like it was made of rice. Then again, it didn't really need one. Its ability to reform no matter the damage she inflicted on it was impressive.

Kotohime's katana moved at speeds beyond what even most yōkai could perceive. It appeared and disappeared at will, nothing more than brief flashes that struck out and vanished in the same instant. Rather than simply saying her blade "moved," it might have been more accurate to say that her katana was instantly teleporting from one location to the next.

With each flash of her katana, one of the many spear-like tendrils that her enemy launched at her was sliced into exactly six pieces. The strangely liquid substance splattered against the ground, creating a puddle, which would ripple before, ever so slowly, crawling back towards the armored being, amalgamating once again. This, too, she catalogued in her mind.

For its part, the strange armored being had yet to move from its spot. It stood there, a sentinel at the ready. Its arms moved while its heels dug in. The spear-like tendrils shot from its hands ten at a time, one for each finger.

That was something Kotohime had noticed early on. Even though it all appeared to be made of the same liquid compound, no other part of its body except for its hands seemed capable of creating those strange tendrils. It also couldn't create more than ten at any given time.

This worked to her advantage. Her speed was such that blocking against ten attacks at the same time wasn't a problem. Her hands moved and her blade followed, arcing paths of light that sliced through each tendril with ease. When Kotohime felt she had her opponent's timing and attack patterns down, she charged forward.

Six tendrils appeared on her right and four on her left, all of which were set to skewer various parts of her body.

Moving with an instinctive grace bred from years of experience, Kotohime's feet danced along the blacktop. Legs bent and thigh muscles bunched underneath her beautiful kimono, preparing for what was to come. With a push, her feet left the ground in a burst of speed.

She shot forward, her body parallel to the asphalt and spinning like a top. In a manner that was similar to a blender, the blade in her left hand spun about so rapidly that it could only be seen as bright silver streaks. The blade created a funnel around Kotohime's body, a whirlpool of steel that sliced apart everything in its path. All ten tendrils were shredded. Her blade spun right through them, cutting them into hundreds of tiny pieces.

Ceasing her spin by creating a counterforce to halt her rotary movements, Kotohime flipped around, landing on her feet just six inches from her foe. She crouched down in a manner that was all predator. The figure tilted its head, its red visor staring at her with an unnatural glow. Swifter than it could track her, she came up and swung her katana.

"Ikken Hissatsu. Sen."

Her blade lashed out an uncountable number of times. Over and over, the katana appeared as instantaneous flashes of silver that continuously moved within split seconds of each other. The flashes, though brief, soon coalesced into an ethereal spiderweb of otherworldly luminescence, and the creature, thing, whatever it was, found itself trapped within the middle of this intricate web of continuous attacks. Unable to move. Unable to block. Unable to do anything. All it could do was stand there and ride out the wave of ceaseless blades assaulting it from all sides.

And then it was over.

Kotohime sheathed her blade, the resounding *click* echoing across the silent road. The thing behind her slid apart, thousands of separate pieces hitting the ground with a wet splat.

Turning around to observe the armored figure, Kotohime noticed immediately that it wasn't dead, despite being turned into several puddles. The mercury-like substance still glowed. Blobs of liquid metal pulled themselves together, congealing into a single entity once more. Like a rising tide, it surged upwards, its undefined form rippling. It began bulging in some places and retracting in others, its body constantly shifting, as if it couldn't decide on the form it wanted to take, until it eventually settled on an approximately human shape.

"Hmm." Gripping the hilt of her katana, Kotohime observed her regenerated foe with the sharp eyes of a warrior. "It seems I will need to use something more powerful than a simple sword technique to defeat you."

It had become clear to her that this thing was impervious to all forms of physical damage—slashing, stabbing, blunt force trauma; none of that would work. If she wanted to defeat this strange metallic being, then she needed to use something that didn't require her to cut it.

But what technique should she use? It would have to be something that could destroy its body in one go. Maybe... yes... that could work, provided she was careful.

The thing seemed to realize that its tendril attacks wouldn't work on her. Its hands shifted, the metal elongating into two double-edged blades about three feet in length. Then it charged at her.

Kotohime met the charge head on. The first attack made by the armored figure was a downward slash with its right blade, which Kotohime redirected when she raised her katana at an angle, allowing the weapon to slide off her sword. She then shifted her stance, her feet sliding across the blacktop as she raised the katana above her head with the tip pointed at the ground. The ringing of steel echoed as her foe swung its blade again, only to discover that her katana was there to meet it. When their weapons locked, she flicked her wrist and the blade grinding against her katana was redirected over her head, following the contours of a crescent.

Her skillful redirect caused her opponent to stumble forward. Reversing her grip on her katana, Kotohime sent an enhanced thrust at the figure with her pommel. The creature, unable to properly ground itself, could do nothing as she hit it with the full force of her youki-enhanced strength. Like the sonic boom of a fighter jet breaking the sound barrier, a powerful shockwave sent the thing hurtling backwards where it smashed into the ground, breaking apart the road and digging a long trench in the blacktop.

"Water Art: Dance of Timeless Erosion."

Before the thing even had a chance to stand back up, water gathered around it. At first, the liquid only appeared as tiny droplets barely larger than a thumbtack. There were a lot of them; thousands, maybe even hundreds of thousands; glittering gems from a hidden treasure, tiny pearls of moisture that remained liquid and unstable. They looked small, harmless, and were surprisingly beautiful.

Then they began to move, swirling around the armored figure like pieces of debris trapped in a tornado. The water droplets picked up speed, the rotatory forces becoming an intense maelstrom of energy, a whirlpool of incredible power that danced around her armored foe. And then the funnel of rotating droplets started to shrink, conforming to the size and shape of the being trapped within.

Water is an unusual element. It is generally very gentle, soft and tender, like a lover's caress. However, it can also be powerful and chaotic, a tempest squall capable of unmitigated destruction in the right circumstances.

It was not wind or fire or earth that created the Grand Canyon. It was water. Thousands of years worth of water eroding the earth, slowly chipping away at it. There was power in water, both terrible and great.

Kotohime, as a Water Kitsune, was capable of controlling this element with the ease of one born into it. Her very blood pulsed with the flow of water. Her technique, **Dance of Timeless Erosion**, was an ability that showed her powers over water to their fullest extent.

The water molecules encased the metal figure from head to toe and continued spinning. The force generated from each droplet, combined with each droplet's continuous motion, took what constituted as several thousand years' worth of erosion and compressed it into several seconds.

When the water finally dispersed, her armored opponent was gone, vanished. Annihilated. Its very molecular structure had been broken down and eroded. The only thing that remained was a strange orb, which Kotohime picked up and placed within her Extra Dimensional Storage Space.

"I see you took care of your opponent, sister." Kotohime turned to greet her younger sibling, who smiled at her as she walked up. "And without receiving so much as a single scratch." The woman's eyes shone with a glimmer of admiration. "I'm always amazed by how powerful you are."

"In a few decades, you will be this strong as well." Kotohime observed her sister, the cuts on her clothes and the blood leaking from her many wounds. Her gaze traveled to her sister's side, where Kirihime held a hand against her torso, carnelian fluids seeping between her fingers. "You are injured. Do you require healing?"

"I appreciate your concern, but you need not worry about me." Demure as always, Kirihime smiled at her elder sibling and brushed off Kotohime's concern. "That thing, um, whatever it was, it was stronger than I expected it to be. I underestimated it and ended up paying the price."

"I see. So, you had to use 'that,' then?" When Kirihime just tilted her head in honest confusion, Kotohime sighed. "Never mind. Let us report back to the others and inform them of this new development."

"Okay."

***

Standing on the roof, a gleaming metallic figure observed the battle's conclusion from afar, watching as the two beings defeated its two brethren. After cataloguing the many attacks used and studying the battle with its high-spec processor, it quickly determined that fighting those two would end in its defeat.

While it had no concept of death, it did have orders to exterminate Heather Grant. Its processor, which functioned on logic, reasoned that it couldn't eliminate its target if it was destroyed.

With no more reason to stick around, it left, disappearing into the night. It would wait for another opportunity to dispose of its target.

***

Kevin's sleep was interrupted by an annoying voice.

"Kevin-sama. Lilian-sama. I must ask that you two please wake up."

"Five more minutes," Lilian, who'd slept with him, didn't appreciate being woken up either.

"I apologize, Lilian-sama, but I must insist that you two wake up now. There has been a new development that you should be made aware of."

With a groan of complaint, Kevin opened his eyes and sat up. Yawning, he raised his arms above his head, his eyes closing as stiff muscles were stretched taut. Sitting up beside him, Lilian rubbed her eyes in a most adorable manner.

"Come along, you two." Kotohime stood before them. "We are having a meeting in the living room."

"Right, right," Kevin yawned again, "we're coming."

When he, Lilian and Kotohime arrived in the living room, it was to see that Kirihime and the others were already there. He and Lilian sat down, while Kotohime gracefully moved to stand beside her sister. The only one not present was Camellia, who he assumed was still sleeping.

"Thank you for waking up so promptly, everyone," Kotohime bowed politely.

"Whatever. Look, I don't want to be rude or anything," Iris started, crossing her arms and giving the swordswoman a tired glare, "but does anyone want to tell me why I had to wake up at this Inari-forsaken hour?"

Unlike Kevin and Eric, who sat on armchairs, and Lilian—who sat on Kevin—Iris had chosen to rest on the floor. Once again, Kevin found himself unconsciously admiring the raven-haired fox-girl; without even trying, the girl somehow made even the simplest of gestures look unbearably sexy. Sprawled regally on her right side, her head resting on her right hand, the kitsune's posture seemed designed to draw all eyes to her. Her sleepwear, a tiny white shirt that stretched tautly across her breasts and showed off her flat stomach and a red thong, ensured that she remained the center of attention.

"My apologies, Iris-sama." The sound of Kotohime's voice gave Kevin the strength needed to look away from Iris, something he was very grateful for. "The reason that I have asked all of you to wake up at such an untimely hour is because just a few minutes ago, a pair of... of... creatures? Robots?" Her nose scrunched up. "I do not know what they were, exactly. Suffice to say, they were hostile, and I believe they were responsible for Heather-san's condition."

Everyone looked at Kotohime in alarm.

"Fortunately, Kirihime and I managed to defeat those things," Kotohime continued. "However, we are now faced with a new problem. The strange foes that we fought are completely unknown to me. They were neither yōkai nor human, but something else entirely."

"So, you don't know what they were?" Lilian looked troubled.

"I do not."

Kotohime went into a brief description of the enemy she and her sister had fought. Only half of Kevin paid attention. The rest of him was trying to ignore the way Lilian's butt felt against his erection.

Lilian leaned back against Kevin's chest after Kotohime finished giving her description. "It sounds like those things were made of mercury. That's the only metal I know of that can become liquid at low temperatures."

"I do not believe it was mercury. While the substance did indeed behave in a manner similar to mercury, it also acted completely differently from that particular type of metal, moving almost as if it had a mind of its own."

Kotohime reached into her cleavage and pulled out a orb. It didn't look like much. It was a sphere about the size of a baseball, silver, but with black veins running along its surface.

"Is that...?"

"Indeed." Kotohime nodded at Kevin. "After I defeated my opponent, all that was left of it was this strange sphere." Holding the orb up to her eyes, the maid-slash-bodyguard's brow furrowed. "I was hoping we would be able to discover what those things were with this, but I confess to being at a loss."

"I think I might be able to answer a few of your questions."

Everyone turned their heads to see Heather standing in the hallway leading to the guest rooms. She didn't look good. She was leaning against the wall for support, and her right hand covered her left side. Her heavy breathing was accompanied by sweat covering her flushed face, as if just standing there took a concerted amount of effort.

"Master! You're awake!" Eric was at her side in an instant. "Are you alright? Is there anything I can do for you? Do you need any help?"

"I'm fine, my young apprentice." Heather gave her student in the ways of perversion a smile mixed with a grimace. She looked back at Kotohime. "I believe I can answer at least some of your questions. Apprentice, help me walk; I seem to be having some trouble moving on my own right now."

With Eric's help, Heather was soon sitting on the armchair that he had vacated, the young pervert choosing to stand behind her.

"I'm sorry for getting all of you involved in this. I would also like to thank you for helping me."

"You are welcome." Kotohime graciously accepted Heather's thanks. "Now, then, I believe you mentioned something about having answers to our questions."

Heather nodded. "Right, it's about those things you fought. I don't really know what those things are, but I do know who created them; a group calling themselves The Sons and Daughters of Humanity."

Iris wrinkled her nose. "Pretty pretentious name, don't you think?"

Heather shrugged. "Don't look at me. I didn't come up with the name. Anyway, The Sons and Daughters of Humanity is a secret organization of the highest level. Very few people know they exist, and fewer still know what their true goals are. I'm not exactly sure who's funding them, but I know they're very powerful, and that they've got some deep pockets."

Kotohime stroked the hilt of her katana, her thoughtful hum momentarily filling the air. "The Sons and Daughters of Humanity... I take it they are some kind of anti-yōkai group?"

"Yes. Their modus operandi is basically to protect humanity from the threat of yōkai incursions." Noticing the disgusted looks being sent her way, Heather raised her hands in a weak gesture of defense. "Hey, don't look at me. I don't really care about yōkai or whatever. I only worked for them because I had no other choice."

"How did you come into their services?" asked Kevin.

Heather squirmed in her seat and laughed nervously. "W-well, you know how it is... these things just tend to happen sometimes."

Everyone deadpanned at her.

"No," Kevin countered swiftly, "we don't know how it is, because these things don't just 'tend to happen.'" Everyone nodded in agreement—even Eric. "So, please, explain it to us."

Kotohime looked at Kevin in approval, causing the teenager to flush a bit and bury his face in Lilian's hair.

Lilian giggled when his hot breath hit her neck and wiggled in his lap. "T-that kind of tickles."

"A-alright, but you guys have to promise not to laugh." Heather eyed all of the people present. "Before I became a member of The Sons and Daughters of Humanity, I was actually a cop."

"I can believe that," Kevin said, and Eric nodded in agreement. While the woman looked sort of like a cheerleader with her blond hair, bright attitude and curvaceous figure, she also had a toughness about her that was reminiscent of several police officers he'd met before.

"Right, so, I actually used to work for the LAPD, however, I was fired for, uh, reasons."

"Reasons?" Several brows furrowed, Kevin's included. "What kind of reasons?"

"Oh, you know…" Heather avoided eye-contact with everyone. "The usual reasons."

"Stop beating around the bush and just tell us!"

"I was caught peeping, okay?!"

Silence.

"Um, what?" Kevin asked, not quite sure he'd heard her properly.

With those words, the dam broken, there was no stopping Heather now. "It all started back when I was younger. Ever since I was little, I've been enamored with women's bodies. There's just something about a woman's figure that drives me wild. The way their breasts bounce, how their butts jiggle, the flow of seamless curves, it's enough to really get my motor running. Kukuku…"

Heather giggled like a perverted old lecher. Her bluish-green eyes glazed over and drool leaked from her mouth, dribbling down her chin.

She eventually snapped back to reality and noticed that everyone was looking at her with matching deadpan expressions—except for Eric, who had stars in his eyes. She blushed, absently wiping the drool away.

"A-anyway, this love for women's bodies soon turned into something more: admiration and the desire to immortalize the beauty of women everywhere, which is why I began peeping—and also because I wanted to use them as inspiration for the books I'm writing."

A moment of silence ensued.

"It's a female version of Eric," Kevin suddenly deadpanned.

"A female Eric has descended upon us," Lilian added.

"At least this female Eric is hotter than the male version," Iris said, which caused everyone to look at her strangely. "What? All of you were thinking it, too."

After several headshakes, the group turned back to Heather.

"Please continue, Heather-san."

"Um, right. So, anyway, I would peep on women and, well, I eventually got caught, like, multiple times. After the... seventh time, I think?" She paused, then nodded. "Yeah, after the seventh time getting caught, the Chief of Police fired me. He said something about how I was breaking the law." She huffed. "I don't see how I broke the law. I'm a woman, they were women; it's not like it's illegal for me to ogle another woman."

"The fact that you would even use the term ogle is reason enough to fire you," Kevin stated with certainty.

"That still doesn't explain how you came to work for these Sons and Daughters of Humanity," Kotohime pressed.

"That came later," Heather admitted. "See, I was pretty down on my luck after that. I couldn't hold a job for very long because I kept peeping on my female coworkers while they were changing. My managers would always fire me after receiving several complaints—or when they discovered the hidden cameras I had installed inside of each locker."

Kevin would have facepalmed, but since his face was buried in Lilian's neck, he refrained.

"I was eventually picked up by a recruiter, who said that my experience as a cop would secure me a job with the agency he worked for. He also said they didn't care if I peeped on women in my free time, so I took it."

"And these people turned out to be The Sons and Daughters of Humanity?" Lilian asked for clarification.

"Yep."

Silence fell over the group as everyone absorbed this latest piece of information.

"Dang," Kevin grunted, "those people don't have very high standards, do they?"

"I think it's more that they just don't care who works for them, so long as that person is skilled enough to be of use," Heather told Kevin.

"Why are these people after you now?" asked Kirihime. "Weren't they your comrades?"

"Because I disobeyed orders, I think, or maybe because I failed to deliver Red over there." Heather pointed at Lilian, who puffed up her cheeks at the new nickname the woman had given her. "I'm not really sure what goes on in the minds of those up top. All I know is that after the debacle in which Red and Swift got away, the agency decided to cut us loose."

"And by cut loose, you mean they tried to silence you," Kotohime stated more than asked.

"Right." Heather nodded. "I'm pretty sure the others in my division are already dead. Our base was attacked and completely destroyed. I was out at the time, so I wasn't there when it happened, but I saw the aftermath. There were a lot of corpses and no survivors."

"How do you know it was these Sons and Daughters people?" asked Lilian. "Couldn't it have been someone else?"

"You mean aside from the killer robots that attacked me?" Heather shot back. "The only people who knew the location of our base are the people in my division and our superiors."

"We also know where it's located," Kevin pointed out.

"No," Heather shook her head, "you know where our holding cells were. That wasn't our actual base, which is located seventy-two miles outside of Phoenix in the middle of nowhere."

"If you knew these people were after you, then why are you still in Arizona?" Lilian asked the question that Kevin wanted to know as well. It didn't make much sense to him.

"Where would I go?" Heather shrugged at her own question. "These guys aren't a small terrorist cell or a tiny drug cartel. They're a large organization that spans fifty-two different countries. They've got spies everywhere. How else do you think they can kidnap so many yōkai without anyone ever knowing it's them?"

No one had an answer for her, and it was this very lack of an answer that scared Kevin the most.

Aside from what Heather had just told them, he had no clue as to who these people were, but he knew one thing for sure.

This would not be the last time he and his friends encountered The Sons and Daughters of Humanity.

Chapter 8

Invitation

"I see. So, both Kotohime and Kirihime are acting as my Lilian's bodyguards, are they?"

"It seems that way, Lord Jiāoào."

Jiāoào sat on a comfortable-looking couch made of red leather. Gold inlays and intricate designs swirled around it in esoteric patterns. The leather squeaked as he shifted. Laying on the couch with her head on his lap, a docile Maddison rested, her dead eyes staring into a void.

His current abode, while still depressingly tiny, had a much more ostentatious appearance now. Large tapestries hung from the wall, their colors a combination of royal purple and gold. The plain white carpet had been switched out for the same purple as the tapestries. He had even added several gigantic columns to the foyer and switched out the boring staircase for a much grander one.

While he still didn't approve of the place and would be glad to leave it, at least now it held the decor of someone befitting his station.

"I should have known they would be here," Jiāoào murmured, mostly to himself. "Kotohime has been my Lilian's personal bodyguard ever since she gained her second tail, and Kirihime has been taking care of her sister and mother for decades." He stroked the underside of his chin with one of his two tails. "Is there any chance you and Maddison could defeat them?"

"Doubtful," Ling's answer was swift and sure. Had anyone else spoken in such a manner, or told him such a thing, they would have been punished. He trusted Ling's judgement on matters such as this, however.

"Which means we cannot attack while either one of them is around," Jiāoào mused.

"In a two on one battle we might be able to defeat Kirihime," Ling said, her three tails writhing agitatedly at the thought of fighting the water user. "However, it would be a close call. She did not earn the title of Yandere Berserker for nothing."

"Hmm." More thinking noises. "What if we went after Lilian while she is at that… school that she is currently attending?"

"We would be breaking one of the few laws that all yōkai must abide by, Lord Jiāoào, in which case, we would have to deal with Davin Monstrang, a yōkai whose power is said to be on par with an eight-tailed kitsune."

Jiāoào grimaced. "That damn Saint is causing me problems without even realizing it."

All yōkai traveling to the US had to go through an immigration process, where their names were put on record. Jiāoào had not wanted to deal with the Four Saints, so he'd simply infiltrated the country by entering the human way. This meant they had to be more cautious than he normally liked.

"If you'd like," a voice spoke up, "I could take care of those bodyguards for you."

Jiāoào looked at the speaker, trying not to show his disgust as he contemplated the suggestion. "No, even if you could defeat these two, doing so would create too much of a ruckus, and I would rather not have to deal with a member of the Four Saints."

"As you wish," a man garbed like a butler bowed mockingly low.

Sighing, Jiāoào relaxed back into his posh, comfortable sofa. His fingers idly scraped Maddison's scalp. Maddison shuddered, but she didn't react to his ministrations otherwise. Jiāoào ignored her shuddering.

"This is quite the conundrum." Thinking about the issue some more, he eventually happened upon an idea. "I want you to enroll in my Lilian's academy. Find out everything you can, and if you see an opportunity to capture her without rousing suspicion, then do so."

Ling bowed before him. "Of course, Lord Jiāoào."

As Ling left to perform her duties, Jiāoào smiled as an image of Lilian appeared within his mind. "Soon, very soon, you will become mine." He looked down at the pathetic excuse for a kitsune resting on his lap. "And then I can get rid of you."

Jiāoào drifted off, thoughts of how he would break Lilian flitting through his mind.

He never noticed Maddison gritting her sharp canines. Nor did he see the single tear that leaked from her right eye.

***

On Monday morning Kevin, Lilian and Iris headed to school with Eric.

Eric did not take the bus to school, because his old man was the principal—a fact that appalled women. They were driven to school by Mr. Corrompere, who somehow managed to sleep through everything that had happened last night.

I guess it's because Kirihime had placed an enchantment on him.

School felt very odd that day. Perhaps it was because of what happened last night, the break in their routine, the knowledge about the anti-yōkai group, and the strange machines that Kirihime and Kotohime had fought, but Kevin and Lilian felt off all day. Going to school, sitting in class, and spending time with friends talking about regular teenage stuff--all of it felt so normal that it threw them for a loop.

"I'm telling you, nobody can beat Kenshin Himura in a straight up sword fight. He's the ultimate badass swordsman, and that style of his is way more awesome than anyone else's."

"You clearly don't know what you're talking about. Kirito would pound Himura's ass into grass."

Kevin let the argument between Alex and Andrew wash over him. Lilian sat beside him, listening to Lindsay as she tried to convince the redhead to join her soccer team.

"Are you sure there's no way I can convince you to join the soccer team? I really think you would be a good addition," the tomboy was saying. "You're really fast, and you've got some serious kicking power."

Lilian smiled apologetically at her friend. "I'm sorry, but I'm not really interested in playing sports."

"Ha… I get it. I'll stop asking, for now at least." Lindsay gave her friend a pout. "But, don't think I've given up or anything."

Lilian's demure giggle rang through the air like wind chimes. "Of course. I would expect nothing less from you."

"By the way, I noticed that Kevin seems kind of tired today." Lindsay leaned into Lilian, a somewhat mischievous grin on her face. "You two didn't do anything inappropriate, did you?"

"Great," Kevin sighed, "Lindsay's become a gossip."

"Hush, you," Lindsay said without taking her eyes off Lilian. "So, did you?"

Lilian tilted her head in curiosity. She appeared genuinely confused. "I'm not sure I understand."

Lindsay gave her a dubious look. "Oh, come on. You know. Did you and Kevin get up to anything…" she leaned forward more and whispered into the redhead's ear, "naughty?"

Kevin took a bite of his pork cutlets as he cast a sideways glance at the pair.

I wonder if I should tell Lindsay that I can hear every word she's saying?

"Naughty?" Lilian's frown grew.

Lindsay nodded emphatically. "Yeah, you know. Like, some healthy adult fun and all that?"

Lilian placed a finger against her lips, her thoughtful mien undeniably cute. "Well, Kevin and I did take a shower together, and we lounged in the bath afterward. We also kissed a lot." Lilian looked at the now red-faced Lindsay, who apparently hadn't expected him and Lilian to have actually gotten up to anything risque. "That might have tired him out a bit, but I don't think we did anything inappropriate."

"How could you say you and Kevin didn't do anything inappropriate?" Lindsay looked scandalized. "Everything you just told me is completely inappropriate. Seriously, you two… and in the bath… how is that not inappropriate?"

"Kevin's my mate. Anything he does to me is not only appropriate, but completely normal."

Lindsay looked like someone had just smacked her in the face with a dead fish. "… Is this another kitsune thing?"

"Ara? A kitsune thing?"

While Lilian and Lindsay spoke of things that Kevin rather wished he couldn't hear, Christine sat down on his other side.

"Hey," she greeted, "you look like shit."

Kevin gave her a bland look. "Gee, thanks. Hearing someone say I look like crap really brightens my day."

Christine blushed. "T-that's not what I—I just meant you look tired!"

"I know." Kevin rubbed a hand down his face. "Sorry, I've got a lot on my mind right now."

"You wanna talk about it?" When Kevin looked at her like she'd said something strange, Christine's cheeks turned blue. "W-what the hell are you staring at me like that for, you idiot?"

"No reason." Kevin's blond hair swayed as he shook his head. "I'm just surprised you're being so, well, so nice."

Christine looked offended. "I can be nice!"

"You yell at me every time we talk."

"Urk!"

"You've also started hitting me whenever we talk, too."

"Gurk!"

"Don't forget the number of times she's beaten up Eric," Lilian added.

"Ugh!"

"Eric deserved all of those beatings," Kevin pointed out.

"True, true." Lilian nodded. "I was just pointing out how violent she is."

"Stop talking about me like I'm not here!" a blue-faced Christine shouted.

"Speaking of Eric," Alex started as he and his brother stopped arguing, "where is he?"

"Don't know," his twin said, "but it's kinda odd that he's not here. Eric's not one to miss out on a chance to try and grope Christine."

"Wha—SHUT UP ABOUT THAT!"

"Justin is also missing," Lindsay added.

"So is Iris," Lilian frowned.

"Eric's probably trying to peep on the freshmen girls while they change into their PE uniforms," Kevin determined. "That, or he's already running from them."

As if on cue, loud, obnoxious wails of agony echoed across the campus, followed by equally loud screams of pain.

"NOT THE FACE! NOT THE FACE! AAIIEEEE! YES, THE FACE! YES, THE FACE!"

A stiff breeze blew through the now silent clearing. Several birds cawed in a most annoying manner.

"Or he's already been caught," Kevin said into the silence.

"And Justin and Iris?" asked Lindsay.

Kevin and Lilian shared a look.

"Last I saw, Iris had convinced Justin to give her a tour of the school," Lilian said.

"Tch! Lucky bastard," Alex grumbled. "How did someone like Justin manage to catch the interest of a babe like Iris? He can't even hold a proper conversation!"

"That's probably why," Lilian mused. "He's so simple-minded that manipulating him is easy for someone like Iris."

Iris had been extensively trained in the art of pleasing and manipulating people. The matriarch had wanted to turn Lilian's sister into a field agent; someone who would travel around the world and gather potentially beneficial information via the seduction of men—and women. She probably would have become their best temptress, too, had she not been so adamant in refusing the matriarch under the claim that "*the only person she wanted to seduce was her Lily-pad.*"

Alex and Andrew looked at each other.

"Think we should start acting dumber to pick up chicks?"

"It worked for Justin, didn't it? I'm sure it will work for us."

Kevin rolled his eyes. "I swear, all of my friends are idiots."

"That's not a very nice thing to say."

"I agree. You might be a Harem Lord, but that doesn't give you the right to make fun of your loyal subjects."

"Shut up! I'm not a Harem Lord or whatever, so stop calling me that! Ugh," Kevin buried his head in his hands, "why couldn't I have smarter and less embarrassing friends?"

"There, there." Lilian rubbed Kevin's back in soothing up and down motions. "I know what will make you feel better."

"What's that?"

Lilian grinned, and the next thing he knew a pair of soft, warm, and smoother than milk chocolate lips were kissing him.

Kevin could have melted into them.

Unfortunately, Christine didn't like their display of affection.

"Da—wh-w-w-WHAT THE HELL DO YOU TWO THINK YOU'RE DOING?! DON'T GO AROUND KISSING IN PUBLIC! THERE ARE PEOPLE WATCHING!"

Lilian clicked her tongue in annoyance after removing her lips from a slightly insensate Kevin. "Considering that Kevin and I are dating, you have no right to tell us what we can and cannot do."

"Sure I do." Christine's baleful glare was colder than icicles hanging from a hut in the Arctic Circle. "Someone has to stop you two from acting so promiscuous in public."

"So you say, but I think you're just jealous."

"Je-je-je—I AM NOT!"

"Are too."

"AM NOT!"

"Yes, you are."

"NO, I'M NOT!"

"No, you're not!"

"YES, I AM!" A pause. It took Christine exactly two seconds to compute what she'd just said. Were her tsundere protocols not already activated, they would have been now. "Y-y-y-y-you...! Shut up! shut up, shut up, shut up!"

"Has anyone told you that your voice is really annoying? Your Seiyuu's not Kugimiya-san, is it?"

"What?" Christine couldn't seem to make heads or tails of that statement.

"Nothing, nothing." Lilian airily waved a hand through the air in a dismissive gesture.

The conversation soon returned to more normal topics after that.

"I was wondering if you and Christine wanted to sleep over this weekend?" Lindsay twirled the fork in her salad as she looked inquiringly at the redhead.

"A sleep over?" Lilian blinked. "I don't know... I mean, Kevin and I..."

Lindsay rolled her eyes while Christine's flared with righteous anger. "You can sleep with Kevin whenever you want. Don't you sleep with him pretty much every night anyways?"

"There's no pretty much about it," Lilian corrected, "we

always sleep together."

Christine gnashed her teeth together. Kevin feared the girl's gums might start bleeding.

"Exactly my point." Lindsay pointed at Lilian with her fork. "You always sleep with Kevin. Surely not sleeping with him for a single night won't kill you."

"Do you two really have to talk about my and Lilian's sleeping arrangements?" asked a mildly embarrassed Kevin.

"Yes," Lindsay responded shamelessly, turning back to Lilian, her doe-like brown eyes sparkling. "What do you say? Come on, say you'll sleep over with Christine and I?"

"Who said I was willing to spend a night with this skank?"

Lindsay and Lilian both stared at Christine, who held their stares for a moment, then looked away with a grumble.

"I don't know." An uncertain Lilian looked at Kevin. "What do you think I should do?"

"Why are you asking me? This is your life; you should do whatever you want. You know, live your life the way you want to and all that?"

Truth be told, Kevin would actually be a little lonely without Lilian. He'd grown so used to having the enchanting fox-girl sleep with him that the idea of not being able to hold her in his arms, to feel her warm body against his, seemed almost foreign to him now.

I guess it's true that a lot can change in three months.

However, Kevin also knew that Lilian enjoyed trying out new things; whether that was playing games at the arcade or traveling to a place she'd never visited before.

Lilian worried her lip for a moment. Kevin could almost see the debate being waged in her mind.

"Lilian," he placed a hand over hers, "I know you want to go, so you shouldn't let me stop you. We're going to be spending our whole lives together, right? A single night won't mean much in the grand scheme of things. Go and have fun."

Like a drill piercing the heavens, Lilian's face broke out into a vibrant smile. "Thank you, Kevin."

Kevin returned the smile. "You're welcome."

Lilian looked at Lindsay. "Okay, I'll come to this sleep over thing."

"Great!" Lindsay cheered. "Now it'll be a true girls' night. I haven't had one of those in ages!"

"Girls' night?" The term made Lilian tilt her head. "What's that?"

Lindsay gasped. Even Christine looked askance at her. "Don't tell me you've never heard of a girls' night?"

"Is that sort of like a girls' day out?"

"Sort of. A girls' night is…"

As the tomboyish blond explained the concept of a "girls' night" to Lilian, Kevin tuned her out and took to observing the surrounding courtyard. He could see a trail of dust expanding across the school yard, at the front of which was Eric, who was screaming for his life. Sweat trickled down Kevin's face when he noticed that his friend's clothes had been ripped to shreds. He began sweating even more when he noticed the horde of enraged girls chasing the boy.

That idiot really worries me sometimes.

"Who the fuck do you think you're talking to, bitch?!"

Kevin's head snapped to his left. Blue eyes narrowed in worry when he saw Iris confronting an angry Chris. On the ground beside Iris was Justin, who looked dazed.

It had been a long time since Kevin had thought about the inu. Even when Chris had become upset after seeing them disembark from Kiara's car, the dog yōkai had merely been a part of the background, a static image.

Such was not the case now.

"Kevin?"

Everyone at the table became startled when Kevin stood up and rushed over to where Iris was glaring daggers at Chris.

"I think I'm talking to a ragged, beaten up dog who doesn't know his place."

"Fucking fox!"

Chris raised his clenched right fist, prepared to deliver a savage punch to the pretty female. Before he could, Kevin leapt into the air, his body spinning like a top.

"Don't-touch-my-girlfriend's-sister Screwdriver!"

"What the—GUAG!"

Spittle flew from Chris's mouth as Kevin planted his feet into the inu's gut, knocking all of the air from the boy's lungs in one fell swoop. He bent his knees, absorbing the shock of impact, his body parallel with the ground. Kevin then used his impressive leg muscles to push off Chris's body, launching the inu several feet back where he crashed into a garbage can.

For all of one second, time stood still.

For all of one second, everyone stared at Kevin in awe.

For all of one second, Kevin felt like the most awesome person in the world.

Then the second was over.

And Kevin landed on his back. On the concrete. Hard.

As Kevin's lungs were deprived of oxygen and his vision exploded with white while pain overloaded his photo-optic receptors, Iris knelt beside his head.

"Feeling manly now?" She asked, her lips stretching from ear to ear in a wide grin.

Kevin raised a shaky arm and gave Iris a thumbs up.

***

Track practice was canceled that day due to the track field flooding. Apparently, the sprinkler system had broken. Coach Raide had not been happy.

Since track was canceled, Kevin had called up Kiara and asked if he could come to Mad Dawg Fitness to get some training in. Once there, he and Lilian found a surprise waiting for them.

"Ms. Grant? What are you doing here? Shouldn't you still be resting?"

Standing on the blue mat that he got his butt kicked on so often was Heather. The blond woman had donned tight black stretch shorts and a sports bra of the same color. She was doing stretches; some of them he recognized, but most he didn't—and could she bend her body. He didn't think it was possible for anyone to be that flexible.

Kevin noticed that the trio of Tall, Taller, and Midget was mysteriously absent.

Heather scoffed as she straightened up. "Psh! What nonsense is this? I'm feeling fine—right as rain, in fact. I really do need to thank you and Red for convincing that maid of yours to help me out. Her healing abilities are impressive."

Lilian puffed up her cheeks in anger, which made her look so cute that no one would ever be intimidated by her. "Don't call me Red!"

"So, what are you doing here?" asked Kevin. "I know you're living with Kiara right now, but I didn't expect to see you until the issue with your former organization has been dealt with."

"Bah," Heather scoffed, "they won't do anything now that their little machines have been defeated. If they did, they'd run the risk of people learning about their existence."

"Makes sense." Kevin turned to Kiara. "I also wanted to thank you for taking her in. I would have let her stay with me but, well—" a helpless shrug, "—my place is a little cramped at the moment."

"I'll bet." Kiara's lips twitched in amusement. "Anyway, the reason she's here is because I thought we'd switch things up a bit. Heather has police training, and is well-versed in both armed and unarmed combat. She'll be able to give you a better fight than my disciples."

Kevin looked from Heather to Kiara, then back to Heather. "So, you're going to help me get stronger, then?"

Heather grinned and raised a clenched hand to her face. "Yep! I heard that you were learning to fight and thought this would be a great way to repay you and your, um, family?" When Kevin nodded, Heather continued. "Right, as a way to repay you guys for everything you've done for me, I've decided to help you get stronger by offering you a different sparring partner."

"This will also have the added benefit of allowing you to see another fighting style," Kiara added. "I know I told you I wouldn't teach you any formalized martial arts, because learning a style of combat like Tae Kwon Do, Aikido, Jiu Jitsu and Muay Thai makes you easy to predict, but I do believe it would be a good idea for you to see other styles. By seeing other fighting styles, you'll not only be able to create your own unique techniques, but you'll also get better at recognizing what style someone is using and how best to counter it."

While Kevin listened to everything Kiara said with rapt attention, Lilian stood beside him, not really listening to the woman, but offering her support all the same.

"Right. I want you and Heather to start sparring now. Your girlfriend and I will watch over on the sidelines."

"Got it."

Kevin turned to Lilian and gave her a quick peck on the lips—

"for luck," he told her.

Lilian was less than satisfied.

"That was not a good luck kiss," the redhead said seconds before she pounced on him.

Kevin didn't think he would ever get used to the intensity behind Lilian's kisses. They were always filled with so much passion… and a lot of tongue action. Kevin tried to keep up with her, but he was so surprised that he could do little except hang on while Lilian ravished the inside of his mouth.

She pulled back after having thoroughly plundered the depths of his mouth with her tongue, a thin string of saliva connecting them. It was broken when Lilian licked his lips, her expression containing a satisfaction that reminded him of Natsumo Uzukami after she pulled a successful prank.

"Now *that* is a good luck kiss."

"Um… right…"

Lilian strolled over to the sideline, an exaggerated sway in her hips, and stood exactly two meters away from Kiara, who she still didn't like. Heather snickered as she moved in front of a dazed and blushing Kevin.

"You ready, kiddo?"

Kevin smacked his cheeks. The action stung, but it also served its purpose; getting rid of his blush and sharpening his focus.

"I'm ready."

Both of them prepared for the sparring match. The difference between the two was immediately apparent. Kevin clearly had no set style, which anyone with combat experience would have been able to tell just by looking at him. His arms, while placed in a basic guard position, were loose and held further away from his face and body than most experienced combatants.

In stark contrast, Heather had taken an open, short stance; the lateral distance between her hind and lead foot was wide, but the general distance between them was not-quite shoulder-length. She also looked a lot more comfortable than Kevin, who had only been sparring for a few weeks.

Kiara held up a hand.

"On three. One. Two. Three. Begin!"

Heather shot forward more quickly than anything Kevin had seen outside of youki-enhanced speed. Fortunately, Kevin was the king of speed and actually saw her coming. When Heather got within range, she swung out with a swift jab, testing his defenses. Kevin stumbled backwards, avoiding the blow by the skin of his teeth. The fist came so close that it grazed his nose. Kevin swore he lost a few epidermal layers.

Two steps forward brought Heather into Kevin's guard. Already tucked into her left side, the fist that she had prepared shot out, striking fast and hard. Heather's torso rotated with the attack, allowing her to put more power behind her punch. Kevin moved to the left, avoiding the attack, but tumbled and fell over in the process. Oddly enough, when he fell, the young man continued rolling backwards until he kipped back to his feet.

Heather raised an eyebrow.

He turned his fall into a roll. Sure, he nearly fell on his ass, but he managed to get up quickly. If I had charged in to capitalize on my advantage, he would have been able to attack me before I could do anything about it. Clever.

Deciding to test the waters some more, Heather moved in. Four steps took her right into Kevin's range. She waited for a moment, but when he didn't attack, she threw another jab.

Her eyebrow rose some more when Kevin's head tilted—no, his entire body was tilting. And his arms were flailing about like a pinwheel. What the hell? Surprise became shock when one of those flailing arms latched onto her wrists, and Kevin, still falling, used the momentum from his fall to pull her down to the floor.

Or he would have, had Heather not acted quickly by jabbing him in the arm with her knuckles, then kicking him in the face when he continued to fall. The young man hit the floor hard and rolled across the mat, but he didn't stay down long. Heather was impressed when he jumped back onto his feet, a small bruise visible underneath his right eye to show he'd been kicked.

"You're pretty durable," Heather complimented. "Most people would have been down and out after getting kicked like that."

Kevin winced as he raised a hand to his newly formed bruise. "Yeah, well, I've been getting beaten up a lot lately. I guess you could say I've built up a tolerance to pain."

Heather shook her head. "It's more than that. If it was just a matter of being durable and able to withstand pain, you would still have a large bruise. I put a lot of strength into that kick, and my legs are stronger than most, yet all you have to show for it is a tiny little mark. That means you've got tough skin."

"I'm not sure if that's a good thing or not," Kevin muttered before the battle started up again.

***

Kevin and Heather renewed their spar seconds later, with the blond woman proving herself to be a more than capable fighter.

Kiara watched for a moment before her dark eyes shifted to Lilian. "I've gotta admit, your mate's really something. You must be proud of him."

Lilian's eyes, which burned with admiration as she watched Kevin spar, flickered to Kiara. She looked away a second later to hide the smile on her face. "I've always been proud of my mate."

"Hn."

They watched in silence for a while longer. Kevin fell backwards after avoiding a powerful punch that would have cleaned his clock. Yet, even as he fell, he grabbed ahold of Heather's extended forearm. His fall turned into a roll and, with a slight heave, he took Heather down with him. The former secret agent, her eyes wide in surprise, was flipped head over heels.

That would have ended with a point going to Kevin, except Heather twisted her body around in midair so that, instead of hitting the mat back first, she hit it feet first.

"What the—?"

In a reversal of roles, Kevin was tossed into the air by Heather, who used her apparently hulkish strength to lift his body from her awkward bridge-like position and throw him across the room. He landed on the mat back first, the air leaving his lungs in a loud *whoosh!*

"I have to wonder, though," Kiara continued while musing out loud. "Kevin's been training with me for over a month and a half now, working his butt off day in and day out to get stronger." She glanced at Lilian, her eyes sharp and almost accusing. "Why aren't you doing the same?"

Lilian's lips thinned. "What makes you think I don't train? I practice my enchantments everyday." Sure, it was on the unsuspecting students and teachers at school, but this woman didn't need to know that.

"I'm not talking about enchantments and illusions, girl." The way Kiara scoffed, as if she thought the idea of practicing enchantments and calling it training was too stupid for mere words to express, made Lilian grit her teeth. "I'm talking about real training. Combat training. I remember how you used the enhancement technique when we fought. It was pathetic. Rather than training what you're already good at, you should be training what you're weak at. It's the only way you'll ever improve."

Lilian turned her head, no longer wishing to look at this woman. What did she know? Kitsune were all about their illusions and enchantments. When those weren't enough, they had their specialized techniques. It was how they were. They didn't need to become physically powerful, not when their illusions, enchantments, and elemental techniques were enough to fend off attacks by other yōkai.

"I can get along just fine without the need to get all sweaty and gross. The only time I want to work up any kind of sweat is when Kevin finally snaps and pounds his meat stick into my honey pot."

"LILIAN! DON'T SAY SUCH EMBARRASSING THINGS!"

"Whoops. Sorry, Beloved!"

"You shouldn't take your eyes off your opponent, kiddo!"

"Gya! My nose! You just broke my nose!"

"Oh, don't be such a baby. Your nose is fine."

"It's bleeding!"

"Noses tend to do that! Now keep that guard up!"

"EEK!"

"Hya!"

Thus the battle continued. It would be long and hard and brutal… for Kevin, that is.

***

Kiara sat with Heather at the dinner table, eating a meal prepared by the blond bombshell; steak and mashed potatoes. It was a simple meal, but that suited her just fine.

"So, what do you think of my protege?"

Heather paused mid-scoop, her spoon sticking into the mashed potatoes. The hesitation didn't last, and she soon had a mouth full of starchy goodness. It gave her time to think up a suitable answer.

"He's not all that good at fighting—he kinda sucks actually, but the potential is there. He's got guts at least." She paused, thinking some more. "I'm honestly not sure how he'll do against yōkai though, which is what he'll most likely be facing if he sticks around with Lilian."

"That is true." With her dinner already finished, Kiara leaned back in her seat and placed her hands on the table, drumming her left index finger in an off-beat rhythm. "Against a yōkai, especially one at a higher level than, let's say, a two-tailed kitsune, he'll be in deep trouble without a weapon of some kind. I've been trying to find something that'll suit him, a weapon powerful enough to help him deal with the more powerful yōkai he's bound to run into, but I haven't had much luck so far."

"Do you think he's even suited to a weapon?" asked a skeptical Heather. "I don't mean to be rude, but he doesn't really strike me as a weapon-using type."

"That's because you're thinking traditionally," Kiara replied, her left hand coming up to her chin. "I'm thinking of getting him a more esoteric weapon. At first, I thought about commissioning someone to create a set of metal gauntlets and greaves to increase his hitting power, but his deceptive fighting style makes using those problematic."

"Yeah, that weird style of his is awfully good at misleading people, though it's really unrefined. It will need a lot of work before he can use it in battle." Her eyes suddenly lit up. "Hey! What if you gave him a weapon with a lot of versatility? Like… like… I know! A utility belt!"

"A utility belt?" Kiara gave Heather a flat look.

"Yeah, a utility belt. You know, like Batman."

"I don't think that would help him match the strength of a yōkai." Kiara rubbed her jaw in thought. "Still, maybe I could commission some kind of strength-enhancing bodysuit…"

"Huh?"

"It's nothing."

Kiara was just about to take her plate to the sink, when her danger senses screamed at her to move.

The ceiling directly above them exploded in a shower of wood, stucco and insulation. Heather and Kiara both reacted quickly, leaping away from the dining room table. A second after they vacated their seats, something heavy crashed into the floor—

and the dining room table.

"What the fuck!" Kiara actually swore. "My table!" A growl. "I don't know who or what this thing is, but the moment I see its face, it's dead!"

No one destroys my stuff and gets away with it!

The dust blocking their view dispersed, revealing the figure that had dropped down through the ceiling. Its bright surface glimmered within the light, despite the amount of dust covering it. Its body, roughly humanoid in shape, stood on two thick legs and had arms that appeared to ripple. A red visor situated on its helmet and shaped like a T scanned its surroundings.

"That's the thing that nearly did me in!" Heather exclaimed in shock. "I thought those two sexy fox-women destroyed it!"

"I'm guessing there was one more." Kiara's eyes never strayed from that visored, bullet-shaped head.

The thing lifted its arms and pointed them at her. Kiara's eyes had just enough time to widen before a hailstorm of bullets were shot from the silver being's fingers. She and Heather both ducked to avoid the lethal projectiles, which ended up hitting her wall and blasting several holes straight through it.

"My wall!" Kiara howled. "Do you know how expensive it'll be to fix that?!"

Anger washed over Kiara like gasoline being poured onto a bonfire. She didn't know what this thing was, robot or whatever, but she honestly couldn't find it in herself to care. This... thing was destroying her condo, which cost a lot of money to build and even more to maintain. There was no way she could let that stand.

This thing is dead.

Unlike Chris, whose shift from human form to yōkai form took time, Kiara's was instantaneous. Her ears quickly sprouted fur and grew longer and floppy as they moved up her head. Her face remained unchanged, as did most of her body, but the nails on her hands and feet grew exponentially longer and much sharper. A single bushy brown tail sprouted from her business suit, jutting out of the small flap in her pants.

With a low growl and a snarl on her face, Kiara used her immense speed to appear right underneath the thing wrecking her home. She placed her hands on the ground, palms pressed firmly against cool tile, fingers splayed. She lifted her legs into the air and tucked them in towards her chest...

... And then launched them forward with enough power to crush a car.

Like the clapping of thunder, Kiara's attack resounded throughout the condo as her feet crashed into the thing's jaw. Despite clearly weighing quite a bit, it flew into the air, back out of the hole it had made in her ceiling.

Kiara followed, jumping through the hole and landing on the roof. She looked up to see the thing still ascending. She must have put more power into her kick than she'd originally thought.

Dark eyes watched as the thing continued soaring. When it reached the apex of its ascent, it began to descend. Seeing this, Kiara shot off her roof like a missile, heading straight for the enemy. Before she reached it, she twisted her body around, her feet swinging about in a fast arc that cut through the air.

A loud bang reminiscent of an explosion echoed across the valley when the heel of Kiara's foot met the back of the metallic being's head. The metal surface pulsated and it was sent flying towards the ground at speed. Kiara's eyes danced with satisfaction as the foolish creature smashed into the street with force. The earth shattered underneath it, the ground cratering as large chunks of road and rubble were upheaved and sent flying.

Kiara landed several feet away, her eyes narrowed as she watched the machine clamber to its feet. This battle was making a lot of noise, and since she lived in a condominium complex, that meant a lot of people were hearing it. Already she could see lights turning on and shouts sounding out. She needed to end this now.

I'll also have to talk with Davin and see if he can send members of the Saint's Brigade to erase the memories of everyone here.

Now there was a fun conversation waiting to happen.

Not wanting to give the mech any time to recover, Kiara shot forward. The pavement cracking underneath her feet. She extended her left hand in a swift punch, her entire forearm corkscrewing as it smashed against the thing's face. The power behind the twisting straight was such that the area she hit splattered like a boulder being dropped into a lake.

The machine skidded backwards, though it didn't go far. Digging its feet into the road, the metal man gouged a trench along the blacktop for several feet before stopping.

Before it could so much as raise its guard, Kiara was there. She had assumed a power stance. Her feet were spread wide, knees bent, arms tucked into her torso. The machine's processor barely had time to register the heat source mere inches from its body before she struck.

Her fists were a blur of impossibly fast motion, visible only as a streak of earth tone colors. They slammed into the metal body like a rampaging bull, pounding away at it. Each time one of the blurring fists struck, large chunks of the creature's body were blown away, the odd metal becoming liquid as it splattered against the ground like mercuric blood.

The attacks became more vicious. Anger fueled movements intensified to the point where each fist contained what seemed to be the power of an entire pantheon of angry gods. Before long, nothing remained of the machine except for silver puddles that glistened in the moonlight.

Kiara eyed the splatters with disdain. Muttering obscenities under her breath, she turned around and began to walk away.

She didn't get far before a most unusual noise reached her. Kiara turned, her eyes narrowing into slits as she witnessed the splatters of silver liquid crawling along the ground. The small pools began to combine, congealing together and growing larger. It then started to shift, its form bulging and expanding and contracting. A head sprouted from the top, bullet-shaped and streamlined. A neck formed underneath, followed by shoulders and then arms. Like a muck monster rising from a swamp, the creature's body emerged from within the silver liquid, the last bit of which crawled along its legs to form a pair of feet.

Kiara's eyes narrowed. "So, Kotohime wasn't exaggerating when she said you could regenerate from any and all forms of physical damage. In that case, I'll just have to annihilate you completely."

Taking a deep breath, Kiara shifted into a new stance. Her left foot slid forward, the right moving back as she bent her knee. She brought her hands together near her torso, her tail also curving around her body, the tip moving into the gap between her hands.

Another breath. The carefully placed locks on Kiara's power were released. The energy flowed out from her body, engulfing her in a red flame of undeniable power. Youki gathered within her palms and the tip of her tail, a tiny ball of bright red that grew larger with each passing second. Rays shone from between curved fingers, a blinding array of vermillion that grew in brilliance until it reached a zenith.

Kiara's hands shot forward, fingers opening like a venus flytrap. However, unlike the plant, these appendages were not meant to capture, but to release. A bright red beam of conical energy shot from within her hands. The compressed youki expanded the further it moved away from her, until the beam was at least twice as tall as Kiara. It struck the machine, its entire form becoming engulfed in bright red, disappearing entirely as the youki washed over it.

The energy put into the attack ran dry, the beam dispersing into thousands of particles. Kiara nodded in satisfaction when she saw that there was nothing left of the creature—or the road. All that remained was a huge trench nearly sixteen meters long. Glistening with refracted moonlight, the entire trench appeared to have been glassed, the blacktop superheated to the point where it had melted down to its base components.

She felt a drop of sweat run down her face.

"Looks like I put a little too much power into that attack." She scratched the back of her neck. "Davin's really not gonna like this…"

Chapter 9

Kidnapped

"It looks like those creations of yours were all defeated. If I had known you were going to send some of the science division's prototype experiments, I would have told you not to bother. Now you've revealed how far along our technological weaponry has come *and* there are several yōkai who now know about our organization, including the big man running this place. I've got to tell you, that move you just pulled--not very smart."

"..."

"I'm not being insubordinate. I'm merely stating the facts, and you can give as many justifications as you want, but it won't change the fact that you screwed up royally. Now you'll never be able to silence Ms. Grant. She'll be put under the protection of Davin Monstrang and Kiara F. Kuyo, neither of whom are pushovers."

"..."

"Very well, though if leaving her alone was going to be the end result of your plan anyway, we should have just let her be from the start."

"..."

"Right, right. Silence those who could reveal our existence, blah, blah, blah. Look, why don't you just give me my orders now?"

"…"

"If I am a smartass, then it's because your people made me this way. My orders?"

"…"

"Same as always, eh? Fine. I'll continue keeping an eye on the yōkai going to Desert Cactus High, as well as the ones Kevin's been interacting with outside of school. Yes, yes. I understand. Justin out."

As the conversation wound to a close, Justin pocketed his cell phone and looked up at the morning sky. Reds and oranges and yellows mixed in streaks and swirls of color. Radiant beams of light shone down from parted clouds, casting patterns along the ground. School would be starting soon.

Justin's lips curled into a smile. "I wonder what today will bring. I'm sure it'll be interesting."

***

Ling wandered the school courtyard, enjoying the brief respite from her normal activities. While she had dedicated her life to Lord Jiāoào, that did not mean she didn't appreciate the small moment of freedom. All around her students and teachers walked. Classes started in about twenty minutes, so she had enough time to get a feel for the campus' layout.

Gaining entrance into the school had been depressingly easy. The man who called himself this educational institute's principal was a pervert of the highest level. She didn't even have to show off any skin. Just appearing before him had turned the man into a drooling sack of flesh. Had assassinating him been her mission, she would have been able to kill him before he could have even registered that something was wrong.

Truly, perverts are a weak-willed group of people.

The buses began arriving, and Ling found a nice place to sit down and observe. She enjoyed watching people go about their daily lives. It was something of a hobby for her.

Of course, she was not just doing this to watch teenage boys and girls do what teenage boys and girls were wont to do.

"A sleep over, eh? Sounds interesting, but are you sure it's alright to invite me along? Won't the tomboy and flatty get angry?"

It wasn't hard to pick out Lilian, Kevin and Iris amongst the crowd. Lilian's hair, a vibrant red very few individuals possessed, stood out starkly amongst the masses. Her sister was also easily noticeable, especially because every male in the vicinity, and even some of the females, would cease what they were doing to drool over her. Even Kevin could be distinguished amongst the crowd; his blond hair, blue eyes and the limp in his step, like someone had repeatedly knifed him in the thigh, made spotting him quite simple.

"Lindsay's already given me permission to invite you along. The only reason I didn't you ask last night is because Kevin and I didn't come home until really late."

"Right, right. You were training with that... dog, right? I don't know how you can stand being around her."

They walked through the crowd. Whispers broke out. Ling, with her youki-enhanced hearing, could make out everything being said. It seemed that some of the men didn't like Kevin for being so close to the two kitsune. The poor fools didn't even realize how dangerous being intimate with Lilian and her sister was—and if Ling had her way, they would never know.

"Kiara's not... okay, she is that bad. But, she's helping Kevin get stronger. If it's to help my mate, I'll gladly withstand her presence."

"Aren't you two being a little biased?"

Iris and Lilian gave Kevin a deadpan stare. A drop of sweat rolled down his face and neck before disappearing into his shirt.

"Right, stupid question. Forget I asked."

"So, when is this sleepover?" Iris inquired.

"We'll be going over to Lindsay's house this Saturday around noon."

"Uh-huh, and how will we get there?"

"Lindsay's mom is going to pick us up."

"Urk!"

Ling nearly chuckled in amusement when Kevin tripped over his own two feet and face planted into the hard concrete.

"Kevin!" Lilian cried out as she knelt next to her mate. Iris hung back and snickered at the teen's misfortune. The redhead tossed her snickering sister a glare before helping her mate stand up. "A-are you alright?"

"Y-yeah," Kevin held a hand to his nose, which Ling noticed was bleeding, "I'm fine. So, Mrs. Diane is going to be..." he shuddered, "... picking you up?"

"Um!" Lilian nodded. "Is that a problem?"

"No, no." Kevin shuddered again. "There's no problem."

"Then why do you look like a rat that's been caught in a trap?" asked an amused Iris.

Kevin sent her a glare. "Hush, you."

Ling watched the group walk off, her mind going over everything she'd learned. Lindsay and Iris would be traveling to a friend's house to spend the night this Saturday. This meant that, for at least one night, the two-tails would not be in the presence of her bodyguard.

It was the perfect time to strike.

***

Kevin and Lilian were lounging in the bath together. It was Saturday, and this was the first time they'd done this since the disaster at Eric's house, in which the perverted teen had walked in on them while they were getting hot and heavy.

Lilian had asked Kevin if he would like to spend some intimate one-on-one time together that morning, claiming she would miss him during the sleepover and wanted to be with him for as long as possible. Regardless of his thoughts on the issue of physical intimacy, he could not deny his mate's desire to be with him—part of him would even admit that he was thrilled by the idea.

After helping each other clean up in the shower, they filled the bathtub with steaming hot water. Lilian even added some bath salts. Kevin would have asked where she'd gotten those, but he already knew the answer and therefore decided to save himself the headache.

With his back against the tub, the water rising up to his chest, Kevin found it impossible to feel anything but relaxed. Lilian rested against him, laying on her left side between his legs, using his right shoulder as a pillow. The tub was small, but that didn't bother either of them. Feeling a bit more adventurous that morning, Kevin softly rubbed Lilian's hips. The lyrical sounds she produced and the warm breathing hitting his neck sent tingles down Kevin's spine.

"This is so nice," Lilian murmured, her voice soft and lackadaisical. She sounded tired. Kevin worried that she might fall asleep if she relaxed any further. "I wish we could stay like this."

"We'll prune if we stay in here for too long."

"I know that. But a girl can dream, can't she?"

Kevin chuckled. He couldn't see her face, which was nuzzled against his neck, but he could imagine the adorable pout she wore.

"We'll do this again. Maybe it can be something we do on weekends, or whatever."

Lilian raised her head and looked him in the eyes. Her own eyes were wide and full of hope. "Really?"

"Really."

Lilian stared at him for a moment longer. Long enough to make his cheeks grow hot. After what felt like fifteen minutes but was really only a few seconds, she smiled, and leaned in to give him a kiss.

"I love this new, more confident Kevin," she mumbled against his lips.

"Not so new," he whispered back, his voice only slightly muffled by her mouth.

Lilian leaned back and gave him a bright, cheerful smile. "Perhaps not," she chirped, "you're still the same kind-hearted person who saved me and allowed me to live with you, even though I sort of screwed up your life."

"Sort of?"

Lilian had the decency to look mildly abashed. "Okay, so maybe it was more than just a little."

"Right, because having someone tell all my friends that we're engaged when we really weren't and trying to intimidate my only female friend into staying away from me is 'more than just a little.'"

Lilian's cheeks puffed up. "So, I was a little overzealous in my attempts to win your affection. I needed a leg up so I could be number one in case the author decided to turn this story into a harem. Can you blame me?"

Grinning, Kevin finally removed his hands from Lilian's hips, placing them against her cheeks and pushing the air out of them. "Yes. Yes, I can." A pause. "Wait. What?"

"What do you mean 'what?'"

"I could have sworn you just said something about a harem."

"You're imagining things."

"No, no. I could have sworn you said something about a harem. And how many times have I told you to stop mentioning people who don't exist?!"

Their skin eventually started to wrinkle and the two were forced to get out. After drying each other off, they got dressed and wandered into the kitchen.

Iris was already sitting down at the table while Kotohime served breakfast. The two-tailed Void Kitsune looked up when they walked in, as did Kotohime.

"Lilian-sama, Kevin-sama. I hope you two had a pleasant shower."

"We did." Lilian was the epitome of good cheer while Kevin blushed. More confident he might have been, but he still couldn't deal with people actually knowing that he and Lilian were intimate.

"You two were in that shower for an awfully long time." Iris's eyes narrowed into thin slits. "You didn't do anything you shouldn't have, did you?"

While Kevin coughed into his hand, mostly to hide the fierce burning in his cheeks, Lilian defiantly stared back at Iris. "Is that a problem?"

Kevin sat down and busied himself with his food, hoping that doing so would hide his embarrassment.

"No, no," the ravenette assured, raising both hands in a defensive gesture. "No problem. I was just wondering if you would let me join you guys next time."

Kevin was so surprised by Iris's comment that the food he'd begun eating went down his windpipe.

"B-Beloved!"

Kevin choked and hacked, pounding his chest as he tried to dislodge the food. Lilian rubbed his back as if trying to soothe the panic he felt at not being able to breathe. When he finally coughed up the last bit of rice, he heartily drank the glass of water that Kotohime presented to him.

"Stop picking on my mate," Lilian frowned at her fraternal twin.

"Who said I was picking on him?" asked a devious Iris. "I was being completely serious. The next time you two decide to take a bath together, let me know so I can join you." She eyed the two with a hungry leer. "I think it'll be fun."

While Kevin tried to pretend he hadn't heard her, Lilian flushed at the imagery Iris's words invoked. She then shook her head, dispelling the images, and sent Iris a mildly flustered glare. "Not happening."

"Aw, come on, Lily-pad. You can't share your mate with your dear sister?"

While Kevin's face turned into a neon sign, Lilian looked away uncomfortably. "You already know my stance on this subject." A pause. Lilian turned back to Iris and frowned. "And I thought I told you to stop calling me Lily-pad."

"You're such a spoilsport, sis." Iris feigned disappointment, then grinned as she turned her attention to Kevin, a wicked gleam in her eyes. "I know, I'll just ask your mate."

Lilian's eyes widened. "Don't you dare!"

"Hey, Kevin, maybe this will convince you to let me join in on your fun." Iris's grin made Kevin feel like a mouse trapped between the paws of a jungle panther. "I'm not wearing any panties. See?" Iris stood and lifted up her skirt.

The reaction was instantaneous. Blood shot from Kevin's nose with the power of a fire hydrant. The chair tipped over from the force of the crimson jet stream, causing him to also topple over. He landed on his back, his head cracking against the hard tile floor. Good thing he was already unconscious due to blood depletion, or that would have probably hurt.

"Inari blessed! Beloved!"

"Fufufu. That was too easy."

"IRIS!"

***

Kotohime was washing the dishes when the doorbell rang. She ignored it in favor of continuing her task. Kirihime, who'd been hanging up the laundry, answered the door instead.

The woman standing on the other side was completely unknown to her. Light brown hair in a short bob-cut adorned her head. The sleeveless pink shirt donning her figure was loose enough that a casual glance would not reveal the slight plumpness of her form. A long white skirt traveled down to her ankles.

Ever the demure young woman, Kirihime clasped her hands in front of her and offered a somewhat shy smile. "Good morning, ma'am. Can I help you?"

The woman didn't say anything for the longest time. She just stared. It was very disturbing.

"Um," Kirihime fidgeted nervously, "ma'am?"

"You are... a maid?"

"Y-yes, I am."

"A French maid."

"We-well, technically I'm from Japan, so..."

"Kevin has a maid."

"Uh... n-not quite." Kirihime hastened to correct the woman. "I am Lady Iris's maid."

"Lady Iris?" The woman squinted at her, as if doing so might reveal the secrets of the multiverse. "And who, may I ask, is 'Lady Iris?'"

Kirhime shrunk under the woman's gaze. "Um, ah, Lady Iris is Lady Lilian's sister."

"Oh..."

Kirihime squirmed as the woman continued to stare. A cold sweat broke out on her forehead. She wanted to look away from this woman, but that would have been impolite. All she could do was stand there and pray for a miracle.

"Hey, Kirihime," Kevin suddenly walked into the living room, "what are you doing standing in front of the—urk!"

"Kevin!"

Using her greater size, the woman pushed Kirihime out of the way and bum-rushed the poor boy like an otaku on a hug pillow. Kevin barely had time to squeak before the woman was on him, wrapping her thick arms around his head and shoving his face into her bosoms.

"Kevin! Just look at how much you've grown! And are those muscles I feel? They are! Oh, you've become delicious enough to eat!"

"Mrrphggrlllle!"

"Yes, yes, you've become such a big, strong boy!"

"MMPPPHHH!"

"What's with all the noise?" An irritated Iris stepped into the living room. She stopped upon seeing Kevin being smothered by a large woman's breasts. A smirk lit her face. "Fufufu, it seems even older women can't resist you, Stud."

"Mm mmff mmph mff mmph!" Kevin's screams were unintelligible, but somehow, Iris managed to make something out of them.

"I don't know if I should," Iris said, sounding uncertain. The grin on her face belied her supposed apprehension. "I mean, you look so comfortable."

"Mrrrmmph!!"

"Iris," Lilian called out as she waltzed into the living room with a bounce in her step. "What's with all the—WHAT ARE YOU DOING TO MY MATE?!"

"Your mate?" The large woman squinted suspiciously at the redhead. Her eyes soon lit up in recognition, however, and she snorted derisively. "Ah, you must be Lilian. The one who stole Kevin away from my daughter."

"Daughter?" It took several seconds for Lilian to realize what those words meant. "You're Lindsay's mom!" Only then did she properly compute the rest of the woman's words. "And I did not steal Kevin from anyone. He chose to be with me of his own volition. Now get your hands off him!"

"Hmph! Why would I do that?" Mrs. Diane's grip on Kevin tightened, pushing him further into her bust. Kevin's squirming and struggling reached a zenith. "Kevin has always appreciated my affection, especially since his mother has never given him enough love. Isn't that right, Kevin?"

"MMMPH mmm Mhppphh Mmmgglllrr!"

"He's not even trying to make sense anymore," Iris noted.

"Mmmpph mmmm!"

"Now that's not a very nice thing to say."

"Let go of my mate!"

"I think not."

"Let go of him right this instant!"

"No."

Over on the sidelines, Kirihime, Kotohime and Camellia watched the odd conversation between Lilian, Mrs. Diane, Iris and Kevin. Although, none of them were quite sure if the conversation between Iris and Kevin could truly be called a conversation… and Kevin just went limp.

"D-do you think we should tell Mrs. Diane that Lord Kevin has passed out?" a worried Kirihime nervously wrung her hands together.

"Hawa."

"We probably should," Kotohime agreed, "but I am positive that Lilian-sama will notice soon enough."

"BELOVED!!"

Kotohime nodded conclusively. "There you go."

***

Lilian and Iris sat in the back seat of Mrs. Diane's car.

It had taken a long while to pry the large woman off of Kevin, and it had taken even longer to leave. Lilian had been adamant on saying goodbye to her mate and refused to go anywhere until he had woken up. It was most fortunate that he'd become used to asphyxiation-induced unconsciousness. He had regained consciousness mere minutes after nearly suffocating to death.

Well, that, and Kevin and Lilian's goodbye—along with the argument that had ensued between Lilian and Mrs. Diane about propriety afterward. The plump woman apparently didn't approve of the intense, open-mouthed kiss, complete with tongue action, that Lilian had given Kevin.

"What an indecent display!" she had said.

Strange words coming from a woman who had shoved a teenage boy's head between her breasts.

Iris watched the scenery pass by in a blur. Sighing, she tucked a strand of raven hair behind her ear and turned to look at Lilian. Her beautiful, red-haired sister looked incredibly depressed. Her shoulders were slumped, her eyes were downcast, and she was twiddling her thumbs in her lap. Iris wouldn't have been surprised if it had started raining over the girl's head.

Smiling slyly, Iris slid over to her sister and promptly squeezed the Celestial Kitsune's right boob.

"Kya!"

Mrs. Diane looked into the rear view mirror upon hearing Lilian's squeal. When she did, her nose wrinkled in disgust and she went back to driving.

Lilian's face turned beet red.

"I-Iris!" she hissed, covering her breasts protectively with her arms. "What are you doing?"

"I just wanted to make sure you were still my sister." Smiling with devious intent, Iris's right hand made creepy squeezing motions not all that dissimilar to those of a certain perverted butt monkey. "Yep, you're definitely still her."

Lilian flushed and looked away. "W-whatever."

"What's got you so down, Lily-pad?"

Lilian glared at her sister for using that accursed nickname. "Nothing."

"Oh, please." Iris rolled her eyes. "I know you better than you seem to think I do. I can tell when something is bothering you." Her left arm went around Lilian's shoulder. "Now what's on your mind?"

Shoulders slumping, Lilian looked down at her sandal-clad feet. "I just... I miss... Kevin..."

"By Inari's rotting testicles." Iris groaned. "It's only been ten minutes since you left him. You can't possibly be missing him so soon." When Lilian's shoulders slumped further, Iris used her free hand to palm her face. "By Inari's hairy ball sack, you need to get a life outside of your mate."

"I don't need a life outside of my mate," Lilian argued. The look Iris gave her in return made the redhead awfully uncomfortable.

"Yes, you do. You need a life, and I'm not just saying that because I don't want Kevin's dirty mitts touching you."

"I so don't need to hear this from you."

"Sa, sa, don't be so down." Iris pulled her struggling sister closer. "Your mate might not be here, but your dear *onee-chan* is."

Lilian looked askance at her sister. "Who the heck is *onee-chan*?"

Iris was just about to answer her sister with a sassy remark—a rather good one, too, if she did say so herself—when something powerful struck the car with enough force that the vehicle was lifted into the air and flipped around like a pinwheel.

Iris felt her world turn upside down. Because she wasn't wearing a seat belt, her head hit the roof. Her mind exploded with pain. Her vision went white. Everything was tumbling, rolling, including her body, which was battered around with bone-jarring force. Iris thought she heard screaming, but couldn't be sure, as the noise sounded like it was coming from across a vast distance.

It took Iris several seconds to regain her bearings. She looked around and noticed that she was lying on her back, on the roof of the car.

"Lilian?" she groaned. "Lilian, are you okay?"

… No answer.

Iris turned her head and her eyes widened in shock.

"Lilian!"

Her sister was hanging upside down in her seat, the straps of the seatbelt keeping her in place. She was unconscious. Her eyes were closed, arms dangling limply above her head as if she were stretching, and her long red hair trailed along the roof. Blood ran down the left side of her forehead from a cut that split the skin like a machete slicing a watermelon.

Iris ignored the pain wracking her body, pushing past it, forcing herself to move. With some ingenious thinking and liberal use of her tails, she undid Lilian's seatbelt and caught her sister in a furry bundle before the redhead could fall and hit her head. The tails brought her sister's limp body over to her, and Iris wrapped her sibling in a tight embrace.

"Don't worry, Lily," Iris grunted, "I'll get you out of here."

It took more effort than she thought it would, but Iris eventually dragged herself and Lilian out of the car. She gently laid her sister's body on the ground and checked the two-tailed Celestial Kitsune for any injuries that she might have had, aside from her head wound.

"It doesn't look like she's injured," Iris mumbled. "She's breathing at least." Opening the eyelids of Lilian's left eye, Iris couldn't see anything wrong with it. Then again, if something was wrong with it, she wouldn't know. It wasn't like she had any knowledge of first aid. "Damn it, I wish I had Lilian's healing powers."

"Lady Iris, I must ask that you step away from Lady Lilian."

Iris looked up and narrowed her eyes. A woman stood before her. Long purple hair was twisted artistically into a bun behind her head. Pale skin, rosy lips, a small nose and wide, almond-shaped eyes made for an attractive face—at least it would've been attractive, were the woman's expression not so bland. Her dead eyes and blank facade reminded Iris of a corpse.

Much like Kotohime, this woman wore a kimono. However, whereas Lilian's bodyguard preferred kimonos in shades of blue with intricate designs on them, this woman's kimono was black with no designs. It had also been clearly modified. The kimono was shorter than what was considered normal, coming up to her thighs instead of down to her ankles. Wide, voluminous sleeves served to create an unusual contrast and looked awkward when combined with the short kimono skirt. Three tails wavered behind the woman's back.

"You…" Iris narrowed her eyes. "I recognize you. You're one of the brat's bitches."

Ling twitched, but showed no other emotion. "I am a vassal of Lord Jiāoào," she confirmed. "Now then, I must ask that you step away from Lady Lilian."

"Like hell I will!" Iris stepped in front of her prone sister's form. "I know what will happen to her if I let you take her. Do you really think I'm gonna let that disgusting freak of nature lay a single finger on my sister? Think again!"

"I see that you are going to be stubborn about this." Ling sighed. It sounded odd coming from such an expressionless visage. "Very well, then. It seems I must force you to step aside."

Iris' instincts screamed at her. She moved swiftly, faster than she ever had before. The area she'd been standing on just a second prior exploded with white light, a large pillar of brilliant fire that rose into the sky. Iris began to sweat just by standing near it.

"I see you managed to dodge my **Fire Pillar**. Impressive."

Iris' eyes went wide seconds before a sharp, unbearable pain speared through her lower back and stomach. She looked down, blinking, not quite able to believe what she saw. Something long and sharp was sticking out of her stomach. It looked like an ethereal sword. Wisps of red and yellow flame flickered before her eyes like a candle caught in a breeze.

"However, speed doesn't matter in a battle between kitsune," a voice said behind her—the voice that belonged to the person who should have been in front of her.

Iris looked up just in time to see the "woman" standing before her vanish.

"That… an illusion…" she gasped, agonized by the fire surging through her veins.

"Indeed. This whole time we were conversing, you were simply speaking to an illusion. The real me was hidden this whole time. Do not worry. I did not hit any of your vital organs. While

Lord Jiāoào wants Lady Lilian for himself, he is not willing to risk war with the Pnévma Clan. You are very lucky in that regard."

Iris could have cursed—she probably would have, too, if she were thinking straight. To think she'd been fooled by something as simple as an illusion!

Her legs gave out, unable to support her weight. She fell on her stomach, raven hair spilling about her face and across the ground. Thanks to how she fell, she could see Lilian lying on the ground several feet away, eyes still closed, legs straight and feet canted inwards. Were it not for the blood on her face, Iris would have almost assumed Lilian was merely sleeping.

A pair of feet garbed in *kunoichi* sandals stopped in front of Lilian. Ling bent down and lifted Lilian underneath her left arm. The redhead dangled limply, her feet, arms, and head swaying as the lapdog of that brat, Jiāoào, stood back up.

Iris wanted to move, to lift her hand, grab Lilian, and pull her sister into her arms. She couldn't, however, because her entire body refused to move, or rather, it was incapable of movement.

That vixen... she must have grazed a nerve ending in my spine.

Ling disappeared, leaving Iris alone, in pain, and trying to come to terms with the fact that she had just let Lilian be kidnapped.

***

Kevin sat in front of the television, staring at the screen. A show was playing, *Furry Tail*, one of his favorites. Oddly enough, it was a story about a world where yōkai created guilds to take on missions and stuff. He had always loved watching this show, and would normally be quoting the anime while he watched. Not today, however. Today was not normal.

Lilian wasn't there. He was far more lonely than he had thought he would be with her gone. His chest ached. There was an abnormal emptiness that threw him off his game. In a way that Kevin simply could not understand, Lilian had become an integral part of his life. Without her there, everything appeared in monochrome.

There must be something wrong with me.

"You look troubled, Lord Kevin."

Kevin shuddered. No matter how many times he heard it, he

would never, EVER, get used to the way these kitsune addressed him.

"I'm just thinking."

"Would you like to talk about it?"

Kevin debated for a moment. He didn't know Kirihime all that well, but still, she was nice. Ever since she and the other two members of Lilian's family had arrived, she'd been nothing but kind to him.

In the end, he decided to explain his problem. By the time he had finished, Kirihime was smiling.

"I think I understand what the problem is, Lord Kevin." Nope. The shuddering would not be going away anytime soon. "You're overwhelmed by the depths of your own feelings for Lady Lilian."

"It's not that. At least, I don't think it's that." Kevin shook his head. "I just don't understand how Lilian's become so important to me in such a short amount of time. I've only known her for three months."

"That is what I mean. You're overwhelmed by how important Lady Lilian has become in such a short amount of time." Kirihime's smile was like a panacea for his troubled mind. It was kind and warm and full of compassion—nothing at all like her sister's smile. "What I think you're forgetting is that you're not dating a human girl, but a kitsune. As a species whose lives are governed by intense emotions, we have no middle ground. It is either one extreme or the other when it comes to matters of the heart."

"But, I'm a human."

"Yes, you are," Kirihime agreed. "However, you are mated to a kitsune. Lilian has offered you everything that she is, freely and without reservation. Unlike a human girl who will always keep secrets from you, Lilian has none. If you ask, she will answer. If you want to know something, she will not hesitate to tell you. She is an open book, and all you need to do is turn the pages to learn more. With that kind of open honesty, combined with the depths of her love for you, is it any wonder that you would eventually feel the same way?"

"I... I guess not." Kevin closed his eyes. "Though I don't know how to feel about that. It's kind of frightening to know that I have a girl who's that dedicated to me." A light smile touched at his lips. "I'm afraid of breaking her heart."

"The only way you could break her heart, Lord Kevin, is if you decide that you don't want to be her mate anymore." A dazzling smile lit up Kirihime's face. "I do hope that never happens. I would hate it if I had to kill you."

Kevin froze. "W-what?"

"Oh, nothing." Kirihime stood up and wiped the imaginary dust off her maid outfit. "Now, then, I think you should stop moping around and—"

The phone rang.

"I wonder who that could be calling at this time?" Kirihime asked as she went over to the phone and answered it. "Hello? This is the Swift residence. May I—oh. Oh, no!"

Kevin stood up, alarmed as Kirihime's body went stock still and her eyes widened in horror.

"Yes, I-I see. Thank you. We'll be there as soon as we can."

As Kirihime hung up the phone, Kevin stepped in front of the woman.

"Kirihime, what's wrong?"

Kirihime shuddered. "It's… It's Iris." She looked at Kevin, tears in her eyes and worry written plain as day on her face. "She's in the hospital. They say she was found unconscious on the road and that she has been horrifically injured."

***

Kevin didn't have a car, nor could he drive. Unfortunately, neither could Kirihime or Kotohime. However, that did not mean they were not without options. Kevin made a call to Kiara, who arrived several minutes later and drove them all to the hospital.

Kevin Swift's mind was a tumultuous storm as he paced around the waiting area close to the operating room where Iris was located. There were so many thoughts whirling through his mind, so many questions, so many worries. What had happened to Iris? Where was his mate?

"You need to relax, boya." Kiara leaned against a wall with her arms crossed over her chest, her calm expression a stark contrast to her disciple's. "Pacing around like that isn't going to help you, your friend, or your mate."

"That's easy for you to say!" Kevin snapped before he realized what he was doing and took a deep breath. "Sorry. I didn't mean to snap at you. I'm just—"

"Worried?"

"Mm."

"I understand where you're coming from, but you've got to calm down. Remember one of the first rules I taught you?"

"A true warrior never acts on emotions alone. They must always keep a calm and collected mind in order to better analyze their current situation," Kevin recited.

"That's right. So, take a deep breath and calm down."

Kevin did just that—or, he tried to. No matter how many deep breaths he took the worry, the anxiety and the fear persisted, a small black ball of negative emotions churning inside of his gut.

"Do not worry, Lord Kevin." Once again, Kirihime's hand on his shoulder served to calm his raging thoughts. "I know that you're worried, but remember, all of us feel the same. Acting out like this isn't going to solve anything."

"Right. You're both right." He tossed them an uneasy smile. "I'm sorry."

"There is no need to apologize. I'm glad you're worried about Lady Lilian and Lady Iris. Your kind and caring nature is truly something to be cherished."

Kevin didn't know why, but he felt a little better.

He looked back at the operating room doors and sighed.

Please be okay...

***

While Kirihime calmed Kevin's emotions with her gentle demeanor, Kiara walked over to Kotohime. The swordswoman was kneeling against the wall, her katana in her lap. Although her eyes were closed, Kiara wasn't fooled. She knew that Kotohime was perfectly aware of everything happening around her.

"Not going to comfort your charge's mate?"

A single eye cracked open. "Should I? He does not need me to comfort him, and even if he did, what would I say?"

"Hn. You may have a point." Kiara leaned against the wall. "But are you sure there isn't another reason you're leaving him to Kirihime?"

"I don't know what you're talking about."

"I think you do. While they couldn't look more different, the boya's personality is strikingly similar to—"

"Do not go there, Kiara-san," Kotohime interrupted, her voice harder than steel and sharper than any blade. "There is no need to bring up the ghosts of the past."

Kiara ran a hand through her unruly mess of hair. "I guess not."

* * *

Though he was no longer pacing, Kevin remained worried. He didn't think anyone would blame him. When the hospital had called and told them that Iris was in the ICU, he'd been shocked. When he was told that her injuries were severe and that she might be paralysed from the waist down, he'd been worried. And when he realized that Lilian was not with her, his mind had nearly gone into a fit. He didn't know what was going on, where his mate was, or what had happened.

"Kevin?" a voice startled him from his thoughts. He craned his neck to see a familiar figure walking up to him.

"Lindsay?"

Lindsay didn't appear to be in the best shape mentally. Her eyes were wide and her hair frazzled. If Kevin didn't know any better, he would have said that she was in a mild state of shock.

"Kevin, what's going on? My mother…"

At the mention of Mrs. Diane, Kevin's eyes widened. With all the worry and anxiety he was feeling about Lilian's absence and Iris's injury, he'd completely forgotten about Lindsay's mom.

"What happened to your mother?"

"She was in a car accident. The paramedics found her car turned over and her strapped to the front seat. Dad's here, too." She bit her lower lip, her eyes threatening to water. "Isn't that why you're here, too? I mean, Lilian and Iris—"

Kevin shook his head. "Iris was attacked by someone, we think."

"B-but Iris was with my mom, wasn't she? She and Lilian were on their way to my house!"

"I know, and Lilian is missing. We don't know where she is."

"Oh." Lindsay's eyes suddenly softened. "Oh, Kevin. I'm so sorry."

Kevin's smile was strained. "Don't be. None of this is your fault."

Lindsay bit her lip. She didn't look convinced. Kevin decided

290

to change the subject.

"How's your mom?"

"She's fine. The doctor said she only has a minor concussion and that she should be back on her feet in a day or so."

"That's good."

"Yeah…"

The door to the operating room opened, interrupting the awkward silence that followed their conversation. A man wearing a standard white lab coat and carrying a clipboard walked out of the room. He looked at the group and gave them all a reassuring smile.

"Ms. Pnéyma is going to be okay. She'll have to stay the night, but she's out of danger." A collective breath was released. "It seems she received damage from a stab wound of some kind. There's a scar where it impaled her in the back and went through her abdomen. The wound was cauterized, oddly enough, and no vital organs were hit. She'll be fine after a few days of bed rest."

"Is she awake?" asked Kevin.

"She is. She's actually requested all of you to join her." The doctor frowned for a moment. "I don't think I need to tell you this, but Ms. Pnéyma is extremely weak right now. She needs a lot of rest, so try not to stay too long."

The group entered the room that Iris had been moved to. Lindsay, at Kevin's urging, joined them.

Iris was laid out on the only bed. The smell of antiseptic filled the room, sharp and poignant, invading Kevin's olfactory senses like a dagger through the nose. He'd never enjoyed that smell and could only imagine how bad it must have been for the kitsune with him. They had a much stronger sense of smell than he did.

"You're all here." Iris sounded weak as she reclined on the bed. "Good."

"L-Lady Iris, h-how are you feeling? Do you need any help? Is there anything I can get for you? Shall I kill something for you?"

Kirihime was the first to Iris' side. Camellia would have been second, but, well…

"Hawa!"

She tripped.

Even while injured, Iris still had the good sense to facepalm. "Gods above, Mom. You're such a klutz. And you," she pointed at

Kirihime, "stop worrying."

"H-hawa... Iris is so mean."

"B-but, Lady Iris, how can you possibly expect me to not worry after seeing you in this state?"

Iris rolled her eyes. Kevin walked up to her bedside. Lindsay and Kiara hung back, while Kotohime remained by Kevin's left side and four paces behind him.

"Are you alright? What happened?"

"Concerned for me?" Upon hearing that mischievous voice and seeing the glint in her eyes, Kevin turned his head.

"I'm only worried because you're Lilian's sister."

"So you say, but I know you can't get enough of me."

"Pfft! As if... like I could ever..."

"Kevin," Iris interrupted, her expression serious, "Lilian's been kidnapped."

***

Lilian had been kidnapped.

How could this have happened?

The words rang out in Kevin's mind, a hollow sound that filled him with self-loathing and a sense of failure. He should have been there. If he had been with her, then...

What could I have done? She wasn't kidnapped by a human, but a kitsune. I... I probably would have been a hindrance.

He stood outside of Iris' room, staring at the wall in shock. According to Iris, one of Jiāoào's "lapdogs" had attacked Mrs. Diane's vehicle, stabbed Iris with some kind of fire technique, and taken Lilian.

Jiāoào had kidnapped Lilian. Jiāoào, the kitsune that Kotohime had warned him about.

What am I going to do? What am I supposed to do?

Kevin pressed a hand against the wall, hunching over as he clenched his eyes shut, fighting against the incertitude that waged war within his mind.

He wanted to go. He wanted to rescue Lilian, but—

"How long are you going to stand there?" a voice said behind him.

"Kiara..."

Kevin turned around to see Kiara stomp up to him. He didn't react when she grabbed him by the shirt and hauled him off his feet.

"Well?" she asked, her face inches from his own. "How long are you going to keep moping? Your mate's in danger! Isn't it your duty to go and save her? Don't you want to rescue her from this guy?"

"Of course I do," Kevin whispered, eyes turning downward, "but I…"

"But you what?"

"I'm just… I'm only human. Every time something bad has happened, Lilian was always the one who saved me. Whenever I was in trouble, she would come to my rescue. It's pathetic, really. I'm so weak and helpless. How could I possibly rescue Lilian when I can't even rescue myself?"

"You…" Kiara seemed shocked, but she quickly hardened her glare to finely honed points. "Listen here, brat! I didn't train a weak little fool who would get frightened at the first sign of trouble! If I didn't think you had a fighting chance against the people who would do you harm, then I would never have trained you in the first place. You should be more than a match for some brat with a chip on his shoulder."

"B-but Jiāoào is a kitsune—"

"I don't care what he is! Everybody has a weakness, even kitsune—especially kitsune. You have training, but what does he have? A couple illusions at most. There's no way someone I trained would ever be defeated by someone like that."

"B-but I've been barely training for a month."

"And he likely hasn't trained at all," Kiara countered. "Now…"

Kiara dragged Kevin so close their noses were touching.

"… are you going to rescue Lilian, or am I gonna have to beat you for being a coward?"

Kevin stared into Kiara's eyes, his mind searching for answers. Could he really defeat Jiāoào? Could he really beat a yōkai, a creature so far beyond him in power that it was almost ridiculous?

Does it even matter? Kevin asked himself. *Why should it matter if he's a yōkai and I'm a human? He kidnapped Lilian. He stole my… my mate from me. Am I just going to let that slide?*

Kevin felt his resolve become like steel. He raised his eyes to gaze at Kiara, whose lips curled into a smirk.

"I take it you've made up your mind?"

Kevin didn't answer with words.

He just smirked back.

***

Kevin entered the room much more calmly than when he walked out.

"Are you doing okay, Kevin?" Lindsay asked.

"Yeah," Kevin smiled at her, "I'm fine. I just needed someone to talk some sense into me."

Kiara snorted, which made him turn slightly to glare at her. He then sighed when the woman just grinned back, and turned to look at Iris.

She still lay on the bed, looking like she'd been trampled by a stampede of Pokemon, but a smirk twisted her lips and a light entered her eyes.

"So, I take it you've decided to rescue my Lily-pad?"

"Your Lily-pad?" Kevin raised an eyebrow. "You mean my mate, right?"

"Hmph." Had Iris not been bedridden, Kevin had the distinct impression that she would have crossed her arms. "You're only a temporary replacement. No one but myself will ever be truly worthy of her."

"There is something seriously wrong with a girl saying that about her own sister," Kevin mused.

"Whatever." Iris became dead serious, which caused him to become serious in turn. "Listen to me, Kevin. You have to rescue Lilian. Jiāoào, he's... he's not a good person. He's the worst kind of scum you can possibly think of, and he's been obsessed with Lilian ever since they first met. I mean, I've always had a thing for my sister, but he's *really* obsessed."

Kevin made a face. "At least you're willing to admit that you're obsessed with Lilian, though it's kinda disturbing to actually hear you say it."

"Yeah, yeah, I love my sister more than I should. Now get the fuck out of here and go rescue her already." Her eyes gleamed like twin bloody moons as she gazed at him. "If you manage to save her before that dickwad steals her chastity, I'll give you a pair of my panties."

"Oh, shut up," Kevin snapped. "You don't even wear panties!"

Lindsay's cheeks blushed bright red at the words. She quickly pinched her nose to keep the blood from escaping.

"Ah, right. I forgot." Iris paused before grinning again. "In that case, I'll give you a pair of Lilian's panties."

"There are so many things I could say to that, but I won't. Do you know where Lilian is?"

Iris looked grim as she shook her head. "No. Sorry."

"I see." The knuckles of Kevin's left hand turned white as he clenched it into a fist.

"Do not worry, Kevin-sama." Kotohime placed a reassuring hand on his shoulder. "I know how we can find Lilian-sama."

***

Juan was just about to sit down on his psychedelic couch when the door to his apartment exploded, showering wood chips and fragments across his abode. A figure darted into the room. He barely had time to blink before he was slammed against the wall, and an unsheathed katana was pressed against his neck.

"Kotohime," despite having the sharp end of a katana caressing his jugular, Juan did not appear the least bit worried, "it seems you have forgotten what I told you the last time you visited."

"No, I remember." The blade was pressed more firmly against Juan's neck. "I just don't care. I know that Jiāoào discovered Lilian-sama was staying in Phoenix because you told him."

Juan would have shrugged, but he feared that even the slightest movement would cause the katana's edge to slit his throat. "Jiāoào offered a large reward for any information on Lilian's whereabouts. It was an offer I could not refuse."

"Where is he?" Kotohime's eyes narrowed. The air grew heavier. Kevin, who'd entered behind the woman, felt a chill run down his spine. "Where is Jiāoào? Where is he keeping Lilian-sama?"

"And why should I tell you that?" asked a defiant Juan. "What can you offer me that would be worth my while?"

"Your life."

"Ha..." Juan sighed. "It seems that you still do not understand—"

"No," Kotohime's voice was cold enough to freeze over hell. "You are the one who doesn't understand. Lilian-sama is my charge. I have been tasked with her protection, and anyone trying to obstruct my ability to protect her is an obstacle that must be eliminated. You, Valsiener-san, have become an obstacle."

"I thought I told you, my name is—" The katana caressed his jugular. A trickle of blood ran down his neck. It was only now, as he stared into Kotohime's eyes, that he realized she really would kill him. "Very well, I will tell you where Jiāoào is currently staying."

"And Lilian-sama?"

"She will be with Jiāoào."

"Give me the location."

Juan, or Valsiener, as Kotohime called him, gave the kimono-clad femme Jiāoào's location.

"I hope you know this transgression will not go unpunished," Juan said after the threat of death by katana had passed.

"If you wish to go up against one of the Thirteen Great Kitsune Clans, then be my guest," Kotohime stared coldly at him. "Your benefactors will not care what I do to you, so long as you remain alive and are able to give them the information they seek. They will not go up against a Great Clan. Not for you."

Juan said nothing to that. Not for lack of having something to say, which he really didn't, but because Kevin had stepped in front of him.

"Ah. Kevin Swift," the horrible Spanish accent was back in place. "It has been a while since I've seen you, no? I hope you are doing well, though," he chuckled, "considering the circumstances, perhaps I am being optimistic."

Kevin didn't speak for the longest time. He just stared at Juan, Valsiener, whatever his name was, with a blank expression.

"You... you are the reason that Lilian was kidnapped by Jiāoào?" he asked calmly.

"Well, I am the one who supplied him with the information on Lilian's whereabouts, but that's about it." Juan shrugged. "I am an information broker. It's what I do. I've got to earn a living somehow."

Kevin's hands tightened into fists, the only sign of what was about to happen.

A loud crack echoed around the room as the blond's right hand crashed into Juan's nose with a loud *crunch!* His head rocked back as blood spurted from his nostrils. His pompadour-style hair bounced and jiggled with the motion.

"Ow…" Juan held a hand to his nose. It was definitely broken. He hadn't realized Kevin could punch so hard.

"You have no idea how long I've wanted to do that," Kevin said before he spun around and walked out of the apartment, leaving a surprised Kotohime and a dazed Juan, holding his bleeding and broken nose.

***

Kevin hadn't walked more than fifteen feet when Kotohime caught up to him.

"Kevin-sama?" she sounded almost tentative.

"So, Juan is a yōkai?" he asked, not revealing his thoughts or opinions. He seemed calm, calmer than she thought he should have been.

"Yes, the young man you know as Juan is indeed a yōkai. To be more specific, he is a half-yōkai—a half-human, half-kitsune hybrid."

Kevin nodded noncommittally. "I guess I should have realized that. The strange quirks, the big hair, and that ridiculous internet-translated Spanish. It only makes sense that he isn't human."

"I somehow feel really insulted by your comments."

"Ah! Sorry, sorry," Kevin was quick to apologize. "I didn't mean that as an insult to you. You and Iris and Kirihime and Camellia are really nice people. Truly. I… you've all become very important to me."

"Ufufufu." Kotohime, in a bout of unusual behavior, ruffled Kevin's hair. "That's very kind of you to say. I think I am beginning to see why Lilian-sama is so taken with you, just a little."

He and Kotohime shared a smile. Maybe it was just him, but he felt like he and Kotohime had just bonded a little. It left him with a heady feeling, a sense of accomplishment.

"I didn't know half-kitsune existed," Kevin said after a moment. "I always thought anyone born with a yōkai parent would be pure yōkai."

"I suppose I can understand that logic, given that our genetics are stronger than a human's." Kotohime paused. "There are some yōkai who, when procreating with a human, will always birth a pure yōkai child. Yuki-onna are the best example of this. However, many yōkai will give birth to half-yōkai when they have sex with a human."

Kevin nodded as he absorbed this small lesson. It was interesting, but...

"Procreation is complicated with you yōkai. Not that I'm surprised."

Kotohime's amused smile was preceded by a chortle. "If you think that is complicated, wait until I teach you about how kitsune genetics affect their elemental affinities."

Kevin wasn't sure if he wanted to know right now, but Kotohime apparently felt the need to explain.

"Kitsune are an unusual breed. Unlike most yōkai, who can only ever be born to a single element, kitsune are among the few that can use every elemental type, depending on the pulse of their blood. A Lightning Kitsune can use lightning; a Fire Kitsune could wield fire; a Celestial Kitsune unleashing light/divine powers, etc."

She paused for a breath.

"When a kitsune is born, the element they're born with almost always comes from the male. There are some who pick up the element of their mother, but those are few and far between. Even rarer than those who gain their mother's element are those born with both. They're a rarity beyond compare, and are highly prized by the Thirteen Great Clans."

"Why did you tell me all that?" Kevin asked. "It seems kind of unnecessary."

Kotohime paused. "Because the author is really bad at foreshadowing?"

"Try again," he ground out.

"Because I felt like you needed to know?"

Kevin and Kotohime stared at each other. Kevin was the one who looked away first.

"Let's... let's just get going," he sighed.

"Ufufufu, of course, Kevin-sama."

They walked into the parking lot, where Kiara was waiting for them with the car ready. She stood beside the driver's door, leaning against the metal chassis, her arms crossed over her chest.

"You know where we're going?" she asked as they walked up to her.

"Yes," Kotohime answered. "Valsiener-san was kind enough to give us Jiāoào's location. It is a little out of the way, but not too far from here."

"Good. Then let's hurry up. I wanna be home in time for dinner."

They all got in the car, Kevin in the back and Kotohime taking the front passenger's seat. Kiara started the engine and they soon took off.

Kevin looked out the window, watching as they left the apartment complex. He didn't see any of the passing scenery, however. His thoughts, his mind and his heart, were all focused on a single thought.

Hang on, Lilian. I'm coming.

Chapter 10

The Difference Between Humans and Yōkai

Lilian's first thought upon waking up was: *"Uga wufuguu muffu..."*

Her second thought was: *"What the hell hit me?"*

Wanting to know where she was, Lilian opened her eyes... and was immediately forced to shut them again as sunlight burned her retinas. Groaning, she felt her head begin to throb, a slow pounding like someone was using her brain as a bongo drum. She felt a strong compunction to return to the blissful darkness she'd awakened from.

"I see you're finally awake, my Lilian."

Lilian's body seized.

No. It can't be. He can't be here.

"How long are you going to feign sleep?"

Ice seeped into her veins. She recognized that voice.

No. No, no, no, no, no!

Wanting to stop herself but unable to, Lilian opened her eyes, ignoring the way they burned. She turned to the source of the voice. What she saw, who she saw, chilled her to her very core, as if someone had dumped her in the middle of the Arctic Circle.

"You!"

Jiāoào smiled at her, either not caring or willfully ignoring the disgust and fear that had appeared on Lilian's face. "Hello, my

Lilian. You haven't changed at all since the last time I saw you. You're every bit as beautiful as I remember. I've missed—"

"What happened to me?" Jiāoào's right eye twitched as Lilian rudely interrupted him. "Where am I? And what are you doing here?"

"You were the unfortunate victim of a rather atrocious car accident," Jiāoào explained calmly. "My vassal, Ling, was fortunately in the area and managed to pull you to safety. You really should be more careful when getting into strange vehicles. You never know what might happen," he chided, wagging a finger at her. "As for where you are, why, you are currently resting within my temporary domicile."

Lilian looked around and finally noticed that she was in a room of extreme opulence. Richly decorated walls painted with intricate designs surrounded her. Tapestries hung from those walls, the symbol that she recognized as the Shénshèng Clan crest imprinted firmly on their front. Dark red carpet lined the floor, and the ceiling was painted to mimic the sky at sunset. Decadence didn't begin to describe the room.

She also noticed that she'd been bound. Her arms, her legs, and even her tails were wrapped in some kind of cloth. She tried breaking it, even going so far as to use reinforcement to increase her strength. But it didn't work, which meant the cloth had been made from the silk of a *Jorōgumo*, a spider yōkai. It was the only known fabric durable enough to withstand youki-enhanced strength. It also absorbed youki, which meant she wouldn't be able to use any techniques to break out.

A sudden feeling welled up inside of her. A chill ran down her spine.

She was being watched.

She looked around and quickly spotted the woman behind Jiāoào.

Like her, this woman had red hair and green eyes. She even appeared to be around the same age. There were only a few general differences, those being the shape of her face and eyes and her body proportions. Lilian could proudly claim that she was bustier and had a slimmer waist than this kitsune. Two tails hung limply behind the other kitsune's back.

It wasn't the other kitsune's physical appearance that Lilian noticed, however. Rather, she saw the glare being directed at her, the insanity in the other vixen's eyes, the way her lips peeled back to reveal sharpened canines…

What… what is this feeling?

Lilian took several deep breaths. She couldn't afford to panic in a situation like this.

She focused back on Jiāoào. "Your horrible taste in decoration hasn't changed, I see."

"And your blunt manner of speaking remains the same as always." A cold smile crawled onto Jiāoào's face. "I look forward to breaking you of that willful spirit of yours."

Lilian shuddered, not just in fear, but in revulsion as well. This boy, she had always hated him, loathed him with her very existence. And now she was caught, trapped within his paws.

"But do not worry too much." Jiāoào reached out with his left hand and his fingers brushed against her cheek. "I'll make you sure enjoy every—"

Lilian sank her teeth into Jiāoào's finger. The boy screamed and tried to pull his hand back, but her canines had pierced the skin. She tasted the coppery tang of blood on her tongue, but ignored it in favor of keeping her teeth clamped firmly on his flesh. Jiāoào yanked his entire arm back, and while it wasn't enough to make her release him, it did make her fall to the floor.

She groaned as her bones were jarred from her impact. Jiāoào used that moment to pull his finger back—a finger that had been peeled of its skin and muscle, revealing bits of the white bone underneath thick layers of crimson fluids.

Lilian felt a moment of vindication. She licked her lips to get the blood off, then spat a glob of it onto the floor. Jiāoào stared at her in shock, as if he couldn't believe she had just done that. She presented him with her most fierce grin, complete with bloodstained teeth.

"You bitch!"

The grin was wiped off her face as a scream resounded throughout the room. It did not come from Jiāoào, but from the woman with him.

Like a storm she surged forward, the intent to harm clear in her eyes. Lilian tried to move away, but with her arms, legs and tails bound, she could do nothing more than wiggle and squirm in place.

Fear seized her.

An icy fist clenched her heart.

How could anyone have such insane eyes?

"Maddison!" The girl froze. Lilian held her breath. "Do not go near her!"

"B-but Master, I—GYA!"

Lilian winced when Jiāoào brutally yanked on the chain tethered to the girl's neck. The redhead jerked, choking noises emerging from her throat. The force he put behind his action was such that Maddison fell backwards, hitting the floor with a solid *thump!*

"Stupid girl!"

"AAAHHHH!"

Lilian watched in abject horror as Jiāoào kicked the girl in the stomach, making her curl her legs into her chest. She was given no reprieve, however, as the next kick was to her face. Blood flew from her mouth as her head jerked backwards. Now lying on her back, the poor girl could do nothing as Jiāoào mercilessly whaled on her.

"I thought I told you not to move!" Stomp. Maddison's nose broke. "You're lucky I even allowed you to breathe the same air as my Lilian!" Kick. All the air rushed from Maddison's lungs. "Fucking bitch!"

"Stop it!" Lilian screamed with tears in her eyes. "I said stop! Why are you hurting her?!"

Jiāoào did stop, if for no other reason than to address Lilian's question. Lying at his feet, Maddison quietly sobbed. "I am disappointed in you, my Lilian. Surely, you understand the need to ensure that pets like her know their place."

Lilian was stunned. "Pet? Make sure she knows her place? She's not an animal! She's a person! A kitsune, just like us!"

"Lilian. my Lilian." Lilian shuddered. Jiāoào's smile frightened her for reasons she couldn't even begin to fathom. "You are far too kind. Maddison is nothing more than a pet, an object for me to pleasure myself with. This... thing may indeed be a kitsune, but she's a failure whose only purpose was to be your replacement until I had you within my grasp."

By this point in time, Jiāoào had healed the bite wounds on his finger. He opened his mouth to say something more, but a knock at the door interrupted him. Jiāoào opened the door to reveal a woman with long purple hair in a ponytail and short-skirted kimono kneeling on the ground.

"My Lord," the woman said, "it seems we have several unexpected guests."

"Unexpected guests?" Jiāoào hummed. "How many?"

"Three. One of them is Kotohime. I've tentatively identified the other as Kiara F. Kuyo."

Kotohime is here?!

Lilian felt a surge of hope. If Kotohime had come to rescue her, then surely everything would be alright. No one, not Jiāoào or this new three-tailed kitsune, could defeat a vixen of Kotohime's caliber, especially if Kiara was with her.

"I see." Jiāoào grimaced with repressed disdain. "So, the great Swordswoman of the defunct Slina clan is working with a dog, is she? That's fine. I shall have them both dealt with. Who's the last one?"

"A human male around fifteen years of age with blond hair and blue eyes. It's the one that I told you about in my report."

Kevin!

Lilian's eyes widened. Kevin was coming to rescue her! Equal amounts of warmth and terror filled her chest. Coming here would put him in incredible peril.

I have to do something!

"I see." Jiāoào's body went through a series of shudders. "It seems that Lilian's toy has come to rescue her. How amusing." His cruel chuckle set Lilian's teeth rattling. "I shall have to give this boy a warm reception, then."

Lilian's eyes widened. He couldn't!

"Ling, I want you to deal with Kotohime. You don't need to beat her, just stall her long enough for me to deal with the human."

"Yes, My Lord."

Ling left the room, and Jiāoào looked at the redhead by his feet. "Maddison, tell Shílì that I have found a worthy opponent for him. After that, you are to guard this door and let no one aside from myself enter. Fail to do so, and I will ensure that you experience so much pain and suffering that you'll wish I had discarded you like the trash you are."

"Yes… Master."

The chain was taken off and Maddison was allowed back to her feet. The redhead sent one last withering glare at Lilian, then marched out of the room.

Jiāoào stared at Lilian for several silent seconds before making one last parting comment. "Enjoy the last few days of your freedom, my Lilian. Once we leave this Inari-forsaken country, I will take great pleasure in breaking you." With that said, he vacated the room as well, the door behind him closing with a light *click.*

The moment she was alone, Lilian began to struggle against her bonds.

I have to break free and help Kevin!

***

Kevin felt his stomach leap into his throat as the car he was in hit a speed bump and became airborne. Sitting within the driver's seat, Kiara laughed like a loon.

"Fear me road, for I AM YOUR DOOM! Hahahahahaha-BWAHAHAHAHAHA!"

They were traveling down a dirt road. Dust and rocks and the gods only knew what else were kicked up in their wake. Ever since they had hit this out-of-the-way desert road, Kiara's driving had taken a turn for the insane.

"Now this is what I'm talking about! WHOOOO!"

"AAAEEEIIIII!"

Kevin could have sworn he saw his life flash before his eyes as the car sailed through the air. When they hit the ground again, he nearly bit the inside of his cheek.

"Kiara-san, must you drive so recklessly?" Kotohime asked, somehow managing to remain poised, the perfect picture of calm, despite Kiara's driving.

Kiara sent her foxy friend a fierce grin. Her eyes twinkled with joy, though Kevin thought insanity was a better term to describe it. "Of course I do. We're off road, Kotohime. Off road means no cops, and no cops means flooring it!"

Kevin clasped his hands together and started muttering under his breath. "Our father, who art in Heaven, hallowed be thy name. My Kingdom come. My will be done—"

"Are you praying?" Kiara asked.

"Yes! How can I not with the way you're driving?"

Kiara merely laughed his words off and stomped on the gas. Kevin shrieked like a little girl as they bolted further along the road, hitting bumps and dips, catching air and slamming back down. The tang of blood filled his mouth as he accidentally bit his tongue. He clenched his eyes shut, praying to God, Izanagi, Izanami, Inari, Allah, Shiva, Ifrit, Thor, Odin, and every other god he could think of to make this crazy woman stop.

"Shit!"

A curse escaped Kiara's mouth. Loud squealing reached Kevin's ears as he was thrown forward, his face thunking against the front seat. He knew that was going to leave a rash come tomorrow morning. The car swerved several times, left and right, left and right. Kevin's face turned green as he fought against the breakfast that threatened to spew from his mouth.

Then they stopped. Suddenly. Abruptly. And without warning.

Kevin quickly undid his seatbelt and was just about to bolt out of the car—

"Hold it, boya."

—when Kiara stopped him.

"What? Why?"

"Because we have company," Kotohime answered calmly as she undid her seatbelt.

Kevin looked out the front window to see that, yes, there was indeed someone impeding them from continuing. Her long purple hair, tied into a ponytail behind her head, flowed gently like streamers caught in a breeze. Her short-skirted kimono reminded him of Kotohime's, except it was all black. He wondered why Kiara hadn't just run her over, but then he noticed the three tails waving behind her and the fox ears that sat twitching on her head.

A kitsune. Great. This is just what we need.

"I shall handle this."

Kevin felt a jolt of surprise. "Kotohime?"

The kimono-clad female offered Kevin a conciliatory smile before stepping out of the car. "You two should go on ahead. I will take care of this one and then catch up with you."

Kiara shrugged and shifted out of neutral. "Alright. I don't expect it will take you very long to beat her anyway."

"Indeed."

***

As she closed the passenger door and Kiara took off, the other kimono-wearing kitsune tried to stop them by shooting a large cylinder of fire from her tails. It was negated before it could travel ten feet by the equally large stream of water that Kotohime launched at it.

Loud hissing echoed across the desert landscape. Steam billowed outwards from where the two attacks met, covering the area in a thick, cloying cloud of evaporated moisture. Kiara used it as a smokescreen, driving right past the kitsune and bursting out of the cloud. Kotohime could hear Kevin's shriek of fear along with Kiara's laughter as the car took off down the road.

Ling made to attack them before they could get too far.

Kotohime did not let her.

Several spikes shot up from the ground almost too quickly for the naked eye to follow. Ling barely avoided the first spike, and only managed to keep from being impaled by the second by launching herself into the air. The third spike erupted from the earth right below her, but Ling's tails burst into flames and she used them to shatter the ice crystal.

"Fire Art: Fire Tail Whip."

Ling landed on the ground several feet away from Kotohime, who smiled congenially at the woman.

"Water Art: Glacial Crystals. It is a rather basic technique, I'll admit, but it gets the job done." Her eyes, sharper even than a hawk's, observed the kunoichi-garbed woman before her. "I do not believe I'll need anything more than basic techniques, not for this battle."

Ling frowned and slid into a combat stance, knees bent, center of gravity lowered, and arms set in front of her in a basic martial arts stance.

"Do not think defeating me will be that easy just because I am a three tails," Ling declared in an emotionless voice. "I assure you that if you underestimate me, it will be the last mistake you ever make."

***

The house was getting closer. Kevin could make out the more intricate details as they drove. It was a massive construct, built to the size of a mansion. It looked like something out of the late

Victorian era, with two spire-like towers standing about three stories high. Red tiled roofing and brick walls made for a stark contrast with the tan desert colors surrounding it.

Before they could go much further, the ground in front of them exploded. Black flames burst into existence and sought to devour the car. Kevin had never seen such flames before, and his eyes widened as the dark fire leapt forward to consume them.

"We're gonna die!!"

Kiara swerved the vehicle, turning hard. They avoided the flames, which reversed course and continued to follow them until they seemed to move out of their range.

The car then skidded to a halt.

A figure had appeared in front of them.

"Looks like this is where we start hoofing it. Outta the car, boya."

Kevin scrambled out of the car at the same time as Kiara. They walked towards the person standing before them, wary of potential traps. None were forthcoming though, and they reached the man soon enough.

Dark hair descended from his crown to frame an effeminately beautiful face marred by dark rings surrounding the man's eyes. His eyes, which were black enough to make the night jealous, stared at them politely, but Kevin could practically sense the insanity rolling off them in waves. He wore a very unusual outfit, black slacks and a black penguin jacket with a white undershirt. Equally white gloves covered his hands. He had four tails swaying behind him, making him the same age as Camellia.

"Is that a butler's outfit?" Kevin asked in surprise. It was, indeed, a butler's outfit.

"You must be the one known as Kiara F. Kuyo." The kitsune gave a graceful bow at the waist. Kevin felt a drop of sweat trail down his face. This man definitely acted like a butler. "My name is Shílì, however, you may call me the Black Butler."

"Ugh." Kevin felt like vomiting. "That was so lame..."

Shílì's eyes widened. "W-what do you mean it's lame? I'll have you know that I spent a lot of time coming up with that nickname. Hours even."

"Oh, please. We both know you stole that name from *Black Butler*," Kevin shot back. "Now stop butchering one of the anime I like and think up your own dang nickname!"

"Your words are harsh, young one, but I can see your point. It wouldn't be a very good idea for me to so blatantly use the name of an anime for my nickname. Copyright issues and all that." He placed a hand on his chin. "So, then, what should I call myself..." After mumbling to himself a little more, the black-haired kitsune nodded. "My new nickname shall be Sebastian Michaelis!"

"That's even worse!"

"Ciel Phantomhive?"

"Not on your life!"

"... Tanaka?"

"Absolutely not!"

"Then what should I call myself?"

"How about you just call yourself by your own name?" asked an annoyed Kevin. "You know, that series of letters you were given upon your birth?"

"Hmm... yes, yes, I guess I see your point. It would not do to rip off of another person's fame. That is, indeed, in very poor taste. And as my master's butler, I must keep myself to the highest standards possible. Very well, then." Another formal bow. "You may call me Shílì. I am Master Jiāoào's butler and servant, his sword and his shield, and I have come to challenge you, Kiara F. Kuyo!"

Seeing that it was finally her turn to play a part, Kiara looked at the man pointing a finger at her with amusement. "Oh? You wanna fight me, huh? I'll admit, I'm pretty curious to see what sort of tricks a four-tails has up his sleeve." She sniffed the air. "Especially one with the powers of darkness."

"Noticed that, did you?" Shílì pouted, as if she'd just ruined his big surprise. "I do not know why I was born with this accursed power, though I shall be the first to admit that it has come in handy."

"I'm just surprised someone like you is willing to serve a brat from the Great Celestial Clan."

"A series of mitigating circumstances led to my fortuitous role as Master Jiāoào's bodyguard and butler. I will admit, it was very difficult at first, but I have since come to terms with and learned to enjoy my work." A strange gleam entered the butler's eyes. "I especially enjoy when it leads me to strong opponents like you."

"Heh." Kiara chuckled and shook her head ruefully. "You really want to fight me?" A smile grew upon her lips and her eyes gleamed dangerously in the light. Kevin could feel the air around him become thick with something frightening. Bile rose up in his throat.

"Indeed I do." The kitsune's smile matched Kiara's. It spoke of danger and insanity, of a bloodlust that could only be sated through brutal combat. "There are few things more enjoyable than fighting and killing a strong opponent."

Kiara slid into a stance that Kevin didn't recognize. He could see that it bore a slight resemblance to Muay Thai, but Kiara remained too light on her feet for it to be that.

"I'm surprised to hear a kitsune say that."

"Not all kitsune go out of their way to avoid a good battle. Some of us actually enjoy pushing our physical capabilities to the limit." Shílì began bouncing on the balls of his feet, his hands dangling loosely at his sides. "For me, there is no greater joy than finding the limits of my strength and overcoming those limits. Pushing my abilities as far as they can go is my greatest joy and happiness."

The air grew thick, and Kevin found it difficult to breathe.

"However, I've not had an opponent who can push me to my utmost limits in nearly a century." Shílì lamented, his arms reaching up to the heavens. He brought them back down and smiled at Kiara. "I hope very much that you succeed in giving me the challenge I so crave."

"I think you've got things backwards," Kiara said, giving him a fanged smirk. "You're the one who I'm hoping will give me a challenge." She looked over at the silent Kevin. "Boya, get going. I'll take care of things from here."

Kevin took a deep breath to steady himself. Slowly, he nodded. "Alright. Thanks."

Shílì didn't stop Kevin as the young man ran past him. He didn't even look the boy's way.

"Not going to stop him?" asked Kiara, an eyebrow raised.

"No. Master Jiāoào has something special planned for him. It is best to just let my master have his way with the young man."

… A moment of silence. Several crows cawed in the distance. Kiara watched a tumbleweed slowly roll between her and her soon-to-be opponent.

Finally...

"...That sounded so wrong in so many ways."

***

When Kevin stepped into the courtyard, someone was already waiting for him.

The person standing before him looked even younger than Kevin, though the two tails jutting from his tailbone said otherwise. Long blond hair tied into a topknot at the back kept his hair out of his face, all except for two bangs which fell down his front, stopping just below his chest. His outfit consisted of a traditional Han Fu robe—a gown of pure white with long, voluminous sleeves and a multi-layered skirt of light purple was visible underneath the robes. A belt with intricate embroideries of a nine-tailed fox held it all together.

A chill ran down Kevin's spine, causing him to stop. An unknown feeling of anxiety passed through him. He felt unnerved by this kitsune's presence. The young-looking yōkai did not speak. He just stood there, staring.

Kevin gathered his courage.

"You must be Jiāoào."

"And you must be Kevin Swift."

"That's right. What of it?"

Jiāoào looked him over, then scoffed. "I cannot fathom the reason as to why my Lilian has pledged herself to you. You're nothing but a filthy, disgusting, lowly human."

The fear vanished at the petulant kitsune's arrogant words.

"And you're nothing but a jerk who goes around kidnapping the girl you want because you know it's the only way you can have her," Kevin snapped back. "At least I gained Lilian's love naturally, unlike you, so spare me your 'lowly human' crap!"

"Tch. You're also incredibly crass, it seems. I wonder, have you always been like this, or is that bluntness something you picked up from my Lilian?"

"Who cares? Look, are we going to get this started or not?"

Jiāoào raised an eyebrow. "You're not going to tell me to, 'hand over Lilian or you'll regret it,' or something of that nature? Isn't that how you protagonist types normally operate?"

Kevin shrugged. "Why bother? We both know that you're not

going to hand Lilian over to me."

"True enough."

"Besides, I don't think we have enough word count for that."

"That is very—wait." Blink. "You can break the fourth wall?"

Now it was Kevin's turn to blink. "The fourth what now?"

"Never mind." Jiāoào shook his head. He must have been hearing things. "Let us, as you humans say, get this over with."

A cruel smile lit Jiāoào's face as he stared Kevin down, his two tails writhing behind him like the abominable tentacles from an amorphous eldritch horror.

"Allow me to show you why we kitsune are superior to you apes."

Chapter 11

Lessons in Badassery

"Fire Art: Fiery Prism, Thirteen Pentagrams."

Kotohime watched as streaks of fire carved lines through the air in the shape of a pentagram. A second pentagram soon joined the first, followed by a third, a fourth, all the way to the thirteenth. She looked around, noting that all of the pentagrams had trapped her inside of what she guessed was a larger pentagram.

"Ara, ara. What an interesting technique." Dust rose as her sandal-clad feet slid further apart. Her left hand grasped the hilt of her katana, while her right held onto the sheath. "Ufufufu..."

Even in battle, the chuckle remained the same.

Ling shuddered.

The blazing pentagrams of destruction closed in on her, intent on turning her into cinders.

"Water Art: Blade of the Water Lily."

Water appeared on Kotohime's katana, covering her blade in liquid blue that constantly rippled and shifted as she moved.

"Ikken Hissatsu. Sen."

Kotohime's sword lashed out, an untraceable number of flashes weaving a never ending trail as the water-covered steel glinted in the light. Each strike of her blade seemed to slice through one of the pentagrams multiple times—dozens, hundreds even. And each flame that was cut by Kotohime's blade burst into dozens of fireflies, tiny bulbs of light composed entirely of fire. The fireflies moved a short distance away, swirling around her in a half-dome entrapment.

"Oh? What kind of technique is—k-ku!"

One of the fireflies latched onto her back, and the flame seemed to burn a hole straight through her skin—no, it felt like the fire was searing her very soul!

More and more fireflies latched onto Kotohime's frame, and each one that affixed itself to her brought even more pain. And yet, despite the amount of pain she felt, the swordswoman had the presence of mind to notice that something was off.

None of the flames had burned her.

"A-an illusion! Gah!"

However, it appeared to be too late by that point. The fireflies swarmed over her, latching onto her, covering every part of her body in their orange and yellow light. Kotohime began to struggle. She started to stagger. Her body fell onto its knees and then toppled face first to the ground. Her firefly-covered figure twitched once, twice, then went still.

"Is that it?" Ling asked, frowning. That seemed far too easy.

She approached the prone corpse cautiously, her eyes wary for any sign that Kotohime might not be dead. However, when she reached the figure, she saw that, indeed, the woman was still.

"It seems I defeated her," Ling murmured, "it appears that she underestimated me, right to the very—what the—?!"

The body before her dispersed into water. A million tiny droplets sparkling in the afternoon sun, which hovered in the air— at least until they all darted towards Ling at unparalleled speeds.

Ling did her best to defend against the attack, but she didn't have time to perform a technique and was thus reduced to reinforcing her body and guarding her vital organs with her arms.

Her body was pelted with thousands of water droplets. It didn't sound very painful, but when those droplets moved faster than 100 miles per hour and were dense enough that their compositional hardness was comparative to diamonds, it hurt. It really, really hurt. With every drop that struck her frame, blood spurted out of a new wound. And there were many such strikes. Before long, Ling's arms, legs and abdomen were covered with small punctures, tiny holes from which crimson ichor poured. They weren't large, nor were they debilitating on their own, but together, they presented a problem.

"Water Art: Tsukuyomi's Wrathful Tears."

Ling turned around, her bloodstained teeth clenched in unmasked pain. Kotohime stood several feet behind her, unharmed. Her kimono didn't have a single cut, tear or burn mark, not even a ruffle or a crease. The expression on her face remained unchanged, placid and calm and composed, as if she were not in the middle of a life and death battle.

"You…" Ling wiped away at the blood making a slow trail down her chin. Some of her non-vital organs must have been punctured. "That was… an illusion?"

"Oh, no," Kotohime responded with a light smile. "While I do have some illusions at my disposal, they do not go very well with my style. I simply replaced myself with a water clone and held its form together during your attack using my youki. You were so focused on watching 'me' burn to death that hiding in the bushes while you were distracted became a simple matter."

"I see." More blood dribbled down her chin. Ling wiped it off. "You are indeed skilled just as the rumors say. However—" A pair of black tonfa shot out from the sleeves of her kimono and into her hands, where they quickly caught fire. "Do not think this means that I am ready to throw in the towel just yet. **Fire Art: Encompassing Torch.**"

"I would expect nothing less."

Kotohime shifted into a relaxed posture. She gripped her katana with both hands, the sheath tucked safely away within her obi. She slid her left foot forward, bending her legs at a precise 45 degree angle. She thought about also using her sheath, but discarded the notion as preposterous. There was no need for overkill here.

A moment of silence passed. Two opponents eyed each other. They moved on some unspoken signal, each preparing to attack before the other.

Kotohime was quicker.

With speed that the other kitsune simply couldn't match, she appeared before Ling in a flicker, a ghostly mirage filled with ill-intent. Her sword was already descending. Ling raised her tonfas above her head in an X-guard to block the attack.

"G-guu..."

The swing never came.

Pain exploded in Ling's stomach as something hard and powerful smashed into her. She doubled over the katana pommel like a foldout chair, right before her body was launched into the air. She hit the ground several feet away, her body rolling for several more yards. Luckily for her, she was on the road. Otherwise, she would have been the unfortunate victim of numerous cacti.

She struggled to her feet and looked up just in time to see her opponent's next attack.

"Ikken Hissatsu. Tsukuyomi no Dansu."

Kotohime began to dance, slowly at first, but picking up speed by the second. Her blade sang, coming in at Ling from seemingly random angles, seeking to slip through a hole in the three-tails' defense.

The younger kitsune did her best to defend against the increasingly speedy onslaught but eventually found herself being overwhelmed. Her tonfas flashed through the air, doing everything kitsune-ly possible to avoid getting injured, but that was like trying to keep a thousand killer bees from stinging. Utterly impossible. Cuts slowly formed on her skin, most notably her arms, which she was forced to use to keep the majority of the strikes from reaching anything vital.

Then Kotohime began to spin. Her body started twirling around with the artistic grace of a ballerina. Her katana came in faster, too, appearing as brief flashes of silver that disappeared seconds later. It moved so quickly that it seemed as if there were multiple blades striking her at once.

The three-tails tried to defend against the storm, but the task proved impossible. There were simply too many attacks coming in from too many different angles. More cuts appeared on her fair skin. All she could do was grit her teeth and hold out against this unfathomable onslaught, wincing as her clothes became stained in carnelian liquid.

And then it was over.

Ling, her body bleeding from innumerable lacerations, fell backwards, hitting the ground.

And then she disappeared, her body bursting into wisps of

smoke and a gout of flame.

"That was…!"

Kotohime turned around and raised her blade. A loud *clang!* rang out across the clearing. The katana Kotohime held in her hands ground against one of the tonfas. Just one. The other tonfa swung in from her left. Ling clearly hoped to slip this one in her guard and strike her unaware. The weapon was even being held by one of Ling's tails instead of a hand.

How cute.

Two people could play at that game.

One of Kotohime's long, white-tipped fox-tails grabbed onto the hilt of the *wakazashi* being carried in the sheath on her back. The short blade slid out with the sibilant hiss of steel, its polished surface glinting in the sun. *Wakazashi* met tonfa in a clash of sparks. Ling's eyes widened before narrowing into a look of fierce determination.

"Fire Art: Three Tails of the Undying Flame."

The temperature rose around them. Three spots on the ground became red hot and boiling, like magma bubbling up from a hidden underground volcano. Fire burst from the ground. Three large pillars rose into the air and took the shape of three flaming fox-tails.

Kotohime did not take her eyes off Ling, but through her peripheral vision, she could see the tails wavering around her, blowing back and forth as if caught in a stiff breeze. The tails straightened up and then descended towards her as one. At the last second, just before the tails struck, the fox-woman in the black kimono leapt back, her left hand enclosing into a fist.

"Constrict."

"Ikken Hissatsu. Bōei."

Before the inferno of tails could coil around her, Kotohime's water-coated blade moved faster than even most yōkai could follow. Flashes of light from her sword's reflection appeared, the number of refractions increasing over time. Soon, Kotohime's sword was moving so quickly that the flashing lights had become a singular, solitary entity, a half-dome that surrounded the four-tails on all sides, a barrier made from an uncountable number of sword strikes.

The fiery tails didn't stand a chance. They burst into steam the moment they touched the barrier, which disappeared as the thick cloud of evaporated water covered the battleground, blocking Ling's vision of Kotohime.

Kotohime tore out of the expanding cloud, the steam splitting apart as she rushed forward, moving on swift feet.

Ling backpedaled. Her tails moved forward and around, surging past her body. They came together, their tips touching. From the tips, a bright yellow, almost white flame appeared. It flickered for but a moment, then morphed into a ball about seven inches in diameter.

"Fire Art: Fire Bullets."

Dozens—no, hundreds of bullets shot from the small sphere of fire, all of them traveling towards Kotohime as indecipherably incandescent streaks. They were all spaced several inches apart, and there were so many of them that it would be impossible for her to dodge them all.

In that case…

"Ikken Hissatsu. Senpū."

Her katana spun in a counterclockwise motion in front of her body. The blade moved so fast that it almost looked like the blades of a helicopter. From the spinning katana, a tornado of wind shot forth.

"Water Art: Tsukuyomi's Surging Waterfall."

The wind soon merged with a jetstream of water, which burst from Kotohime's four tails as if it had been launched from a geyser. Water and wind combined to form a torrential flood of inconceivably fast motion. Power of nature given form.

The water tornado engulfed the fire bullets, snuffing them out quicker than a candle in a hurricane.

Ling's eyes were impossibly wide as the attack struck her with the full force of a tempest condensed into a small tornado. The attack slammed into her body… and barreled straight through it as though it wasn't even there. Ling's body flickered once, and then it was gone.

Instincts born from years of combat saved Kotohime. She turned, her blade already raised. A tonfa struck it. Sparks flared like dying souls lost in the wind. She pushed the offending weapon away, then tilted her blade down and to the left so the tip pointed towards the ground. The second tonfa struck moments later and slid off her blade. That was when her *wakazashi*, still held in the grip of her tail, struck.

Ling was knocked off balance as the short sword slammed against her tonfa, which she'd just barely managed to raise in time to avoid having her throat slit. Her balance shot, she could do nothing as Kotohime's katana swung down.

And hit nothing.

Like a ghost wavering in a breeze, Ling's body disappeared, leaving only a strange smokey substance behind. The smoke, from which cries of anguish could be heard and the faces of undying phantoms lost in a phantasmagoric realm could be seen, surged forward, trapping Kotohime and wrapping around her.

"W-what is—gah!"

Kotohime fell to her knees. Her body felt cold. Chilled. Numb. Like she had just put one foot into the realm of the dead. Her vision darkened and she struggled to keep her form cohesive.

In the same manner that she had disappeared in, Ling reappeared in front of Kotohime. She looked down at the four-tailed kitsune, dark eyes filled with a merciless cold.

"Spirit Art: Braying Spirits of the Underworld."

"G-gu... this is..."

"This is one of my most powerful techniques. You feel it, don't you? The numbness spreading through you is a sign; your body is shutting down. First, your muscles will grow cold and begin to atrophy at an extraordinary rate. Your organs will cease functioning next; first the minor ones, then the major. Your heart will be the last to stop, and then your soul will be pulled out of your body and carried on to the Sanzu river. It is a technique that not even a four-tails can escape from once trapped."

"I see."

Ling's eyes widened. That voice—it came from behind her!

Pain erupted from her chest, along with a lot of blood, which arced through the air in an almost graceful manner. Ling looked down to see a katana protruding through her chest, bright red liquid dripping from its gleaming surface. She blinked, turned her head...

... and met a pair of dark eyes smiling at her.

"How..." Ling hacked up several globs of blood. "How did you...?"

"How did I escape from your technique?" Kotohime finished

for her. "The best way to avoid getting hit is to not be there when the attack is coming. I knew from the moment you used that technique with those fireflies that you are not a pure Fire Kitsune. You are a hybrid, a combination of fire and spirit."

"It would also explain why your abilities exceed those of a regular three-tails," Kotohime continued.

"Ha… ha…" Ling's breathing had become labored and her eyes half-lidded. "So you… figured it out… I-I suppose… I should have expected this… from… the Blood Princess of the Slina Clan."

"Indeed, but do not feel too bad. You did very well for one so young. I was impressed by your abilities."

"Heh, to be praised by you…" A bloody smile made Ling's lips twitch. "I suppose… there are worse things to hear… before I die…" Ling took one last shuddering breath before her body became limp. She slid off the blade, crumpling to the ground, where she lay still.

Kotohime eyed the woman for but a moment. Ling's ponytail had come undone and her hair was splayed across the ground. Her eyes were half-lidded and dull. Blood leaked from between parted lips that breathed no more.

Kneeling down, Kotohime placed a hand over Ling's face, closing her eyes. "You did well," she praised. "May you find peace in eternal slumber."

She stood back up.

Looking off into the distance, where she felt an incredible surge of clashing youki, Kotohime found her placid smile returning. "Ara, ara. It seems Kiara is having a lot of fun."

***

Kiara grinned as her aura engulfed her. Flames of power licked her body, an ethereal inferno that surrounded her, encompassed her, yet did not burn her. Her large, brown and bushy tail wagged behind her, as if to emphasize the excitement she felt at the fight to come.

"Are you ready, foxy?"

Shílì's grin matched Kiara's. "I am merely waiting for you to start." A slight bow at the waist. "Ladies first, you understand."

"Heh, a gentleman during a battle. What an unusual fox."

Deciding to take Shílì up on his invitation, Kiara started the battle by slamming her left fist into the ground. Tremors rocked the earth. Large cracks appeared along the surface. From those cracks, several dozen shards of rubble burst from the ground like a hail of spears, shooting straight at Shílì.

A grin crossed his face. Before the fragments could hit him, his tails moved forward. On the tip of each tail was a small black flame darker than midnight. They moved with lives of their own, writhing and turning and twisting.

"Void Art: Fork Bullets."

A multitude of small projectiles shaped like forks were fired from the dark spheres. Each Void fork struck the rubble flying towards him. The dark flames spread across each makeshift projectile, consuming then, devouring them until nothing remained.

"So, that's Void fire," Kiara muttered, a shiver crawling up her spine. Even from where she stood, she could sense the flame's hunger; it seemed to possess a sentience of its own, irrespective of the one who summoned it.

"Is this the first time you've seen the Void?" inquired a curious Shílì.

"Hn. So what if it is?"

The dark grin on Shílì's face unnerved Kiara. "The Void is the inevitable end of all things. It is the means as well as the conclusion. The Void is the absence of concept; it is nothingness beyond dimension, boundary, or measurement."

Shílì looked down at his hands, clenching and unclenching them. Dark shadows played across his face, preventing Kiara from seeing anything except his chilling grin that stretched from ear to ear.

When he looked up, Shílì's eyes held equal amounts of reverence and madness.

"No one truly understands what the Void is... or why it's so malevolent. Perhaps it is not the Void itself, but the whispers of dead gods who are not really dead, of beings ancient and powerful, descending into madness that transcends the boundaries of time and concepts. In the end, no one really knows. All we have are theories... and the whispers."

Kiara's tongue felt thick and swollen as she listened to this man. She didn't know why, but the words he spoke disturbed her, filling her mind with vile images and delusions of suffering.

"Being one who has never touched the Void, never heard its sirens' call, you probably won't understand." Flames of the darkest black flared into existence above the tips of Shílì's tails. "The Void hungers, Kiara," he whispered, his haunted voice bordering on dementia. "It's only desire is to consume everything. And we who touch the Void hear the whispers in our hearts and minds. Every day and every night we're forced to listen to them; gods, beings descended into madness, whatever they are, imploring us, tempting us with whispered words, demanding we destroy all, that we hasten this world to its final demise. It haunts us, drives us to madness! We are forever slaves to its will!"

The flames roared into an inferno. Kiara's eyes bulged.

"The Void! Is! Merciless!"

Black flames rushed her, speeding across the ground, consuming everything in its path. She could feel its intent, its desire to consume everything, increase in potency the closer it came.

Her body blurred. She rushed backwards, moving faster than she ever had before. The Void followed. Even as she kept track of it, the flames shifted and morphed to form a giant creature, long and serpentine, perhaps a dragon or a snake. It surged forward to swallow her whole. It did indeed appear to have a mind of its own.

In an attempt to delay the all-consuming flames, Kiara's fists smashed into the ground. A large chunk of earth jutted up to block its path. Black fire splashed against the pillar from all sides. The flames were slowed, but not stopped. They crawled along the earth pillar, creeping across its surface like the black tendrils of a demented god.

Kiara moved backwards. Her incredible agility and speed allowed her to put a good deal of distance between herself and the Void fire. She hoped it would be enough.

"You should never take your eyes off of your opponent."

Kiara jumped to her left just in time to dodge a tail that speared into the ground. She moved, her body twisting to face the Void Kitsune. Her fists shot forward. Her aura, the red flames that were the physical manifestation of her power, shot forward as well, taking the shape of a spear.

It struck Shílì's body, which exploded into dark tendrils,

becoming rapidly expanding tongues of fire. The Void fire descended upon Kiara faster than she could move out of the way. Knowing this, Kiara launched her fist into the ground, causing it to explode just as the Void fire struck.

***

Shílì watched the explosion of black flames from a distance, entranced as the sentient fire, full of malice and hunger, greedily consumed everything around it. When he felt that the flames had enough to eat, he forcibly dismissed them, grunting just a bit as his mind strained against the Void's will. There was nothing left of the area struck by the malicious flames, just charred ground.

"Ha…" Shílì looked disappointed. "Is that all she had? I had expected much more from someone who was proclaimed as one of the strongest warriors of this time."

"Then it's a good thing I'm not the kind of gal who's willing to disappoint."

Upon hearing the voice, Shílì turned, only for his left cheek to be met by a powerful fist.

The attack struck, the blow clapping more loudly than thunder in the middle of a storm. Shílì's face seemed to cave in where the fist met it, until the power generated from the punch sent him flying backwards.

He struck the ground some distance away, plowing into the earth with undeniable force. Gravel exploded all around him. His body was propelled forcibly across the ground, dirt and debris spraying everywhere. He came to a stop several dozen yards away, lying on his back and looking at the sky.

"Hehehe… hahahaha… HAHAHAHAHA!"

He began to laugh, uproariously, joyously, like a child who'd just been told that Christmas was coming two months after it had ended. Shílì climbed to his feet, shaking his head and wiping the blood from his lips, still laughing. There was a grin on his face, which he directed toward the female inu warrior.

"Excellent! Truly excellent!" He cried, spreading his arms wide. "Never have I been hit so hard. You are truly an exemplary member of your species!"

"Glad to see you approve." Kiara slid into another stance. "You're pretty strong yourself, and since you've proven to be so capable, how about we take this up a notch?"

"Very well. I look forward to seeing what you've got in store for me."

More Void fire appeared—small black dots that hovered around Shílì, orbs of infinite darkness that seemed to absorb all light; the absence and negation of concept.

"Entertain me."

"Void Art: The Infinite Oblivion."

The orbs of darkness merged together, combining and growing, swelling like a rising tide. Actually, come to think of it, the Void fire looked a lot like a giant tidal wave…

Kiara blinked.

"… That cannot mean anything good."

"Sa…" Shílì grinned. "Die now."

***

The wave fell. The fire spread. Everything was consumed. Plants disintegrated within seconds. Animals were engulfed in darkness, disappearing beneath the encompassing wave of absolute destruction.

Kiara avoided that fate.

High above the ground consumed in dark flames, she flipped and corkscrewed through the sky. Kiara oriented herself towards Shílì, who stood within a small circle, a clear patch of undamaged, pristine land amidst a plane of annihilation.

Shílì looked up as she descended, her body twisting and flipping. Her leg struck out as she dropped down on the black-haired fox-man with a powerful heel drop.

The ground cracked underneath the power of her attack. A large crater formed in the earth, with Shílì standing at its epicenter. With his left arm raised above his head, holding the woman's ferociously powerful leg back, the Void kitsune grinned.

"Good. That's very good. You've got some serious power."

Kiara pushed off the arm, flipping over and landing on the ground several feet away. All around them Void fire continued to burn, devouring everything within sight. Only the area they stood on was kept safe, protected by Shílì's will.

Standing up from her crouch, Kiara clapped the dust off her hands. "You'll find that I have a lot more than just power."

She took a deep breath, her chest puffing up as oxygen filled her lungs…

Then she roared.

A storm emerged from her mouth. A torrential flood of powerful winds tore the ground apart. The land was ripped to shreds.

Shílì jumped, ascending above the powerful tempest. The storm continued moving, even with its target no longer there. The five-tails then bore witness to something amazing. The gale-force winds smashed into his Void fire, pushing it, splitting it. The black fire which had no beginning and no end was blown apart, dissipating back into nothingness.

"Well, now." A low, impressed whistle emerged from between his lips. "That was impressive. I don't know anyone else who can destroy Void fire like that. And to think, that was just an exercise in manifesting raw youki into a physical attack." He shook his head. "Truly, your prowess continues to amaze me."

"Then allow me to amaze you some more!"

A shadow fell over him. Shílì looked up in time to see Kiara descending from the sky head-first. Her hand was outstretched, forming a fist clearly meant for him. Covering her body from head to toe in red was her aura, blazing away like an infinite bonfire.

Shílì tried to block the attack by crossing his arms, putting him in a disadvantageous position. When Kiara's fist struck Shílì's forearms, the fox with five tails was blasted away at speeds that surpassed even the fastest sports car.

He hit the ground. A loud, earth-shaking rumble followed his descent. Another crater formed in the earth, this one nearly twice as large as the previous one. The earth shook violently. Rifts appeared as the ground split apart. Dust rose into the sky, a mushroom cloud of smoke that ascended like the aftermath of a nuclear explosion.

Kiara landed on the ground some distance away. She walked over to the edge and peered down. A frown formed when she saw that Shílì was missing. There was only a small hole where he had been.

"Did he dig a tunnel underground?" Kiara wondered, then shook her head. "No. He's not an Earth Kitsune. He should not have the ability to dig a tunnel, and the Void is not something that can be used for such delicate work." She pondered the problem a bit more. "Then it must be…" Her eyes widened. "An illusion!"

"Exactly!"

Kiara turned around and was just in time to see the fist before it smashed into her stomach with the strength of a cannonball. She didn't even have time to wheeze as she soared through the air and slammed into the ground several yards from the crater, creating yet another crater.

Kiara tried to suck in a breath that would not come. She attempted to fill her lungs with oxygen that refused to enter her mouth. Everything hurt. Her lungs, her chest... they felt like something heavy, a 70 ton anvil, had been dropped onto her chest, crushing her bones and compressing her body.

A groan escaped her. Blood leaked from between her lips. Kiara struggled to get up, wincing every time her muscles screamed in protest. That attack had been stronger than anything she'd ever felt before.

"So, this is the strength of a kitsune with five tails." A pained chuckle emanated from within her blood-filled mouth. "Damn. And here I thought Kotohime was strong." Kiara spit out several globs of carmine liquid and climbed to her feet. Her legs wobbled, but quickly stopped as her youki began to strengthen her body. "I'm gonna need to be more careful."

"I am pleased to see that you are still alive." Shílì walked over to her, seemingly both curious and happy. "Hehe... Truly, I have not faced an opponent as worthy as you in many years. To think you would survive my reinforced punch. I put everything I had into that attack, you know?"

"We inu can never be outdone when it comes to physical strength," Kiara boasted. "There are very few creatures in this world with more strength in their muscles than us. However, those few yōkai whose physical prowess exceeds ours all lack our durability, which is second to none."

"Indeed, your species appears to be a most hardy stock. That attack would have killed any kitsune with less than at least six tails, even if they were using reinforcement. You were able to survive it with nothing but the natural durability given to you by your species' genetics. That's very impressive."

"Let's see if I can't leave you even more impressed."

Without warning, Kiara rushed Shílì with every intention of bringing the fight to him. Her straight jab struck out with hurricane force. Her foe tilted his head, his hair getting blown in his face as he avoided the attack.

He could not avoid the follow-up.

Now!

The fist that missed Shíli unclenched and grabbed the back of the now surprised fox's head. The surprised face didn't last long. It became replaced with a pained grimace as Kiara brought his head down to her knee, the loud *crunch!* of breaking cartilage echoing across the vast desert landscape.

Shíli's head snapped backwards. His spine arched along the curvature of his back as it also bent in an attempt to keep his head from flying off his body. Blood sprayed from his nose, a fountain of vermillion gore that splattered the ground, staining the earth.

"That was a good hit..." His abdominals flexing, body contorting in a boneless manner, Shíli's spine twisted back into its proper alignment. He grinned at the gobsmacked Kiara. "Very good indeed. Let's see you do that again."

A fast and furious battle of fists followed Shíli's proclamation. The air around them burst as their strikes canceled each other out and created miniature explosions of displaced air, sending their hair and clothes whipping about them as if caught within a terrible and mighty hurricane. Cracks formed along the ground as the displacement of incredible power lashed out at everything around them.

Kiara saw the tail coming before it attacked. She hopped backwards, dodging the mighty blow that descended from above. The ground where the tail struck not only split open as if the mighty hammer of a god had smashed into it, but a gigantic pillar of Void fire ruptured from the surface.

Kiara set herself in a wide stance; knees bent, center of mass lowered, fists tucked into her torso. She called upon her aura, and the red youki came to her, caressing her mind and soothing her body like the touch of a lover. She channeled her power into her fists, encasing them in a brilliant flame of the darkest crimson.

"HA!"

With a mighty shout, the fists shot forward. The aura extended from her fists and plowed into the pillar of Void fire, blasting a hole right through it. The fire, unable to maintain its consistency, dispersed into the wind.

The aura attack continued forward, the ground breaking apart. Shílì saw the attack coming his way. His tails rose into the air, extending to incredible lengths and twisting around each other until they morphed into the shape of a drill. As the aura attack came near, the five combined tails smashed down on it, destroying the attack in a single blow.

Kiara had to cover her face with her arms as dust and rubble flew everywhere. It pelted her skin. It didn't hurt, but it was annoying.

"More! MORE!"

The dust parted as a large cylinder of Void fire lanced out of it. Looking more like a beam of black energy, the fire raced towards Kiara, who moved swiftly to dodge the attack.

"GYAA!"

She wasn't fast enough. While she avoided getting smashed full-on, her left hand got caught in the cylinder of the malicious inferno. She gritted her teeth, fire lancing through her mind like a spear, and looked down at her now burnt appendage. Her hand was no longer there. What's more, the Void fire was beginning to ascend up her forearm. It crawled across her skin, devouring flesh, muscle and bone with ease.

Kiara flared her power and channeled it into the arm, which slowed the fire down, but did not halt its advance. The fire continued consuming her arm inch by agonizing inch.

"G-nnngg!"

Pain flooded her nerves as the fires consumed more of her appendage. Kiara dropped to her knees, her right hand grasping her arm just above the shoulder, as if that would somehow stop it from spreading.

Shílì walked out of the dust. "It seems you were caught in my last attack." He looked disappointed. "And here I was hoping you would last a bit longer." The dissatisfaction only lasted for a few seconds. "Ah, well. Such is life, I guess. You've given me a good fight, and for that I am truly grateful." His gentlemanly aura returned and he bowed at the waist, a show of respect for the first worthy adversary he'd had in centuries. "Thank you for putting up such a magnificent battle."

"It... this fight... isn't over... yet..."

"Eh?"

Her teeth grit hard enough to make her gums bleed, Kiara glared at the five-tailed kitsune.

"Don't... underestimate... ME!"

A roar filled with her tenacity and will resounded across the landscape. Kiara, in a move that stunned her foe, gripped her arm tighter and pulled. Flesh was torn, muscles were ripped, and bones were shattered in a spray of blood and gore that painted the ground. Kiara tossed the remains of her arm at Shílì, who was too stunned to do anything as it smacked him in the face.

"Gah! Blood in my eyes!"

"I'm not done yet!!"

With a cry not unlike that of a samurai charging into battle, Kiara launched herself across the ground.

With blood staining his eyes, Shílì completely missed the fist that plowed right into his chest.

More blood was spilled, but this time, it wasn't Kiara's.

Shílì stared at the arm stuck in his chest all the way up to the elbow, his eyes blatantly showing his disbelief. He then looked up, focusing not on the appendage sticking through him, but instead on the woman who'd just shoved her forearm into his chest.

Kiara's glare was fierce even though she was clearly in pain. Her sharp canines were bared, her nose was scrunched, and her eyes had narrowed into a look that screamed "I will not be beaten!" It was...

"Beautiful..."

"Wh-what?"

Shílì's shocked expression shifted into a sincere smile. "Thank you for allowing me this most beautiful release..."

Kiara watched, blinking as the light faded from Shílì's eyes. His body slumped against her, forcing Kiara to the ground as her exhausted legs were unable to hold their combined weight. She took a deep, shuddering breath, then slowly eased the corpse of her now deceased opponent onto the ground.

After staring at the dead kitsune for nearly a full minute, the pain and exhaustion finally caught up to her. Adrenaline, which had been pumping through her veins, keeping her body going long after it should have given out left, finally left her system. Kiara slumped to the ground, lying on her back, staring up at the midday sky...

Wait. Midday sky?

"Just… how long was I fighting that guy for anyway?"

"I'd say you've been fighting for about an hour or so."

"Kotohime." Kiara blinked as the woman in question marched into her field of vision. The raven-haired femme stared at her upside down, or was that right side up? Either way, she gave her rival and friend a smirk. "I figured you'd win your battle. Che, you only had to deal with that little three-tails."

"Indeed." Kotohime seemed amused. Her eyes glittered mischievously. "I was most fortunate. I do not think I could have won against your opponent. It seems you've gotten much stronger since the last time we fought."

"Yeah, well…" Kiara would have shrugged, but she didn't have the strength. "What can I say? Ever since you first defeated me all those centuries ago, I became determined to surpass you. Heh, I promised myself that I would never lose to you or anyone else ever again."

"It shows."

Several tails wrapped around Kiara, gently lifting her off the ground and cradling her body like a baby.

"Now then, please allow me to heal you. After that, you and I can meet up with Kevin-sama and Lilian-sama."

"Oh? Has the kid rescued her already?"

"Not quite."

Kiara was tempted to ask Kotohime about the strange smile that had appeared on her face, but decided she was too tired to even care.

She looked over at the giant structure that stood a little over a mile away.

I wonder how you'll do against your first yōkai opponent… boya.

Chapter 12

A Human's Determination

The moment Kevin had closed the distance between himself and Jiāoào, he knew that something was very, *very* wrong.

This fact was confirmed seconds later when his fist passed right through Jiāoào's face as if it wasn't even there.

Kevin stumbled, his body also passing through Jiāoào, who appeared to have become a ghost or some kind of hologram. The two-tailed kitsune's body flickered once, twice, and then vanished.

"What the—" Kevin's eyes widened. "An illusion—oof!"

Something impossibly strong impacted Kevin's back, sending him sprawling to the ground. His face met the hard cobblestone pavement. He heard as much as felt his nose being smashed between his head and the ground. Blood gathered in his nostrils, seeping down his mouth and chin. He didn't think it was broken, but it definitely hurt.

He pushed himself to his feet, eyes warily tracing the area. He couldn't see anyone, and that was the problem. Jiāoào had disappeared.

"That's right, ape. This is all an illusion. **Kitsune Art: Hidden Realities.** From the very moment you entered this courtyard, you were trapped within my illusory world. And now, I will show you the difference between us. I will show you why we kitsune are superior to you hairless monkeys in every way possible."

"Guh!"

All of the wind left Kevin's lungs as something long and furry struck him in the gut. He was lifted off his feet and launched into the air. For a moment, everything seemed still, including time. However, that moment came to an end when Kevin's back had a painful meeting with the earth, causing him to gasp as his mouth uselessly tried to suck in oxygen that wouldn't come.

Gritting his teeth, Kevin pushed past the pain and rolled away from his current location. He knew better than to stay in one place. Kiara had taught him that.

It was a good thing that he had taken his teacher's words to heart. Something invisible struck the ground mere seconds after he had vacated his spot. The cobblestone shattered, tiny fragments filling the air and pelting Kevin's body.

Kevin scrambled to his feet.

"Ho? You dodged it."

"You can't expect me to stay in one place, can you?" Even as he asked this question, Kevin was already on the move. He didn't know where Jiāoào was, but he realized that the best way to avoid getting caught by his opponent's attacks was to present the two-tails with a hard to hit target.

"No, I suppose I can't. Even an ape such as yourself must have some kind of self-preservation instinct."

"Again with the ape thing. Your insults need to be more unique. They're completely lacking in originality."

Kevin's body moved of its own accord, juking left and right, moving in constant zigzags, and rolling along the ground at random. All around him the earth was struck by something he couldn't see but instinctively knew were Jiāoào's tails.

"My apologies," Jiāoào's voice was full of sarcasm. "Insults and comebacks have never really been something that I strived to become competent with. When you're of a superior species such as myself, your actions tend to speak for you."

"Tch." Kevin rolled across the ground. The air above him *swished,* and he knew that he'd just managed to avoid a tail. He could feel the displaced air buffeting his hair. "I don't see someone who's superior to me. All I see is an idiot who thinks he's some big-shot because he's got supernatural powers."

"I would recommend shutting that mouth of yours," the comment, spoken in a tone of ice, echoed around the courtyard, "but it won't matter. You'll be dead soon enough. **Kitsune Art: Kitsune-Bi.**"

Kevin would have snapped a retort, but in that moment a brilliant flame exploded in his face. Kevin screamed in pain as his skin was burned. He could feel the heat searing his flesh.

Lilian had once told him that the Kitsune-Bi, or Fox Fire, wasn't powerful enough to cause damage unless a lot of youki was put into it. However, that didn't mean it didn't hurt. It did. A lot. A hell of a lot.

Acting on instinct and fearing for his retinas, Kevin closed his eyes so that he would at least be able to keep from going blind.

This proved to be a mistake.

Something powerful smacked him in the chest. Kevin could almost hear his bones snapping as he was knocked to the ground. Pain detonated behind closed eyes. Acid dripped down his ribcage. He wanted to pass out, but the pain kept him from being able to enter that blissful state of unconsciousness.

With his lips peeling back to reveal bloodstained teeth, Kevin willed his body to move past the pain. Lilian was counting on him to rescue her. He couldn't afford to fail now!

He moved swiftly, rolling across the ground. Several minor tremors rocked the earth as what Kevin could only presume were Jiāoào's tails struck the cobblestone with force. Disregarding the agony in his body, Kevin scrambled to his feet. However, the moment he did, one of the two tails struck him in the stomach.

"Gggnnn!"

Putting all of his strength into his actions, Kevin latched onto the appendage before he could be sent flying. It was difficult—more than difficult. His body screamed at him, begging him to let go, lie down, and curl up into a ball around his battered torso.

He ignored it.

Lilian is counting on me!

"What the—let go of my tail!"

The tail moved. Kevin's feet left the ground. The tail swung through the air in violent jerking motions, obviously an attempt to dislodge him. Kevin tenaciously hung on, refusing to let go.

"Get off! I! Said! Get! Off!"

The tail swung down, smashing into the ground with incredible force. Kevin's back cried out in agony as the cobblestone underneath him cratered. Jagged shards of rock stabbed into his skin, piercing him and causing more pain. His mind became unfocused, an attempt to dull the screaming torment that rendered his body inert.

His vision blurred, but he managed to make something out of the blurriness. A figure. Jiāoào. The kitsune stood before him, looking down at his beaten body, smirking with the sort of superior haughtiness that rich people exuded when they were looking at those less fortunate than themselves. Jiāoào's eyes glinted with malicious pleasure, like a sommelier tasting a fine wine.

"You see? I told you that I would show you how weak and powerless you really are. Now look at you, lying on the ground, utterly defeated by me." Jiāoào's tirade was halted, his superior expression wilting into a frown. "What are you smiling about?"

Kevin's smile, which had appeared during Jiāoào's diatribe, was reminiscent of a cat that had eaten a canary. It was so wide that it almost forced his eyes shut. "I can see you now."

Jiāoào only had a second to ponder those words before Kevin acted. He placed his hands on the ground on either side of his head, palms pressed firmly into the broken cobblestone. Kicking off the ground, he lifted his legs, tucked them into his chest, and then thrust them forward.

Bang! Kevin's powerful legs impacted against Jiāoào's stomach, firing off like a shotgun. The air left the kitsune's lungs. His eyes bulged. His body was lifted off the ground and into the air, making an almost graceful arc as he soared. Kevin would freely admit that it was one of the most beautiful things he'd ever seen. Then again, that might have just been the euphoria from seeing the smug smile getting wiped clean off his opponent's face.

Kevin climbed to his feet while Jiāoào landed on his back with a harsh *thud!*

He could feel blood trailing down his back and the pain of several rocks embedded into his flesh, but Kevin ignored that in favor of watching his opponent wheezing on the ground. He chuckled—or he tried to. He stopped when his chest flared up in agony. It was a sharp pain, like a spear was being slowly pushed between his floating ribs. Still, he could not help but be amused by the sight of the supposedly powerful supernatural being writhing on the ground.

Kevin straightened and took a deep breath. This was it. The moment he'd been waiting for. This was his time to shine.

He pointed at Jiāoào as the kitsune struggled to sit up...

... and began ranting.

"Just who the hell do you think I am, furball?! I don't care if you are a supernatural creature of incredible power! Kitsune, inu, yuki-onna, whatever! Don't underestimate me just because I'm a human! I have no intention of letting myself being defeated by the likes of you! So, come at me with your tails! I'll just rip them clean off! Come at me with your illusions! They won't make a difference! Come at me with those vaunted Celestial powers! I'll prove to you that just because you've got abilities that I don't, it doesn't mean you're stronger than me!"

Jiāoào's face scrunched up in a mask of anger. Outrage poured off his frame like water from a broken valve. He got up, wincing and glaring at Kevin, who returned the fierce look with a grin that bared his teeth.

"You..." An ugly snarl crossed Jiāoào's face. In that moment, the two-tails had never looked more inhuman. "I'm going to kill you! Brutally! Painfully! You're going to regret ever being born!"

"Did you just say porn?"

"I said born!"

"No, no, no. I'm pretty sure you said porn."

"Y-y-y-you—grrr! That's it! You're dead!"

That's it.

Kevin concealed the smile that threatened to pop onto his face at the sight of Jiāoào rushing towards him like an idiot.

He's so angry he's not even thinking straight anymore.

Kiara was a good teacher. Cruel. Sadistic. Merciless. But, still, a damn good teacher. She had taught him more than just how to throw a punch, more than just how to kick. She'd taught him how to fight, how to struggle, and how to take down opponents that he had no right beating.

"Listen to me, boya."

"Do you have to call me boya?"

"Yes. Now shut up and pay attention. As a human, you lack

the many powers and abilities that we yōkai have. However, that doesn't mean you are without weapons. What do you suppose is your greatest weapon?"

"Um... my mind?"

"Heh, good guess. That's correct. Your mind is the greatest weapon you have. So, use that mind to come up with better ways to beat your opponents. If you ever find yourself overwhelmed and outmatched, if you're ever in a fight where no opening presents itself, then all you need to do is create your own opening by using that devious little mind of yours. Got it?"

"Um, yes, I think so."

"Good, cuz I hate having to repeat myself."

Kevin had learned. He had listened and done as instructed, and he had learned to create his own openings. That was what the banter was for, to learn more about his opponent. Jiāoào believed this battle to already be won, never once thinking that he could be defeated by a mere human. He was sadistic, arrogant, and prideful.

In his sadism, Jiāoào had toyed with Kevin and given him time to plan his attack.

In his arrogance, Jiāoào had let himself grow complacent and open to retaliation.

And in his pride, Jiāoào had given Kevin the means to create his own openings.

Now it was time to show this arrogant kitsune what a human could do when given the proper motivation to fight.

***

Lilian was at her wits' end. Nothing was working. Every attempt she had made at getting out of the stupid bindings had failed!

Lying on the ground, she panted and puffed. Sweat coursed down her skin, soaking her body and the bindings that kept her from moving freely. The rough material, now slick with her sweat, grated against her skin, rubbing it in all the wrong ways and making her feel like she'd gotten a severe case of rug burn.

She looked up at the ceiling, her chest heaving. It hurt. The stupid bindings were wrapped tightly around her chest, too.

"Ugyu…" A strange noise escaped her throat. "Why is this so difficult? Dang it! I have to get out of here! Kevin needs me!"

She knew that Kevin was strong. She'd spent the last two weeks watching him spar against Kiara's disciples and then Heather. Each time he fought, Kevin grew just a little stronger, became just a little better. The dog-woman had mentioned something about the boundless potential of humanity shining in Kevin. Lilian didn't know anything about that, but she knew that Kevin was becoming stronger every day.

But, he still wasn't ready to face off against a yōkai. He just wasn't. As painful as it was to admit this about her mate, she knew that he lacked the strength needed to defeat even a two-tails like herself. It had nothing to do with skills or physical prowess, and everything to do with the supernatural powers yōkai possessed. One month of training could not defeat the abilities and techniques that yōkai were born with naturally.

I need to get out of here!

Lilian was about to renew her struggles when something grazed her skin. It stung, and she felt blood dripping down her hand—something sharp. She felt around for a moment before touching the object again. Long handled. A ring at one end. At the other, a leaf-shaped blade. In a flash, Lilian realized what it was. Her kunai! She'd completely forgotten about it until now!

"Ha! I love foreshadowing! Thank you for this!"

You're welcome.

Ignoring the blood dripping down her hands, causing them to become slick, Liliam fumbled with the kunai. She grasped the hilt and then proceeded to cut the fabric binding her hands and wrists. Jorōgumo silk was incredibly durable, and it could withstand the enhanced strength of a three-tailed kitsune, but it couldn't handle something sharp.

She sliced through the silk with relative ease. When her hands were free, Lilian cut the bindings around her legs and chest. She was just about to cut the ones constricting her tails when the door slammed open with a loud *bang!*

"I knew you'd try to escape if I left you to your own devices long enough."

Maddison walked into the room, her glinting green eyes betraying her intentions. Madness had consumed her. The way she walked, her heavy breathing, that insane smile, and those quivering pupils that were wide and unsightly told Lilian as much.

"Now I can kill you and claim that you tried to escape. Then Jiāoào will have no choice but to accept me as your replacement. He won't throw me away."

Insane giggling bubbled up from her throat. Lilian tried not to shiver at the sound, but didn't quite manage it. Yet even with the fear coursing through her body, she felt a sliver of pity for this woman. Maddison was obviously broken, a living doll whose sanity had been shattered into a million pieces by Jiāoào's cruelty.

"You could just let me go," Lilian tried to appeal to whatever compassion remained within the other girl. "You could say that I knocked you unconscious and escaped."

"Oh, no. No, no, no, no. That won't work. That won't work at all," Maddison chided Lilian. "If you were to escape, he would throw me away anyways. It's better to just kill you now. If you're dead, he'll have no choice but to accept me."

The face that looked somewhat similar to her own smiled. Bile rose up in Lilian's throat. Maddison marched over to Lilian, who had only just managed to scramble to her feet.

"Now be a good little bitch and die!"

With a surge of motion, Maddison's two long tails snaked around Lilian's throat and lifted her off the ground. Lilian's legs automatically kicked out in protest, and her hands flew to her throat in a futile gesture as she tried to suck in oxygen through her constricted airways.

"Stop struggling and just die already!" The grin on Maddison's face grew impossibly large, splitting her face in half. Emerald eyes grew big and round. Pupils dilated and became disturbingly small. "Die! Die! Die! Die!"

"Ce… Celestial… Celestial Art…" Lilian rasped, struggling to speak with her throat almost completely closed off. "**Celestial Art… Light… Sphere!**"

"GYA!"

Maddison's tails released their grip on Lilian and dropped her to the floor. The redhead covered her face with her hands, and Lilian looked at the damage that her attack had done. Maddison's face had become covered in ugly burns, red splotches that marred her skin.

"MY EYES! OH, GODS, I CAN'T SEE! YOU BITCH!"

Two long red tails became a riot of activity. They crashed into the walls, the floor, the ceiling—anything and everything. The bed was overturned and shattered into splinters, feathers and springs. The dresser became wood chips that scattered along the ground. The window shattered into thousands of irreparable fragments.

Lilian tried to dodge, but her tails were still bound by the *Jorōgumo* silk. Because of this, she couldn't enhance her body with youki. She'd barely even managed to produce that light sphere.

One of the tails smacked into her, sending her crashing into a wall. The air left her lungs in a *whoosh!* She slid to the ground, coughing and wheezing. Maddison had recovered by this point, and her maddened eyes glared at Lilian. Forgoing the use of her tails this time, she wrapped her hands around Lilian's throat and started to strangle her fellow kitsune.

The hands wrapped around her delicate neck were impossibly tight as Maddison squeezed the life out of her. Lilian's eyes bulged out of their sockets. She tried to think of a way out of this; tried to think of something, anything, that could save her from this crazy bitch.

That's when she saw it. Her kunai. It was lying just a few inches from her left foot.

If I can just reach it...

While her hands tried to keep the other kitsune from choking her to death, her left foot reached over and attempted to grab the kunai. Rasping noises bubbled from her throat, a choked gurgling sound from deep within her esophagus. Her heel touched the cool metal ring. Her vision was starting to get spotty. She slid her foot backwards along the ground, taking the kunai with it. Maddison chanted "Die! Die! Die! Die!" like a mantra as Lilian took one hand off the other kitsune's forearm and reached for the kunai.

"That it's! Just die! Die for me, please! You're no longer needed! I refuse to let myself be thrown away! I won't allow you to—Gurk!"

Maddison ceased ranting. She opened her mouth, but only wet rasping sounds emerged, along with several streams of blood that ran down her chin.

Lilian, her teeth grit and her eyes narrowed with unusual ferocity, twisted the kunai she'd plunged into the other kitsune's chest. The hands around her throat slackened, allowing her to gratefully suck in a lungful of air.

Maddison fell onto her backside. She looked down, staring at the small metal object piercing her heart. Rivulets of blood ran down her body and stained her clothes.

Her eyes went back to Lilian.

"W-why...?" Tears gathered. "All I wanted... was to not be thrown away again... I just... I just..." Her eyes glazing over, Maddison went limp and fell onto her back.

She didn't get back up.

"Oh..." Lilian's body went into a series of shuddering. She wrapped her arms around her legs, which she had curled into her chest. Tears leaked from her eyes to streak down her cheeks.

She'd just killed someone... she had... and this person was...

"Oh, no..."

Gasping sounds escaped from her lips as she tried to breathe. A different type of constriction had blocked her throat. The shuddering increased.

"Oh, please no..."

Her eyes wide, Lilian cried as she realized that she had just murdered someone who had been broken, unable to think straight. Someone who, through no fault of their own, had been backed into a corner.

"I can't believe it..."

She had killed someone. She had killed someone. Why? Why had she done it? Surely there had been another way. That girl hadn't needed to die.

"Kevin..."

She wanted to see her mate. She wanted him to hold her and tell her that everything was going to be okay. She wanted him to tell her that she hadn't done anything wrong.

Kevin... I need to see Kevin.

"I'm sorry," Lilian whispered as she slowly clambered to her feet. Her body shuddered and swayed as she was overcome with a sense of vertigo. She raised a hand to her face, covering her mouth to keep herself from throwing up. She looked down at the two-tailed kitsune and shed several more tears. "I am so sorry, but I can't let you kill me. I need to save my mate."

That's right. Her mate was in danger. She had to protect him. She had to...

The earth suddenly screamed.

About a mile or so away, a large pillar of black flames rose into the air, as if hell itself had decided to invade the Earth.

"What is that?" Lilian asked herself, then shook her head. "Focus, Lilian. Kevin needs you."

Sparing one last sorrowful glance at the dead kitsune, Lilian ran out of the room.

***

Kevin noticed something odd about this kitsune. Ever since the battle had started, there had been something strange about Jiāoào. It was on the tip of his tongue, but he hadn't fully realized just what that something was until the battle had turned in his favor.

A tail tried to smash into him from above. Kevin moved to the side as swiftly as his name implied. The tail created a small indent in the ground. Kevin stomped on it. Hard.

"Gya! My tail! Damn you!"

Jiāoào tried to punch him, but it was oh so sloppy. Kevin stepped to the left and forward. His right hand came up, almost gently nudging the fist wide and sending Jiāoào off-kilter. The two-tailed kitsune practically stumbled into his left hook.

"This is…"

Eyes narrowing, Kevin waded into Jiāoào's guard. His right hand redirected the sloppy jab thrown at him. At the same time, his left hand shot forward in a swift straight. Jiāoào's nose broke under his assault.

"Damn you! Damn you, damn you, damn you!"

Two tails came at him from either side, trying to hem him in. Kevin knew from his lessons with Kotohime that those tails packed a wallop. A kitsune's tails were the strongest appendages they had, because they were where all of their youki was stored. Even without reinforcement, their tails were capable of lifting boulders with ease.

Throwing himself forward, Kevin rolled along the ground. The tails struck the spot he'd been standing seconds too late. Kipping back up to his feet, he bashed his forehead against the underside of Jiāoào's jaw.

"Gah!"

Jiāoào stumbled backwards. A hand came up to his mouth.

Blood leaked from between his fingers, dripping onto his stupidly extravagant robes. Kevin would have smirked, but he was too busy dealing with his realization.

"You can't use Celestial techniques yet, can you?"

Even with a hand covering his face, Jiāoào's shamed blush was visible for Kevin to see.

"W-w-what?! Shut up! Of course I can!"

"Then why haven't you used them already?"

The blush deepened.

"I-I-I-I—th-that's—I just don't feel like it, okay?! You're not worth the effort!"

Jiāoào seemed to have taken several lessons in tsundere.

"And you shut up, too!"

Kevin blinked. "But I didn't say anything."

"Not you! I'm talking to the author!"

"The author?" Kevin's eyebrows twitched. "Oh, great! You mean to tell me I've got to deal with another one?! How many of you foxes are gonna talk to this imaginary idiot?"

I rather resent that.

"You wouldn't understand," Jiāoào snapped. "The fact that you don't even know what I'm talking about proves my superiority."

"That doesn't prove anything of the sort! All it proves is that you're crazy!"

"I'm not crazy! You're just an idiot!"

"Who're you calling an idiot?!"

Before the argument could continue, a loud explosion rocked the area. Kevin and Jiāoào turned their heads just in time to see a large pillar of black flames shooting into the sky.

"Ha…" Jiāoào sighed. "That Shílì… he's really enjoying himself too much."

"Whoa…"

Kevin, too, found himself entranced by the surreal display. He didn't know what the strange fire was, but he was getting some really bad vibes from it. Even though the distance between him and the fire was vast, he still felt a strong urge to run away.

Unfortunately for Kevin, he had forgotten the cardinal rule of combat.

Never look away from your opponent.

"Oof!" Kevin grunted as a tail smacked into his stomach and stole his breath. He was lifted into the air, but before he could get too far, another tail snaked around his leg. "Oh, crap. This is not good—WAAAA!"

The tail slammed Kevin onto the ground, hard. The air left his lungs. His back screamed in protest. The rubble still piercing his skin dug into his muscles, sending molten iron dripping through his nervous system.

"Uagh!" Kevin coughed up blood. The tail lifted him up again. This time it swung him into one of the pillars, which cracked as he hit it. With a whimper, he fell to the ground, which sent lances of agony up his side.

"It seems our roles have reversed again." Jiāoào chuckled. "Just as it should be."

He picked Kevin up by his ankle again. Dazed and unable to think straight, Kevin dangled limply in Jiāoào's grasp.

"Did you really think you had what it takes to defeat me?"

Slam! Kevin's vision went white as pain overrode his mind.

"Fool. I'm a kitsune."

Smash! Kevin's body broke against the fountain in the center of the courtyard.

"I'm superior to you in every way possible."

The tail lifted him again and began to spin Kevin around.

"And now, I'll prove it to you!"

Jiāoào let go of Kevin, who flew through the air like a Gundam being launched from the Archangel.

Blurs flew past Kevin's vision. He could see nothing but streaks. His stomach dropped into his feet. The urge to vomit nearly overwhelmed him. All he could do was squeeze his eyes shut.

Then his body hit the door.

And all he knew was pain.

He could feel hundreds of small needles stabbing into his skin. They hurt, a lot, but he soon found out that this pain was negligible compared to what came next.

Kevin gasped as his body impacted with the hard tile floor. The tiny wooden needles penetrating his skin were pushed further into his body. He could feel the sharp cobblestone shards in his back tear apart his flesh. The world tumbled around him, but he could see nothing. All he could do was feel the agony of his bones being jarred, of his skin being stabbed, ripped and torn apart. He knew nothing but pain. It hurt so much! He wanted everything to stop—

"Gooaaa!" Kevin's eyes widened as his back slammed into something hard. His mind dimmed. Everything became blurry. Darkness encroached upon his vision. He felt tired. So tired. All he wanted to do was rest. Yes. That sounded good. He would just close his eyes and go to sleep—

"BELOVED!"

—The scream jolted him back into awareness. He knew that scream.

Lilian!

"Gu... ha... ngg..."

He twitched and struggled to move, but his muscles spasmed in agony and seized up. His body refused to do what he told it to. He had reached his limit, it seemed.

"Inari-blessed! Beloved!"

Kevin's vision became filled with red, strands of silk that caught fire from the low light filtering in through the windows. He saw green as well. Two emeralds glistening with unshed tears. A face, one that he couldn't forget even if he tried, an apparition of loveliness and beauty like something out of an evanescent fantasy, stared at him with worry.

He tried to call her name, but his mouth wasn't working.

"Inari-blessed, you're hurt!" Lilian's cried out. "Hold on! I'll heal you!"

His body was lifted. He couldn't feel it, he couldn't feel much of anything, but he could tell because Lilian's face was closing in on him. Closer and closer. Kevin's ocular perception was filled with worried gem-like irises.

Warmth. Kevin's body became engulfed in an odd warmth. It was different from when you curl up underneath a blanket or sit beside the fire. This warmth came from inside of him—no, it came from the girl kissing him...

Wait. What?

Kevin blinked several times, his mind finally beginning to realize several things he'd missed in the past few seconds. The first was, of course, Lilian's lips pressed against his own. He also thought he felt some tongue action going on, but that could have just been the delusions of a teenage mind. The second thing he noticed was that he felt better. A lot better. His back no longer protested with each movement. He could no longer feel the splinters digging into his skin. Even the cobblestone rocks seemed to have disappeared, and his previously torn muscles felt brand new.

The kiss ended and Kevin absently realized that, yes, there had been some tongue action going on there.

"Lilian?" Kevin's mind still felt disoriented.

"How are you feeling?" Lilian asked, her tone still fraught with worry.

"Good." And a little confused. "Really good. You healed me?"

Her smile was warm, tender and loving. Kevin turned into a pile of goo. "I did."

"Don't your healing powers come from your tails?"

"They do."

"Right, so, why did you kiss me?"

Kevin and Lilian stared at each other for several silent seconds. Lilian's cheeks turned red. Kevin thought he would die of moé.

"… Because I wanted to?"

Kevin stared at her some more. Then he reached up and his hand found purchase on the back of her head, where his fingers threaded through her hair.

"Good answer," he said, right before he pulled her lips back down to his.

"W… what the hell is this?!"

The screech put an end to what might have been one of the most epic make out sessions since Louise Francoise Leblanc de la Valliere almost had sex with Saito Hiraga in a small boat floating in a lake in the middle of her father's estate—which had also been interrupted.

"Please don't make references that only a few people will get," Lilian stated flatly.

Sorry. I couldn't help myself.

"Whatever. Just don't make a habit of it, okay?"

I won't. I promise.

"You know," Kevin started with a dry look etched on his face, "I'm really getting sick of listening to you talk to imaginary people like that."

… I'm not imaginary…

Lilian giggled. "I'm sorry, Kevin."

Kevin deadpanned. "Somehow, I don't believe you."

Their small moment finished, Kevin and Lilian eyed the source of the screech. Jiāoào stood near the busted entrance, his jaw hanging open and his eyes wide and round. His face was pale, like he'd just witnessed the woman he'd obsessed over for nearly two decades making out with the boy he'd been trying to kill a few seconds prior.

"Lilian…" Jiāoào trembled. "How could you… you're choosing him over me? How… why… I don't… I don't understand!" Jiāoào shook his head, as if trying to deny what lay in front of his eyes. "What does he have that I don't?!"

"A pair of testicles," Kevin muttered, eyeing the boy's long hair.

"Shush, Beloved. There's no need to antagonize him."

"Yes, dear."

Lilian tossed him a smile before giving Jiāoào a flat look. "There are a lot of things he has that you don't, Jiāoào. Unlike you, Kevin is kind and compassionate. He's also strong, both in mind and body. He's protective of the people close to him and actually cares about their happiness. You, on the other hand, are selfish and only care about your own happiness. But, most importantly…"

Lilian's eyes strayed to Kevin for a moment. He tilted his head, obviously confused, but she just smiled and turned back to Jiāoào.

"Most importantly, he wants to stand by my side as an equal, rather than treat me as though I'm subservient to him. I don't want someone who's going to treat me like a slave. I don't want to be treated like someone else's property. I want to be free to make my own choices, whatever those choices are, and know that my mate stands beside me, supporting me just as I'll support him. That's not something a spoiled brat like you would understand."

Jiāoào stood there. His mouth opened and closed, but no sound came out.

"I think you broke him," Kevin said.

Lilian sniffed. "Good."

"I-I see," Jiāoào said at last. A creepy grin spread across his face. He also began chuckling in a manner that freaked Kevin out. "Kekeke… so, you've decided to spurn my love for you."

Lilian rolled her eyes. "You never loved me, Jiāoào. I was just a prize for you to flaunt."

Jiāoào wasn't listening. He remained lost within his own little world, which continued crumbling down around him. "Kekekeke…" More creepy laughter. "Very well. I see how it is. You don't want me. You're denying me."

Lilian's expression seemed to say "duh." So did Kevin's.

"In that case… in that case I will kill you right here! If I can't have you, no one can!"

Jiāoào rushed towards the prone forms of Lilian and Kevin, his eyes glinting with insanity, showing them that he had clearly lost his last marble.

"You and your precious mate will both—"

"Keep-your-filthy-tails-away-from-my-girlfriend Kick!"

"—GURK!"

Kevin, after slamming his heel into Jiāoào's jaw with a flying jump kick, landed on his feet and stood protectively in front of his girlfriend.

"Don't think for one second that I'm going to let you touch a single hair on my mate's head!" The declaration, complete with the "one hand on hip and the other pointing at foe" stance, brought a bright blush to Lilian's face. "Come anywhere near her and I'll show you why you shouldn't underestimate us humans!"

"I think you already did that, Kevin."

"Oh." A pause. "In that case, I'll do it again!"

"Right."

Jiāoào stood up, one hand on his bloody jaw, trembling.

"You… you… YOU DAMN HUMAN!"

He rushed forward again—

"SQUEEEE!!"

—And was sent back down after Kevin punted him in the testicles.

"All right! Time to clean this guy's clock."

"Kevin, you can't possibly mean to fight him on your own! That's dangerous!"

Kevin turned to Lilian as Jiāoào struggled to his feet. "Of course I do. I can't turn my back on this. If I'm going to prove that I'm strong enough to stand by your side, then I have to do this."

"But Beloved!" Lilian pleaded. "He's already injured you so much! I don't... I couldn't bear the thought of seeing you hurt like that again."

"Lilian..." Kevin knelt down beside her. He cupped her cheeks, using his thumbs to gently wipe the tears from her eyes before they could fall. "Please believe in me. If you can't believe in your own mate, then who can you believe in?"

Words were not spoken for the longest time. Jiāoào stood up and began to run at them again, his wordless battle cry letting them know that time was running short.

"Okay," Lilian whispered. "I'll believe in you." She gave Kevin her most brilliant smile. "I'll always believe in you."

"Heh." Kevin grinned. "Just hearing you say that makes me feel like I can take on the world."

Jiāoào finally closed the distance between him and the young couple, his clawed left hand prepared to tear them both limb from bloody limb.

"Now you'll both DIE!"

"Swift Headbutt!"

Kevin headbutted Jiāoào in the face. Again.

"Gah! My nose! I think you actually broke my nose this time!"

Kevin cracked his knuckles. "I'm gonna break a lot more than that!"

What followed was not a fight, for that term implies that the battle between the opposing forces was fair. The fight between Kevin and Jiāoào was not fair at all. Jiāoào, whose mind had lost itself to madness, didn't even bother using his tails, or his illusions. He just ran at Kevin with no plan and no purpose.

It didn't work.

Jiāoào came at Kevin again.

Kevin punched him in the face.

"Gah!"

"That's for trying to force Lilian into mating with you when she clearly doesn't want to!"

Stumbling back, his mind disoriented from the pain, Jiāoào didn't even see the two fingers heading his way.

Poke.

"Inari dammit!! My eyes! You poked my eyes! Who the hell does that?!!"

"I do that!" Kevin declared. "That's for kidnapping Lilian and thinking you can get away with it!"

His hands covering his eyes, Jiāoào was unable to do anything as Kevin rammed a fist into his stomach.

"Oof!"

He doubled over, spittle flying from his mouth.

"That's for hurting my mate's sister!"

Kevin's elbow came up and slammed into Jiāoào's jaw, breaking it.

"Gruak!"

"I have absolutely no clue what that's for, but dang, did it feel good!"

Kevin grabbed Jiāoào's head in a clinch and, just like he'd seen Kiara do and just like Midget had done to him several times, he slammed the two-tailed kitsune's head into his knee.

"GUAG!"

"And that one was for hurting the people I care about!" He did it again. "For causing Lindsay's mom to get sent to the hospital!" Once more. "For being the cause of my mate's suffering!" Two more times. "For every self-centered thing you've ever done!" Three.

By this point, Jiāoào was barely functioning. He stumbled around like a drunken idiot who had decided to start off the new year by drinking an entire beer bong's worth of Jagermeister. His dazed eyes stared at nothing and everything, and drool leaked from his mouth.

Kevin wasn't finished.

"And this one… this one is for me. My finishing move!"

Kevin darted forward, leaping into the air, his feet oriented towards his opponent.

"Final technique! Ultimate Combustion of Manly Prowess Heel Kick Attack!"

Like an explosion going off, Kevin's feet crashed into Jiāoào's face, which seemed to literally cave in as it was struck. Kevin thought he could actually feel the fox-boy's face cracking underneath his shoes. He bent his knees, momentum carrying him forward. With one final shove, a last strain of Kevin's legs, he used Jiāoào's face as a springboard to push himself into the air—and this time, Kevin remembered to flip around so that he landed on his feet.

Jiāoào flew through the air and smashed into the ground several feet away. He rolled along the marble floor, his body flailing limply, stopping when he crashed into a pillar. Jiāoào twitched once, his muscles spasmed, and then he lay still, staring at the ceiling with a blank look in his dull eyes.

Kevin clenched a fist up to his face, a symbol of victory. "And that's how you kick some serious butt!" he declared, just before his body sagged and he stumbled forward.

"Kevin!"

He would have fallen, but Lilian rushed to his side. She wrapped her right arm around his torso, then she slung his left arm over her shoulder for additional support. Kevin leaned against her, his body sagging further as all of his strength left him.

"Ugh... why do I feel so tired?"

"Well, you did just fight against a kitsune," Lilian pointed out, "and you must have been fighting pretty hard before I got here. While my Celestial powers can heal all of your wounds, they can't heal fatigue. You've probably spent all your energy by now."

"Ha... I guess," he sighed. "Still, I feel so lame now. I had such a strong finishing move. It was so awesome. To have my battle end with me barely able to stand is just..."

"Don't be too hard on yourself." Lilian smiled and kissed his cheek. "You did amazing. I don't think you realize how incredible your accomplishment is. You, a human with no supernatural powers, just defeated a kitsune with nothing but your fists."

"And my feet."

Lilian nodded. "And your feet. That's an incredible achievement. I don't think any other human could have done that."

Kevin's face became hot. Really hot. Like someone had taken a flamethrower to it. He just knew that he was blushing. Dang it! Hadn't he gotten over this already?

"Ah-ahahaha! T-thank you."

"Ufufufu, have I ever told you that you're absolutely adorable when you blush?"

"Urk!"

"You see, Kiara-san? I told you that Kevin-sama would be finished with his battle by now," a voice suddenly said, interrupting his banter with Lilian.

"…" Kiara didn't answer for some reason.

"Ara, ara. it seems you've lost too much blood, ufufufu.."

"…" still no answer.

Kevin and Lilian turned around to see a figure—no, two figures—standing near the entrance.

"Kotohime! Kiara! I did it! I—what the hell happened to you, Kiara?!"

"Don't worry, don't worry." Kotohime walked further into the room, carrying a nearly unconscious Kiara over her shoulder like a sack of rice. "She's perfectly fine."

"Ffine? FINE?!" Kevin shrieked. "Her entire left arm is missing!"

"Actually, it's more like just her forearm."

"LIKE THAT MATTERS!"

"You worry too much." Kotohime offered Kevin her brightest, most beautiful smile. "It is true that she no longer has an arm, but it could have been a lot worse. While I cannot bring her arm back, since it was lost to the Void, I have healed it to the point where she will no longer have to worry about bleeding to death. Like I said, Kiara-san will be just fine."

"Why don't you say that when she isn't dangling limply from your shoulder?" Kevin deadpanned.

"Ufufufu, you hear that, Kiara-san? Kevin-sama is underestimating you."

"…" Kiara didn't answer. Kevin wasn't sure if she could answer. She didn't even look conscious anymore.

Kevin took several deep breaths. He needed to, because otherwise he was afraid he might do something stupid, like deck Kotohime. Which would have been bad. Very bad.

"Whatever. I guess as long as she's alive, that's all that matters."

"Exactly." Kotohime looked quite pleased to see that he had come around to her way of thinking. "Now then, why don't we return home? It is nearing dinner time now, and I would like to start cooking as soon as possible."

"Right."

The group walked out of the mansion and were traveling across the courtyard when Kevin suddenly stopped.

"Kevin?" Lilian asked upon noticing this. "Is something wrong?"

"There might be. I just realized something."

Both Kotohime and Lilian appeared curious. "What's that?"

"Kiara is the only one of us who can drive. How are we going to get home?"

A heavy silence descended upon them.

For once, Kotohime actually seemed mildly embarrassed. "I-I hadn't thought about that…"

Lilian was much more… concise.

"Hawa…"

"How many times do I have to tell you not to use your mother's catchphrase?!"

Truly, the role of *tsukkomi* fit Kevin well.

Chapter 13

The Halloween Party

Due to Kiara not only being unconscious but also missing her left arm, Kevin had been forced to drive the group to the hospital. Kotohime didn't know how to drive, and Lilian knew next to nothing about cars.

They were stopped by no less than fifteen police officers.

Each of those officers let them off with a warning.

Oddly enough, neither Lilian nor Kotohime needed to use an enchantment to accomplish this. Then again, every officer who pulled them over happened to be male. They had all taken one look at Lilian and Kotohime before being turned into a drooling mass of hormones.

Truly, Kevin sometimes felt disgraced by his own gender.

After they arrived at the hospital, Kiara was taken into emergency care. Kevin, Lilian and Kotohime had been shooed off, so they ended up popping into Iris's room.

"I am very pleased to see that you have all made it back safely." Kirihime's smile had been tender and gentle when she had said that. Really, that woman was just too nice for her own good. Kevin was actually worried that some jerk might take advantage of her incredible kindness someday.

Camellia had also been quite pleased to see them. She had hugged all three of them while bawling her eyes out. Lilian had been bawling, too.

Apparently, Camellia and Lilian's version of bawling one's eyes out included massive amounts of "hawa."

Iris had also been pleased to see them, or so Kevin liked to think. He could never tell with her. She'd greeted them in the same manner as always, pulling her "Lily-pad" into a hug, then spouting off some kind of sexual innuendo to Kevin, which had thoroughly embarrassed him and caused Lilian to facepalm.

While he didn't know exactly how pleased Iris was to see him, even he could tell that she had been impressed when Lilian told her the story of how he'd beaten the crap out of Jiāoào.

"Well done, stud," Iris congratulated. "Beating a kitsune is no small feat for a human, especially one without any weapons... even if Jiāoào is a complete pansy. For that, I think you deserve a reward."

Iris then placed something into Kevin's hands. It was white and kind of lacy. They seemed so familiar...

"This is... are these panties?!"

"Kukuku. Indeed they are!"

"Iris," Lilian had sighed, "You're just so..."

"Lovely? I know."

"I was going to say perverted, but whatever."

Kevin held onto the panties for several seconds, his face scrunching up as if in deep thought. Finally...

"Wait a minute. You don't wear panties."

A long awkward silence ensued. Everyone looked at each other—everyone except for Camellia, that is, who just smiled and looked adorable.

Kevin looked back at the panties in his hand. Then at Iris. Back to the panties. His face scrunched up further. Then he looked at Iris again.

"Iris," he said with feigned calm, "whose panties are these?"

"Kukuku..."

"I don't like the sound of that laugh."

"Eep!"

All eyes turned to look at Kirihime. Her cheeks were flushed a brilliant red, and she was squeezing her thighs together.

Kotohime twitched. "Don't tell me..."

"L-Lady Iris..." A completely red-in-the-face Kirihime gave her younger mistress a pathetically sad look. *"When did you... I didn't even notice..."*

Iris grinned as she waggled her fingers at Kirihime. *"I've got the magic hands."*

After that embarrassing interlude was over and done with, the doctor had come in to announce that Kiara was out of danger, but that she would be required to stay in the hospital due to massive blood loss.

Kevin had tried to visit Lindsay and her mother, but he learned that his friend had already left and that Lindsay's mother was still resting while not accepting any visitors.

Iris was cleared to leave that day. Her injuries weren't too bad, especially since Kirihime had discreetly healed them while he and Kotohime had gone to save Lilian. They all traveled back home and arrived at the Swift residence in time for Kotohime to get started on dinner. That night, the kimono-clad beauty made a feast to celebrate Kevin's first victory against a yōkai.

"You have done something very impressive," she told him. "Few humans could ever beat a yōkai with their bare hands, regardless of the number of tails they have. That you have managed to do so after one month of training is nothing short of astonishing." She ruffled his hair, much to Kevin's annoyance. "You should be very proud of yourself."

"Here, here!" an oddly cheerful Iris had said. "I really should give you another reward... Oh! I know! How about I give you some of my pubes?"

"IRIS!" the shout came from both Kevin and Lilian.

"Hahaha! I'm kidding, I'm kidding. I shave down there," she said, which did absolutely nothing to reassure them. Then she made another suggestion. "How about I give you some of Lilian's pubes?"

"Don't offer to give away something that isn't yours to give!" Lilian shouted. "And that part of my body already belongs to Kevin! He doesn't need you to offer my pubes to him when he could just ask for them himself!"

It was a thoroughly shamefaced Kevin who ate dinner that night.

After dinner, Lilian wandered off to take a shower. That had been half an hour ago. Kevin spent that time playing video games with Iris.

"Ha! You think you've got me beat! Take this!"

"Great... another button masher. Just so you know, if you break my controller, I'm going to make you buy a new one."

"Aw, stop your worrying. Now... let me see blood!!"

Iris, it seemed, enjoyed playing video games as much as Lilian. Kevin wondered if it ran in the family.

"Ugh... I can't believe I lost... stupid game..."

Or maybe not. A small droplet of sweat rolled down Kevin's face as Iris tossed the controller onto the ground and sulked. Somehow, even her sulking looked incredibly sexy.

"You just need to play some more." Kevin turned his head so he wouldn't be caught staring. Fortunately, Iris didn't seem to notice.

"Whatever."

"I wonder if Lilian's out of the bath yet."

Iris gave Kevin a flat look. "You're her mate, aren't you? Why don't you just go in and check?"

"W-well, I guess I could..." Kevin scratched at his cheek. The idea definitely had appeal. "But, she said she wanted to be alone this time. I-I don't want to be a bother..."

"By Inari's furry ass, how can someone be such a badass one moment and a complete loser the next?"

"Hey!"

"Seriously," she gave him a stern look, "you shouldn't even have to think about crap like this. You saw the look on her face. I know you did." Kevin nodded. He had indeed seen the look on Lilian's face, the smiling facade she'd put on to reassure everyone. She'd been wearing it since the rescue. "She doesn't want to be alone right now. She's just saying that because she's confused. And you, as her mate, must be the one who helps her deal with whatever her problem is."

"Yeah, you're right."

"Of course I'm right." Iris rolled her eyes. "Now get going."

"Thank you, Iris." He tossed her a smile. "Despite your attitude, you really are a caring person."

"Pffft! The fact that you would say something so stupid shows that you don't know me very well."

Kevin left an oddly flustered Iris in the living room and traveled to the bathroom. He knocked on the door, but entered when no one answered. The bathroom was empty, showing that Lilian had finished her shower. And if that was the case, then there was only one other place she could be.

He found her standing by the window in their bedroom. He couldn't see her face, but he didn't need to. The shaking of her shoulders told him enough.

"Lilian?"

The fox-girl stiffened. She hastily rubbed at her eyes. Kevin walked into the room and up to her. By the time she turned around, her tears were gone, but not the redness or the swelling.

"Hey, Kevin." She tried to be cheerful, but Kevin could see the way her lips quivered. "Sorry I didn't come into the living room to play video games with you and Iris. I meant to, but I started thinking and I guess I got caught up in my own thoughts."

"What were you thinking about?"

Lilian turned around. She didn't say anything at first, but Kevin knew she would. Just as Kirihime had told him, he was her mate. She wouldn't keep secrets from him.

"It happened before I found you in the entrance hall," Lilian's voice, softer than a spring breeze, barely reached his ears. He moved in close, until he stood directly behind her. He could see her reflection in the window now, along with the barely contained tears in her eyes. "I... there was this girl, a two-tails like me. She and I looked really similar. I don't know how Jiāoào got his hands on her, but he said that she was being used as my replacement until he could get the real thing."

"The more I hear about Jiāoào, the more I wished I'd given him an even more painful beating." His words caused Lilian to smile, but it was fleeting. She sighed and placed a hand against the window, palm flat and fingers splayed. Her arm was trembling.

"They had me bound in Jorōgumo silk, a type of silk made from the threads of a Jorōgumo, a spider yōkai. It's very strong and can absorb enough youki that a two-tails like myself can't use the enhancement technique to break free. If it weren't for that kunai you bought me, I wouldn't have been able to escape."

Kevin listened silently. Lilian took a deep breath.

"During my escape attempt, this girl came into the room and tried to kill me. She kept saying this stuff about not wanting to be thrown away, about how Jiāoào would have to accept her if I wasn't there. I think she knew that Jiāoào would dispose of her the moment we left for his family's palace."

While Kevin's heart constricted at the knowledge, Lilian began to cry, her tears creating two glistening trails that wound down fair cheeks.

"Jiāoào twisted that poor girl into something broken and hideous. I could see it. He did so many horrible things to her, things I can only begin to guess at, and I... I killed her..."

Lilian's tears poured down her face in earnest now.

"I killed her. She kept coming at me, trying to strangle me and she kept screaming and screaming and I killed her! I killed her, Kevin! I tried to wash the blood off in the shower, but I kept seeing it on my hands! I killed her! It was so easy! One minute she was trying to kill me and the next I stabbed her in the chest! I killed her and I don't know what to do! I-I've never killed someone before, but now I have and I'm afraid! I'm afraid of myself because I can murder someone else so easily! And I'm afraid that you'll hate me because I've become a murderer! I don't know what to do! I-I—"

All words fled when Kevin turned Lilian around and embraced her. He didn't say anything. What could he possibly say to help her? He'd never killed someone before. Any words of wisdom or comfort and understanding that he could have said would have rung hollow. The only thing he could do was give her his support and love. So that's what he did. It was enough.

That night, Lilian cried herself to sleep in her mate's arms.

***

Halloween arrived two days after Kevin had rescued Lilian. That night Kevin, Lilian and Iris went to the Halloween party being hosted at their school.

From the moment they walked in, Iris became the center of attention with her slutty maid outfit—girls, boys, teachers, it didn't matter. All drooled at the sight of her.

Kevin couldn't blame them. Iris looked like sin made flesh on the best of days. That night her every pore seemed to ooze sex appeal.

He and Lilian also received a number of looks, though not

nearly as many as Iris. Some of it was certainly due to Lilian, who looked gorgeous in her white satin gown with a sleeveless purple overshirt, golden shoulder pads, and a jeweled tiara with the Triforce symbol. Her blond hair might have also been cause for some of those looks. She'd dyed it that night. It went well with her pointy elven ears.

Kevin's outfit might have been another reason. How many people wore a green tunic and a sock-like cap of the same color, white linen pants, leather boots, and had a sword and shield strapped across their back? Not many.

The Halloween party was taking place in the amphitheater, a gigantic room located within the same building as the gym. The teachers had clearly gone all out that year. Orange and black streamers hung from rafters high overhead and were long enough that he could reach out and touch them. Jack-o-lanterns sat on tables and in corners, and one huge, grinning jack-o-lantern found itself situated in the center of the room.

"Ho… look at all these different costumes," Iris said, glancing around at all the people. "Mine's still the sexiest." She sent off several winks. Sixteen boys and thirteen girls suddenly passed out from blood loss.

"Would you stop that already?" Kevin grunted in annoyance.

Iris' smirk was devilish, hotter than a freaking stove and absolutely sinful. "Jealous?"

"Hardly." Kevin looked at Lilian walking by his side. When she saw his gaze on her, she tilted her head inquisitively. He smiled, and affectionately squeezed her hand. "I already have my princess."

Lilian's beaming smile contained the brilliance of a thousand suns. "Oh, Kevin, you know just what to say to make my heart go *doki-doki waku-waku*."

"Doki-waku what now?"

"Hmph!" Iris crossed her arms under her chest. "Whatever. Anyway, I think I saw Slowpoke somewhere in the crowd, so I'm gonna go bum some money off him. See ya."

Lilian and Kevin watched the sexed-up kitsune wade into the crowd. Kevin tried not to notice the alluring sway of her hips.

He leaned over to whisper in Lilian's ear. "I don't see anyone dressed as a Slowpoke in here."

"I think she's talking about Justin," Lilian whispered back. Kevin suddenly felt annoyed, both because Iris would try bumming money off his friend and that he hadn't been able to yell at her for attempting to do such a thing in the first place.

"Dang vixen."

"My Lord!" a voice suddenly boomed over the din of music and conversation.

"Stop calling me that!"

Eric Corrompere walked up to them. Kevin took one look at his friend's costume, and then wondered if Eric had been dropped on his head as a child. There were way too many bandages and not enough actual fabric for him to even consider that as clothing.

"Eric... that costume is..."

"It's awesome, right?" Eric looked at himself and grinned.

"Not the word I was going for," Kevin mumbled.

"I think horrendous is the word I would go for," Lilian agreed, her nose wrinkling in disgust.

"Of course, it's not as awesome as yours and Lilian's." Eric looked at their costumes and began sniffling.

"Oh gods, he's crying again."

"Maybe we should have worn something less extravagant?"

"To think." Sniffle. "That My Lord is so great." Sniffle, sob. "That he can even convince his girlfriend to wear couple's cosplay with him." He turned away, his shoulders shaking.

"What is Eric doing?" Alex asked his brother.

"Don't know. Hey, Eric, what are you doing?"

Eric's body shook some more.

"I'm not even worthy of looking at him." Another sob. Eric got down on his knees and bowed before Kevin. "I'm just not worthy!"

"Oh, for Christ's sake! Get up, Eric! Everyone's starting to stare at us!"

Eric didn't get up. He remained prostrated on the ground. While Lilian giggled into her hand, Kevin decided to ignore the crying idiot on the wood paneled floor. He turned to look at the two newcomers.

Alex and Andrew wore what Kevin could only assume were a samurai and a ninja costume respectively. Alex had donned a black one-piece suit, had a sash tied around his waist, wore tabi ninja sandals and the distinctive ninja headgear, which Kevin thought looked more like a ski mask than a ninja mask. His brother, on the other hand, was wearing light blue hakama pants and a traditional dark blue men's kimono. Strapped to his side was a sheath with an obviously fake katana. He also wore geta sandals.

"Are those the costumes you two bought?" Kevin looked at his friends' outfits. "Not bad."

"Yeah, well, they're not as good as yours, obviously." Alex glared at Kevin's costume, as if his stare would make it spontaneously combust. "Seriously, where the hell did you get those?"

"We ordered them online," Lilian answered. "They were custom made! Check it out!" She gave a spirited twirl, which caused the hem of her dress to flare a bit. "Isn't my costume beautiful?"

"It's definitely the most amazing costume I've seen so far," Andrew nodded in agreement, "but I don't think it's the costume that makes it look so pretty. Isn't that right, Kevin?"

Kevin grunted as Andrew nudged him in the side with an elbow. "If this is some unsubtle way of trying to tell me how lucky I am, then you can stop it. I'm already aware of that."

While Lilian started drawing more attention to their group just by being her normally vibrant self, Christine walked up to them.

"K-K-K-K-Kevin!"

"Hey, Christine!"

Kevin paused to get a look at Christine's costume. Alex and Andrew whistled.

For Halloween, Christine had chosen to wear a downright jaw-dropping yukata. It was light blue and shimmered when she moved. Starting from the hem and moving up in a whirlpool pattern were thousands upon thousands of white snowflakes. A dark blue obi held it together.

There seems to be a lot of Japanese-themed costumes in our group.

"You look amazing." Kevin's complimented with a bright grin. Christine's face appeared to undergo spontaneous combustion.

"Guh..."

A struggle clearly took place within the girl. Her body

shivered and her face became mottled with blue. Steam poured from her ears and the temperature took a sudden plummet. Kevin shivered, his breath misting as he exhaled.

"W-what is this? Why did it get so cold all of a sudden?" Alex asked.

"I don't know." Andrew shivered. "Maybe the alignment of the planets has created a hole in the fabric of the universe, and the Frost Giants have come to this world in order to turn it into a neverending winter."

Alex stared at his brother. "You're an idiot."

"Hey! You shouldn't call your brother an idiot! I'm not an idiot!"

"I'm not even gonna deign that with a response."

"You just did!"

"T-t-t-tha… tha…"

Christine emitted odd noises from her mouth, like the choked gurgling of a dying animal. Her face scrunched up further, pale blue lips trying to form words that refused to come out.

"What's up with Christine?"

"Don't know, but something is seriously wrong with this girl."

Fortunately for the young yuki-onna, Eric finally noticed her presence.

"Ah! Gothic Hottie! How wonderful to see you here! And in such a beautiful dress! Why don't you come back to my place where we can take it off and—Balthazar!"

Everyone stared at the twitching, moaning pile of flesh formerly known as Eric.

"The heck did he just say?" Lilian asked.

"I think it was a name," Kevin answered.

"Bal-tha-zar? Huh, what an odd name."

The fortuitous *tsukkomi* act served to calm the snow-maiden down. She looked at Kevin and smiled, though her cheeks still remained a little blue.

"Thank you. You look… really nice… too…"

"Thanks! I'm really glad we decided to go with these costumes." He looked down at his green tunic, white linen pants and brown boots. "I think these actually kind of suit me."

"Mm."

"Is Lindsay with you?" asked Lilian.

Christine looked at her for a moment, then shook her head. "Last I saw, she was with her friends on the soccer team."

Kevin tried not to let himself feel hurt. He really did. But, it was kind of hard not to feel pain when one of his friends had decided that she wasn't sure if they could remain friends any longer.

"It's not that I don't want to be your friend, or even that I don't want to be Lilian's friend. It's just... my mom was injured because she got caught up in Lilian's problems. I'm sorry. I don't want to hurt you or Lilian. I really like you both and want to continue being you guys' friend, but I just... I need some time to figure things out."

Kevin had promised to give her that time. He understood where she was coming from. What happened to her mom only happened because the person who'd attacked the car her mom had been driving was after Lilian. Lindsay was finally beginning to realize that she, and her family by extension, were in danger simply by being associated with a kitsune. Kevin could do nothing less than give her the time she needed to decide on whether or not she wished to continue being their friend. It still hurt.

"Kevin..."

"I'm fine." Kevin tossed Lilian a smile, grateful for her presence and the soothing warmth of her hand on his back.

"S-so, Kevin," Christine was back to blushing, "I was... I wanted to... would you be willing to talk to me... in p-p-p-private, I mean."

Kevin blinked. What an odd request. Still, he didn't see why he couldn't oblige her.

"I'll go and find Iris," Lilian said. She leaned up and gave Kevin a swift kiss on the lips. "She's probably turned your quiet friend into a drooling sack of hormones by now."

"Ugh, now there's an image I didn't need to see."

Lilian waded into the crowd, disappearing from sight. Kevin and Christine left the amphitheater and found themselves in a hallway. Kevin felt amusement when he noticed that it was the same hallway that Christine had saved him in two months ago.

Christine stood before him. Her eyes would look at him, dart to the left, then the right, before looking at him again. It was... well, it was really quite cute, actually.

"Is everything alright?" asked Kevin. "You seem kind of nervous."

"I-I-I-I..." Christine paused, gulped, and then forced her blush down. "I'm fine. T-thank you for your concern."

Kevin scratched the back of his head. "There's no need to thank me. You're my friend. It's only natural that I would be concerned about you."

Christine frowned. "A friend?"

"Pardon?"

"It's nothing."

Kevin didn't think it was nothing, but decided not to argue. "So, what did you want to talk about, exactly?"

"I just wanted... no, I have something that I need to tell you."

Christine placed a hand against her chest, clutching the fabric of her yukata. Kevin grew worried when the snow-maiden's face started to become blue again.

"I...the truth is I... I'vealwayslikedyou!"

A pause.

"Um, what?"

Christine flushed, but now that she'd said it once, she was able to repeat it, and in such a way that Kevin could actually understand it. "I like you."

"Ah." Kevin grinned. "I like you, too."

"No. Not like that, you idiot." Christine actually rolled her eyes. "I mean I... I like you in... *that* way."

It took Kevin a couple of seconds to realize what "that way" meant. When he did, his face went through a series of emotions: shock, surprise and *"oh my god, I think someone just confessed to me!"* being the first three. His face then gained an expression that was best described as a combination of embarrassed, pleasure, and ashamed.

"I... wow... I never knew that."

Christine deadpanned. "You didn't? All this time I spent with you and you never once suspected that it might be because I have feelings for you?"

"Ah, well, you kept hitting me and getting angry all the time, so I just sort of assumed you didn't like me."

"You… you really are an idiot, aren't you?"

Kevin's cheeks puffed up. "That's not very nice. I'm not an idiot. I've got the third highest grades in my class."

"That's not what I meant."

"Still, I suppose I should have suspected something," Kevin mused. "I guess there was some truth to all those times Lilian called you a tsundere, after all."

"Urk!"

"I mean, thinking back on it, all those times that you got really angry and violent, those were, like, classic tsundere moments."

"Geh!"

"Really, I'm almost ashamed of myself. As an anime fan, I should have recognized the signs. I don't know how I missed them."

"Can we stop talking about how I'm a tsundere already?!"

"Right." Kevin offered the girl an apologetic grin. "Sorry."

"W-w-w-whatever." Christine crossed her arms and huffed. "So, um, about what I said…"

"Christine." Kevin's smile was gentle, but it was mixed with guilt and sadness. "I'm sorry. I like you, I really do. You're an amazing person. You're kind, you're fun to be around, and you're super cute."

Normally, Christine's cheeks would have flushed at being complimented so much, but she had already worked out where this was going. Instead of getting embarrassed, she merely looked resigned.

"But you like Lilian, right?"

"That's right." Kevin nodded. "Lilian and I are mates. She's important to me. I like you, but I love Lilian."

"But how can you know that for sure?" asked Christine. "How can you know that you love Lilian? We're fifteen. We don't know what love is."

Blond hair swayed as Kevin shook his head. "I used to think that, too. That I couldn't possibly know what love really is because I'm too young, but I'm beginning to think that age isn't all that important when it comes to matters of the heart."

"But you've only known her for three months!"

"I've only known you for about three months as well," Kevin pointed out.

"That's not true," Christine blurted, "you and I have—eep!" Christine clamped her hands over her mouth.

"Christine?"

"It's nothing."

"It's clearly not nothing," Kevin frowned.

Christine began to look irritated. "Look, if I say it's nothing that means it's nothing, okay?"

"Um, no," Kevin determined, shaking his head. "Not okay. You don't get to decide what is and isn't nothing all on your own. Something I said clearly bothered you, but I can't even apologize because you won't tell me. Do you know how that makes me feel? It makes me feel like you don't trust me. You say you love me, but relationships are built on trust, Christine. If you can't trust me, then —"

"How can I trust you when you don't even remember me?!" Christine exploded like a geyser. A very cold geyser.

"So we've met before," Kevin murmured as Christine huffed and puffed.

"Obviously," was her biting reply.

Kevin thought back to when he might have met her. He recalled a previous conversation with Christine, where she had told him that she used to live in Alaska, which he had visited back when he was younger.

Hm...

"W-what are you doing?" Christine squeaked like a frightened mouse when Kevin got into her personal space.

"You..." Kevin squinted, as if doing so would help him see her more clearly. "Are you Ice Girl?"

"DON'T CALL ME THAT, YOU IDIOT!"

"Doof!"

Kevin was sent sprawling to the ground from Christine's mighty fine pimp slap. He held a hand to his red cheek, gawking at the girl who, after calming down, stared at him in shock.

"Ouch," Kevin muttered, "did you have to hit me?"

"S-sorry," Christine mumbled, looking down at the hem of her robes. She then glanced shyly at Kevin as he stood back up. "So, you... you do remember me?"

"Well..." Kevin rubbed the back of his neck, "I remember Ice Girl, but I hadn't realized that she was you. As I recall, you were very shy back when we first met—and you weren't as prone to violent outbursts. It took me the entire time I was there to break you out of your shell."

"W-whatever," Christine huffed. "I haven't changed that much."

Silence. A number of crickets chirped, adding their music to the awkward moment.

"W-what are you looking at me like that for? I haven't changed."

"Christine, back when we first met, you were more likely to hide in a corner than to beat the crap out of someone for upsetting you."

"Eep!"

"In fact, I distinctly remember you crying when several bullies picked on you."

"Ugh!"

"And I clearly remember this one time where I beat some of those bullies up for you, and you ran over to that corner and began to cry—"

"Alright, alright! I get it! I was a lot different back then!"

"Yes, you were."

Kevin smiled at Christine, who turned her head.

"You still haven't answered my question," she mumbled to change the subject.

"Question?"

"My question. How can you know that you're in love with Lilian when you've only known her for three months?"

"Ah, that question. I'm not exactly sure what to tell you." Kevin shrugged helplessly. "I'll admit, I don't know everything about Lilian. I'm sure it'll be a long time before I do. But, I don't really think I need to know everything about someone to love them. Lilian and I, we just sort of work. She's bright and vibrant and cheerful. She has a love for life that I've never seen in anyone else. Her personality, her emotions, that openness she displays all the time, I envy her ability to be so honest with herself."

He chuckled in a self-deprecating manner.

"To be honest, when I first met Lilian, I was actually kind of jealous of her."

"Jealous?" Christine wrinkled her nose. "Of her?"

"Weird, I know, but Lilian is just so open. She has no trouble speaking her mind. She says what she wants to say, does what she wants to do, and she doesn't care about what anyone else thinks. In comparison, I was a shy kid who couldn't even talk to a single girl without fainting or running away."

"You talked to me just fine," Christine said, referring to their meeting at the arcade.

"And you can thank Lilian for that. It's only because of her that I'm like this now," he fired back. "If it weren't for Lilian, I doubt you and I would have ever met. Re-met? Whatever. My point is, we wouldn't have become friends again. Even if I had met you before Lilian, I wouldn't have been able to speak with you because of my... girlphobia?" Kevin scrunched up his face, then decided to just roll with it. "Yeah, let's go with that."

"Girlphobia?" Christine couldn't believe what she was hearing. "You were... afraid of girls?"

Kevin blushed, just a bit. "Not quite afraid, really, just too shy to talk to them."

"Same difference." Christine blew out a deep breath. "So, that time when you got me that... stupid cat... from the claw machine, the only reason you did it was because of Lilian?"

"I got you that cat because I wanted to," Kevin told her, "but without Lilian helping me get over the anxiety I felt around girls, I can guarantee it would have never happened."

"And just how did she manage to help you get over your... issues?"

Kevin absently recalled the hundreds of times that Lilian had tried to seduce him, either by prancing around naked, leaving the restroom door unlocked while she took a shower, or by wearing sexy lingerie and posing on his bed—desensitization at it's finest.

"By being really, really tenacious."

"I see." Christine closed her eyes. "I... I guess I should have expected this." She smiled at him, but it was a very bitter smile, the smile of someone who had lost without ever realizing it until it was too late to win. "I mean, you two are dating already. It was stupid of me to think you would fall in love with me just because I confessed."

"I'm sorry." Kevin knew that contrite apologies wouldn't really help, but he had nothing else to give.

"No. It's fine." Christine sniffed. "It's not your fault."

Kevin didn't know why he felt so guilty at the sight of Christine's embittered smile, but he did. He felt like a jerk.

"Well!" The smile became cheerful, but Kevin knew it was fake. Christine never gave such bright smiles. "I think I'll go back to the party. You should, too. I bet your mate's looking for you."

The girl didn't spare him another glance. She walked past him and went on her way.

"Christine."

She stopped.

"Are we still friends?"

Christine clenched her hands into fists. Her knuckles, already snow white, turned nearly translucent as they shook. They relaxed seconds later. She turned around and presented him with another smile. It was an honest smile, despite the tears that were starting to glisten down her cheeks.

"Of course we are," she said before disappearing around a corner, walking in the opposite direction of the amphitheater.

Kevin closed his eyes and sighed. He felt bad—horrible even —but he knew this was for the best. He liked Christine, but only as a friend, and he needed to let her know that. Leading her on, giving her false hope, it would have only hurt her more in the end. It was like ripping off a bandaid; better to get it all out of the way at once, than to let it fester and scab.

Kevin re-joined Lilian and his friends. They eventually found Iris bumming money off of Justin. He noticed Lindsay looking at him a few times, but whenever he looked her way, she would be looking at something else.

They partied well into the night, staying up until ten pm before traveling home.

Christine hadn't been seen at the party after their conversation.

***

It is a well-documented fact that all kitsune, especially females, possess an almost unhealthy obsession with their bodies. Every kitsune bears a strong urge to shape their body into an exemplar of beauty. While nature certainly does an excellent job for them, many kitsune feel that isn't enough. Even though the overall standard of what it means to be "beautiful" is something that most of the world's population has come to a general consensus on, each individual often has their own quirks and ideas on what it means to be "truly beautiful."

Looking at the female members of the Pnéyma clan, it becomes immediately apparent that "beauty," as defined by them, can be summed up in two words: tall and voluptuous. Each member of the Pnéyma clan is tall of stature and has a humongous pair of jugs--except for one of them.

Even Iris and Lilian, the second youngest members of the clan, are purveyors of incredible beauty. While not as tall as the others, they are still growing, and they are already quite shapely in all the ways that matter.

In order to fully grasp how the concept of beauty within the Pnéyma clan works, one needn't look any further than the clan's matriarch.

Delphine Pnéyma has, for the past seven centuries, been considered one of the most beautiful kitsune to ever grace the earth. She is the possessor of a beauty envied by all, and is considered the pinnacle of what a "pure" Pnéyma clan female should look like.

Tall with big breasts.

Sure, she has a magnificent pair of legs, wide hips and a shapely rear along with nine perfectly groomed silver tails, but most people are too busy admiring the ginormous beach balls on her chest to notice.

The kitsune in question sat upon a chair, a dais really, one befitting the matriarch of the most powerful spirit clan in the world. Kneeling before her, below the steps that led to her throne, was one of her daughters.

Aster, much like her mother, possessed incredible beauty. She was tall, not taller than her mother, but tall enough that she easily met the standard set by the matriarch. Her breasts, while also not as large, were more than large enough. Then again, it was pretty much impossible to have breasts larger than the matriarch's. The fact that she also had a twin sister, who was identical to her in every way possible, only made her that much more attractive to those outside of the clan.

Too bad they'd both unilaterally stated that they were only into each other.

Delphine was listening to a report from her daughter. While

none of the females of her clan were allowed to leave the clan estate (except on holidays and extended vacations), she had divvied up the task of sorting through the information from her various spies to her daughters. She believed it was important to help them learn and grow as kitsune.

It had nothing to do with the fact that she disliked the idea of more paperwork.

Aster and her sister had been given the task of sorting through information that arrived from France. It was their job to keep an eye on the political climate of that country, both human and yōkai.

She had been just about to tell Delphine something interesting when shouting reached their ears.

"I-I am sorry, Lord Shénshèng, but I cannot allow you to pass!"

"Please step aside, young man. I hold no quarrel with you. However, should you choose to block my path, then I will be forced to take action."

"Lord Shénshèng! Please stop! You have not been granted permission to enter—"

The doors burst open. Delphine watched dispassionately as one of her guards, a grandson of hers, flew into the room and landed on the ground with a dull thud. He had a hole in his chest that steam still rose from.

"Was that really necessary, Shinkuro-kun?"

"I would like to make a strong suggestion that you never call me by that name again," the one known as Shinkuro spoke as he stepped into the room. "Then again, I have a feeling that my words will fall on deaf ears, so I shall not bother."

Like a good portion of male kitsune, Shinkuro Shénshèng was an exemplar of their species, combining all the masculine sex-appeal of an alpha male with the pretty boy looks expected of a *bishounen*.

Like most Celestial Kitsune, Shinkuro had blond hair; long golden locks tied into a ponytail that reached down to his waist. His clothing shimmered with each step he took. Intricate designs crawled along the stately garment, symbols of power that were arcane and esoteric. His robes were resplendent, if a bit ostentatious. Nine blond fox-tails writhed behind his back in clear agitation, contrasting starkly with his emotionless facade.

While Delphine noticed all of this at a glance, she was the only one. No one else could even look at him—his mere presence commanded those weaker than himself, demanding they kneel before him, that they accept him as their liege. It wasn't a technique. Like all kitsune who were gifted with the ninth tail, his very presence bored down on those near him when his youki was unleashed; an omnidirectional force that crushed everyone under its weight.

"Ma... there is no need to be so angry," Delphine replied with a placid smile that did nothing to put the angry man at ease.

Shinkuro stopped several feet from the dais, right next to Aster. Although his face appeared calm, expressionless even, his presence, the essence that made up Shinkuro Shénshèng, showered all those present with unrestrained rage. The rage of a king. The fury of an emperor.

"No need to be angry? After what your granddaughter did to my youngest, I believe that I have every reason in the world to be angry."

"Ah, yes, your son." The placid smile remained, but the quality had changed. Whereas before the smile would have put people at ease, now it had taken on a condescending edge. "The one who went off without your permission, traveled to America, kidnapped my granddaughter, and sent his attendants after my family. Is that the one you are talking about?"

"Please do not try to place the blame on my son. His actions were indeed reckless and hasty, but we both know who is truly at fault. You promised Lilian to me. Though I am loathe to allow a girl bred from that *Shinkuror*, that traitor of a kitsune that you called a son to mate with my own flesh and blood, you still made that promise—and I will admit that her talent for the Celestial arts is unsurpassed amongst the youngest generation in my clan, even my own children. That is all moot now. My son has become a vegetable. He refuses to talk. He hardly eats. He cannot even go to the bathroom without aid."

"And whose fault is that?" asked Delphine. "I did not force your son to go after my granddaughter. I did not tell him of her whereabouts. I specifically kept any and all information about her a complete secret--as per your request, I might add. If anyone is to blame for your son's state, it is you for being negligent."

Shinkuro closed his eyes. "You believe this to be to be my fault?"

"Of course. You are the one who did not keep your son on a strict enough leash. You are the one who refused to do something about him when his ego led him into making reckless decisions. You call yourself an enlightened being, however, rumors have been spreading, Shinkuro-kun. Rumors of your youngest owning sex slaves, of breaking young women, both human and yōkai. It is enough to make one wonder if you Celestial Kitsune are truly the compassionate beings that you claim to be."

Shinkuro opened his eyes, and for the first time since he had barged in, there was true emotion within them; a fierce and burning anger. "What you're claiming is preposterous. I would know if my own son was committing such heinous acts."

Delphine shrugged. "You are free to believe whatever you wish. I cannot stop you. It does not change the fact that rumors have spread. That you claim ignorance of these rumors is troubling, but that is beside the point."

Shinkuro's face twitched as he regained control over his emotions. Delphine smirked.

"You claim that I promised my granddaughter to your son. However, I remember making no such promise. I told you that we would try to come to a mutually beneficial arrangement by setting up mating ceremonies between a man of your choosing and my granddaughter, Lilian, to see if she found herself interested in one of them. I never said that these ceremonies would end in mating. You simply decided to indulge your son's insatiable lust by trying to force me into giving you that which is not yours."

Shinkuro frowned at Delphine. The pressure he'd been releasing in small quantities suddenly increased. Those in his general vicinity gasped, their lungs deprived of oxygen, falling to the floor, hands clinging to their chests as they curled up into the fetal position. Matters only got worse when Delphine upped the ante, unleashing her own oppressive aura.

If the aura wielded by Shinkuro could be considered divine, the aura of one who commanded all to bow before him, than the one that Delphine unleashed was cold and bone-chilling, the tender caress of death's embrace. All those in the room felt it, the icy hands clenching their hearts. The presence Delphine pressed upon them was every bit as impressive as the one wielded by Shinkuro.

"Very well. I see that your beliefs on this matter will not change," Shinkuro's voice was more calming than a gentle ocean breeze. However, none of those who heard it felt comfortable. "However, do not think this is over, Lady Pnévma. You might be willing to try and slide around your sins, but I am not. You have committed a grave injustice against my clan and I. Every action has consequences, and the actions that you have taken this day will have dire consequences indeed. I hope, for the sake of your clan, that you are prepared to face them."

"We shall see," Delphine smiled, seemingly unbothered by Shinkuro's not-so-subtle threat.

With those parting words, Shinkuro exited the great hall. Delphine extended her senses, feeling him as he left the Pnévma estate via the Shrine Realm Gate.

"Are you sure this decision was wise, Mother? This is going to cause a lot of problems for us and our allies."

Delphine turned her head towards her first daughter. Daphne was a kitsune whose extraordinary beauty nearly matched her own. She was tall, about as tall as Delphine herself. Her long silver hair was tied into a series of intricate braids arrayed around her head in beautiful artistry. Her clothing, an off-white toga shaped somewhat like a dress, showed off her tall, busty figure. Daphne, as Delphine's first daughter, was the princess of their clan, and she would one day take over when the matriarch decided to retire. She had seven tails.

"It will be fine," Delphine assured her daughter. "The three Great Clans of Pnévma, Gitsune and Bodhisattva have never gotten along. This was simply an attempt to see if we could come to some kind of accord. To be honest, I did not expect it to work anyway."

"And what about Lilian? Surely you intend to punish the girl for her insolence."

Daphne was a firm believer in supporting the clan. Acting in self-interest was anathema to her, and Lilian's incredible selfishness was something she could not abide by.

"Ma, ma. I think punishing her is a little harsh, don't you agree?"

"But Mother! Surely you can't just—"

"We shall speak no more of this matter, daughter of mine."

Daphne stiffened as the matriarch's words cut through her like a knife. Her body shivered in fear. As the oldest and the one who would eventually lead the clan, she was allowed a certain amount of leeway when it came to how she spoke to her mother. That did not mean she could argue with the matriarch, however, especially in a public forum.

"Yes, Mother."

Delphine's placid smile put her daughter at ease. "In due time, you will come to understand that what happened this day was not Lilian's fault, my dear. For now, though, do your best to put it out of your mind."

"Yes, Mother."

"Now then," Delphine turned back to Aster, who'd had the good sense to remain silent while the more powerful kitsune were talking, "you may continue your report. I believe you mentioned something about one of the yōkai villages located in the Alps being destroyed by an unknown party."

Delphine leaned back on her throne, resting her left elbow on the armrest and placing her left cheek in the palm of her hand.

"I am curious to know more."

AFTERWORD

Welcome to the afterword, home of the place where I randomly spout nonsense. Just kidding.

So, here we are at the end of book 4 to the American Kitsune series, A Fox's Family. I feel like this volume, in particular, is a bit of a doozy. In all honesty, it was the hardest one for me to write, and not because I was suffering from writer's block or something like that. The content of book 4 was brutal compared to the other three, I think, especially for a story that started off as a slapstick romcom anime parody.

A Fox's Family is a story that has equal amounts of light-hearted humor and dark moments that show how horrible people can be to each other. One of the aspects of this story that I wanted to focus on was the difference between the human world and the yōkai world—the kitsune world in particular.

One thing that I wanted people to understand here is that the kitsune world isn't all tropes and comedy. Kitsune are a very long-lived species. They can live for hundreds, even thousands of years. Many of the kitsune that were alive when slavery was legal in the human world, and where the sex slave trade not only thrived but was considered perfectly acceptable by societies at large, are still alive today. These kitsune govern their world, and they have a policy that a lot of people who are stuck in their ways, unable to adapt to change, tend to follow—if isn't broken, don't fix it.

I also wanted to present a contrast between the relationships of Kevin, Lilian, and their family with the relationship that Jiāoào had with Maddison and the girls that he enslaved. This was done to show the massive difference between cultures, but also to show the difference between characters. I think showing how Lilian and Kevin's relationship has progressed, and then comparing the way that Kevin and Lilian treat each other over how Jiāoào treats the girls under his yoke shows how much Kevin and Lilian care for each other.

Jiāoào made this story incredibly hard to write. If you hated his guts every time he showed up on the page, don't worry—I hated him, too. He was honestly one of my least favorite characters, but I think he made a good villain—for a spoiled brat.

Whelp. I think I have done enough writing for now. I hope you all enjoyed this book. It traveled away from the comedy of my previous three books, but I like to think that this didn't detract from this story.

CPSIA information can be obtained
at www.ICGtesting.com
Printed in the USA
LVHW032351130519
617745LV00010B/377/P